DAVID TALLERMAN

Prince Thief

FROM THE TALES OF EASIE DAMASCO

**ANGRY
ROBOT**

ANGRY ROBOT
A member of the Osprey Group

Lace Market House,
54-56 High Pavement,
Nottingham NG1 1HW
UK

www.angryrobotbooks.com
A royal pardon?

An Angry Robot paperback original 2013
1

A catalogue record for this book is available
from the British Library.

ISBN 978 0 85766 267 5
Ebook ISBN 978 0 85766 269 9

Set in Meridien by EpubServices

Printed and bound by CPI Group (UK) Ltd, Croydon, CR0 4YY.

For Mum,
With love and thanks.

CHAPTER ONE

As meetings to decide the fate of a city went, this one was looking a lot like the prelude to a riot.

Of the gathered audience, only a few were paying attention to the stage where I'd somehow found myself; the rest were turned to bawl at a neighbour, or to spew invectives at the rows behind them. Half a dozen self-contained arguments had broken out along the length and breadth of the room, any of which might explode into violence at the slightest provocation.

Then again, perhaps it was all that could be expected of a seating plan that placed bankers besides extortionists, veteran warriors between crime bosses and cloth magnates.

"Settle down!" bellowed Alvantes from the front of the stage. He was gripping the lectern with the whitened knuckles of his one hand, while trying to keep the stump of his recently injured other arm from view.

I doubted it was improving Alvantes's mood that the only venue he'd been able to find for this meeting was the hall Castilio Mounteban had so recently used for the same purpose: Mounteban, the self-same scheming crook that Alvantes had fought to roust from power hardly a day before; the man who had somehow united the disparate factions before us, had then held them together with little more than threats and promises; Mounteban who, in short, was a hundred times better at this sort of thing than Alvantes himself.

"We have to at least discuss the possibility of surrender," Alvantes cried – obviously not feeling his audience's mood was quite volatile enough already. "We know the King is on his way. We know he intends to end the Castoval's independence, and by force if necessary. If we fight and lose, we'll be crushed. If we negotiate, we might still avoid the worst reprisals."

He hadn't finished the sentence before a dozen of those listening were on their feet, howling over each other to see who could make himself heard first.

"Avoid reprisals? Perhaps for yourself, Guard-Captain." From his thick accent, not to mention his knotted hair and fur-trimmed cloak, it was easy to recognise the speaker as a survivor of the warlord Moaradrid's recent invasion; one of those who'd chosen to back Mounteban rather than attempt the trek back to his distant northern home. He had a point, too. Since Mounteban had plotted against the King and Moaradrid's crimes had included the murder of his son, Prince Panchetto, it was hard to imagine his highness looking favourably on either allegiance.

If he thought Alvantes would be spared, though, the northerner's grasp on recent events was shaky at best. Given that the King had already tried to execute him once, given that he'd had his father murdered in the street for aiding our escape from the royal dungeons, it was a safe bet that Alvantes's name placed highly on our lunatic monarch's "to kill slowly" list.

In the meantime, the racket was only getting louder. From beside Alvantes, Marina Estrada cried out, "Please, this isn't helping anyone."

Estrada might have been running a town until recently, not to mention orchestrating the resistance effort against Moaradrid and helping Alvantes to liberate this very city – but just now, she might as well have been trying to put out a forest fire with a thimbleful of water.

Her words were swept away like spilled milk in a rainstorm, and even the fierce northerner's bark was already being drowned out. "You think you got problems?" roared a huge man with scar-latticed skin and a scruff of shorn hair. "If the King don't do for us, the Boar'll have our necks on the block before the day's done."

If his appearance hadn't already given it away, the use of that particular nickname for Alvantes would have identified the man. He belonged to one of the criminal fraternities that had given Mounteban his initial leverage in the city; if I remember rightly, he went by the name of Holes Morales, in honour of all those he'd left in shallow graves outside the walls of Altapasaeda. And once again, his logic was sound: half of those here would have faced imprisonment at the very least under the old order.

A variety of similarly rough-looking characters were bickering to make similar observations, but the voice that actually made it to the surface was of an altogether different tenor. It was a squeal more than a shout, yet its note of sheer desperation was enough to cut through the uproar. "Guard-Captain Alvantes, what about those of us innocent of any wrongdoing? Will the King care that we were tricked and cajoled into treachery?"

I recognised Lord Eldunzi, eldest scion of the house Eldunzi. Considering how quick he'd been to turn his coat, I felt he had a cheek. Perhaps some of the families had gone along with Mounteban against their will, but I suspected that, for most, the chance to trade profitable subservience for unrestrained wealth had been too good to miss.

Well, that more or less covered the three factions Mounteban had persuaded to share power in Altapasaeda: a resounding "three against, nil for" vote in favour of negotiation.

Not for the first time, I regretted letting Estrada talk me into taking the stage with her. I supposed she'd meant it as acknowledgment of my recent efforts in the city's rescue. However, given how quickly our heroic liberation of Altapasaeda had turned sour, I would far rather my part be hurriedly forgotten.

I did my best to shrink into the background as Alvantes leaned forward and raised his voice once more to drown the clamour. "All right! You don't want to surrender. Neither do I. Yet you all agree you're not willing to fight. Who do you expect to defend Altapasaeda if not its own people?"

"Isn't that your job?" someone piped up from towards the back.

"With what?" Alvantes cried. "A few dozen exhausted guardsmen and amateur soldiers?"

"*With what*? With those bloody giants is with what!"

That comment brought a steady roar of approval. Good luck to Alvantes explaining the concept of giant pacifism to his unruly audience – for how could anyone who hadn't witnessed it believe that the terrifying creatures we'd brought here could barely even be persuaded to defend themselves? It was only because I'd accidentally stolen a giant and even more accidentally befriended him that I'd come to understand; for Saltlick and his people, violence was something alien and utterly abhorrent.

"The giants won't fight for us," Alvantes said simply. A note of defeat was starting to enter his voice, and he was hardly trying to restrain it. After everything he'd been through to save this city, everything he'd sacrificed, I could see that the churlish defeatism he was up against was grating upon his good intentions. Then there was the fact that the very threat he was striving to protect his home from was the king he'd served dutifully all his life. All things considered, it wasn't a good day to be former Guard-Captain Lunto Alvantes.

It was only about to get worse.

"What about Mounteban?" someone heckled from towards the centre – and at the mention of that name, the atmosphere in the room changed immediately, as though every light had dimmed or the temperature abruptly climbed.

There was a pause, uncomfortably long, and then another voice echoed, "Yeah! Where's Mounteban?"

"Mounteban! Where is he?"

"We'll talk to Mounteban!"

In a moment it had become a chorus, that one name resounding down the length and breadth of the hall.

Alvantes stood it for a full ten seconds before he broke. Then he lashed a foot into the lectern and it tore loose with a thunderous crack, to burst into pieces on the tiles below. Alvantes stood, sides heaving, eyes roving across his suddenly-silent audience – as though challenging them to acknowledge his outburst, or to so much as whisper that hated name again.

"This meeting is over," he spat, and stormed from the stage.

Outside, the city was in chaos.

Roughly half the populace had chosen to stay at home, and were in the process of barricading those homes against any and every threat. Such was generally the case here in the wealthy South Bank, where some of the families had the sort of resources that could fend off even a royal army – for a while, at least.

The other portion of the city's inhabitants had decided that the best place to be right now would be anywhere but Altapasaeda. These had bundled their possessions onto whatever modes of transport or beasts of burden came to hand – horses, donkeys, handcarts, their own or other people's children – before heading swiftly for the nearest city gate.

Whichever exit they chose, they wouldn't get far. Every gate was closed, and protected by a mixed squad of guardsmen and the irregular soldiers Estrada had brought here. Alvantes was calling it a temporary measure to keep both city and surrounding countryside from falling into further turmoil, but I couldn't help wondering how temporary it would turn out to be. As the disastrous meeting had made abundantly clear, Altapasaeda had a short enough future ahead of it if its own populace weren't willing to stay and defend it.

Just then, however, Alvantes seemed oblivious to anything but his own seething frustration. Where anyone got in his way he simply barged through, leaving horses whickering and men and women shouting in his wake. I followed a few paces behind, still unable to think of anywhere better I could be while the city was busy tearing itself apart, and Estrada struggled to keep pace with Alvantes.

She gave him five minutes, waiting until we were near the inner border of the South Bank district before she said, "You know they're just afraid."

Alvantes didn't look back. "Of course they're afraid. Cowards are always afraid."

"Lunto–"

"What?" he said. "You think I'm being unfair?"

"I think there are bigger questions we have to face."

"Because I think that what's unfair is handing this city back to Castilio Mounteban when we've only just wrestled it out of his filthy grasp. What's unfair is that he's relaxing in comfort when he should be resting his neck on the block in Red Carnation Square. I think..." Alvantes finally caught himself, and the last of his anger came out in a sigh of bitter vexation. "I think you're right as always, Marina... and I'm glad beyond measure that you're here, if only to stop me doing something I might regret."

Estrada reached to touch his arm, careful to choose the one that still had a hand attached to it. "I know how hard this is for you."

Finally pausing to face her, Alvantes managed the weakest of smiles. "It's hard for everyone. You must be worried about Muena Palaiya."

"I doubt the King will stop to bother with one town," she said. "It's if Altapasaeda falls that they'll have something to worry about. The best thing I can do for my people right now is to be here helping you."

"Helping me? Only, it seems no one much cares what I think." Much of the bitterness had returned to Alvantes's voice. "They'd prefer to put their city in the hands of a self-serving crook."

"*Bigger questions*, Lunto. They think of you as part of the old order. Then, the minute you walk through the gates, they hear the King's marching an army on their city. They're going to have to learn to trust you. In the meantime–"

"Yes, I know. In the meantime, they want Mounteban. Good old honest Castilio Mounteban, the people's hero. Well if they want him so badly, maybe they deserve him."

Alvantes set off pacing again, and this time Estrada left him to it. She had her own reasons to despise Mounteban, just as I did – in her case, an amorous attempt that had gone far too far, in mine a deranged assassin sent after my life. In fact, it was arguable that we both had more reason to hate him than Alvantes did. Yet just then I felt remarkably unfazed by the prospect of having the man I'd risked so much to depose weasel his way back into power. Perhaps it was only the shock of discovering that my best efforts to do the right thing had led to nothing except disaster, but ever since the King's message had arrived I'd found it hard to care about much of anything.

We'd barely passed the border of the South Bank, marked by an arch of twisted iron decked and twined with flowers, before our objective presented itself. Since his defeat, Mounteban had been confined to his rooms in the Dancing Cat, the inn he'd made his base of operations. It was a luxurious establishment, perched upon the edges of the rich Upper Market District and the mansion-filled South Bank. Until Mounteban had taken it over, the Cat had catered solely to wealthy patrons resting on their way home from an exhausting day's shopping. The question of just what Mounteban had done with its original proprietor was one of the many left to hang before the more pressing business at hand.

There were two guardsmen on the main entrance, both of whom I recognised from Alvantes's trusted inner circle. Inside, another sat at the bottom of the stairs, on one of the few chairs still intact. Most of the remaining furniture had been smashed to smithereens in the violence that had led up to Mounteban's capture – a fight this man had seen his share of, if the bandage around his arm was anything to judge by. Lastly, at the head of the staircase stood waiting Sub-Captain Navare, former undercover agent in the Suburbs beyond the northern wall. Seeing Alvantes starting up the stairs, he threw a smart salute.

"Has he given you any trouble?" asked Alvantes, sounding almost hopeful. He had wanted to throw Mounteban in the dankest depths of the city prison, and only Estrada's caution had kept him from doing it.

"Quiet as a temple rat," replied Navare. "I think he's been asleep."

"Or else quietly prying off those planks we nailed across his window?"

"I put a man in the yard," replied Navare, "looking out for precisely that. Not a word from him so far."

Alvantes didn't quite hide his disappointment. Brushing past Navare, he made to knock at the heavy panelled door, caught himself, and slammed it open instead.

Already doubting my part in this latest turn of events, I didn't much feel like following after, but Estrada was close behind me, and I couldn't think of a decent enough excuse to make my exit. I fell into step, entering the room a little cautiously, and edged into a corner so as to be well out of whatever came next.

The room was certainly luxurious, a wide and airy space with brilliantly white walls hung with tapestries and rich, patterned carpets on the floors. The furniture was all of dark wood, and more solid than that demolished by the ruckus in the taproom; the desk and broad bed might even have been sturdy enough to survive that violence.

However, I suspected the extravagance had been inherited from the inn's true owner, for imprinted upon it were signs of an altogether more austere personality. The desk was literally buried in maps and other papers, with just enough arrangement to suggest the inklings of some order. The bed looked as if it hadn't been made in weeks; the rugs were scuffed with countless boot prints. My sense was that Mounteban had chosen this location as a compromise, between what he was accustomed to and what he knew would be expected of a man who could run a place like Altapasaeda.

As for Mounteban himself, he certainly didn't look like he'd been relaxing. Sat before the desk, he looked, in fact, like someone for whom sleep had become a distant memory. His eyes were shadowed, and despite his bulk and copious beard, his face looked drawn. He had flinched at Alvantes's entrance, and now he stared up, with a bravado that didn't quite hide the tension beneath it.

"You can relax," scoffed Alvantes. "If you were going to be executed, I wouldn't have bothered to come in person; I'd have sent the city's sewer cleaners. No, it's quite the opposite, Mounteban. We're letting you go."

Mounteban's face didn't change; neither the veneer of courage nor the strain it failed to mask. "I don't understand."

"What's not to understand?" Alvantes spat. "You've won, damn you. Altapasaeda will get its independence, whether it wants it or not – or else be burned to the ground by its own king. And you've poisoned the place so thoroughly that no one will listen to anyone besides you. So get up. Get out. If you really claim any shred of good intentions then make those scum you brought together understand that this city hasn't a chance without their help."

"They're asking for you, Castilio," said Estrada. "The alliance you brought together is falling apart. They won't listen to us. And if they don't listen to someone, the King will simply march into Altapasaeda in a week's time, with no one to hinder him."

Mounteban's only response was a stiff nod, as though he'd weighed what they'd told him and found it credible.

"No gloating?" asked Alvantes, disgust dripping from each syllable. "No grand speech? Not going to explain again how you decided to elect yourself prince of the city for its own good?"

"Do you think I want this any more than you do?" Now that he wasn't anticipating an imminent demise, some of Mounteban's self-possession was beginning to return. "Whether or not you believe it, I *did* have Altapasaeda's best interests at heart."

Alvantes gave him a ghastly smile. "Of course you did."

"Still," continued Mounteban, "I knew when I started that it might come to this."

"You thought the King might come knocking if you absconded with his city? How astute."

"I thought there might be *some* reprisal. So I planned for it... which is more, it seems, than you did, Guard-Captain."

Alvantes lurched forward, fist clenched. "I said I'd let you talk to them, Mounteban. I didn't say what state you'd be in when you got there."

In a moment, Mounteban was on his feet, sending his chair clattering to the floor.

"Stop it! Both of you." Estrada had advanced too, arms outstretched, as though she'd keep them apart by brute force if need be. "And grow up, damn it! There's more at stake here than your petty squabbling." She turned fiercely on Alvantes, who looked both surprised and sheepish. "Leave him alone, Lunto. This isn't helping anything."

If he'd realised, as I had, that Estrada was playing subtly to Mounteban's ego, Alvantes's wounded expression gave no sign. He stamped to the far side of the room and turned half away, as though not quite willing to admit he was interested in anything Mounteban had to say.

Estrada, meanwhile, gave Mounteban a moment to right his chair and sit back down before she said, "Understand, Castilio, that I will never forgive you for the things you've done... to me or to this city. But I'll work with you now, if that's what it takes. So if you really care about Altapasaeda, tell us your plan. There's no time for us to play games."

"Of course," Mounteban replied, all surface calm restored. "I was never the one who wanted a conflict, Marina. I'd have gladly worked with you both from the beginning."

Alvantes gave a snort of derision, silenced abruptly when Estrada glared at him. "All right," she said. "We're listening."

I could tell that was what Mounteban had been waiting to hear, for all his old arrogance had returned as he asked, "I trust you're familiar with the name of the Bastard Prince?"

Alvantes glowered. "A northerner myth. A phantom to scare the royal court."

"Not so," said Mounteban. "The boy is very real."

"Wait a minute," I said. Thus far, I'd been deliberately keeping out of the conversation – but having only recently heard of this mysterious Bastard Prince, I realised I couldn't keep down my curiosity. "Tell me if I'm understanding this right. King Panchessa sires a child on some northerner wench and then covers it up. That child grows up to be Moaradrid, notorious invading warlord, kidnapper of giants and all-round madman."

Mounteban nodded, with the disinterested air of one teaching obvious lessons to a stupid child.

"But Moaradrid is dead," I continued. And no one in their right mind would ever refer to him as a boy. Suddenly, I understood. "You're saying Moaradrid had a son too?"

"His name is Malekrin," Mounteban agreed. "The Bastard Prince, illegitimate son of an illegitimate son. The King's only possible living heir."

"But surely he hasn't any real claim to the throne?" put in Estrada.

"For our purposes," said Mounteban, "it hardly matters. What's important is that the northerners believe it – and that, even after Moaradrid's failed rebellion, they're willing to fight over it. If you're aware of the Prince, Marina, I'm sure you're equally familiar with the name Kalyxis?"

Alvantes's expression soured even further. "That witch."

My inquisitiveness genuinely piqued now, I said, "Let's assume that not everyone has your or Alvantes's grasp on the politics of far-distant lands."

"Kalyxis," said Mounteban, "is King Panchessa's one-time paramour, Moaradrid's mother, Malekrin's grandmother... and just as she did with his father, she's been grooming the boy as a potential saviour of the far north. As obvious as it would seem that she's motivated by spite, she has a remarkable knack for telling her people what they want to hear."

"It sounds like you two have a lot in common," observed Alvantes.

"Just so," Mounteban agreed, ignoring the obvious slight. "Which is why I sent a messenger to her proposing an alliance. I haven't received a reply, but then given the distances involved that's hardly surprising. However, it seems to me that Kalyxis and the Prince are still our best hope. Perhaps they can be persuaded to send support, or to harry Ans Pasaeda from the north, forcing the King to cut short his visit. Perhaps just the threat of an alliance will be enough to make Panchessa think twice."

"I appreciate that you've put thought into this," said Estrada carefully, "but do you really think it could work? And even if it did, as you just said yourself, there's no way anyone could travel so far and return in time. Altapasaeda can't stand against the King for more than a few days."

"A difficulty, for sure," agreed Mounteban. "But there *is* a way."

There was something in the way he emphasised those last words that made everyone, even Alvantes, suddenly more attentive. "Go on," Estrada told him.

"A tunnel, running west from the palace, through the mountainside. It was built, or perhaps more likely discovered, by the first prince... this in the days when a Castovalian revolt seemed more than likely. At the other end are a dock and a ship. If my sources are correct, even Panchetto wasn't so confident in his own safety as to leave the passage and vessel unmaintained. It should still be there, and seaworthy."

"This is all nonsense!" growled Alvantes. "I'd have heard of such a thing."

"Apparently not," replied Mounteban. "Then again," he added with smug good cheer, "Panchetto always did like to keep the City Guard at arm's length."

Alvantes was clearly ready to storm back across the room, but catching Estrada's eye he thought better of it. "Anyway," he said instead, "in case it's escaped these 'sources' of yours, the palace is occupied. I doubt the Palace Guard would take kindly to us traipsing through. Unless, of course, you've somehow managed to deal with them too?"

"That proved... untenable," admitted Mounteban, his brief upturn in mood evaporating. "I'd hoped that, left to their own devices, they'd eventually see sense."

The Palace Guard were notorious in Altapasaeda for many things: their fierce loyalty to the crown, their moral flexibility in its service and their comprehensive training in its defence, especially where that defence involved the use of disproportionate violence. One of the things they'd never been known for, however, was seeing sense – and with their beloved prince dead, it was a safe assumption that they'd be less inclined than ever. Taking all that into account, it was a fair guess that Mounteban's plan had been more along the lines of "wait them out and hope they eventually starve". In fairness, it was probably the best anyone could have come up with.

"However," Mounteban continued, "there's no need to march into the palace. Because the passage has a second exit, which opens outside the city... beneath your own barracks, in fact, Alvantes. No doubt its designers anticipated a less extreme emergency where retreating to the protection of the City Guard might prove useful. Had the Prince trusted you enough to reveal the location of that second exit, our problem would be solved. Still. When it comes to entering the palace and finding the entrance, one man might conceivably succeed where a larger force would be sure to fail."

"I'm not convinced this passage of yours even exists..." began Alvantes.

"It does," Mounteban cut him off. "And it's our one chance of drawing aid to Altapasaeda before the city falls. You'd never have come here if you had another."

Estrada and Alvantes shared a long look. I assumed there was some unspoken communication passing between them, for how else were they to discuss the possibility of a truce with Mounteban, who they'd gone to such lengths to depose, when he was sitting right there? He was all swagger now, not even bothering to look at them – but I doubted even he was truly arrogant enough to assume that they'd unquestioningly put their enmity for him aside to pursue so desperate a plan.

"Altapasaeda needs help," Estrada said finally. "And there's nowhere in the Castoval left to offer it. Frankly, Castilio, I'd don't trust this scheme of yours. There's far too much that could go wrong, and no guarantees even if it doesn't. But I don't see any other choices, and every moment we spend seeking one brings the King closer to our gates."

"I don't like it," agreed Alvantes, "but it's all we have. So I'll go along with it... until you give me the slightest inkling that you can't be trusted in this, Mounteban."

"Let's take the threats as said and heard," replied Mounteban, with studied dignity, "and start preparing while there's still a chance of success. The first question is who to send into the palace."

"I think I could arrange a suitable diversion," conceded Alvantes.

"The walls and the courtyard will be the hardest part," Mounteban said. "How long would this diversion last?"

"Long enough, I think."

"So, if someone were to scale the walls... perhaps to reach a window..."

I couldn't take it anymore. It wasn't so much what they were saying, but that I could feel Estrada's eyes on me, boring into my skull in search of the conscience she seemed convinced was in there. "All right!" I cried. "Why not spare us all a little time?"

Mounteban and Alvantes turned my way as well – and it was only seeing the surprise in their expressions that I realised how badly I'd misjudged. What I'd taken for none-too-subtle hinting in my direction had been no more than the honest back and forth of observations, it appeared.

Yet, with my mouth open and working, I found I couldn't simply back down. "Haven't we been here before?" I said. "Oh no, something needs breaking into! Who can we possibly ask? Who do we know who used to break into things all the time? Who will no one miss when it all goes wrong?"

"Damasco–" Estrada began.

I realised then that, though Alvantes and Mounteban might not have had any intention of involving me, Estrada truly had.

It was there in the gentle cajoling with which she spoke my name. Why couldn't the woman just leave me alone?

And even more infuriatingly, why, when I knew she was manipulating me, could I not stop myself from talking?

"Spare me," I said. "We've danced this dance enough times. Sooner or later, whatever I say, you'll talk me into it, so just this once let's get it over with. You want me to break into the palace? Fine! I'll do it."

CHAPTER TWO

It didn't take long for the cracks to start showing in our new alliance.

We were leaving the Dancing Cat, with Mounteban in tow and Navare and another guardsman hovering awkwardly behind, no one having bothered to inform them about the fragile coalition. "I have a few men in mind to send north," said Mounteban, offhandedly. "Men with some nautical background."

"Freebooters, you mean?" retorted Alvantes – and the way Mounteban tensed suggested the dig had struck its mark. "Not a chance. For all we know, this treaty with Kalyxis is intended to serve you and you only."

"Then go with them, Guard-Captain," said Mounteban. "I'm sure they'd be grateful for your guidance."

"And hand you back Altapasaeda? Never."

"I'll go," put in Estrada.

"That's absurd." Alvantes's reply had the abruptness of a reflex, and it was clear he'd realised his mistake almost before he'd closed his mouth.

It would take more than belated regret to make Estrada go easy on him. "Are we really having this conversation again?"

she snapped. "Do I need to list the qualifications that make me every bit as suitable for this as you?"

"It isn't that," Alvantes said hastily. "But you're needed here, and given the dangers involved–"

"For whatever it's worth," put in Mounteban, "I think Marina would be an excellent choice. From what I've heard, Kalyxis has little affection for men, to say the least. Sending a female leader would show respect, and understanding of her position."

"Her position as a professional rabble-rouser?" said Alvantes. "I hardly think–"

"I'll take some guardsmen with me, if you can spare them," Estrada interrupted. "And one of the giants, if Saltlick agrees. They have a way of ensuring people pay attention."

"Marina..."

Estrada rounded on Alvantes, throwing our small parade into chaos. On any other day such drama would have drawn attention on the streets of Altapasaeda, where gossip was a currency second only to gold, but amidst those still-chaotic streets it passed unheeded. "Listen to me," she said. "If we're agreed that this is our best option then one of us has to go. It can't be Castilio. It can't be you. Who does that leave?"

I didn't even try to make out Alvantes's mumbled reply. Estrada's comment had struck so perfectly with the muddle in my head that everything else had fallen into background noise. She hadn't suggested me as a possibility for the trip north, probably hadn't so much as considered me – and where once that might have caused offence, now I realised I was glad. This foolhardy expedition was none of my concern, and that was exactly how I wanted it.

Of course, my own brush with death would arrive much sooner. Since my outburst in the Dancing Cat, one half of my mind had been gazing in horror at the other, the part that had so blithely thrust me once again into harm's way. Yet, having had time to analyse my brash-seeming decision, I'd come to realise that inspiration had hit me as I'd listened to Mounteban – struck with all the jolting clarity of a lightning bolt. And it had much to do with my depleted money bag and the events that had filled it to brimming not so long ago.

I could see now that ever since Ludovoco had arrived, bearing the message from the royal court that had turned Altapasaeda upside down, I'd been in a sort of stupor. Perhaps that was only to be expected. But what had demoralised me wasn't the threat of Panchessa's arrival; after the events of recent weeks, the mere likelihood of danger was becoming harder and harder to take seriously. No, what had truly thrown me was the shock, like ice water flung in my face, that all my recent attempts to do good had been for nothing. Every menace I'd stood against, each tyrant I'd struggled to depose, had only given way to something worse.

Now here we were, Mounteban's sins forgiven with an ease that had never been shown to my own comparatively minor transgressions. I'd never be truly accepted by Estrada and Alvantes, and given how misguided their efforts had proved, that was no bad thing. Their plans were doomed – and as long as I tied my flag to their mast, so was I. Here was a chance, though, surely a last chance, to turn my fortunes around. Because as full as the palace might be with peril, it was every bit as full of wealth.

One last job. I'd said it before, but this time I'd make certain it was true. If I left the palace alive, I'd also leave it rich. And after that, nothing would keep me in this doomed city.

Ahead of me, Alvantes slowed, and I just barely avoided tripping over his heels. Roused from my reverie, I realised we'd come to a halt before a building I recognised. I'd passed obliviously through the entirety of the Market District, and now here we were somewhere close to the north wall, gathered before an ugly structure of bare grey stone.

It was amazing that the odour hadn't warned me, really –
for now that I was paying attention, the ancient stink of rotted
flesh climbed into my nose and refused to let go. The building
had been a tannery until quite recently; as I understood,
the owner had decided that skipping town would be more
palatable than trying to pay his inordinate gambling debts, and
it had fallen vacant a month ago.

The reason I recognised it was presumably the same reason
we were standing before it now: there were very few empty
buildings in Altapasaeda large enough to house a hundred
giants. Even then, a better solution could probably have been
found had everyone not had more pressing worries. As it was,
since the giants weren't inclined to complain, the decision had
been swiftly made and forgotten.

Whatever the giants' nasal failings, what was suitable for
their habitation remained repulsive to mere men. Alvantes
gathered himself with a visible effort, scrunching his nose
against the stink before pressing through the gap in the open
double doors. Estrada went next, then Mounteban, and I
followed behind, sparing a sympathetic glance for Navare and
his fellow guardsman, who were experiencing this olfactory
horror for the first time.

Inside, I focused all my willpower on not retching. The
fixtures and furnishings had long since vanished, no doubt
stolen by competitors or sold by disgruntled creditors, the only
evidence of their vanished presence the geometry of cleaner
patches amidst the thickening dust. However, stripping the
great room to bare boards and walls had done nothing to wipe
away the vile, mingled odours that had seeped into them over
the years.

If it bothered the giants even slightly, they gave no
indication. They'd settled themselves in clumps around the
room, their presence making the considerable space seem
almost cramped. There was little light in there, nothing but

dim beams descending from openings near the ceiling, but the gloom didn't seem to concern them either.

Saltlick was on his feet and rushing over almost before we'd entered, his usual broad grin of greeting spread across his face. Seeing him, I felt a sudden surge of resentment on his behalf. What right did Estrada have to ask for anything more from him or his people? They were only still here because Saltlick had offered their help in rebuilding after the recent violence. The giants had already done more than enough for Altapasaeda, more than enough for Alvantes and Estrada.

I thought of pointing out as much, but I'd missed my moment: Estrada was already leading Saltlick to one side, while he hunched to catch her low-spoken words. Well, he was an adult, wasn't he? More than that, Saltlick was the closest thing the giants had to a chief now; all that kept him from the post was the absurdities of giant custom. If he couldn't be trusted to stand up for his people, who could?

So instead of trying to contribute my twelfth onyx-worth, I went to wait outside, where there was something at least approaching fresh air to be breathed. I watched the traffic of desperate people, the overladen carts and bickering families, and marvelled at how – even in Altapasaeda, where rumour was lifeblood – word of the King's approach could have spread so very quickly.

A few minutes had passed before Estrada called me back in. She looked paler than before, and shaken. It was there in her voice, too, as she said, "Saltlick's agreed to accompany me northward himself."

"Protect Marina," agreed Saltlick.

"He needs to be here," I said. There had been something in his tone as well – weariness, a hint of resignation – that had resuscitated my anger. "Can't you see that? He's their leader. How can you even consider dragging him off on this madman's errand?"

Estrada gave a half shrug, obviously uncomfortable. "Because he insists."

"Protect Marina," repeated Saltlick, more certainly this time.

It struck me then that he might not like being discussed as though he weren't towering right before us. "Saltlick," I said, "your people need you."

Saltlick motioned, picking out one giant who looked, to me, much like the rest. "Shai Mek will lead. Take people home."

"*Without you?*"

"Not for long," he said.

"Not unless..."

Not unless you die out there. But I didn't finish putting the thought into words; I knew better than to assume Saltlick hadn't thought through the ramifications of what he was about to do. Instead, I looked to Estrada, struggling for some appeal to her decency. Seeing her expression, though, I realised she was far from oblivious. Perhaps she'd have taken her request back if she could have.

She couldn't. Saltlick's mind was made up, and the damage done.

"You needn't worry," Estrada told him. "I'll make sure you get back in one piece."

Saltlick smiled, perfectly trusting. It would never have occurred to him she might do otherwise.

If anything, his faith only added to her obvious discomfort. "Well," she said, "we'd best start preparing."

Saltlick, taking her hint, started towards the giant he'd indicated earlier – and as he did so, looped a finger into the crown he wore at his neck, ready to tear it loose.

"Wait!" Mounteban, who'd hardly seemed to have been paying attention until then, took a quick a step forward.

Everyone, myself included, turned to look at him, expressions ranging from curiosity to Alvantes's outright suspicion.

"Saltlick, perhaps it's not my place," Mounteban said, "but should you really give up the crown? Won't it confuse your people, when it's taken them so long to accept the notion of having a new leader at all? Better, surely, if this Shai Mek simply acts on your behalf."

I wondered briefly how Mounteban knew the recent history of the crown – how I'd used it as a replacement for the giants' lost stone of leadership to trick them into following Saltlick. But *of course* he would know. Mounteban made it his business to know everything that might possibly be of use to him. And what he knew, he used. So what was his angle this time?

The worst of it was, I agreed with him. To say the giants weren't amenable to change was like saying mountains weren't amenable to change. It had taken little short of an earthquake to get them moving; if Saltlick left the slightest ambiguity as to who was in charge and then failed to return, who could say if they'd ever make it home?

Saltlick's slow nod told us he'd reached a similar conclusion. "Speak to people," he said. "Explain."

"Maybe we should wait outside," Estrada suggested.

We trooped out, everyone but me trying not to make a show of gulping the unpolluted air. I listened to the rumble of Saltlick's voice from within, the thick syllables of giantish falling like pebbles on a sheet of slate, and forced myself not to think about what was coming next.

I stared up at the palace walls, as the white-cobbled square behind me turned into a lake of gold beneath the lowering sun. I'd have much preferred to play my part in darkness, while Alvantes had argued that daylight would make his end of the plan seem less suspicious. This time, with night still a good hour away, was the compromise we'd agreed.

Once there had been spikes lining either edge of the wall. Rumour had it that Prince Panchetto had had them removed for purely aesthetic reasons. While it was undeniable that prongs of metal as long as a man's arm would clash badly with the palace's luminous facades, its brilliant murals, its domes of duck egg blue and spires of gold, it was equally true that they'd have gone a long way towards stopping me doing what I was about to attempt.

Back in the days when the palace had still contained its prince, there would have been guardsmen observing this side of the wall as well as the other, but whatever conflicts had occurred between the Palace Guard and Mounteban's regime had put paid to that. Still, under most circumstances, a wall as high as three tall men would have posed a considerable obstacle in itself. Even without the spikes, the upper edges had been carefully rounded to resist a grapple, and the surface was smooth as porcelain.

I, however, had something on my side that every potential interloper before now had surely lacked. "You understand what you have to do, don't you, Saltlick? This needs to be *quiet*. No just hurling me over."

"Quiet," Saltlick agreed, in what passed for him as a whisper. He'd already knelt down to cup his hands at the level of my feet.

"I don't want you to get carried away," I emphasised.

Saltlick solemnly shook his head.

"Well. All right."

From directly below, Saltlick's misshapen head looked all the more odd and turnip-like, the muscles of his upper body more like lumps in an overstuffed mattress – and no length of acquaintance could quite quash the nervousness I felt looking up at a living being twice my own height. Yet this time I realised it was neither Saltlick's ugliness nor his fearsomeness that was causing me to stare at him. "You don't have to go with them," I said. "I know you feel you have some sort of duty to Estrada. But Saltlick, if you ever had you've more than paid it.

You could leave. Take your people home. If you're here when the King arrives, there might never be another chance."

He met my eyes then – and hard as I always found it to judge that misshapen face, it was obvious I wasn't telling him anything he hadn't already considered. Still, despite the moment's hesitation, Saltlick shook his head once more.

I'd learned from long experience how stubborn he could be, especially when he was doing what he thought was right, and outside the walls of a palace filled with paranoid guards was hardly the place for a lengthy debate that I'd inevitably end up losing.

I shrugged resignedly, put one foot into his cupped hands and reached out to clasp his arm. I'd barely made sure of my hold before he was lifting me, as lightly as if I weighed nothing at all. Before I'd even quite registered the motion, the top of the wall was looming within reach. Its rim, smoothed to a gentle curve, offered nothing for my fingers to grip. I scrabbled frantically, caught between the desire to be quiet and fear of my skull splitting like an egg on the paving slabs below.

Abruptly, I lurched higher, as Saltlick heaved my feet to his own head height – and then higher still. I knew from the way we were swaying that he must be practically on tiptoes. It wasn't helping; in fact, he'd only made things worse. The wall was so wide that the far edge was still out of reach, while his thrust had snatched the nearer edge from beneath my fingers. I was teetering, held by nothing but Saltlick's tenuous grip.

I wanted to cry out. I knew it would be suicide. Instead, I flopped towards the wall, scrabbling at its smooth surface. Reaching until I thought my shoulder would tear from its socket, I managed to hook three fingers over the far edge. It was curved too, but less so; my grip held. Saltlick, perhaps understanding, chose that moment for another, incremental push.

He must be standing straight as an arrow; it was now or never. I flung up one leg, dragged with fingers that were knots of fire. My body seemed impossibly weighty, the bulk of a lifelong glutton rather than a half-starved thief. Feeling Saltlick strain to propel my other foot, I gave everything I had to exploit that fractional momentum, kicking and hauling both together. Groaning through gritted teeth, I dragged myself up, flopped onto my back along the wall's broad summit.

I'd made it – but I'd hardly been silent. If a dozen guards were waiting on the other side, it was better I found out now, while I had a chance to change my mind. I rolled over, struggling to angle my head towards the inside edge without exposing myself. At least, with the sun drawing low above the westerly mountains, I wouldn't be silhouetted. Laid flat as I could make myself, I peeked into the courtyard.

The yard beyond the wall was deep in gloom. I had to strain to see figures – two far to my left outside the double doors of the coach house and another quite close on my right. Had they been looking up, they'd have surely seen me too. That they weren't told me they either possessed more subtlety than the average guards or else they'd failed to catch the sounds of my clumsy ascent. Under the circumstances, I'd no choice but to gamble on the latter.

Quiet as I could manage, I slipped off my backpack and drew out the length of rope I had stashed there. I'd purchased it not an hour before from Franco, the city's finest and most cantankerous supplier to those in the shadowier trades. He hadn't been pleased to see me, what with me recently leading Alvantes to his door, but there was no enmity in the world that would make Franco turn away good hard coin. The rope was light and heavily padded, designed to deaden sound – and, as usual, Franco's craftsmanship was beyond reproach.

Now it was only a matter of waiting – and of hoping no one was sharp-eyed enough to spot me.

Alvantes's diversion was simple. In a sense, it was hardly a diversion at all; or, not unless we were found out. After all, he was – or had been – Guard-Captain of Altapasaeda. With the city wrested from Mounteban's grip, it made perfect sense that he should pay a visit to his former colleagues of the Palace Guard. I didn't know what he meant to say to them, nor did I much care. They couldn't very well ignore him, and the question of whether he was there as friend or foe should be enough to keep them occupied for a few minutes.

What it came down to, then, was whether Alvantes's arrival would be enough to disrupt the palace's meticulous security. If discipline triumphed it wouldn't be, and the Palace Guard were nothing if not disciplined. However, they'd been isolated for weeks now, likely with little word from the outside world, their defences probed by Mounteban's forces. My only hope was that those travails had been enough to wear down their iron efficiency.

The main gate was blocked from view by a corner of the palace; I heard Alvantes's arrival rather than saw it. It began as raised, overlapping voices, and soon after came the crash and clatter of heavy objects being moved, no doubt an entrance being cleared in the barricades.

I wasn't the only one to have noticed the sudden din. The guard to my right cried out something I didn't catch and gestured to his companions, one of whom returned a shrug and called clearly, "Who knows?"

The first guard then paced over to the other two and they shared a brief conversation, none of which I could make out. At its conclusion, he hurried back to his post. As he regained it, one of the two opened a small door beside the larger coach house entrance and they both disappeared inside.

Not ideal. I'd hoped all three might leave together. Perhaps it was the best I could expect, though. The lone guard was some distance away, his attention on the continuing tumult from around the corner. Moreover, waiting for a better opportunity was only likely to bring the other two back. No... *this* was my chance.

I fed one end of the rope down the outer side of the wall until it went taut, as Saltlick caught hold of it. The other end I unrolled into the courtyard. With a quick tug of breath, I grasped a length, rolled off the wall's summit and swung down hand over hand. I struck the dusty cobbles with a jolt, but it was better than I'd have fared had I jumped; at least I didn't drive my shinbones into my ears.

A glance told me the lone guard hadn't looked my way. I tugged twice on the rope, my prearranged signal with Saltlick. Sure enough, it went slack, as he released his end. I hauled the rope back over, rolled it in quick loops around my forearm and stuffed it back into my pack.

Not for the first time, it struck me that Saltlick was better suited to thievery than his size would suggest. His part in this endeavour was done, though; I was on my own now. I could just make out his attempt to leave quietly as a muffled swishing, as though someone were sweeping the vast square. The next time I'd see him would be when I opened the tunnel beneath the barracks, if all went to plan. If it didn't, I'd missed my chance for a goodbye – but that would probably be the least of my worries.

I took the briefest instant to get my bearings and then made a dash to, and through, the small entrance by the coach doors. Within, the coach house was dark, its lanterns unlit. The first thing I saw was a carriage parked just inside the entrance; instinct sent me scampering to duck between its high rear wheels. Only then did I notice the damage there, the snapped-off arrows sunk into the wood, and recognise the vehicle for what it was. This was the carriage I'd escaped in after Moaradrid murdered Panchetto, a journey I'd passed in the gruesome company of the Prince's beheaded corpse – and I couldn't but shudder at the memory.

I made a brief investigation of the room from beneath the carriage, satisfied myself that there were no feet in view, and gratefully set out again. The coach house ran on into deeper gloom, but there were stairs ascending to my left and I took them. Knowing how narrow my window of opportunity was, knowing how much I was pushing that window by adding a diversion of my own, I took the steps as rapidly as I dared, straining my ears for any hint that I was charging into trouble.

At the first landing, I elected to continue up another flight, and then another and another, until I could go no higher. The Palace Guard were sure to have concentrated their efforts on the lowest level, where intruders might conceivably enter. By the same measure, I was confident that Panchetto's rooms would be on the highest floor, for what prince ever had his bedroom in the cellars? Anyway, what I'd seen of Panchetto told me he'd have wanted a good view from which to look down on the little people.

What else? I knew from my previous visit where the guest quarters were, having robbed them quite methodically. It was a safe bet Panchetto wouldn't want his own rooms bordering directly onto those. It made sense, in fact, that the servant's quarters should be closer, so that there was never a risk of a princely whim failing to receive its proper pandering. Put it all together and my tenuous evidence pointed towards the western wing.

In any case, I had to start somewhere. I peeked to satisfy myself the passage was empty and darted left. Things would have been simpler had the palace been designed according to any sort of logic; common sense would have dictated a single main corridor circumnavigating the entire floor, but common sense had clearly never stood a chance in the face of royal capriciousness. Time and again I had to divert around some needless obstruction – first a fountain that had no right to be four floors from the ground and then a great light well, illuminating a small and apparently sealed off garden.

It would have been less frustrating had every corner not required another pause to make certain I wasn't charging into the arms of the Palace Guard. I could frequently hear footsteps, sometimes near, sometimes the faintest patter, and raised voices calling to and over each other. It was safe to say that Alvantes's arrival had been more than enough to focus the guards' attention, after their weeks of forced isolation. Still, the fact the diversion was working only made it more likely that I'd barge into some isolated sentry curious as to what all the fuss was about.

As it turned out, though, it was the one time I didn't look that nearly gave me away. My nerves were strung to breaking point by the palace's wilful design, and a long streak of safety had made me careless. I raced around a corner and had taken three steps before my brain acknowledged the guard ahead. By the time I'd skidded to a halt, I was certain he must be aware of me, about to look round at any moment.

However, the corridor was long, my soft-soled shoes all but silent on the patterned tiles, and his gaze was trained away from me – towards the ongoing ruckus caused by Alvantes's appearance, no doubt. I retreated, literally walking backwards for fear of taking my eyes off him. I pressed myself around the corner I'd so recently burst from, held still until the blood stopped pounding in my ears.

Lucky. I'd been lucky. More than I deserved for such sloppiness.

And another thought, following close behind: what was there left to guard up here but Panchetto's vacant quarters?

It seemed unfair to expect any more of fate, and I was already mulling over the impossible-seeming task of making my entrance without the guard's noticing, when a voice – distant but clear, presumably issuing from the far end of the passage – called, "Namquo, get here. There's trouble downstairs."

I didn't witness the man named Namquo's response; but a moment later, I heard the tap of feet receding down the hall.

I refused to let myself consider. I'd freeze if I did. I burst round the corner once more, ran to the door hanging, hoping my rapid footsteps were quieter than the booming of my heart. I actually saw the guard's retreating back as he disappeared round the next corner, and for an instant it seemed certain he'd hear and turn. Then he was gone, and I was plunging through the curtain, exertion and fear making my chest quiver like a beaten drum.

It was worth it. Before I'd even really taken in the sight before me, I knew it was worth it. As the rush of fear passed, I only became more certain: of all my less than wise, not always savoury undertakings, here was the one that might actually justify the risks.

For Prince Panchetto's chambers were a thing of beauty, of exquisiteness that mocked even the possibility of imperfection. Where an edge or surface could be painted, gilded, studded with jewels or inlaid with precious metal, it had been, and always with the most astounding artistry. More, there were so many cushions scattered round and so many sumptuous rugs upon the mosaicked floor that it was as though the space had been designed with a toddling child in mind.

Now that I was here, however, one obvious question that I'd somehow hitherto ignored made itself inescapable: what was I actually looking for? Did princes keep gold and jewels loose in their chambers? Would Panchetto have even possessed coin when he hardly left the palace, never wanted for anything money could buy? Having spent so little time with royalty, I found it impossible to say – but I had my doubts.

I'd made it this far, though, and I couldn't bear the thought of leaving empty handed. I pushed through a silken hanging, into a room dominated by a bed fit for a small household, curtained with fine cloth of interlacing crimson and blue. Bed aside, there wasn't a single piece of furniture in there, so I pressed on, through another hanging into a slightly smaller room, where a bath as large as a good-sized cottage was sunk into the floor.

I was about to turn back when something caught my eye: a box set with polished bronze and lapis lazuli perched on one edge of the oceanic bath. On impulse, I scurried over, drew back the lid – and almost keeled over in my delight. It wasn't the oils and perfumes within that had set my head spinning, expensive though they no doubt were. No, it was the bottles that contained them: the flasks of cut crystal, with their jewel-encrusted stoppers of gold and silver. Melted down, the gold alone would keep me comfortable for a year.

I unslung my pack, loosed the straps and began to fill it. I went carefully at first, but soon realised it was wasted effort. Like everything else, the flasks had been designed with the clumsy Panchetto in mind; I could probably have flung them at the wall without them breaking. Instead, I crammed them in by the handful, heedless of how they clinked and rattled.

Too late did it occur to me that breaking my prizes was the least of my worries.

No, it was the noise I was making I should have been paying attention to. It was a mistake unworthy of a seasoned thief – and all the more so because it took a hand clamping my shoulder to make me realise it.

"Whoever you are," a leaden voice declaimed, "you sure as hells aren't Prince Panchetto."

CHAPTER THREE

My mistake had been assuming there would only be one guard watching Panchetto's chambers.

Or else it had been not keeping an eye out; or perhaps breaking into the palace in the first place; or maybe just ever returning to Altapasaeda. The more I thought about it, the harder it became to think of some point that I could definitively say *wasn't* a mistake to work forward from.

In the meantime, the vice-like grip on my shoulder was doing unpleasant things to the circulation in my arm. I could already feel my fingers starting to go numb. "If you can just give me a minute to explain..."

He released my shoulder abruptly. Whatever relief I felt vanished the instant I realised it was only to clasp my wrist and wrap my arm efficiently – not to mention, excruciatingly – behind my back.

"Aaaowww," I wailed, "there's no need to–"

Another twist, very slight and utterly agonising, was enough to make me shut up.

"You can tell it downstairs," he said. My guard, whose face I still hadn't seen, had perfectly mastered the forced boredom of the professional law enforcer. We might have been discussing the weather on a particularly dull day for all the interest in his voice.

Still, his professionalism couldn't be faulted. He had me on my feet in a moment, and moving straight after, all achieved with only the subtlest manipulation of my pinned arm. I was helpless as a newborn kitten in a snake pit. My choices extended to doing precisely what he wanted or having my shoulder dislodged from its socket.

He led me at a steady march, taking a different route to the one I'd arrived by. I could hardly see where we were going for the tears stinging my eyes, but the passages looked more or less like the ones I'd navigated on the way in. The same could be said for the stairwell he manoeuvred me into and the descending levels he steered me down.

Without its prince and the bustle that had gone with his residency, the palace was sunk in a silence that worked wonderfully to channel any sound. By the second flight I could clearly make out voices, drifting from some distant other wing. One of them I felt sure belonged to Alvantes, and I could make out enough of his interlocutor's replies to realise their voice was familiar as well, unlikely as that seemed.

On the ground floor, the landscape changed: here was the region intended for eyes other than the palace's regular inhabitants, and the decor became suitably more grand and gaudy. My guard led me along wide passages and on through the sculpted gardens that dominated the interior yard, thoughtfully choosing a path where rich-scented flowers climbed around great edifices of cane.

By the time we drew near the far side, the conversation ahead was growing discernible. The first sentence I heard a part of distinctly was Alvantes's, "...an amicable solution. Without shedding of blood."

"I think that point is past," replied the second voice.

"And food? Fresh water? Supplies of medicine?"

"Oh, yes. We have all of those. Enough for a very long time."

Alvantes's next comment was muted, and I missed it. The reply, however, was perfectly clear. "So you see? You have nothing at all to bargain with."

It was the note of contempt that did it, with its particular undercurrent of arrogance. *Of course* I knew that voice. Hadn't I spent days in its owner's company? Commander Ludovoco, of the Crown Guard: the man who'd escorted Alvantes and I to Pasaeda, only to arrest us on its doorstep; the man I'd last seen delivering the King's declaration of war and plunging Altapasaeda into disarray. I'd seen enough of Ludovoco to know that he was a conniving bastard, a political thug with his own distorted agenda and scant regard for the wellbeing of others.

I'd given no thought, though, to where he'd disappeared to after dropping his wasp's nest into our laps. It should have been obvious. Where else than here, where he could work best to be a thorn in the side of the Altapasaedan defence? Alvantes had come here to reason with the Palace Guard, to try to persuade them to stand down now that Mounteban was no longer a threat – and perhaps it might have worked, had they not known that relief was mere days away.

All of which meant that Alvantes had just placed his life in his enemy's hands. Under the circumstances, I doubted he was going to be pleased to see me.

There was a curtained aperture ahead and my guard shoved me hard into it, without quite releasing my arm, so that for a moment I was afraid I'd get tangled in its thick folds. Then I was through, and gawping at a large room that opened far above to the sky. It was a sort of patio, with a sunken area in the middle meant for players or musicians perhaps, and around the outside, seats, tables and decorated alcoves.

On the outer tier stood Ludovoco, along with twenty or so men from the Palace Guard. Half a dozen of them bore crossbows, which they held levelled at the occupants of the lower level – those being Alvantes and five of his city guardsmen. Beside Ludovoco was a man I distantly recognised from my time living in Altapasaeda, someone I knew only through reputation and the occasional public glimpse: Commander Ondeges, head of the Palace Guard. He was older than Ludovoco, his black hair flecked thickly with grey. Other than that, I could tell little about him; he had one of those chiselled, purposefully expressionless faces that I was starting to consider a prerequisite for dangerous positions of authority.

"Commander." My guard addressed not Ondeges but Ludovoco, which I found surprising. He sounded not only more alert than he had upstairs but conspicuously nervous. "I found *this* in his highness's chambers, sir."

Seeing me, Alvantes's eyes widened. "Damasco!"

Ludovoco glanced at him with disdain. "You seem surprised. Are we to believe this wasn't part of your plan?"

"If it was, I'd hardly have meant to get caught," I pointed out.

Ludovoco ignored me. "Is that his?" he asked, nodding towards something behind me.

"His pack, sir," explained my guard. "I think he was taking something out of it, maybe."

I hadn't even considered what had become of my bag. Evidently the guard had been attentive enough to bring it with him.

"Check it," Ludovoco told him.

I heard a dull clink as my guard flung the pack upon a low table beside the door, a scuffing as he drew open the cover. I still couldn't see his face, but a little of his stoic professionalism had slipped as he said, "A rope, Commander, and... er... bottles, mostly. Lots of little bottles." He obviously hadn't taken any time to wonder what I'd been doing in the Prince's bath chamber.

"A saboteur, is it? Or an assassin?" Ludovoco con-templated me, as if I were a slug crawling across his dinner plate. "Are they poisons? Some incendiary, perhaps?"

Perhaps my guard was ignorant of royal bathing practices, but I doubted very much that Ludovoco couldn't recognise bath oils when he saw them. Likewise, he had no reason to be quite this suspicious of Alvantes's motives. In any case, we were on Ondeges's turf, not his; what was Ludovoco doing, coming here and pulling rank like this?

Alvantes scowled. "I assure you," he said, "I knew nothing about this. I came here in good faith, to try and..."

"Spare me," said Ludovoco. "Please. I'm a busy man. In fact, to move matters to a swift conclusion, I'll propose a deal. Tell me, without prevarication, what your scheme here was and I'll let your men go."

"I've told you," said Alvantes with dignity, "I knew nothing of this degenerate's actions. Moreover, I won't bargain with the fates of my men, who are servants of the crown every bit as much as..."

Ludovoco cut him off with an upraised hand. It said a lot about the man that he could silence Alvantes so easily. With the same hand, he picked out one of Alvantes's entourage, a man I knew vaguely as Godares. To the palace guard beside him, Ludovoco said, "Kill that one."

The crossbowman hesitated – but only for an instant. In one economic motion, he lodged the bow against his shoulder and pulled the trigger.

Godares's mouth was just opening, perhaps to protest. It formed into a perfect "O" as the bolt struck. At such close range, the impact lifted him from his feet and carried him with it. By the time his body finally struck the ground, it was brokenly splayed, with his own blood already pooling beneath him.

Alvantes had made three swift steps towards Ludovoco before the other crossbowmen realised what was happening.

Once they did, however, they were quick enough to aim their weapons at him. Alvantes's weathered face seemed black with rage. My mind threw up an image, so clear that I could barely doubt its reality, of him pressing on, his body tattered with bolts, to crush Ludovoco's throat with his one good hand.

If Ludovoco was pondering a similar scene, he hid his unease perfectly. He didn't so much as consider Godares's corpse; his eyes held Alvantes pinned. "So you see," he said, "I don't make threats, idle or otherwise. You'll tell me what I want to know."

"You'll pay for that." Alvantes's voice was a growl, the words almost lost in the depths of his hate.

"Unlikely," said Ludovoco. "And again, you're wasting time." He raised a hand once more. His eyes strayed idly over Alvantes's surviving men.

"Wait!" Alvantes cried.

Ludovoco didn't lower the hand. "You have something to tell me? You didn't come here to make peace. So what was it? Quick now."

"I know your type," said Alvantes. His voice had returned to something like normal – except that now it was almost *too* normal.

"Do you really?" asked Ludovoco, without much curiosity.

"Good family. Wealthy. Close to the royal court. Yes, I know your type," Alvantes repeated. "We're not so different, you and I."

"Hardly a compliment," Ludovoco observed, "coming from a former provincial captain to a commander of the Crown Guard."

"Perhaps. But I *did* attend the Academy. I'm sure you did too. I was in a duelling circle; who wasn't? You though, I think you were one of the serious ones. Those who were in it for the blood. Am I right?"

"That I duelled at the Crown Academy?" said Ludovoco. "That I enjoyed it? Certainly."

"Then I challenge you, Commander Ludovoco," said Alvantes. "By the bonds of the Academy and for the murder of guardsman Pietto Godares. If you have any spark of honour left in you, you'll fight me now." Alvantes looked around the room, his gaze taking in faces, weighing them. "Or shame yourself in front of these men."

Ludovoco's lips curled in a tight smile. "I don't know what you imagine you'll achieve. Other than a swift and bloody death, that is."

"Justice," said Alvantes. "For the good man you just killed."

"Really? If you say so." Ludovoco reached one hand to his waist and, seemingly without conscious thought, loosened his sword in its scabbard. "And when I win, you'll tell me what I want to know."

"*If* you win."

Ludovoco stepped down to the lower level. "I'll be careful to wound you. In the gut, perhaps. It will provide a focus for our conversation."

His tone was so casually sadistic that I couldn't resist a shudder. How long before his attentions turned in my direction? Alvantes, however, seemed unconcerned. In fact, he was looking not at Ludovoco but at me – *really* looking at me, I realised, for the first time since I'd entered the room. As he saw that I'd caught his gaze, he let it drift to my left, and my own eyes followed automatically. Yet all I could see was an alcove carved into the wall beside the entrance. A fat vase sat there, glazed in yellow and umber, resting upon a pedestal at roughly waist height.

It only occurred to me then that my guard was no longer holding my arm. He was hovering close, to be sure – but I had both my hands free. And that vase looked heavy.

Alvantes drew his sword, tapped the flat to his forehead in salute.

Ludovoco mimicked the gesture with his hand, but contemptuously – a parody. Then he dropped the hand to his waist and flicked his blade loose, raising it in one neat motion and at the same time relaxing into an on guard stance, as though it were all the most natural thing imaginable.

Alvantes took a step back, squared up. He had none of Ludovoco's grace. Before it, his one-handedness looked horribly disabling – more than I'd ever have thought it could. I'd seen him fight, seen how little he'd let his injury slow him. This was different, though. If what he'd said were true, Ludovoco was a stone cold killer, trained to hunt out any weakness and use it to demolish his opponent. And one hand against two was a very great weakness indeed.

Alvantes was many things, but he wasn't a fool – at least not the kind of fool who would jeopardise the lives of his remaining men to revenge the death of one. Which meant that whatever he had in mind, it was more than a simple duel.

Or so I hoped. There was hatred enough in Alvantes's eyes to make me think that he'd really convinced himself he could beat Ludovoco, and maybe his men as well. Ludovoco, meanwhile, was edging in a slow semicircle around the makeshift arena, the faintest of smiles on his lips, the rest of his face dreamily sedate. I thought of a cat toying with its prey – but this was something even worse than that. Ludovoco was taking pleasure in imagining just *how* he'd play, once the time came.

It didn't take long for his patience to exhaust itself. Suddenly Ludovoco was moving, feet dancing in quick sidesteps, blade outstretched and weaving. Alvantes drifted back behind it and then span aside, curling an offhand blow away.

Ludovoco stepped into space and nodded, as though the exchange were a performance they'd been acting out and he acknowledged that Alvantes had kept to his part. He shifted his pose, tucking his free arm behind his back; another mockery, perhaps? Briefly, he resumed his semi-circular drift, more clearly predatory this time. Then he lashed out again.

That altercation was over almost before it had begun. Alvantes easily tipped Ludovoco's blade aside. The next went the same way – and the next. Between each, Ludovoco retreated; let a few moments pass by. He wasn't trying to penetrate Alvantes's defence, merely testing it.

I'd have expected no less. With every advantage his, it made sense that he'd take time rather than risks. The only thing I found strange was Alvantes letting him get away with it. The fact that he was willing to defend sat badly with his lust for vengeance. Damn him, why did the man have to be so damned cryptic?

Abruptly, Ludovoco switched hands, shifting his blade from one to the other with a casual flip, and was off again, with a whirlwind of strikes to Alvantes's left side. Ludovoco fenced every bit as ably with his off hand, shifting constantly to keep the pressure on. Though Alvantes defended every blow, his stance was too unnatural to maintain for long. Without as much as a glove to protect his bandaged stump, his only recourse was to fight across his body.

Finally, Ludovoco relented once more. It was clear in his face; everything Alvantes had said of him was true. He was enjoying himself, fighting to wear Alvantes down by degrees. Ludovoco's features were still, but every so often the twitch of an eyebrow or lip would betray the tension keeping them in place. I felt sure it was only iron self-control that stopped him cackling with glee.

Everyone's attention was on the fight now. Even the men whose express function was to keep their crossbows trained on Alvantes's guardsmen had let their weapons loll. I could sense my own guard, close behind my right shoulder; he'd edged forward to better view the action. The vase Alvantes had indicated was to my left – just out of reach. I edged the fraction of a step nearer, hoping against hope that my guard was too engrossed to notice.

Luckily for me, Ludovoco chose that moment to press his attack once more. Blade high, he dashed off a rapid sequence of strikes, the tip of his blade dancing figures-of-eight towards Alvantes's face. It was clear even to me that the fight had changed – that Ludovoco was done with toying.

He wasn't the only one. Alvantes twisted, side-stepped, let Ludovoco's blade slip past his right side and smashed an elbow into Ludovoco's shoulder. Not giving him an instant to react, Alvantes lashed out a foot for Ludovoco's knee – and though Ludovoco recoiled in time, he still staggered. Alvantes swung for Ludovoco's heels and then pressed close, clubbing at his opponent's hand with his sword hilt, once and twice, so that blood splashed from his knuckles.

This wasn't duelling. It was the kind of brutal, dirty street-fighting that had no place in a duelling ring – but which a city guard-captain might well pick up over the years. Ludovoco was too good to be kept off his guard for long, but Alvantes had chosen his moment perfectly. They were fighting now before Alvantes's own men, and any crossbow shot aimed at them was as likely to strike Ludovoco.

Alvantes pressed his attack once more, abandoning any hint of style for raw, calculated violence – and making sure that wherever Ludovoco was, he made a mess of any clear shot the palace guards might risk in his defence. Alvantes's men, meanwhile, already had their own blades out, and were pressing towards the nearest arch, with no one making any effort to stop them.

Ludovoco's face was set with cold fury at the fact that he'd let himself be played, that he was *still* being played – for though he was capable of defending against even so vicious and undisciplined an attack, the need to protect himself against not only Alvantes's blade but his feet, knees and elbows had thrown him badly. His anger, however, was nothing to Alvantes's manifest hatred. Perhaps he knew he couldn't win this fight, but I had no doubt he'd draw every drop of Ludovoco's blood he could to avenge his murdered man.

Whatever opportunity Alvantes had hoped to gain, it wasn't going to get better than this. No one was paying me the slightest attention. My sentry was twitching beside me, undoubtedly unsure if he should be heading off the retreating guardsmen or rushing to aid his commander; he was hardly even looking my way.

It came as no surprise when Alvantes darted a glance my way and bellowed, "Now, Damasco!"

I didn't need to be told twice. My arm was still half numb from the guard's attentions, and once I might have let that stop me. Lately I'd been through a lot, though, and grown intimately familiar with pain. Thus it was that I managed to grasp the vase beside me, despite pins and needles lacerating my wrist and shoulder – and thus it was that I managed to smash it into my guard's face.

I even succeeded in not screaming as I did it – though a scream might have been manlier than the yelp I came out with. My guard fared better, making not the slightest noise as he took two slow steps backward to collapse through the curtain, his head negotiating a perfect arc on its way to the floor.

The horrid thud of his skull against the tiles was blessedly masked by my own footsteps, as I snatched up my pack and pounded past, back the way we'd come.

CHAPTER FOUR

I was surprised to realise I had a fair idea of not only where I was but where I was going. Mounteban had insisted I spend an hour poring over plans of the palace – without ever feeling the need to explain where he'd found those plans – and now, almost unbidden, the details were returning.

I was in the east wing, somewhere near the main entrance and nowhere near where I wanted to be. The only way into the sublevels that my memory threw up was towards the kitchens, in the northwest corner. Since the palace was essentially a vast quadrangle, even getting that far meant covering quite a distance.

I couldn't tell what was happening behind me – except that a lot of people were running, and many of them apparently in my direction. Whether that meant the duel had been called off, whether Alvantes and his men were making a break for it, I didn't know or much care. I had more than enough trouble of my own approaching.

Seeing the chance of a shortcut as I met the corridor around the inner garden, I vaulted through a wide window arch, rolled through a bed of crimson blossoms and crashed into the line of low shrubbery beyond. That brought me out near a paved pathway, with a little cover and a significantly extended lead. I was nearing the far side before a shout let me know my pursuers had me back in sight.

Leaving the gardens via a mosaicked arch, I saw what I was looking for: a descending flight of stairs. I took them four at a time. It wasn't often I had an advantage, over anyone or anything. Right then, however, I was unencumbered by weapons or armour, being chased by men with more than their share of both. Even without that, I was better built for speed than those muscle-bound clods. Lastly, I was following a precise mental map through regions of the palace its guards might never have encountered. All in all, I was startled to realise I'd gained a decent lead.

What I *couldn't* do was lose them. I doubted this lower level had ever been cleaned as fastidiously as the rest of the palace, and it certainly hadn't been touched since Panchetto's death. The tiles I sprinted across were thick with dust. Even without looking back, I knew I was leaving a trail that anyone could follow. My only chance of losing my pursuers would be to stay ahead until they gave up – and from what I'd heard of the Palace Guard, that meant no chance at all.

It only occurred to me then that Mounteban's secret passage, which I'd been running towards all this while, might not be the best of my options. It might not even exist; I had no reason to trust Mounteban, or to put faith in his information. Even if it were real, wouldn't I have done better to flee the palace by a more conventional route, and the city soon after?

Too late now. And if the passage *was* real, it offered the easiest route out of both palace and city that I could hope for.

Another flight of steps led me into a yet lower level; one that, from the thick grime on the flagstones, was rarely entered these days. The walls were of a different stone to those above, stained with mildew, and echoed my footsteps hollowly. There were brackets of soot-blackened iron but no torches, so that the only dim light filtered down from the stairwell and failed as I penetrated deeper. By the time I reached the door at the far end, it was all I could do to feel out the keyhole sunk into its ancient timbers.

I bent over, panting, straining my ears for any sound of footsteps. There was only a faint rumble, as of distant earthquakes; but I knew that unless my pursuers had abandoned the chase altogether, they couldn't be far behind. I unslung my pack and fumbled inside, grateful that my captor had only made the most cursory of searches. Probing beneath the clinking vials, I felt the cold touch of metal, and drew it out.

The key was nearly as long as my hand, and complicated, eight teeth jutting awkwardly. The lock must be fiendish, and I was glad I wouldn't be trying to pick it. Instead, I slipped the key in and turned it.

Or at least I tried to. The key fit perfectly, but it was stiff. I applied both hands and threw my weight into it; this time, in a series of heavy jerks, the key clicked round. There was a metal ring beside the keyhole, so I gripped it, pushed with all my strength. The door gave, but barely. How often would crews be sent to check the boat, assuming it was more than a figment of Mounteban's imagination? Once a month? Once a year? It wouldn't take long for hinges to grow rusted down here. I put my shoulder to the door, dug my heels against the damp slabs and drove with all my strength.

For once, being half starved was an advantage. It didn't take much of a gap for me to be able to press through. I pushed the heavy door shut and, with great relief, locked it behind me. Even with every guard in the palace working together, it would take them a good hour to break it down – assuming, of course, that no one else had a key.

Less to my liking was the weighty dark pressing around me. With great care, I put my bag down and fumbled inside until I found the tinderbox I had stashed there. Lying upon my stomach, I placed the tinderbox before me, plucked out the flint and iron, and scraped one against the other above the tin until a spark found the char cloth inside. With the tiny light that gave, I drew out and lit the oil lantern Mounteban had given me, a neat little device that looked more ornamental than useful.

Once its wick was alight, however, the lantern just about served its purpose. I could make out the walls and ceiling, not with any detail but as a more solid black amidst the gloom. I reclaimed my pack and set off at a run; less because of the guards beyond the door than for my doubts that the miniature lantern's oil reserve would last until I reached my destination. Mounteban had assured me it would suffice if I hurried, but that was a vague notion indeed, and I was already weary from my race across the palace.

Thinking about Mounteban brought to the surface a thought that had been prying at my mind all day. Back when this had all begun, Mounteban had supposedly been retired from a life of crime, leading a relatively quiet life as owner of Muena Palaiya's most notorious bar. I'd always suspected his retirement was a sham, but only now did I fully appreciate how thorough the lie had been. The ease with which he'd gathered other criminals to his cause during his time as Altapasaeda's resident tyrant suggested a network fostered over years or decades; and what kind of a man had stolen plans to the local palace in his possession?

Mounteban had mentioned that the staff had left the palace soon after Panchetto's death, at the order of the palace guard. It was conceivable that some enterprising manservant had known about the key to the secret passage, thought to secure it, had smuggled out the maps as well or else drawn them from memory and then decided to approach Mounteban. Yet I had a curious sense that this went deeper. Could Mounteban have known about this for longer? Maybe for years? What else might he have hoarded away like some villainous magpie, and to what ends?

I remembered something Mounteban had told me, long ago. *We know everything*, he'd said. Had it been mere braggadocio, or a glimpse into the mind of a criminal genius? I hated to give him that much credit, or any credit at all, but time and again he'd proved himself a dangerous man to underestimate.

My lamp was already noticeably dimmer. How far had I travelled? In the diminished light, the tunnel seemed almost featureless. It ran straight, but all I could see in front or behind was deepening darkness.

Then, brutal amidst the silence as a boulder hurled into a pool, a reverberating crash rushed down the passage and over me. Another followed – and this time I recognised it for what it was. So I *did* have the only key. On the other hand, those mammoth blows were such that I couldn't believe the door would hold up long.

I picked up my pace. The lantern flame jogged with me, weaving wild shadows across the walls. The noise continued, steady and remorseless as a war drum – but worse was when it stopped, with one last splintering crack. Because the silence that followed could only mean the door had offered less resistance than I'd hoped; it meant I no longer had the tunnel to myself. Most of all, it meant Ludovoco had no intention at all of letting me go.

Though I'd already spent most of my strength, I broke into a faltering run, and kept it up for as long as I could bear. Once my muscles were filled with slow-burning fire, I relented to a fast walk, and tried to judge whether other footfalls echoed my own. No luck. As deep underground as I must be, every sound was deceptive.

Logic told me I must have twenty minutes' lead or more on my pursuers; but it was hard to trust logic as I stumbled along in that close darkness. I had no doubt they'd be narrowing the gap, and even if they weren't, pursuit was hardly my only reason for haste. By the time I reached the junction, my lantern was less than half as bright as when I'd set out, and every step set its timid flame quivering.

One branch of the passage continued the way I'd been travelling; the other broke to the left and inclined gently. Unless I'd altogether lost my sense of direction, the choice was obvious, and I hurried into the turnoff.

This time, I didn't have far to go. After five minutes of what felt like slight ascent, I realised I'd come to the tunnel's close. There was no question about it – and I stopped and stared, dumbfounded. Because the door I'd been expecting wasn't a door at all. The tunnel ended in blank wall.

It took me a minute of mounting alarm to notice the faint, irregular outline towards the wall's edge; only that and the lever jutting from beside it suggested it might be anything but a dead end. It seemed we'd underestimated just how little Panchessa's ancestors had trusted the City Guard. I doubted there was any way short of a sledgehammer to breach that entrance from the barracks side, even assuming you could find it.

How long since it had last been opened? Had it ever? A fresh wave of panic swam over me at the thought that I might be trapped down there in the blackness, cowering while I waited for the palace guard to find me. Before my lantern could blink out altogether, I set it down and yanked at the lever with both hands.

It gave just slightly. I could smell the faint tincture of old grease. It might have been months or years since the mechanism had been oiled – but it *had* been oiled. I leaned my whole weight into the lever and it groaned. I lifted my feet from the ground, so that nothing held me but the slim beam of metal – and only when it started to move did the possibility that it might simply snap cross my mind.

It didn't. Rather, ever so slowly, the lever edged downward. As it did, the wall before me shifted, dust shivering from the old stones. A great section, almost the entire end, began to edge outward, opening like any normal door. By the time the lever was horizontal I could see faint moonlight softening the wall's outer edge. By slow degrees, it opened, wider and wider – and then it stopped.

The mechanism complained; the lever moaned alarmingly. I strained my eyes against the failing lamplight, and finally saw why the hidden door had stuck. Had I ever considered this far ahead, I'd have guessed immediately. The barracks had been burned almost to the ground during Mounteban's time in power. What reason was there to think this secret passage should come out in one of the few sections to have escaped the fire?

It hadn't, of course. The door had come up against a beam as thick as my thigh. Beyond, I could see dim outlines of other obstructions, more timbers and chunks of masonry and mounds of dirt overflowed from the heat-shattered walls. Expecting the mechanism to push through that wreckage was like expecting me to dig to the surface with my fingers. Moreover, the moment I slackened pressure on the lever, the door began to edge shut. I didn't know how long I'd have the strength to hold it – or if I once let go, if I'd ever get it open again.

Under the circumstances, there was only one thing to do. "Help!" I wailed. "I'm down here! Estrada, Saltlick... please, they're coming! It's dark! Someone, anyone, *help me*–"

"Be quiet, Damasco! We won't work any faster for you bellowing at us."

Estrada's voice – and just then, it was sweeter than any music. A moment later came a resounding crack, closely followed by another. Stones rained from above, a great wooden balk came crashing down, scattering debris – and in its wake a massive shape plunged into view. It was only when it moved that I realised it wasn't some chunk of the demolished barracks.

"Saltlick?" I asked.

"Easie!" Saltlick greeted me with such casual good cheer that we might as well have chanced upon each other in the street. He easily shouldered the beam aside, thrust out an arm to hold a leaning hunk of wall in place. The door opened a little further, then came to rest once more, this time against Saltlick's foot. More stones bounced down to glance off his back, but he hardly seemed to notice.

There came a scrabbling from the shadows behind him. A moment later, Estrada ducked beneath his outstretched arm and brushed past me. She acknowledged me with a terse, "Damasco," and called back, "Hurry, before it all collapses!"

There followed a stream of indistinct figures. First came Navare, who greeted me with a quick nod before hurrying on. Of the rest, half were in guardsmen's uniforms, men I dimly recognised, and the rest were obviously Mounteban's freebooters, looking powerfully disgruntled with the company they'd found themselves in. Every fourth or fifth man carried a lantern, so that the passage was soon bright with ruddy light.

"All right. Now you, Saltlick," said Estrada.

I realised, suddenly, what was about to happen... but too late. Even as I let go of the lever, even as I flung myself forward, Saltlick was in the gap. I came up hard against his leg, bounced backwards. As he crammed himself through the too-small opening, dust billowed round him. Loose bricks tumbled past his feet, piling in the diminishing gap. Beyond the door, it sounded as if the entire barracks was settling to fill the hole that Saltlick had vacated.

"No!" The door was still open a crack, but I didn't think for a moment that I could squeeze through – or if I could, get past the rubble on the other side. "No no no!" When Saltlick only hung his head contritely, I rounded on Estrada. "This wasn't our deal!"

"Fine. I'm sorry, Damasco," she said calmly, "but what's done is done, and you might as well make the best of it."

Did I detect that familiar look in her eye? That look that said, *I know you better than you know yourself, so why not just let me decide what happens?* "You planned this!" I hissed. "You *want* me dragged into this ridiculous expedition of yours."

"Why would I possibly want that?" Estrada asked – and before I could begin to formulate an answer, she'd set off to catch the buccaneers and guardsmen, who'd already pressed on without us.

"I'm leaving," I muttered. "First chance I get. I won't be pressganged into another of your suicide attempts."

In the immediate future, however, I had no desire to be left amidst the rapidly descending darkness. I hurried after Estrada, just as my exhausted lantern sputtered out the last of its life. As Saltlick shuffled behind me, bent almost to hands and knees by the low ceiling, I heard a crunch that could only have been its annihilation beneath a giant foot.

When I drew near to Estrada, she glanced back and said, "When you were making all that noise, Damasco, you said someone was coming. Did you mean the Palace Guard?"

Amidst the horror of realising I was caught up in another of Estrada's hare-brained schemes, I'd almost forgotten the far more immediate danger. "I gave them the slip," I lied, "but it won't take them much effort to pick up my trail."

"And Lunto and his men?"

"I don't know." Not quite a lie this time, though I had a fair idea. The likelihood of them fighting their way free from a palace full of highly trained soldiers was remote, to say the least. Still, I wasn't quite ready to admit that – not to Estrada, not even to myself. "I'm sure they're fine. You know Alvantes."

"So what went wrong?" she asked.

Yet again, my brain automatically resisted the honest answer; it was the suspicion in her voice that changed my mind. Just because she was right, it didn't make her assumption that it was my fault any less insulting. "A misunderstanding," I said. "To do with a few of the Prince's personal effects finding their way into my possession. I could have explained it easily enough if anyone had cared to listen, and if Alvantes hadn't started swinging his sword around."

"Oh Damasco, you *didn't*."

"Didn't what?" I snapped. "Commit a victimless... I won't even use the word *crime*. A redistribution of no-longer-required wealth."

"I thought you were past all that," Estrada said, sounding more sad than angry.

A part of me wanted to explain my motives in precise and comprehensive detail, to point out how her meddling had done nothing but bring the Castoval to the edge of ruin, to propound my new understanding that so-called heroism brought nothing but trouble for all concerned. But even if she listened, what good would it do? "It seems you were wrong," I replied sullenly.

Estrada shook her head – and the disappointment in that gesture cut me more than I'd have imagined it could. Then, as if she'd already dismissed me from her thoughts, she called to the next figure in line, who happened to be one of Alvantes's buccaneers, "We need to hurry. We have company down here."

He made some sullen reply, grunted to the man before him. It barely passed for language, but it had the desired effect. Seconds later, as whatever message he'd passed forward reached the end of the line, the entire column picked up pace.

Estrada matched her speed to the man ahead and I did my best to keep up.

It didn't take us long to reach the junction. I'd almost expected to see our assailants closing from the direction of the palace, or at least the distant glow of their torches; but the only lights were those of Estrada's party, melting the blackness of the branch to our left into wavering pools of honey and amber. Given how straight the passage ran, the lack of any sign of pursuit meant we had a respectable lead – or that the palace guardsmen had given up altogether.

If I'd assumed that might be enough to make Estrada slacken our pace, I couldn't have been more wrong. Whether she was erring on the side of caution or whether, as I came to suspect, she was simply punishing me, she let our column keep up its unreasonable speed. Soon my sides were burning once again and my breath coming in shudders; but the guardsmen showed no signs of flagging, Mounteban's buccaneers seemed unconcerned, and Estrada herself wasn't so much as short of breath. Of course, none of them had endured the travails I'd already been through that day. I had every right to be exhausted, and it was only stubbornness that kept me from pleading with her.

As it happened, however, it wasn't me who eventually brought us to a halt. Estrada glanced over her shoulder for the first time since we'd left the junction, perhaps beginning to doubt whether our pursuers existed outside of my imagination. "Wait," she called. "Everyone, wait!"

Relieved as I was, I couldn't imagine what could possibly warrant a full stop – until I turned and saw that Saltlick wasn't behind us.

For one strange moment, it seemed as if he'd vanished altogether. It was only when I concentrated that I realised a patch of the distant darkness was lumbering towards us. As Saltlick drew closer, as the lanterns illuminated his hulking form, it became more and more clear why he'd been lagging. He was bent double by the low ceiling, almost crawling on hands and knees. He looked miserably uncomfortable, and the rough walls and ceiling had lashed scratches across his arms and head.

"Oh, Saltlick! Why didn't you tell me you couldn't keep up?" Estrada asked him.

His look of horror at the very prospect was all the answer she needed. Saltlick was always the dependable one; it was against his nature to be the cause of problems, however small. Now here he was, placing us all in jeopardy and not able to do a thing about it.

"It's all right," Estrada told him. "It's not your fault. We'll just have to let you set the pace."

If she meant it to sound comforting, it hardly came out that way. Anyway, it was easier said than done. How exactly did twenty people match their speed to the giant crawling along behind them? Suddenly, Estrada's insistence on bringing Saltlick was looking ludicrous indeed, and I could hear the rumblings of discontent from further up the line. The loyalty of the men supplied by Mounteban was doubtful enough already and this surely wasn't helping.

The night wore on – or so I assumed. It was frightening how quickly even the memory of daylight, of a sky above, had vanished in favour of the conviction that this subterranean channel was all the world there was. After a while – minutes perhaps, a couple of hours, a day for all I knew – I muttered to Estrada's back, "How far can it possibly be?"

"All the way beneath the western mountains," she replied, without looking back.

"Which is...?"

"A long way."

At least, thanks to Saltlick, I'd been able to recover my strength a little, and the added light of so many lanterns meant an opportunity to properly examine my surroundings. Alone, I'd thought the passage was blank-walled, little more than a mineshaft. Now I could see it was far more than that. The vertical supports were all of stone, and every one was patterned, in curious swirls and designs I could make no sense of.

I couldn't believe that Pasaedan royalty had fashioned this sunless way, however desperate they might have been for an escape route. It was clear, though, from the clumsier workmanship, that the ceiling had been extended a good way upwards at some point. Had it not been, we would all have had to duck, and Saltlick couldn't have moved at all.

The passage brought to mind the ancient tunnels behind Muena Palaiya where I'd first met Estrada – and I remembered the strange stories I'd heard over the years about those fathomless warrens. The deeper we travelled, the warmer the air became, and the more my nerves began to torment me. The final straw came when exits began to appear to either side, their arches too low for human traffic. What had Mounteban got us into?

"How do we even know which is the right way?" I asked Estrada, my voice a little tremulous.

Estrada showed me what she held in her hand, a map much like the designs of the palace I'd studied. This one, however, looked more like an abstract representation of a spider's web. I assumed the dotted line running more or less straight across its middle was our route. Given how many opportunities to go wrong it offered the careless navigator, I couldn't take much comfort from it.

I soon realised, though, that all we really needed to do was keep to the main tunnel, readily identified by its heightened ceiling. The answer to the side passages was simply to ignore them – even when odd shambling sounds seemed to drift from their mouths, or the splash of dripping water, or unidentifiable, musky odours. I tried to tell myself that with guardsmen and buccaneers in front of me and a giant behind, I was probably as safe as I could be anywhere.

As it turned out, however, it might have been better had our route been a little more intricate. Had that been the case, we might have stood a chance of losing the palace soldiers.

I was never sure what tipped Estrada off; whether it was some noise I'd missed or just a lucky guess. But out of nowhere she called another stop, and when the line had shuffled to a halt, sent word for the lanterns to be masked. It took me an effort of will not to protest. The thought of absolute darkness was almost more than I could bear. Only knowing how Estrada would ridicule me kept my mouth shut. Still, my heart sped up with every light that went suddenly black, until by the time there was only one distant glow left, it was hammering a tattoo in my ears. I held my breath, trying and failing to ready myself for that last plunge into total obscurity.

It took me the seconds my eyes needed to adjust to appreciate that total obscurity *wasn't* what I was surrounded by. Deep gloom, certainly, but I could make out Estrada's silhouette before me, and trace the border of my own outstretched hand. I turned and – seeing only the outline of Saltlick's bulk – knelt down. Just visible between his legs, far back in the passage, was a dim glow, like a glint in the pupil of a mammoth eye. I couldn't see movement, but that didn't mean much; the slightest turn in the passage would be enough to hide our pursuers from view.

"They're close," I said, "and gaining." I was surprised by how calm I sounded.

"We just need to keep our lead a little longer," Estrada said. "I'm sure we're nearly there. They can't possibly follow us over open water." Then, to the group at large she called, "All right... unmask the lanterns. Pick up the pace. They've found us."

Pick up the pace – as if it were that easy. Saltlick had been travelling as fast as he could since the beginning, and I wasn't about to let him fall behind again. What made it all the more excruciating was that, with our lanterns relit, there was no way to judge whether the palace troops were closing on us. Likely we'd only know when arrows or sword blows started raining upon Saltlick's back – and given his resistance to complaining, perhaps not even then.

"Can't you go a little faster?" Estrada asked him, though it was obvious he couldn't.

Saltlick's expression was pained beyond measure. He shook his head, and even that slight gesture brought dust shivering from the ceiling.

Estrada considered only briefly. Then she bellowed up the line, "Run, all of you! Prepare the boat... we'll catch you up!"

We? Was Estrada's plan that hacking their way through Saltlick and me would keep the palace guards occupied long enough for her and the others to make their escape? Right then, I'd have put nothing past her.

Soon the nearest lantern was only a distant glow, leaving us travelling in thick darkness. I was briefly amused, and then horrified, by the thought that if the next man in line got too far ahead we'd have to depend on our pursuers for light. However, even as the glimmer shrunk to nothing, I realised we were past the point of needing to rely on it. The walls were charcoal now, not black, and lightened ahead. Somewhere in that direction was natural light.

When the passage opened, finally, it was both sudden and dramatic: one moment the dark around us was the closeness of stone-chiselled walls, the next a cavernous space, the outlines of which I could barely distinguish. We'd come out in a huge cave, its domed ceiling descending to a distant line ahead, where it gave way to the faded blue of an early morning sky. We'd travelled through the entire night.

The shale beneath our feet ran down to a wooden jetty, and from that a wide pier extended towards the cavern's distant mouth. The rest of the party were already upon the pier, and nearing its far end – where the means of our deliverance lay, chopping slightly in the creased grey water.

To call it a disappointment was an understatement. I'd feared that the boat might be absent, or left to rack and ruin beyond any hope of saving us.

It had never even crossed my mind to worry that there might be two of them.

CHAPTER FIVE

How had it not occurred to anyone? *Of course* there would be two boats. This was the Ans Pasaedan royal family. There was no way Panchetto could have fled a revolution with anything less than a boatload of servants; what would he have done if he needed his nails trimmed three days into the voyage and the Head Nail Trimmer wasn't there to do it? Now that the evidence was before me, I was amazed he'd stopped at anything shy of a flotilla.

Of course, that didn't mean I wasn't cursing his name. One boat for us, one for our pursuers, and no hope of escape. Unless...

"Saltlick, could you sink that second boat? Punch a hole in its side or..."

But there was no point even finishing. Saltlick, dragging himself from the passage mouth like a cork popped from a bottle, could hardly even stand upright.

In any case, Mounteban's thugs were already busy at work on the second craft. Both vessels were moored at bow and stern and gang planks had been left on the jetty, which the party had already hurried to set in place. Now, the city guardsmen were dashing to ready the boat to my right, preparing the sails and fitting oars into oarlocks, while a half dozen of the buccaneers worked with wicked-looking knives on the cables holding the other. Even as I watched, one of the aft ropes split and coiled away.

By then, I was nearing the end of the jetty, with Estrada just ahead of me. It occurred to me that a flung oil lamp would make short work of the second boat; but the men had already extinguished their lanterns, I was hardly about to take the time to relight one, and knowing my luck there was a real chance I'd miss anyway.

Instead, I spared a moment to glance behind me. Saltlick was now halfway between the tunnel mouth and me, struggling to close the gap between us. Then, even as I watched, the first of the palace soldiers stole into the light. He blinked hard, struggling to make sense of the scene before him. Then he raised his crossbow and fired. The bolt missed Saltlick's left foot by the slightest of margins and hammered into the pier.

Another soldier stepped from the darkness. He too carried a crossbow, he too was briefly dazzled, took the measure of his surroundings, set his bow and fired... and the only difference was that his aim was considerably better.

Saltlick went down on one knee, with such a shock that the planks seemed to ripple and buck. I couldn't even tell where he'd been hit at first, until he tried to stand and I saw the bloodied shaft protruding through his shin. He took a step, nearly toppled sideways, and I could see him realise just as I did that this injury was something worse than the many hurts he'd shrugged off in recent weeks. I had to fight the urge to rush to him, to try to support him – because there was no possible way I could.

"Come on!" I roared, instead. "Damn it, Saltlick, get your lazy giant hide over here!"

Both soldiers were struggling to reload their weapons, even as their colleagues spilled from the tunnel mouth, drew swords and began to narrow the distance between us. Meanwhile, Saltlick hobbled closer – but each step pumped blood onto the salt-stained timbers, with every second or third he'd stumble, almost fall.

"Done!" bellowed one of the buccaneers from behind me, and as I looked the last rope quivered and coiled, like a snake drowning on the chopping water. The boat was already beginning to drift; the men on board simply flung themselves overboard, as though swimming were no less troublesome than walking. A few swift strokes brought them back to the pier.

When I turned back, Saltlick was almost up to us – and the palace soldiers weren't far behind. The buccaneers were hurrying past me and up the gangplank of our boat, Estrada had led the way, and it occurred to me that apart from Saltlick and the men hurrying to kill us, I was the only one left on the jetty. I darted across the plank, hardly noticing how it shivered beneath me, and flung myself aboard.

As soon as I had my feet back I was at the boat's side, ready to cajole Saltlick some more. But he'd already caught up, and was poised at the end of the pier, wavering as he struggled to balance on his good leg. He eyed the gangplank nervously – for as long as it took another crossbow bolt to whistle past his eyes. Then he took one stride out onto it, another... and the plank split in two.

The splash was titanic, a column of brine that geysered above my head and opened like a flower, crashing water into the boat. The point where Saltlick had gone under was hidden from my view by the angle of the boat's side. I'd once seen giants wade through a river almost as deep as they were tall, but could they swim? Given that their mountain home was landlocked, I doubted it.

"Wait, what are you doing?" I shouted at two guardsmen hacking the last of our tethers to the pier. They looked at me in confusion, and only hesitated when they registered the utter panic on my face. I glanced round, hoping against hope for some miracle to materialise. I could almost feel Saltlick sinking into the chill waters, as though he were a stone tied round my waist.

"There! The net!" It was bundled neatly on the starboard side, perhaps an emergency measure for if the Prince ate all the food on board. When no one seemed to understand, I dashed over and tried to drag it myself. It was heavier than I could have guessed, and all I managed was to tumble backwards, with a cry of frustration.

By then, all eyes were on me. Those who hadn't seen what had happened were giving me the kind of looks normally reserved for people who gibbered to themselves in public. But there *were* those who had seen, and Navare was among them. In an instant he was at my side and calmly unfurling the net, signalling his men to help us. I steadied myself with a vast effort and put my back into the work. Still, it all seemed to be taking so long – and through every moment, I couldn't escape that sense of Saltlick sinking like a leaden weight into the depths.

"Get it overboard!" I bawled.

But my guidance was no longer necessary. Navare was directing, with short gestures and brief, snapped commands. In a moment the net was shaken loose and dashed over the boat's side, with Navare, ten guardsmen and myself straining to weigh down our edge.

For all that, the shock when Saltlick caught hold threatened to wrench my arms out of their sockets. I'd been so certain he was at the bottom of the sea that I'd hardly thought to prepare myself. Even if I had, I could never have anticipated how damned heavy he was. With a dozen of us straining in a knot of arms and legs against the boat's side, it still seemed certain we'd be dragged overboard – as if we were fishermen who'd snared some prodigious monster from the deeps. It was impossible to imagine we could hang on; already, the craft was tipping alarmingly.

Then huge fingers closed over the boat's side, and some of the tension went out of the net. The fingers sprouted an arm, a couple of guardsmen grasped onto that, and Saltlick loomed into view. I let go of the net; I couldn't have held on a moment longer anyway. Spray splashing around him, Saltlick hauled himself over, crashed to the deck.

I heard rather than saw the snap of the last rope holding us in place, the thud of the anchor being hefted onto the deck. It was all I could do to crawl out of the way, to let the oarsmen take their places.

I lay back, exhausted, as we pushed our way out towards the cave mouth and open water.

It didn't take the palace soldiers long to recover the second boat.

It started as a speck barely visible in the cave mouth, unthreatening as a fly drowned in a drinking cup. Yet it meant only one thing: for reasons I couldn't begin to guess at, Ludovoco had no intention of giving up the chase.

It was sheer chance that our numbers about equalled those of our pursuers. As the hours wore on, it became apparent that their nautical knowledge was no better or worse than ours either. They couldn't catch us; even if they could have, there wasn't much they could have done. But nor could we lose them. There were times when we would find some current and draw away, when fog or darkness would obscure them for a while. Those breaks never lasted long, however, and never gave me much hope that we'd seen the last of our persistent new friends.

The fact that all they could do was keep pace with us begged a question that troubled me more with each passing hour: what did they hope to achieve? The likeliest explanation was that the palace guardsmen were readying for a fight when we arrived at our destination – and perhaps they'd already guessed where that might be. If Ludovoco had realised we were seeking an alliance with Kalyxis and the far-northern tribes, it was too great a threat for him to ignore.

Then again, maybe they had no plan at all, and were only trailing us as spies. Either way, the frustration lay in not knowing – and more than that, in their inescapable presence. Just because our adversaries posed no great threat while we were on open water, that didn't mean we could risk their getting too near, let alone ignore them.

I did my best, however, and tried to lose myself as well as I could in the routine of the days. There was something hypnotic in watching the water slide by, the ever-present mountains drifting past. On their farther, Castovalian side, those mountains rose in gentle, wooded hills that softened their stark outlines; here, they presented their backs to us, a rugged wall of stone that jutted and receded like the fortifications of some gargantuan city. Every so often there would be a beach of grit and pebbles, its edges smudged by the driving surf, and even more rarely a narrow cove of white sand, with knotty trees eking out a slim existence on its crevassed slopes, but for the most part there were only the cliffs, climbing in layers and topped with jagged pinnacles that scratched the sky.

The boats were fast, surprisingly so for their size. They were also unlike anything I'd seen, very different from the craft that plied the inland waters of the Casto Mara or for that matter the skiffs that fished from the eastern ports of Goya Mica and Goya Pinenta. They were high in the stern and bow, and also higher at the sides than the river boats I was used to. Within, a half dozen thwarts made room for twelve men to row in tandem, six to either side – and row we did, for the wind was strictly against us, an unsteady billowing that brought spatters of rain from a dull, iron-grey sky.

It soon became apparent that someone at some time had made the judgement to sacrifice royal comfort for royal safety, for there was no shelter on board. A complex arrangement of hooks and pegs in the stern suggested some way to rig a canopy, where presumably Panchetto could have lazed and watched others labour on his behalf; however a quick search of the holds had revealed nothing that could be hung there. At least there was water, and food as well – all of the dried or salted variety and much of that past the point of being edible, but enough to complement our supplies in an emergency.

We worked the oars in shifts, through the day and night. No one was spared, not me and not Estrada, not even Saltlick, though it took an hour's hard work to balance the other rowers enough that he didn't send us curving off route, and it was clear that the effort caused him pain. I'd found myself worrying more and more about him; for while Estrada and Navare had managed to get the bolt out and wrap his leg, fresh blood continued to splotch the bandage and he still strained to stand. It wasn't like Saltlick, who normally recovered from injuries the way others did from hangovers.

All of it – worry for Saltlick, the unsheltered cold of the nights, the shifts of hard labour, the lack of decent food and the ever-present menace of our shadows from the Palace Guard – worked to drag at my already miserable humour. By the second day I could hardly bring myself to speak to anyone, and the fact that everyone on board was too busy to notice only aggravated me more. By the third day, I knew my mood could sink no lower, and that there were only two things likely to relieve it: reaching our destination or a good fight. Given that we still had a day or more of travel before us, it was clear which was more likely.

As for a suitable sparring partner, there could be only one choice. I couldn't bring myself to torment Saltlick, the guardsmen had done nothing to incur my ire and Mounteban's buccaneers were too frightening for me to so much as go near them. No, there was only one person I had good reason to vent my anger at: the woman who'd led me to be on this accursed boat in the first place, who had driven me into danger after danger since the instant I'd set eyes on her.

All that was missing was the opportunity. Estrada had slipped into her mayoral persona from the moment we'd set out, conferring with Navare, tending to Saltlick, acting as go-between for the guardsmen and buccaneers – who were urgently in need of one – and generally behaving like the interfering termagant she was. She'd hardly spoken more than a word to me and when she had, my abrupt answers had discouraged her from trying again.

I'd thought we might get through the rest of the journey that way, and if the prospect added to my irritation, I was also a little glad. I'd taken by then to fantasising about how I'd wait until we landed and then disappear at the least opportune moment, or of twenty other ways I could make it clear that I'd been an unwilling passenger, practically a kidnappee. Better that, I'd decided, than a slanging match I might conceivably come out the worse from.

I should have realised Estrada was too much the busybody to leave the decision in my hands.

It was late in the third evening, the waters fading from the colour of dried blood to the purple of stale wine. Sick to death of our resident cook's culinary efforts, which had yet to extend much beyond hard biscuit, dried olives and salt meat, I'd ended up leaving a good proportion of my meal, for all that my stomach was growling. In frustration, I pushed my bowl away and it tipped over, spilling its miserable contents.

I pondered trying to clean the mess, decided it hardly warranted the effort. When I looked up, Estrada was standing over me, swaying in time with the boat's motion. "What's wrong with you Damasco?" she said. "I've never seen you turn away food unless you were actually poisoned."

I glowered at my overturned bowl. "Whatever I'm turning away, I'd hardly call it food."

"You're eating just as well as anyone aboard, and doing less work for it than most." Estrada sighed, ran a hand through tangled hair. "I know you didn't want to come along, but..."

"But what?" I cut her off. "You had no right to drag me into this mess!"

"Well if you'd kept your fingers to yourself," she said, "we wouldn't have had half the Palace Guard after us, and perhaps we could have cleared a way into the barracks for you."

"And if *you* had minded your own damn business," I spat, "the Castoval wouldn't be about to be wiped off the map by its own king."

Her eyes went wide – with shock, resentment or both. "That's absurd, Damasco. Is that really the best you can do?"

I'd already said more than I meant to; what was there to do now but press on? "You know, Estrada," I said, "since you decided to make nice with Mounteban, I've been thinking over something he told us. I never took it seriously at the time, and I never took it seriously when we were trying to kick him out of Altapasaeda, but now that we're all the best of friends I've been giving it a little more consideration. Just why did you feel the need to start a fight with Moaradrid anyway? It was Panchessa he wanted a war with, not us."

Whatever I thought I'd seen in her expression, the anger had altogether burned it away now. "You think I should have left Moaradrid to make a bloodbath of Ans Pasaeda? Hurt more innocent people and then, sooner or later, come back and do the same to the entire Castoval? You think I should have let him make murdering slaves of the giants?"

I jabbed a finger towards Saltlick. "And you're so much better? Remind me why Saltlick isn't leading his people home right now, like you *promised* him he would be. What I think is, you started a war you don't know how to finish. I think we wouldn't be worrying about the King hanging us in the streets if you'd just let Moaradrid do what needed to be done."

Her hand came up at that, and I thought for a moment she'd strike me. Then she let it drop, and her voice was quiet as she said, "What's this about, Damasco? I mean, really? What is it you think I've done to you?"

It was the last question I wanted to answer just then, and I fought to think of a way out of it. Yet even as it did, the words were frothing inside me, bubbling up like a geyser, and there was nothing I could do to keep them down. "What did you do? I trusted you, damn it! You and Alvantes... the great and noble heroes of the Castoval! I thought... I was actually starting to believe it might *mean* something. We topple Mounteban, peace is restored, everyone's happy. Now look at this mess! Even if we survive, what good's ever going to come out of any of this?"

I felt a hand on my shoulder and looked round to see Navare behind me. "Step down, Damasco," he said, calm but firm.

I shook him off roughly. It wasn't that he was ordering me around; it was the pity in his voice as he did it. I could feel the emotion welling in me, the frustration and disappointment, and I knew it was myself I was angry with as much as Estrada – perhaps more so. What kind of fool had I been to believe, actually to let myself *believe*, that the universe could have some role in mind for me beyond a brief, pathetic life of petty thievery?

Just for a moment I considered telling Navare what I thought of him, too. But four guardsmen were already watching our altercation with a little too much interest. Instead, I stormed away – as far as I could, anyway, which was to the other end of the boat.

••••

On the fourth day, the wind changed, and in no uncertain terms. The crew barely had time to get our sails up before we were caught by its breath and dragged forward, the already considerable speed we'd been keeping almost redoubling.

It did nothing to make me feel any better. In fact, I was close to the point of throwing myself overboard by then. Perhaps the palace soldiers would pick me up; maybe if I gave back Panchetto's bath ointments they would forget the whole stupid business. Even if they didn't, even if they left me to drown or put me to torture, it couldn't be worse than what I was currently enduring.

Since I couldn't quite work up the final degree of desperation needed to take the plunge, however, that day passed much as the others had – uneventful unless you considered the crew's incessant struggles to keep our craft on course as events, which I didn't.

Late in the afternoon, I overheard Navare comment that we were passing the northern edge of Pasaeda and so, if the wind kept up, less than a day from our destination. By that point, even the prospect of a relief from my nautical torments could do nothing to lift my spirit. It had long since occurred to me that if the northerners were anything like their reputation, if Moaradrid had been any representation of their national character, we'd be lucky to live long enough even to explain our presence. On the other hand, death might not be such a terrible alternative to sitting in a stinking tent for days while Estrada played diplomat.

As it turned out, however, Navare's optimism was ill-founded – and I had more immediate worries than foul-tempered northerners or their inadequate hygiene.

Our first intimation of trouble came when the boat behind us changed its course. Until then, they'd held close to our wake, trailing us like a guilty hound at its master's heel. Now, for the first time, they'd set a line significantly different to ours

– drifting further out to sea, until soon they were almost out of view.

"What are they up to?" I asked the nearest person, who turned out to be one of the buccaneers, a man whose shaven head was tanned to the colour and consistency of old leather.

He turned deep-set eyes on me, and I thought he wouldn't answer, or perhaps would stab me for wasting precious seconds of his life. Then he said, in a voice every bit as weathered as his face, "Maybe they know something we don't."

I didn't have the courage to press further. In any case, vague though his answer had been, I thought I'd followed his implication. I'd already grasped from overheard conversations that no one in our crew had sailed this course before, that our navigation had been based on a combination of tavern gossip and a few tattered charts Mounteban have given to Navare. The fact that our pursuers had tailed us so closely had suggested they were no more familiar with these waters than we were.

As I gazed towards the other craft, settled now into a course that placed them roughly parallel to us, though far behind, I realised there was another, equally valid explanation. I'd assumed they were trailing us; I'd accepted that they had no means to attack us. So far as I knew, no one on board had reached a different conclusion.

But there *was* another possibility, and my sun-scarred friend had summed it up perfectly. What if they knew something we didn't? What if they'd simply been waiting?

I looked to starboard. We were passing a long tract of gravel beach, its rocky line slipping uneasily into the sea, so that even quite far out I could see the black tips of rocks, and beyond that swirls of white water. I looked again to port, and to the other boat there, now just a brooding smudge between the ocean and the late afternoon sky. And as I glanced from one to the other, a pressure began to build inside my head and chest – a sense of purest dread.

I was about to shout out, though even as I opened my mouth I wasn't quite sure what I'd say – when the world fell apart. The angle of the boat shifted entirely, taking my feet and everything else with it, spinning the sky around my head. The roar of the waves transformed into a crash like a fist crunching kindling, though amplified a thousand times – and what made it more awful was that it was coming from directly *beneath* us.

Now I understood why the other boat had pulled away, and what it was they knew that we didn't.

If I hadn't, the spur of rock gouging through the bottom of our hull would surely have answered any remaining questions.

CHAPTER SIX

It was impossible to tell when I left the boat; impossible, as the sea flooded in, to say what was inside and what was out. For a moment, I couldn't even tell sky from sea – but the flood of icy brine into my throat answered that one quickly enough.

I floundered, clutched for where I thought the boat's shattered timbers must be, realised they weren't and went under – was *sucked* under, as if the water below were hollow and I was being dragged into the gaping void.

I didn't get far. My ankle dashed against what could only be a rock, and as the impact rocked me over, my head glanced off another. I felt the skin tear and a deep chill, as though the salt water were trying to drain into me. Searching with my good ankle, I made contact with something hard and jagged, kicked off.

I broke the surface, gasping. Through blood-slick hair and stinging salt, I saw the boat, sheared almost in two, flopping on the rocks like a gutted fish. There were men swimming, a couple just floating, one clutching to the mast. I couldn't see Estrada; I couldn't even see Saltlick, and that seemed so absurd that I tried to sway myself around to look for him.

All I succeeded in doing was slapping the breath from my lungs, as a wave tossed me against a jut of broken timber. I recoiled, disorientated, and found there was nowhere to go but down. The waves closed back over me, and somehow my feet were facing up towards the surface now. The more I flailed, the deeper I seemed to carry myself. My head stung, where the cold had settled. My ankle, by contrast, was on fire.

I was dragging myself down and down. Every time I thought I'd righted myself, the dimming light of the surface only faded further. I was sure I'd hit more rocks, and the prospect terrified me; it only came to me far too late that the alternative was drowning a little deeper. By then, the chill and fire both had moved into my lungs, working to push out whatever air was left there, leaving my head and foot merely numb.

I wanted urgently to breathe; air or water, I didn't care which. Only some small instinct kept me from trying, and I knew I couldn't listen to it for much longer. The darkness was descending, or else I still was. Either way, I might never have time for that last breath if I didn't take it then. I knew how good it would feel – as good as anything ever had. Whatever came after, it would be worth it...

Something closed around the scruff of my neck and suddenly I was moving again, the darkness cascading away. I took the breath I'd been longing for and of course there was nothing but water. When I tried to choke it up, there was nowhere for it to go – and with that realisation, light exploded in my eyes, noise sluiced through me. It could only be dying, though I'd somehow imagined death would be quiet and this was anything but. In hopeless desperation, I tried for one more, final breath...

Air smashed into my chest, just as water gushed out in a great splutter. I took another breath, another, each one pumping what seemed a bucket's load of seawater back into its rightful home. Only on the fourth breath did the light begin to congeal into a picture, the sound resolve into the pound of waves.

I was further from the boat, which looked almost nothing like a boat now. Even as I grasped what had happened, why I was alive, I swung a little in Saltlick's grip and he came into view. He was battered and bloody, hanging one-handed from a crest of rock, holding me half-free of the ocean's savage churn. He gave me one glance, managed the palest shadow of a grin, and began to move.

I'd never felt so helpless in my life. Saltlick's path was a crude concourse of rocks, some thrusting from under the waves, slick with foam and thrashed with white water, most just beneath its surface. It would have been lethal even without his wounded leg or a sodden thief hanging from one fist. For all Saltlick's agility, I was sure he'd slip at any moment and plunge us both back into the depths, or else dash my head into jelly against the reef. I'd have pleaded with him to put me down if I'd thought I could possibly speak, or that he could possibly hear.

Then Saltlick finally *did* let go, and I fell to my knees, still hacking up water – but infinitely relieved to feel something solid beneath me. I'd have stayed that way, probably passed out that way, but the sea was already sucking round my legs and if there was one thing I wanted to be away from, it was the sea. With a hand on Saltlick's knee, I dragged myself back to my feet, not sure until the last moment that my ankle would hold me.

We were stood upon the beach I'd seen before. Though it ran almost out of sight in either direction, it wasn't much more than a crescent of gravel flayed by white-edged waves. There were other figures crawling or staggering their way up it, clustering into bedraggled knots, one or two even trying to haul in salvage from the boat before the sea sucked it away. I spotted Estrada nearby, half-supported by Navare, and was surprised by how much relief I felt.

But that wasn't the time for relief. For seeing Estrada, I saw too where she was looking – saw where the other boat had landed further up the shore, run aground on the dismal shale. Already men were tumbling from its side, their uniforms drab and salt-stained but their drawn swords vivid in the early evening light.

Our party were already gathering themselves, the guardsmen drawing their own blades, the buccaneers producing wicked-looking dirks from the sheaths they wore low behind their backs; even Estrada had a sword in her hand, though I'd never noticed her wearing one. They'd have made an intimidating sight if one amongst them hadn't been half drowned, or if the palace soldiers hadn't been closing with such grim and steady composure.

Fortunate, then, that I wasn't the only one with sense enough to read the odds. "Fall back!" cried Navare – and though his voice was weak against the crash of the surf, everyone turned to look where he was pointing. What Navare had spied, what he was already leading us towards, was a gully in the cliff side, its upper edge breaching onto the higher ground above. There was no trace of a path and it was too hard a climb for men in our state, but about its base were a half-ring of boulders that had slid down in some earlier age, and those offered a better point of defence than anywhere on the beach.

There was a little false bravado at the prospect of so swift a retreat, but mostly everyone seemed glad of a hope, however slim, that they might not have to lay down their lives on that miserable shore. I wasn't quite the first to arrive at the boulders but I came close, finding unexpected energy in tormented muscles. Even Saltlick failed to outpace me – and I couldn't help noticing how heavily he still favoured his good leg.

Inside, the crude crescent barrier was less of an obstruction than it had appeared, with a wide gap on one side and considerable space within. Fortunately, its best protection lay on the side the palace troops were approaching from, and even the open span was narrow enough to defend. I climbed a little way up the incline, the better to see what was happening while playing as small a part in it as possible, and watched as the others fit themselves into gaps under Navare's direction – so that in a mere few moments, the natural barrier really had come to look like a fortress in miniature.

The resulting battle didn't take long; as long as it took our opponents to realise that, with their crossbow strings wet and momentarily useless from the time at sea, even a few injured and half-drowned men could hold that boulder enclave against them. In fact, from my perspective – and it was true that my only contribution was a couple of thrown stones that came closer to hitting our side than theirs – it all seemed more a sham than an actual combat. There was some rattling of sabres, much shouting, and perhaps a thigh or shoulder nicked somewhere along the line. But the resulting retreat was eager and orderly enough to imply that the palace soldiers recognised a hopeless cause when they saw it.

Then again, what reason did they have to hurry? If their goal was to keep us from our destination then they'd already achieved it. If they wanted us dead, they had time enough for that as well. Fighting an unfavourable fight in the deepening gloom was a risk they had no need to take.

Estrada watched them go, squinting against the darkness as the last ruddy sunlight spilt against the waves and drained into their furrows. She waited until they were back around their own boat, and continued to watch until there was no light to watch by. Navare, meanwhile, posted sentries at the more conspicuous gaps in our defence and set others to looking after the injured – a difficult task when, if you counted cuts and scrapes, almost everyone fell into that category.

Having already clambered down by then, I'd confirmed to my satisfaction that neither the wound on my ankle nor the gash on my forehead were likely to prove fatal. A tentative inspection had confirmed that both were skin deep, and the saltwater had done a decent job of cleaning them. Still, I felt tired unto death – as though a part of me really had drowned out there, and what Saltlick had hauled from the depths was nothing but a tattered shell.

Once Estrada and Navare were confident that we'd seen the last of the palace guardsmen for at least the immediate future, Navare called everyone together. "We'll need a fire," Estrada began, "if we're going to last out the night."

"Especially since there's every chance they'll come at us again before dawn," Navare agreed. "I doubt we're the first boat to fall foul of those rocks, so there might be driftwood out there somewhere. After what you've just been through I won't force anyone, but a couple of volunteers would be acting in all our interests."

"I'll go." I wasn't certain what impulse made me say it. I was dressed for the task, it had to be said, my dark clothes and cloak already disappearing into the twilight. That in itself was hardly a reason to risk my life, however. Then again, perhaps that was just it. I didn't anticipate much within our enclave besides a drawn-out death. Outside at least I could weigh up possibilities and maybe see something I was missing.

No one tried to argue with me – though I couldn't help wondering, when Navare sent out a couple of his men who'd also volunteered in different directions to my own, if it wasn't his way of saying he didn't expect me back. I was assigned the stretch of beach directly ahead – which meant at least that the death cries of the man to my right might alert me to approaching danger.

I squeezed through a gap in two boulders. The narrow band of sand that clung to the base of the cliffs was silvery in the moonlight, rippled as oft-worn fabric. Beyond it, below the strip of lead-grey gravel that made the greater part of the beach, the sea frothed and seethed like an old man sucking at his teeth.

I'd overestimated the good my cloak would do me. Beneath the moon's hoary glow, I stood out just as clearly as I would have clothed in the brightest motley. I considered scurrying back to the defence of the rocks, but what betrayed me was also in my favour, for I could see clear to the landed boat and its entourage of soldiers, and I could make out one of Navare's men moving between them and me. Out there, at least I'd have plenty of warning of an attack – and I could think, without the stink of twenty waterlogged sailors in my nostrils.

Or so I'd imagined, anyway. By the time I'd reached the waterline, I was beginning to realise that whatever thoughts my exhausted mind might offer, they weren't the useful, escape-enabling sort I'd been hoping for. It seemed the ocean depths had pummelled all the fight out of me, and I found it hard even to remember why I'd been so angry at Estrada. The truth was that I was at a loss. I'd failed at thievery, failed at heroism, and now here I was in the arse end of nowhere, staring death in the face once again and lacking the energy to much care. If there were any fairness in the world I'd be in a tavern at that moment, narrating my legendary adventures in exchange for cups of wine, and thinking fondly of the part I'd played in returning Saltlick and his people home.

A nice dream. But it had burned to nothing the moment Alvantes and Estrada had made their truce with that villain Mounteban, and now all I could do was wander down this beach grey as ashes, remembering it fondly.

I shook myself. No use in getting maudlin. I'd survived this far, and through worse than this. Maybe I'd never be regaled for my heroism, maybe the King would put Altapasaeda to fire and the sword, maybe Saltlick would never see his distant home again, but there would always be taverns – and surely that was enough to keep me going for one more night at least?

It was hard to see much past the turns of the cliff that closed either end of the beach, but I didn't think I'd be swimming out. It crossed my mind that there must be timbers from our boat around, that perhaps I could turn one into a crude raft. A ludicrous plan; the water would be freezing by now, and there was no reason to imagine I'd fare better on the rocks for a second attempt. I turned around, stared back towards our rocky barbican. More realistically, once I'd recovered a little I might be able to climb that ravine in the cliff side. Yet the best I could hope for would be to snatch a few uncomfortable hours rest and make a try before dawn, and I doubted I'd get halfway like that. No, it would take more strength than I had to make that tricky ascent in the dark.

I could see no option except to attempt the fool's errand I'd come out there on. I might as well make a try of it before I returned empty handed. To my astonishment, however, less than a minute had passed before my eye snagged on something that looked like bleached bone and turned out to be ancient wood, desiccated and salt-stained. After that, I began to hunt seriously, drawn by the prospect of a little warmth – and sure enough, Navare had been right. Some of my tiredness turned to enthusiasm as I chanced on more chunks of weatherworn timber, and for a while the quest fully absorbed me.

My excitement waned quickly. Aside from the first piece I'd discovered, nothing I found was much more than a sliver; we'd have a scanty fire indeed if the others hadn't fared better. Still, at least I'd shown willing. I was beginning to regret the previous day's outburst at Estrada, and maybe my small haul would offer a means back into her good graces.

Then, as I turned back, something else caught my eye. It was difficult to make sense of at first; a pattern upon the rocks nearest the shore, a curious checked design drawn over the weed-decked stone. Finally, after a few moments of staring, I understood what I was looking at: a net, snagged on one of the higher protrusions and draping down, most of its length beneath the water. It could only have come from our boat;

probably it was the same we'd used to haul in Saltlick at the dock.

I continued to watch the net for a minute longer, as new thoughts turned over in my mind: memories, and the first spark of an idea. Maybe there was a way off this miserable shore after all, but I couldn't begin to guess how I'd make it work.

I'd sleep on it, I decided, and assuming I was still alive, perhaps the morning would offer some insight. I headed back to the boulder wall and was a little pleased by how warmly everyone greeted me – until I realised it wasn't me they were glad to see but the burden I carried.

Paltry as my stock of firewood was, I'd done better than Navare's guardsmen. As it turned out, though, even a pitiful fire was better than nothing in such cramped surrounds. With twenty men, one woman and a giant crammed into a space the size of the average peasant cottage, it didn't take long for the chill to evaporate. Propped with a boulder at my back, I could hardly claim to be comfortable, but with the fire's brisk heat on my face and a vast weight of fatigue closing over me, I was at least relaxed, and blissfully near to sleep.

Still, I wasn't as irritated as I might have been when Estrada came to sit beside me. "Will you talk to me, Damasco?" she asked.

"I'll talk. I can't guarantee I'll listen," I told her. But, whether from tiredness or because it was hard to stay angry when we'd likely soon both be dead, there wasn't much bite in the words.

"You don't have to if you don't want to," Estrada said. "All I wanted to say was, I've been thinking about what you said before, on the boat. And maybe, in a way, you're right. I could have done things differently."

"You mean, better?"

"I mean *differently*. I mean, it's easy to look back at your actions and realise they didn't work out the way you'd hoped."

Estrada propped a hand against dark hair still slick with brine and gazed into the fire. "Alvantes told me what you did when you were travelling with him... using the money you'd stolen to help the giants and the villagers on the Hunch."

"And what a waste that turned out to be," I said.

"But you tried. He would never tell you, but I think he respected you for it. And so do I... I respect that you *tried*. Here's the thing, though, Damasco: doing the right thing isn't about gestures. It's about working out, as well as you can, what people need to make their lives better and then trying as hard as you can to give it to them. A few coins can't do it. Fighting wars can't either. And you don't always get to win."

"Then what's the point?" I said. "If trying to do good is just as likely to cause harm, why not just leave well alone?"

She shook her head. "I wonder myself sometimes. Of course I do, damn it! Did you think it hadn't crossed my mind that some of this might be my fault? I did what I thought I had to... what I thought *someone* needed to do to set things right. And looking back, I can see that maybe all I did was make them worse. Maybe that's what I did. I don't know."

I could tell this wasn't how she'd intended the conversation to go; there was a note of pained emotion welling in her voice. Flailing for some reassurance to offer and finding nothing I said, "Things don't always work out how you expect them to."

Estrada offered me a wan smile. "No. They don't. Goodnight, Damasco."

Watching her go, I couldn't shake the feeling that I'd accidentally told Estrada just what she needed to hear. Perhaps, at least, I'd die with one less enemy to my name – and I was a little glad for that.

I closed my eyes and let the darkness fall, dragging me down with it.

●●●●

I woke to a hand roughly shaking my shoulder and to a different shade of gloom, this one lit by the last dying embers of our fire. My eyes ached with fatigue; my mouth felt like it had been salted and left to dry for a week. It seemed a preposterous act of cruelty that anyone should have dragged me out of sleep, even such muddled and comfortless sleep as mine had been. I registered Navare to my left – it was he who was manhandling my shoulder – and when I tried to look away, realised Estrada was kneeling to my other side.

"Are they attacking?" I mumbled. It seemed the least alarming explanation of why those two should by hemming me in like hungry vultures.

"Not yet," Navare said, "but it's only a matter of time."

"Then what?" I racked my tired brain for a reason anyone would wake me before dawn that didn't involve imminent death. "Do you want me to collect more firewood?" I tried.

"We have a mission for you, Damasco," Estrada said. "I won't pretend it's not dangerous... but it's a better chance at surviving than anyone else has."

I swung my head in her direction, took a moment to let my eyes focus. It was maybe an hour before sunrise, I realised, the light already beginning to turn just faintly. "A mission?" I repeated, for want of anything useful or intelligent to say.

Estrada's face was grimly set. I suspected that whatever she was about to ask, however arduous the task she had in mind, she expected to be demanding far more of better men that me before this day was done. "You and Saltlick climb out," she said. "You follow the coastline north. Once you reach Kalyxis's camp, you try and persuade her to send help for us. There's a chance we can hold out for a couple of days; a boat could be back here before then. But whether or not she'll do that, you *have* to get aid for Altapasaeda... before it's too late."

A dozen things had gone through my mind as Estrada spoke, and half of them had almost made it to my lips. It was all I could do not to point out what a weight of responsibility this was to heap on the shoulders of one poor, mostly-retired thief and his wounded giant friend: the lives of everyone around me and the fate of a city and its people, possibly all of the Castoval.

Then there was the most obvious question: why me? Yet I'd guessed the answer to that one almost before I'd thought to ask it. I was no fighter. Neither, for all his strength, was Saltlick. When push came to shove and shove came to swordplay, we'd be more of a hindrance than a help. This way at least we stood a tiny chance of being useful. In any case, the greatest likelihood was that we'd plummet to our deaths, adding our corpses to the makeshift defences, and that too would be usefulness of a sort.

There was one more thought, though – and if it was hardest to ignore, it was the easiest not to give voice to.

Because Estrada's plan had occurred to me too, as I'd drifted fitfully in and out of sleep. It had started when I'd seen the netting strung on the rocks, so reminiscent of the rider's harness Saltlick had worn when I first met him, and had gained form through the long night. If Estrada hadn't suggested it, I would have myself.

And, though I couldn't have said why, I'd never felt more guilty for anything in my life. It was such a powerful torrent of emotion that I almost declined – almost suggested that she, or Navare, or *anyone* go in my place, almost said that I'd sooner stay and fight and die so that someone other than me could take this slender chance at safety.

I didn't, though. Of course I didn't.

What I actually said was, "Fine. How soon can we leave?"

CHAPTER SEVEN

Any idea that I might be getting the safe or painless option lasted fully as long as it took Alvantes's men to prepare the harness Saltlick would be wearing.

Its essential elements were gathered in a predawn raid on the beach by three of Navare's men: the net, some straggling lengths of rope and a broad timber plank that had recently been part of our boat's flank. The remaining components, mostly metal rings and leather straps, were pillaged from a pair of bags and a torn brigandine that had been rescued during our unexpected landing.

The end result, prepared hastily without proper tools or any great skill, was a pale imitation of the elaborate harnesses that Moaradrid's army had saddled the giants with. Wearing it with clear discomfort, Saltlick looked dejected and somehow less giant than usual. I felt sorry for him – but his humiliation was hardly the worst of it. No, the worst part was that I'd be hanging off that junk pile while Saltlick attempted his death-defying climb.

"This is a terrible idea," I pointed out, trying my best to make the observation sound constructive.

"It is," agreed Estrada. "Absolutely. If you have any better suggestions, I'll be glad to entertain them."

"Well... I was thinking. On his back, Saltlick might make a serviceable raft."

"And you might make serviceable ammunition for a catapult," said Estrada, "but we haven't a catapult, Easie, and we haven't any more time to waste. If you're going to do this then please, do it now, while there's still a chance you'll make it back in time to help us."

I looked up at the rugged cliff side, and then over Estrada's shoulder, through a gap in the boulders, to where the second boat waited on the water's edge, black as a beetle in the scant light before sunrise. "All right," I said, "I'm going. I just wanted to make my position clear. That way, when Saltlick falls off and we crush you all, you won't waste your last breath blaming me."

Estrada reached out suddenly, wrapped her hand around my forearm and pressed her wrist against my own, in something between a handshake and an embrace. "Tell yourself what you like, Easie. I know you can be brave when you need to be. I'm asking you to do this because I *trust* you to do it."

For a moment, my heart swelled. Then I remembered who I was talking to. Speeches were Estrada's weapon of choice, and self-delusion had also proved high on her list of talents. "Let's hope you're right," I said, pulling my arm free, "because I don't much like the idea of walking home."

Of everything, it was the wind that bothered me the most.

I'd hardly noticed it on the beach, where the boulder wall had sheltered us; but halfway between ground and summit, hanging from a giant, it was harder to ignore. A gale howled and whistled over the cliff face, and the gully we were in seemed particularly to provoke it, as though the rock had crumbled in that particular place just to frustrate it. Currents whipped at the netting I clung to, made it quiver like unsettled water. Breezes plucked at my clothing – and if I hadn't already felt like a target for those two crossbows I knew were somewhere below, their strings undoubtedly dry by now, then my cloak whirling behind me would surely have done it.

All told, however, wind-chilled, scared and uncomfortable though I was, it was safe to say that I had it easy. Saltlick was the one with the truly demanding part to play – and it was only a shame that my survival relied so completely on his.

If the sloping gully was shallower than the cliffs to either side, it was still a difficult ascent; difficult, that is, for an uninjured human. I knew Saltlick was agile. I knew he could climb, for I'd seen him do it. But though the surface was uneven, rare was the gap or ledge that was wide enough for a giant's hands. In their absence, he was forced to rely on brute strength – and from the caution with which he moved, from the way he kept off his hurt leg, I could tell that was a commodity he had far less of than usual.

The last thing he needed was the weight of the harness, or the weight of me for that matter. I could tell he was suffering. And the more he suffered, the more he slowed; the slower he went, the harder it became. The pain coming off him was almost tangible, as though it were radiating through strained muscles, steaming from his pores.

I looked down. The world span, readjusted, and there was Estrada, small and far below. Of its own accord, a small part of my brain estimated the distance, what it would be like to plummet across it and what exactly landing would feel like. All of a sudden I found myself shaking so hard that I almost lost my grip, and I grasped the net frantically.

I had to do something. Saltlick was exhausted, he was hurt, and I knew with a cold certainty that he wasn't going to make it. "Wait," I said. "Just wait, Saltlick."

He paused, hugged the cold stone. His breath was coming in ragged shudders. He'd never admit he was worn out; not because he was stubborn or arrogant, as a man might be, but because he was too damn decent to stop. He'd climb until he reached the top, or until he died trying – and if I'd had any doubts of the likelier outcome, those torn gasps of air were all the evidence I needed.

"Are you all right?" I asked him. "Can you hold on?"

Rather than answer, Saltlick nodded – and the netting danced beneath me.

"All right! Stop that. Can you move in any closer? *Don't* nod. If you can do it, do it."

Saltlick grunted, a low rumble. I took it for a no, until he began to shift. By degrees, he moved to splay his hands and feet, flattening against the stone.

I gritted my teeth, tried to push from my mind the image of the beach far below. I'd thought I could climb at least half the cliff face – well, this might not be the half I'd set my sights on, but here was my chance to prove it.

"Hold still," I told Saltlick. "Whatever you do, hold still."

I crept to the very edge of the net and – realising how I'd set Saltlick trembling, his fragile balance disturbed – hurled out a foot in panic. I scrabbled at stone, certain I could feel Saltlick's grasp slipping, and dashed out my left hand for a lip of rock. With that hold, I abandoned the netting altogether, throwing my whole weight against the rock wall, hoping my tenuous grip would be enough.

Only when I was sure I wasn't about to fall did I dare hiss through gritted teeth, "Are you all right, Saltlick?"

"Good," Saltlick agreed.

"I'm going to climb past you," I told him. "I'll find you a path."

Not waiting for an answer, I began to do as I'd said. I'd been right; it was far easier for me than for Saltlick. Whatever ancient catastrophe had carved this rut and deposited the boulders below, it had left a smashed and rugged surface in its wake. The hardest part was overtaking Saltlick; the worst moment the one when I realised that what I'd mistaken for a jut of stone was in fact his fingers. Saltlick being Saltlick, he didn't even protest, merely clung on for the instant it took me to understand that stone didn't squish that way under a boot heel.

"Argh... sorry! Damn it, hold on..."

I shifted my weight, hauled myself higher, narrowly avoided repeating my mistake by trying to use Saltlick's head as a foot rest and finally reached a point where I knew I was clear of him. Already, my limbs were beginning to ache. I pushed the discomfort aside. Whatever pain I was in, Saltlick was hurting more. It was a mere matter of hours since he'd last saved my life; just this once, I had to at least try to return the favour.

So I climbed – and the climbing was hard enough. But all the while, a part of my thoughts were occupied in plotting Saltlick's route, spying any ledge or fissure that would accommodate his fat fingers and bulbous feet, while I pointed them out in breathless gasps: "There... do you see? No, not that one, to your left. Got it? Now, your right foot... the hole. *That's* it. All right, now the hand again..."

I'd never concentrated so hard. All sense of where I was or what I was doing soon vanished, reduced to simple mechanical processes: Move my hands and feet; move Saltlick's hands and feet; hang on; put aside the pain. Thus it was that when the slope petered into a steep rut, and then a soily incline that I could ascend on hands and knees, it hardly occurred to me that the ordeal was almost done. Even as I hauled myself over a rim of matted grass and tangled roots, my mind was still feverishly questioning what would or wouldn't support a giant foot.

It took Saltlick crawling up beside me and flopping into the long grass to make me realise we'd made it. I lay still, letting my fatigue subside, and my brain return to something like normal operation. Only when I had my breath back and thought I could view the landscape without measuring it for giant-sized handholds did I try to look around.

Upon our right, the cliff side continued in a series of abrupt rises that eventually dissolved into a mountain range. Or rather, the jutting corner of one – for, tilting my head, I could see the march of the peaks back towards the Castoval, and with less effort their encroachment inland, until the point where they became ghostly on the horizon, merging into distant, rolling hillside. If my geography was right then somewhere on the other side of those nearest mountains lay the Ans Pasaedan capital of Pasaeda.

Looking to my left, I saw that the mountain range, bleak though it was, might be as interesting as the view was about to get. In a sense this land was much like what I'd seen of Ans Pasaeda: tracts of grassy steppe reaching farther than my eye could measure. In Ans Pasaeda, however, there had been towns and cities, farmland, often a river in sight... whereas here in the far north there was nothing. If I stared I could make out faint undulations in the turf, the hint of shallow hillsides, and surely there must be water running somewhere, for the grass was vibrant enough.

For all that, the landscape was uncompromising in its emptiness. Where there were trees, they clung in knots, as though afraid of what might happen should they stray too far apart. Nowhere was anything that deserved the name of a forest, or even a wood; compared with the endless verdure of the lower Castoval, or even the sun-scorched reaches of the Hunch, it all seemed desperately barren. All I could hear was the occasional screech of hunting birds and the crash of the sea, as it beat and beat against the shore behind us. All I could smell was a faint hint of peat, sea salt, and the grass itself.

So *this* was the far north. Now I could see why Moaradrid had gone to so much trouble to leave. And small wonder no Ans Pasaedan king had ever made much effort to seize this inhospitable land; I was only surprised they'd never taken the time to wall it off.

I turned my attention back to Saltlick. He was sat on his backside, legs outstretched, hands perched on knees. His eyes were closed; his breath came in short tugs through half-closed lips. The bandage on his hurt leg was showing splotches of fresh blood, bright against the wormy grey of his skin.

"Can you stand?" I asked, doing my best to sound gentle.

As if the question had been a command, Saltlick struggled to his feet. He swayed for a moment and then, planting his feet firm as any tree roots, offered a vigorous nod.

I wasn't fooled. Then again, I had no choice. I had to reach Kalyxis's camp, had to bring back help for Estrada and the others – and Saltlick was my only transport.

"Are you ready for this?" I asked him. "You'll have to go fast – as fast as you can."

"Ready," Saltlick agreed.

Of course, I hardly needed to tell him. In fact, I could see from the grim set of his jaw that he was already excavating whatever reserves of strength he had left; my contribution would more likely be to stop him running himself to death. If anyone was prevaricating, it was me. I wasn't sure that I could bear to watch Saltlick cripple himself. I didn't know if I could choose between that and dooming Estrada and the others. Those just weren't the sorts of choices I was used to making.

"Ready," Saltlick said again – and this time it was an order, however politely phrased.

"Fine," I said. "Kneel down."

I grasped the netting and hauled myself onto his back. As the harness creaked and groaned, I was reminded again of how feeble an imitation it was of the ones devised by Moaradrid's troops. The best I could hope for would be to hang from Saltlick's back, my head just above his shoulder to afford some view of what lay ahead.

I took a deep breath. The next few hours weren't going to pleasant for either of us. I was about to say "let's go," but Saltlick didn't give me the chance. With a muscle-wrenching jolt, we were off.

••••

The countryside didn't improve as the day wore on.

That was my impression, anyway, based on the sliver I could see of it: grass and more grass, the land still undulating faintly beneath an overcast sky, the sea still whipping itself into frenzy against the rocks to our left. Here at least there was a little variation, for the cliffs appeared to be petering out as we headed north, often broken by beaches like the one where we'd inadvertently landed. None of it, however, was the least bit engaging or distracting; and if I'd ever needed a distraction, it was then.

The harness Saltlick had worn when we'd escaped from Moaradrid had been bad enough. Compared with Navare's makeshift alternative, it might have been a carriage lined with goose-down pillows. I was literally hanging from Saltlick's back, held by nothing except my feeble grip, and flung against his shoulders by his every stride. Not trusting to my flagging strength, I'd wrapped my wrists inside the thick cord, so that even if I was fortunate enough to pass out I'd still remain hanging. But what aided my survival did nothing for my circulation, so that the prospect of tumbling from a fast-moving giant seemed more attractive with each passing minute.

All the while, Saltlick's limp was worsening. As much as he tried to compensate, to carry his weight on the other leg, I could feel his mounting distress with every bound he took. He was keeping up a startling pace, but I couldn't shake the doubt that he'd never do it again; that perhaps he might never even walk for the harm he was doing himself today.

But what could I do? He wouldn't stop now, not even if I pleaded with him. My only option lay in not thinking about Saltlick, in concentrating as well as I could on our journey and its goal.

Yet only as the day ebbed towards evening did I think to consider the obvious. I didn't know much about the far north or its denizens, but I'd heard they were nomads, living in tents and moving whenever the mood struck them, perhaps in forlorn hope of finding some part of their land that wasn't drab and ugly. Probably the chance of our running into Kalyxis and her tribe was almost non-existent; likely the encampment I was seeking had long since been packed up and moved to some other equally dismal corner.

I should have known I didn't need to worry. When had I ever had to look for trouble when trouble was so very good at finding me?

I'd demanded a break, supposedly to consider our route but in truth because I couldn't bear another moment of being tenderised against Saltlick's back. As I stood massaging bruised wrists and staring north along the diminished coast line, I thought I felt the barest tremor through my feet.

I was about to dismiss it as imagination when the riders appeared – came out of nowhere. One moment there was nothing but the barren wilds, their rich green drained almost to blue by the daylight's fading. The next, there were a dozen riders thundering towards us – and as I turned, thinking vaguely of escape, another ten behind us, arriving impossibly from the direction we'd just come.

With the cliff at our backs, there was nowhere to go; nothing to do but wait. They surrounded us in a half-circle, gliding into place without a word. The party that had arrived behind us carried the delicate bows of horse archers – not loaded as yet, but I had no doubt that they could arm and fire in half the time it would take me or Saltlick to reach them. The others kept their free hands loose at their sides, close to the hilts of narrow scimitars in fur-trimmed sheathes.

Even if our location weren't a sure giveaway, I'd have recognised them easily as northerners. Their skin was a good shade darker than my own olive brown, and deeply marked by a life in the open. Their hair was braided and bound with wire. Nowhere could I see a scrap of material that hadn't begun as a living thing; they wore leather and fur aplenty, but not so much as a ring of metal or a neckerchief of cloth.

They didn't seem nervous at the sight of Saltlick. In fact, their expressions gave nothing away at all. I waited a few seconds in the hope that one of them would say something, if only to give some indication of whether they'd come to greet or murder us. Then I raised a palm in tentative greeting, flinched as twenty hands clenched on bows and sword hilts.

"Ah... good evening," I said. "We're looking for a lady by the name of Kalyxis. I don't suppose you'd be kind enough to point us in her direction?"

As it turned out, they would.

For once something had gone right for me – if being captured by barbarians and escorted under armed guard could possibly be considered right. Since it got us where we were going, I was willing to give this latest twist of fortune the benefit of the doubt.

One moment there was nothing but empty prairie, the next we were cresting what appeared to be the shallowest of rises and abruptly there was a whole town spread beneath us, its low structures altogether hidden by the wide basin it occupied. The town extended all the way to the shore, and most unexpected were the two long jetties protruding there and the fleet of boats clustered round them. I'd never even suspected that the northerners might have boats; I'd always imagined saddling horses to be the length and breadth of their technology.

Only as we descended did I begin to realise that large though the town was, it was by no means permanent. There were carts and horses everywhere, along with a few burly oxen. I saw that what I'd taken for buildings were in fact large, circular tents patched from dyed and painted skins, though they looked as solid as if they'd been built from wood and stone. It occurred to me that this whole place must be portable, just as I'd expected; I'd been right in principle, but completely failed to grasp the scale.

Then again, how did that explain the harbour, and the boats moored there? Those could hardly be taken apart and hauled away. No, this was something more than a temporary dwelling, a brief pause in a life of nomadism.

Worries for another time – for it was apparent that we'd reached our destination. Having marched us through the unpaved streets, our escort had come to a halt before a tent considerably grander than those about it. In front was a low plinth, and on that sat a dozen chairs. All but the centre two seated men of various advanced ages; the middle pair, however, raised somewhat above the others, were occupied by a strikingly tall woman with chalk-white hair and a skinny youth who didn't even look up at our approach.

Still some distance away, our escort dismounted and approached on foot. They stopped when they'd halved the remaining distance, and each man dropped abruptly to one knee. "Strangers," one said. "Found approaching from the south. They asked for you by name, lady."

That settled any doubts: the woman was Kalyxis, mother to Moaradrid and former paramour of King Panchessa. For all that her hair was so starkly white, her skin showed no lines, and her face still possessed a stern elegance that might in flattering light be taken for beauty. It was certainly hard to credit that she was old enough to be anyone's grandmother.

At that thought, I spared a glance for the sour-looking youth beside her, who sat with his shoulders hunched, gaze fixed on one unexceptional patch of dirt. He looked to me like a northern variation on the template of anonymous street ruffian, with nothing distinguishing in his morosely set features. Yet he was dressed almost as finely as Kalyxis herself, in a cloak of rich, dark leather hemmed with black fur and studded with beads of silver. I could only assume that here was the notorious Bastard Prince – and that the epithet had been chosen as much for his temperament as his parentage.

Kalyxis watched me for long moments, with the sort of interest a hunting bird would pay some speck on the horizon that might or might not be prey. When she spoke, her tone was imperious, and almost devoid of any northern accent. "Who are you and what are you doing in Shoan?"

"My name's Easie Damasco, the giant there is Saltlick and... wait... *this* is Shoan?"

I'd heard the name in reference to Moaradrid – "Moaradrid of Shoan" – and assumed it must be his home town. I'd imagined a few filthy tents and half a dozen horses, in so much as I'd considered it at all. Moaradrid had been impressive enough, it was true, but I'd taken that as a rarity achieved only by dint of much effort and pillaging. Yet what I was seeing here wasn't so far from my idea of civilisation; rough and ready, no doubt, erring towards the savage in its decor, but for all that not so basically different from the average Castovalian town.

Kalyxis extended an arm in a sweeping gesture, fingers caressing the distant landscape as though it were the hide of some great and half-tamed beast. "All this... all of this is Shoan. The free lands of the north."

In fairness, I thought, you could hardly expect anyone to pay for them – and the thought made it dangerously close to my tongue. Instead, I said, "You'll have to excuse my ignorance. I don't get up this way very often. Or, now that I think about it, ever."

"Which, I believe," said Kalyxis, "brings us back to my question. Though with time and much of my patience wasted."

"Ah." I struggled to marshal my thoughts into something like working order. "Well, you got our message, of course? I mean Castilio Mounteban's message."

Kalyxis's eyes narrowed. "That? An obvious trick... though the messenger would not be persuaded to admit as much." Her gaze unfocused for the smallest moment, and I tried not to wonder what qualified for persuasion here in Shoan. "Even if it weren't," she continued, "it's hard to credit that this

Mounteban would send two such as you: a skinny wretch and a monster. More likely you're spies, or else a pair of swindlers. We will need time to deliberate."

Biting my tongue once more, this time against the urge to point out that at least one of us wasn't a swindler, I said, "Well, there's the thing. We could really do with your help sooner rather than later. At this very moment, King Panchessa is marching his armies on the Castoval. As it happens, though, that's actually our least urgent worry right now. The reason we're a few envoys short of a delegation is that we were shipwrecked further down the coast... and the rest of our party are in trouble with some very dangerous people... so, what I was hoping, is–"

"Chain them up," said Kalyxis, to no one in particular. "We will consider."

I wondered if I dared argue – and, given what was at stake, if I dared not to. Yet just as I'd decided that, for once, nothing I said could make matters significantly worse, I realised Kalyxis's gaze had left me and fixed on Saltlick.

"First," she said, "tell me, what is that?"

I assumed at first that she meant Saltlick, and it took me a moment to realise she was pointing not at him but at the crown around his neck. I'd grown so used to seeing it there, to its fresh function as the giant badge of leadership, that I hardly noticed it anymore. Now, however, with Kalyxis's finger beginning a line that ended in that circle of glittering metal, I found my blood had suddenly turned cold.

"That...?"

I could lie. I was *good* at lying.

Only, nothing would come. A dozen untruths flitted through my mind, each more absurd than the last. But there was no getting past the fact that she was pointing at a crown, and there were only two crowns of note that I knew of. Since this wasn't Panchessa's, it stood to obvious reason that it was the crown of the princedom of Altapasaeda.

Perhaps it was fortunate that Kalyxis's patience ran out then – though it hardly felt it. "The crown of Altapasaeda," she said. "If nothing else, this Castilio Mounteban keeps his promises."

I froze.

How could Mounteban have promised her the crown? He *couldn't* have known where it was, not when he'd written all those days ago. Maybe he'd meant it metaphorically, then, or else intended some scam, for if he believed the true crown lost it would have been easy enough to craft a fake. What better present to offer a woman with delusions of royalty?

Then, of course, Mounteban had seen the opportunity to deliver the real crown into Kalyxis's hands – and he'd manoeuvred us accordingly. I'd been played; betrayed yet again by Castilio Mounteban. Even two countries away, he was still pulling my strings.

"The thing is..." I started, for no other reason than that my mouth felt like it should be doing something.

Kalyxis, ignoring me, merely pointed.

One of her men moved forward. "On your knees," he told Saltlick.

Saltlick looked at me questioningly. I gave him the slightest nod; we had nothing to bargain with, nothing to offer or threaten. He crumpled to his haunches and bent forward. The Shoanan didn't even have the decency to appear nervous as he reached, cut the crown loose with a swift stroke and caught it in his free hand. Without once glancing up, he crossed to Kalyxis and held it to her.

Kalyxis took the crown, turned it thoughtfully in her hands. When she looked up, her eyes on me were merciless as any hawk's; if there'd ever been any doubt as to whether I was prey, it had vanished.

"Good," she said, "now chain those two up. We've much to think upon this night."

CHAPTER EIGHT

Like many a ruler before her, Kalyxis wasn't one to think through the finer points of her orders.

Thus it was that the actual logistics of chaining up a giant without said giant's permission were left to a hastily gathered contingent made up from a dozen of the more savage-looking Shoanish warriors. For all their conspicuous muscle and their scars and their clothing made of animals they'd likely killed with their own bare hands, it was obviously a function that nothing in their previous experience had prepared them for.

Had time not been a factor, it would have entertaining enough to watch. The Shoanish brought long spears and circled around Saltlick, regardless of the fact that he'd moved not a finger against them and had followed all their orders with his usual polite good nature. That done, much pointing and unnecessary threatening conveyed us as far as a large tent on the west of town, close to the harbour.

Inside, I saw that six large metal rings protruded from the ground, presumably secured to posts beneath the dirt. Two chains ran from each, to end in leather straps. The moment we entered I was forced to my knees, and my wrists and ankles efficiently strapped behind my back.

Securing dashing thieves was one thing, though; doing the same to giants quite another. There was much muttering back and forth, as if they imagined Saltlick hadn't yet worked out their intentions. However, with every man only able to communicate with his neighbours without breaking the circle, it was impossible for any real discussion to take place. No one seemed to be in charge, and as each minute passed without any sign of unanimity, so tensions in the enclosed space rose like the heat before a summer storm.

With as much reason as anyone to desire a swift outcome and my extremities already growing numb, I was ready to cheer when one particularly rough and ugly Shoanan finally broke ranks. My gratitude evaporated quickly when he paced to me, drew a knife from his belt and put the curved blade to my throat.

"Do you hear me, monster?" he barked at Saltlick. "Twitch a hair on your head and I'll show you what the inside of your friend's throat looks like."

"Um..." There was obviously an art to speaking with a blade at your throat that I hadn't grasped. Nor was it something I felt comfortable practising; even that one syllable had brought me dangerously close to gaining a new orifice. "Will... you...?"

"Shut up," said the Shoanan holding the knife. But he did ease the pressure a fraction.

"Look... can you just...?" I was all ready to explain that Saltlick was harmless as a fly, and only at the last instant did it occur to me how unwise sharing that information might be. "He'll... he'll listen to me."

My guard gave that a little thought. "Then tell him you don't want to try and learn breathing through your neck," he said, and eased up ever so slightly more.

I supposed I couldn't begrudge him his caution; I'd just pointed out that the cart-sized wall of muscle across from us would do exactly what I told him to. "Saltlick," I said, "I order you to stay still. However much you might want to tear someone's arm off or rip out their heart and eat it, you won't do any such thing. Do you hear? Just for once, restrain your inexhaustible lust for blood."

I accompanied it with a clumsy wink, in the faint hope that the signal would mean the same to giants as men. Saltlick probably imagined I'd gone mad; but since there'd never been a possibility of him doing anything but politely sitting still, it hardly mattered. All that was important was persuading our captors not to waste the entire night in securing him.

To that end, at least, my words seemed to have achieved something. My new friend eased his knife away from my neck and beckoned over a couple of his companions. This time, it didn't take long for a consensus to be reached. It was hardly the one I'd been expecting, though – for together, the three of them then hurried outside.

It wasn't long before they were back, however, this time with armfuls of rope and chains. An end was in sight; but even with a dozen men working together and Saltlick crouched still as a statue, it still took them the better part of an hour to secure him to their satisfaction. By the time the Shoanish had finished, hardly a part of him wasn't criss-crossed with rope, metal, leather or wood – for rather than remove his harness, they'd figured it into their construction – and the whole elaborate web secured to every one of the remaining hoops set in the ground.

Finally, they appeared satisfied with their masterwork, and I felt the time was right to move onto more meaningful concerns. "All right," I said. "It's safe to say we're not going anywhere. Saltlick won't be eating anyone who doesn't want to be eaten. Now, can we please speak again with Kalyxis?"

"You'll speak to Kalyxis when Kalyxis wants to speak to you," replied the Shoanan who'd threatened me earlier.

"Which will be...?" I asked.

"When she says."

As helpful an answer as I'd expected. My attempt at ambassadorship was a disaster, and if I didn't think of something quickly, there was no doubt that I'd have the blood of Estrada, Navare and the others on my hands, not to mention a few thousand Altapasaedans. My slender remaining hope was that these fastidious barbarians would leave us alone now that we were trussed beyond any reasonable hope of escape.

Even that was too much to ask of my miserable luck. Ten of them trooped out but two remained, and, with initiative beyond the average guard, chose to make their vigil not from outside the tent but from within. It was a completely unfair strategy, and of doubtful professionalism; clearly here in the far north they were ignorant even of traditional guarding etiquette.

The minutes dragged by. I was growing close to despair. It was hard to believe that tying your guests to the floor was a preliminary to accepting their heartfelt pleas for help, even in Shoan; more likely, Kalyxis was busy pondering dramatic and amusing ways to execute us.

Then, just as I'd all but given up hope, I noticed our two sentries start and look behind them. A third figure had drawn up the tent flap and, as I watched, spoke briefly to them in hushed tones. I didn't hear what was said, but the two gave us a last hard glance and followed the new arrival outside, dropping the flap behind them.

I doubted the three of them had gone far. In all likelihood it was just a changing of the guard, or a brief break to share some revolting northern liquor brewed from bits of dead horse. Nevertheless, it was the best and only opportunity I'd had, and I refused to waste it.

"Saltlick," I hissed, "I know you can break those ropes, so get on with it. We don't have all night."

Saltlick eyed me mournfully. It might have been because he was exhausted from his day's running; it might have been because I was wrong and he was too tightly bound for even his colossal strength to prevail. Knowing him, though, I suspected it had more to do with guilt at the prospect of undoing all of our captors' hard work.

"Look," I said, "I have a plan. But I'm going to need your help."

Truthfully, I had no plan at all, no idea what I'd do if Saltlick could liberate us. It would likely achieve nothing. Yet knowing what hung on my actions and sitting there unable to move was killing me just as surely as our guards would if – or more realistically, when – they caught us. Anyway, I always thought best on my feet. There was a chance *something* would come to me, if only I could get free.

Because Saltlick still didn't look convinced, I added, with all the urgency I could muster, "Quickly! Every minute we waste here could cost Estrada and the others dearly." Another bluff, of course; for all I knew, this was the worst possible thing for Estrada. Maybe Kalyxis was at this very moment preparing to help us and all I was doing was jeopardising that.

But it wasn't a possibility I was prepared to entertain. I *had* to be free. I couldn't just do nothing.

Anyway, it seemed I'd finally gotten through to him. I'd hardly noticed at first how hard he was straining; he was so tightly trussed that his exertions were almost invisible. Now that I concentrated, though, I could see subtle motion: a chain link bulging here, a rope strained to its limits there. Looking back to Saltlick's face, I understood that his expression showed not his usual dull placidity but the most intense effort, locking his features rigid.

Too late it struck that he really might not have the necessary strength. On his best day, I doubted any measures could hold him; even weakened by torture, I'd seen Saltlick tear through ropes thicker than these outside Moaradrid's camp. Today, however, he'd run himself half to death, perhaps beyond the point of healing – and that after being almost drowned, battered on rocks and climbing a cliff. There *had* to be limits even to Saltlick's vast strength. Maybe today was the day I found them.

A chain link popped, with a delicate *ting*. One rope rippled like smoke and fell in coils into the dust. The following pause dragged on for so long that I started to wonder if that wasn't it, if those small achievements hadn't sapped the last of Saltlick's vigour. Then a section of rope thinned, unravelled and came apart, all in a moment. A leather strap ripped. Navare's scratch-built harness, surely the weakest link in the entire arrangement, gave one deep, wailing groan, before the beam over Saltlick's shoulders snapped clean in two and crashed to the ground.

I glanced nervously towards the door flap, expecting angry northerners and sharpened blades to come flooding in at the sound. Neither one materialised. Even as another chain lashed the ground, as two and then three more ropes split, our privacy remained undisturbed. It was perplexing, and perhaps I'd have questioned it more had it not been so hypnotic watching Saltlick free himself. Once when I was a boy, a band of travelling performers had passed through our village, and one of their number – a giant himself by any normal standards – had performed a similar stunt. Impressive as it had seemed, it was nothing to what Saltlick was doing now. Even battered and fatigued, the power in those muscles of his was phenomenal.

When he was done, when all that remained was a nest of torn rope, shattered chains, scraps of leather and splintered wood, Saltlick climbed shakily to his feet and trudged over to me. He reached behind my back and fumbled with the straps there. I heard a tearing sound, another, and with that I could move my wrists and ankles once more.

Unfortunately, since my appendages were utterly numb by then, I had no choice but to flop onto my side and lie like a beached fish while my circulation returned. Once I had a little feeling back I rubbed my hands together, despite the throb of pins and needles, and when they were usable again began to massage life back into my feet.

All the while, Saltlick watched me steadily. His skin was beaded everywhere with tracks of blood, where ropes and chains had nicked the flesh. He looked inexpressibly weary. It occurred to me then that even if I did have a plan, I would have no idea how to incorporate him into it. Even if I had a chance at escape, even assuming escape might achieve some useful end, I could hardly drag Saltlick around town without someone noticing.

A noise came from behind me. It was so subtle, like the sough of wind through grass, that I hardly registered it at first. By the time I recognised it for what it was, a blade slicing through the thick hide of the tent wall, and by the time I'd turned around, there was already an almost man-sized opening there – not to mention the almost man-sized figure crouched in the gap.

In the half-light, it took me a moment to recognise the sullen youth from earlier; he was the one who'd sat beside Kalyxis, the one I'd figured for the Bastard Prince. That moment was exactly as long as it took him to cross the short distance between us and bring his knife up.

The knife was a piddling thing compared to the one I'd had recently at my throat, not much longer than my hand, and I struggled to find either it or him intimidating. "You should put that down," I said, "before someone gets hurt. Someone, of course, meaning you. It wouldn't be very princely to accidentally chop your own thumb off, would it?"

"You know who I am," he said, ignoring my advice. "So *are* you a spy then? Like my grandmother thinks?"

Was that really the conclusion Kalyxis had come to? She was even more paranoid than I'd imagined – or else the standard for royal spies was uncommonly low these days. "Everything I told her was true," I said. "We need her help."

The youth scrunched his face into an even denser scowl. "Well, I don't care either way. I need *your* help, and you're going to give me it. I heard you can command that thing?"

It took me a moment to understand what he meant. "That *thing* has a name. He's called Saltlick."

"That's no name," he observed with disdain.

I considered explaining that the blame for that lay with his father's idiot thugs and their inability to pronounce Saltlick's true, giantish name; however, the information was neither politic nor pertinent just then, and I had bigger questions on my mind. "He'll do what I ask him, so long as he agrees with it. But why would you need our help? Aren't you supposed to be royalty around here?"

"Pah!" The youth spat into the dirt. "A prisoner more like. The only one anybody listens to round here is my grandmother. Do you know what it's like to grow up with everyone thinking you're going to be some sort of legendary hero?" He looked me up and down. "Of course you don't. Anyway, they can all go rot in the cold hells. I'm getting out of here. And you and your monster are going to help me."

"What's in it for us?" I asked, for no real reason other than that I was finding him intensely irritating.

"Are you an idiot? You get out of here." He waved the knife in my direction. "And I don't make that stupid-looking face look any stupider."

I'd never been a fighter. I'd never truly cared for knives. I'd always preferred to talk my way out of danger, or run my way out on those not infrequent occasions when talking failed to do the trick.

But you couldn't live a life of crime for as long as I had without picking up the odd thing along the way. And I knew without doubt that this Bastard Prince was standing too close; he was holding the knife too far across his own body.

I ducked forward and sideways, caught his wrist with my right hand and grasped his shoulder with my left. Then I shoved hard. I stopped when he let go and before his arm popped out of joint – but only barely. I let him get out one brief whimper before I kicked him hard in the arse; while he stumbled forward, I picked up the knife.

"So have you even got a plan?" I asked. "Or are we just walking out?"

"You..."

"Manners," I suggested, tapping the blade against my open palm. "Because *if* we're leaving, it's on my terms."

Not that I actually *had* terms. But surely a prince, especially this prince, must be a useful card to have up my sleeve. Might the palace soldiers trade him for the lives of Estrada and the others? After all, the King must surely be itching to meet his unruly grandson.

When, rather than answer, the youth merely stood glowering at me, I racked my memory until it coughed up what I was looking for and said, "Look... Malekrin, that's your name, isn't it? You don't want to be here. I certainly don't want to be here, and neither does Saltlick. Since that's the one thing we all have in common, what say we concentrate on it?"

"Everyone calls me Mal," the boy said sulkily – and in a way that made me suspect that absolutely no one called him that, however much he might like them to.

Still, it couldn't hurt to try to get on his good side, assuming he had any such thing. "Mal, is it? Fine. Care to share your escape plan, Mal?"

To my amusement, he did perk up a little at that. "There's a boat I use," he said. "It should be big enough, even for... that *creature*, whatever you call it."

"Saltlick," I reminded him. "And I don't know if you've noticed, but he tends to draw attention."

"Hardly anyone's awake at this hour," Malekrin said. "And those that are won't be looking in our direction."

He spoke that last with confidence. Did he know something I didn't? If so then every minute I spent stood questioning him was a minute wasted. Coming to a swift decision, I said, "Hurry up, Saltlick; we're getting out of here."

"Plan?" Saltlick asked. As usual he spoke volumes with a single word – for there was a powerful note of doubt underlying that one syllable.

"Yes. *This* is the plan. Trust me, all right?"

Saltlick nodded. He *did* trust me, the poor, lumbering fool, and I'd never felt worse about the fact. Even I could see this was no sort of plan, and the odds of it helping the others were practically non-existent. Yet this opportunity had fallen into our laps, and I couldn't imagine a better one coming along any time soon.

Malekrin had already ducked back under the improvised flap he'd made, and I hurried to follow. Saltlick made a brief effort to squeeze through the existing gap and then, realising its hopelessness, reached with both hands and tore the thick hide almost to its highest point. I winced at the noise; but no one called out the alert, no one appeared from the darkness.

As Saltlick hauled himself through the widened breach, I couldn't but notice how badly he was limping. He could hardly put any weight on his wounded leg. He wouldn't slow us down, his height would compensate for that, but I hated to see how he was suffering – and all for nothing.

As Malekrin led us past a gap between two tents, something even more arresting than Saltlick's plight drew my attention. In the distance, an orange glow hung over the camp town, as though the sun were just beginning to rise there. Then a tongue of brilliant yellow licked into sight, followed by a pale gust of smoke. Something was burning, and burning fast; even as I'd watched, the fire must have doubled in size.

Malekrin had told me no one would be looking our way, and now here was something on fire, conveniently far from where we were. "Your handiwork?" I asked.

Malekrin gave me an unprepossessing grin. "It wasn't easy, delaying it like that."

"And you're not worried about setting fire to your own people's tents?" I asked, trying to keep any suggestion of judgement out of my voice.

"It's just a store for hay, they won't miss it," he whispered back dismissively.

If I'd had doubts about Malekrin being Moaradrid's son, they were starting to diminish. Disregard for the lives of others and a passion for setting their property on fire were certainly qualities Moaradrid had possessed in abundance. I was even starting to see a similarity in the boy's face, even if he had none of his father's hawkish intensity. "Did you have something to do with the guards leaving as well?" I asked.

"Of course. I told them relief was on the way and they were urgently needed to clean out my grandmother's latrines... a punishment for taking so long to restrain you. They weren't happy about it."

"I don't imagine they were," I agreed.

Malekrin ducked around the corner of a tent and I stayed close. He was leading us by an indirect route to the dockside; keeping away from the main thoroughfare, weaving instead through the clusters of high-sided tents that bordered it. The shadows were thick there, for the night sky was overcast and there were no torches lit. Even if the town had been thronged with people, we'd have stood a chance of moving Saltlick unnoticed.

When we came out, there was nothing between us and the harbour but a stretch of gravelly sand. I could see no one. As we hurried across the intervening distance, I wondered again at the size and number of the craft moored there. What exactly did a tribe of nomads want with a fleet of what could only be considered ships? What was Kalyxis up to? She'd struck me as the kind of woman who by her nature would always be up to something.

I could have asked Malekrin, but we were already hurrying towards the end of the leftmost wharf by then, Saltlick crashing behind us, and I decided questions could wait. This was going to be a short trip indeed if anyone saw us leave. The boat Malekrin came to a halt before was tied amongst a flotilla of smaller vessels, craft presumably kept for fishing the nearby waters. His was no more impressive than any of the others; another statement, maybe, of how highly these people really considered their bastard prince. Regardless of whether his claims of being kept like a prisoner were true, he obviously hadn't been living like any kind of royalty.

"I call her *Seadagger,*" Malekrin said, with obvious pride.

Even in such dire circumstances, I struggled not to laugh. "You can call it whatever you like... but if you're saying it out loud, let's stick with 'the boat', all right?"

Malekrin gave me the filthiest of looks, and hopped aboard. "Your pet monster better not sink her," he said.

"Saltlick's good with boats," I lied, thinking back to the time he'd once rowed Estrada and I to safety and almost drowned us all in the process. However, Malekrin's craft was larger than that measly rowboat had been, and though it had clearly been designed to be sailable by one man there was space for a couple more.

I leapt aboard. Malekrin had already brought out a pair of oars, and between us we manoeuvred the boat as close to the wharf as we could manage. Once it was brushing the timber, Saltlick knelt down and lowered himself in. His sudden weight set the craft rocking distressingly, but he was quick to crawl towards the centre. After a minute, though we were drenched from head to toe, we'd at least returned to an even keel.

Malekrin cast off the mooring rope, shoved us free and began to set sail. Whatever his failings of character, he'd been honest about his ability to handle a boat, for it took him hardly any time to get the small craft rigged, behind the wind and out into open water. We were free – and readying to leave the far north, Shoan, or whatever the damned place was called. So far as I could tell, no one had seen us go.

But how long could it possibly take them to realise we were missing? Or that their insufferable so-called prince was gone, and his boat too? Not long, I knew.

And after that, with us stranded at sea, how long could it be before I found out the punishment for kidnapping Shoanish royalty?

CHAPTER NINE

Unbearable as every aspect of his personality might be, Malekrin had one redeeming trait: his seamanship was excellent.

He soon had us scudding before the waves, aided by a hard wind driving down from the north – a direction he'd dismissed as a course of escape without any contribution from me. "There's nothing to the north," he'd said, "except barbarians."

I'd refrained from pointing out that there was nothing but barbarians to the south either, at least until we passed the border into Ans Pasaeda. I supposed that never having seen a city, Malekrin considered horse riding the highest expression of culture and tents the epitome of architecture. What use was there in disillusioning him now? If we should somehow make it to Altapasaeda, he'd learn the truth soon enough.

At any rate, I was grateful that Malekrin expected no contribution from Saltlick or me in the running of his beloved craft. Saltlick had immediately lain himself out in the stern and within seconds his head was lolling, tectonic snores rattling from his throat. Whatever last spark that had been keeping him moving was vanished, and I suspected he might sleep for days if we left him to. Malekrin eyed him with contempt, and turned the same look on me when I struggled into the crook of Saltlick's arm – the only space on the boat now free – and drew my cloak over me. But he didn't say anything, and I interpreted his silence as confirmation that he could manage well enough without us.

However, there was one matter I knew I had to attend to before I surrendered to exhaustion. Around a yawn, I said, "You know, I think the best person to help you is Marina Estrada... one of the friends I tried to tell your grandmother about. She's mayor of a little town; I'm sure she could find you somewhere to start your new life."

"I can look after myself," muttered Malekrin.

"Really? If I was you I'd take whatever help I could get. Anyway, we'll have a better chance of getting to safety with Estrada and the others on our side."

Malekrin gave a grunt that I took for, if not agreement, then at least acknowledgement of what I'd said.

"The thing is," I went on, "there's a... *situation*. We shouldn't just go blundering in."

"I'm not an idiot," Malekrin said, "and I heard what you told my grandmother. Your friends are in trouble."

"All right," I admitted, "they're in trouble. And you can do what you like, but I have to try to help them. So keep a look out for a beached ship, will you? There are rocks nearby, so be careful."

"Fine," he agreed, in a tone that implied it was anything but.

It was all I reasonably could hope for. I had my plan now, desperate as it might be. If Estrada and the others were still alive, if they'd managed to resist the palace guard for this long, then I'd have to find a way to bargain Malekrin's life for theirs. There were plenty of assumptions involved, not least that anyone would actually *want* the brat alive; but I was too tired for second guessing, and there was no way my dwindling consciousness was going to offer anything better.

I let my head fall back upon Saltlick's armpit, trying hard to ignore the pungent odour of giant sweat, and closed my eyes.

I woke to Malekrin kicking my leg, with more enthusiasm than he'd shown in anything else up to that point.

"Ow! Stop that," I mumbled, trying to curl into a ball.

"Shush!" he spat. "I've found your damn boat."

That was enough to make me open my eyes. It was still dark, but the night was softening above the cliffs on our left and sunrise couldn't be far away. As Malekrin had said, the boat was in view – though not quite as I remembered it. It took me a few moments to appreciate what had happened: that the tide had been out when the palace guard had landed and now was in, so that the boat was sitting in low water, some distance from the diminished shoreline.

Suddenly, with no conscious thought, I realised that my simple plan was evolving. Because out upon the beach, I could see blunt silhouettes backed by a dying fire; the contingent from the palace was still camped there. Conversely, I couldn't see anyone aboard the boat. If we could secure it, could capture their only means of leaving this wretched shore, then that was just as good a bargaining tool as Malekrin's life. With the two together, they might even listen to me.

"Can you get us closer?" I whispered. "I mean, without anyone on board seeing, or us running aground?"

Malekrin considered. "We're shallower than they are. We could row in if I stow the mast... it would be easier without the monster in the way."

"His name's Saltlick," I corrected automatically. "Do your best, will you?"

Malekrin was right, though; Saltlick's bulk filling half the small boat made it tricky to take the mast down, let alone to do it without noise. Even in that, however, the boy worked with deft efficiency. While I worked with an oar to stop us drifting, he dropped the sail and tidied it away, then hammered out the pins that kept the mast in place and, with my assistance, lowered it along the boat. We had to prop one end on Saltlick's chest, and he still didn't stir; his breath was coming in shallow tugs by then, and his skin looked pastier than ever in the greying gloom.

Taking an oar each, we nudged closer and closer to the enemy vessel. With the current on our side, it took us a mere few minutes to edge within the shadowed lee of their port side. Throughout our approach, I'd seen no one, nor any sign of activity from the camp upon the shore. The only noise was the lap of the sea against their flank and the creak of straining wood, enough between them to mask any sound as we brushed alongside the larger craft.

Now came the difficult part. For all I knew, there might be a dozen men sleeping within, hidden by their boat's high flank. Once I was sure Malekrin had us under control and we weren't about to drift away, I eased up from a crouch, palms flat against the other vessel's side. I'd need to be standing to see over; not easy when the surface beneath my feet was in constant motion. Moreover, I couldn't shake the conviction that all I'd see if I succeeded was a palace soldier staring back.

I eased my head above the summit. No one was looking my way, but that wasn't quite the relief it might have been – for ahead, staring out towards the shore, two shadowy figures stood guard. We wouldn't be taking the boat without a fight.

I ducked back, held up two fingers to Malekrin, pointed to left and right.

"Why can't the monster fight them?" Malekrin whispered.

"He's not a monster," I muttered, "and he doesn't like fighting." Ignoring Malekrin's look of incredulity, I added, "Can you handle the one on the left?"

"Without my knife?"

I took it from my pocket, handed it to him. "But *don't* hurt them," I mouthed. "Let's not make things worse than they are."

"It might be nice to know who I'm fighting."

"Bad people. That's all you need to know."

"And what about *Seadagger*?"

I suppressed a groan. I couldn't care less about his stupid *Seadagger*, but it would hardly do to have Saltlick drifting out to sea. Of course an anchor was too much to ask of so small a boat. I looked around for a protrusion to tie off against on the larger vessel, found nothing.

Damn it, this plan was getting more out of hand by the minute! For a long moment, I fought to resist suggesting that we simply sail on, head for Altapasaeda alone. Estrada, Navare and Alvantes's guardsmen could surely look after themselves.

Only, they were outnumbered, many of them had been hurt in the shipwreck – and more than that, I imagined myself trying to explain to Saltlick what I'd done, saw vividly the anger and disappointment in his face. Even if I could live with the thought of abandoning Estrada, there was no way I could bear that look.

I glanced round for a weapon. Seeing the mallet Malekrin had used earlier, I slipped it into a pocket. "Give me the rope," I whispered, "and be ready."

Malekrin passed the thick mooring rope to me, and with much discomfort, I clenched it between my teeth. Then, not giving myself any more time to think about it, I grasped the upper edge of the larger boat and swung myself up.

Again, though I'd moved as silently as I was able, I was certain I'd come face to face with two angry palace guardsmen – but as I rolled down the other side, they were still stood in the prow, staring away from me. I spat out the rope and looped it round the nearest rower's bench, tying a hasty knot. Then I gave the cable a tug, wishing I'd thought to establish the signal before I went.

Thankfully, Malekrin understood. In an instant he'd clambered to join me, moving soft and fast as a greased cat. Evidently, sailing wasn't the only hobby he'd occupied himself with back home – for no one moved like that unless they'd spent time getting into places others wanted them kept out of. I gave him a nod of approval, which he ignored.

Taking the mallet from my pocket, I wished I'd given Malekrin the man on the right. I'd picked the bigger of the two for myself, and not only was he better armed, he was infinitely more disposable.

Too late now – and at least I still had the element of surprise. I started towards my man; felt more than saw Malekrin move on my left. My eyes flicked from my diminutive weapon to the nape of my opponent's neck, and I wondered what chance the one had against the other. An arm's length away, I readied my swing, took one more brief step...

Something creaked beneath my foot – and though it sounded exactly like every other creak that cursed boat had made, nevertheless the man before me turned his head a fraction. Adjusting too late, I swiped his temple, lost my grip, and watched the mallet spiral towards the sea.

The splash of its final impact was masked by the crunch of his fist against my jaw.

He was fast, I had to give him that – though my appreciation of his athleticism was dulled by pain, first from his punch then my head smacking timber, as I lost my footing and tumbled back. I tried to regain my feet, reconsidered when I realised that would only put my face back in the way of his fist. That brief indecision cost me dearly; before I knew it, his hand was around my throat and dragging me to my feet, his other clenched and drawn back for another blow...

"Get off him!" Malekrin had his knife to the second man's throat. "Or your friend gets the closest shave of his life."

I cringed. Had he really said that? I fought the urge to apologise: *he's young, you see, his quipping needs some work.* Under the circumstances, however, I was prepared to let it go – for the man I'd been fighting, or rather being savagely beaten by, now had his hands off me and above his head.

"Good choice," I told him, successfully hiding my embarrassment. "My partner means business."

I darted to grab a length of rope from the stern and hurriedly bound his feet and hands, my heart hammering all the while lest he realise how illusory our advantage was. Once I had him secured, I turned my attention to Malekrin's man. And only once I had them both safely trussed did I dare to consider breathing normally again. We had their boat – and I had the infamous Bastard Prince. My plan was actually *working*.

At no point had it occurred to me I'd make it this far, and I hardly knew what to do next. I moved to the prow, looked out towards the shore. Compared with when I'd last been here, there was quite a camp beneath the cliffs now: two large tents, presumably stowed in the boat for just such a crisis, sat side to side of a wide fire pit hemmed with stones, from which a lazy thread of smoke lost itself in the slate grey sky.

As the blood rush from my brief tussle began to subside, I realised it was clear what I had to do. I'd try to make contact with Estrada, assuming she was alive to be made contact with. As much as the idea of bartering Malekrin had a certain appeal, it might yet prove unnecessary; if Navare and his guardsmen swam out here and secured the boat, we might make our escape without trading either words or blows with the palace soldiers.

Ready to put my plan into action, I spared once last glance for the camp on the shore. I could still see no one, and now that fact sent a vague chill of doubt through me. Did the lack of a sentry mean there was nobody left to guard against? Had I returned too late?

Then I realised someone *was* there – and likely had been all along.

He'd been standing against one of the tents, indistinguishable in the gloom. I'd only noticed him now because he'd moved a little. As I watched, he did so once more – and I knew with cold certainty that he was looking back, straight at me. He took a full step forward then, outlined before the glimmer of firelight, and bellowed, "Who in the hells are you?"

That he was even asking suggested he'd missed the recent scuffle. Did that mean I could bluff my way out of this? But by the time I'd thought it, a second figure had joined the first, appearing so far as I could judge from the mouth of the second tent. They took half a dozen more quick steps, hurrying towards the line where pale surf scoured the ash grey beach.

"Easie? Is that you?"

The voice was familiar as it was inexplicable. "*Estrada*?"

"How did you get there?" she called back. "And who's that with you?"

The questions barely registered. I was too busy looking for anyone aiming a bow or holding a sword in her direction; for any hint at all that she was being threatened by the man behind her. Yet, as my brain began to process what Estrada had said, it struck me that hers wasn't the tone of someone being intimidated – more that of a woman annoyed at being woken at too early an hour.

Then her question finally sunk in, and I realised she was referring to Malekrin, who'd moved up beside me without my noticing. "This is Malekrin," I called back. Catching the scowl he threw me, I added, "Though his many friends call him Mal." I refrained from pointing out that we knew him by an altogether different name; that news could wait until I understood what was going on here.

"And what are you *doing*?" cried Estrada.

"I'm... We're... That is..." I coughed into my fist, not sure why I felt so embarrassed when I'd clearly just done something terrifically heroic. "What we're doing is that I've just captured their boat," I concluded, with all the bravado I could manage.

"Oh, Easie." Even at such a distance, I recognised all too well the embarrassment in Estrada's voice. "I think you need to come ashore right now..."

On Estrada's insistence and against my better judgement, we freed the two palace guardsmen, neither of whom showed much in the way of gratitude. It seemed best to make a hasty exit, so we recovered Malekrin's boat – in which Saltlick, astonishingly, was still fast asleep – and rowed hastily for the shore.

There, I presented Malekrin to Estrada and finally woke Saltlick, who was both befuddled and overjoyed to see her. Introductions and reunions complete, Estrada took me aside, a little way from the camp, to where a hard-faced and vaguely familiar man stood waiting. "Easie, meet Commander Ondeges," she said, "captain of the Palace Guard in Altapasaeda."

Ondeges looked me up and down. "The thief," he observed, "who stole into the palace."

"If this is about those bath oils someone vindictively hid in my bag," I said, as the memory clicked into place, "then I'm afraid I lost them when you shipwrecked us."

Estrada's expression turned to one of mortification. "I hope this won't jeopardise our arrangement?" she asked Ondeges.

To my surprise, Ondeges's reply was to offer me his hand. "Just now," he said, "my interests lie more in the future than the past."

I shook, striving not to wince as his fingers clenched around mine. "You've come to... an understanding then?" I managed. "One that doesn't involve trying to kill each other, I mean?"

"We've reached an agreement," Estrada said. "Commander Ondeges has certain questions regarding the events of recent days that he'd like answering before any more blood is shed."

It was Ondeges's turn to look uncomfortable. "My first loyalty was to Prince Panchetto," he said. "After that…"

He let the sentence trail away, but I thought I'd understood. "Isn't Ondeges a Castovalian name?" I asked.

Ondeges nodded. "My family live in Altapasaeda. So do the families of many of my men. If I'm to tell them to raise arms against their own people, it's an order I need to hear from the King himself."

Taken aback as I was by Ondeges's honesty, it was easy enough to appreciate his position. Ludovoco had appeared from nowhere and in no time at all had supplanted his command, not to mention plunging Altapasaeda into chaos and potential war; and was it any coincidence that Ondeges had been sent on this mission to the middle of nowhere while Ludovoco stayed behind? No, it was clear why Commander Ondeges might have questions in need of answers; I was only impressed that someone in his position would have sense enough to ask them.

Rather than say that, however, I settled for something more diplomatic. "I'm sorry about the… ah, misunderstanding. The one where we tied up your men and tried to steal your boat, I mean."

Ondeges's mouth creased into a smile; for a moment he looked younger, less careworn. "I'm sure it's not a mistake you'll make twice," he said. "Now, if you'll excuse me…" And with that and a nod towards Estrada, he turned back towards the camp.

I watched him go, my thoughts awhirl. Despite everything Ondeges had said, I hadn't quite let go of the notion that this might be some sort of ambush. Then again, I'd seen firsthand what an insufferable bastard Ludovoco was. Whatever doubts Ondeges might have had about his fellow commander's presence in Altapasaeda, they were exactly the kind of weakness a skilled ambassador like Estrada could play on.

Which led me to one inescapable conclusion: "I rushed back here for nothing, didn't I?"

"We've been waiting for you since yesterday," replied Estrada. She had the decency to sound a little guilty.

"That's gracious of you. Do you realise Saltlick ran himself half to death?"

"I'm sorry, Easie," she said. "I didn't know this would happen."

"Really? No idea at all?"

Estrada gave an awkward half shrug, a gesture that spoke volumes in itself. "I had to try talking. If it meant avoiding fighting and more people being hurt, of course I did. I had no way to know Ondeges would listen."

"So, in a sense," I said, "we were really just the backup plan?"

"Not at all. We still needed you to get help for Altapasaeda."

Shit! I'd been so quick to castigate Estrada for sending me on yet another fool's errand that I'd forgotten just how horribly I'd botched that part of my mission. Of course, thanks to my actions, there was a fair chance Kalyxis actually would have sent some of her warriors our way – but it was safe to assume that helping us would be the last thing on their minds. Perhaps I wasn't in a position to be hurling criticisms after all.

Then again, when had that ever stopped me? "That didn't go so well," I said. '"How would it, when Mounteban sent us into a trap? Well, of course he did, he's *Mounteban*. Only a moon-eyed imbecile would think to trust him for even a second."

Estrada glared at me. "Just tell me what happened."

"Kalyxis saw us coming is what happened. We weren't there to recruit help for Altapasaeda; we were delivering its crown to her. And if any alliance comes out of it, I doubt very much we'll be on the guest list."

Estrada winced sharply as I spoke, as though the reality of what had happened were a knife drawn across her flesh.

"Damn it!" she said, and then, "Damn you, Castilio!" She turned away, took a deep and shuddering breath. "We have to hurry. We need to get back to Altapasaeda."

"Damn right we do. But first, you need to tell me what these terms you've agreed with Ondeges are."

"I surrendered," she said, still not looking at me. "Those are the terms. I surrendered and Ondeges makes sure no one gets hurt."

I glanced after Ondeges, now busy organising the dismantling of his small camp. He struck me as the honourable type, but once we got back to Altapasaeda, it would be Ludovoco calling the shots, not him. How much would Ondeges's word be worth then?

My eyes wandered further, to where Malekrin stood kicking pebbles at the water's edge, far enough away from the work to make it clear he had no interest in helping. "Maybe we've got grounds for renegotiation now," I said.

Estrada had followed my gaze. "I'm not even going to ask how you managed to steal the Bastard Prince."

"Ah. I thought you might recognise the name." When she finally turned back to look at me, I offered her a weak grin. "The truth is, it was Malekrin's idea more than mine. Turns out he doesn't much like being a figurehead in his grandparents' war."

"Does he know who he's dealing with?" Estrada asked.

"You mean, does he know he's just landed in the lap of the Altapasaedan Palace Guard? No. And I think that until we know where this is going, we should keep it that way. The same goes for Ondeges."

Estrada nodded thoughtfully. "You might have given us a chance after all, Easie. But until I understand Ondeges's loyalties a little better, I think you're right. We have a slim advantage now; let's try and keep it until we need it."

As if he'd somehow heard what we'd said, despite the distance and the tumult of waves and the rasping screech of seabirds, Malekrin left off his idle kicking and turned to scowl at us. Then he looked away, back out to sea.

I thought about Kalyxis. I thought about what I'd seen of the King during my brief, unpleasant time in Pasaeda. I thought about how alike they'd seemed in many ways, the similarities of nature that perhaps had drawn them together all those years ago for their brief, disastrous fling – an affair that in due term had unleashed an infant Moaradrid upon the world. All three of them had seemed to me propelled by hatred, utterly disregarding of the little people who happened to stray into their paths. How much of this conflict between Panchessa and Kalyxis was for the reasons they stated, the goals they threw out to their followers? And how much of it was just to sate whatever darkness drove them?

"You know," I said, "I think it might take more than one barbarian brat to head off this particular war."

Just as Estrada had told me, her hope for mine and Saltlick's return had been the only thing keeping the now combined party of freebooters, city guardsmen and palace soldiers from starting back to Altapasaeda.

Thus, while the tide receded and the morning sun rose above the waves, the shoreside camp was hurriedly dismantled and stashed aboard. Navare and his people even worked alongside the palace contingent, though there was obvious distrust and not the slightest camaraderie evident between the two factions.

However, just as my mood began to lift a little at the prospect of leaving Shoan behind, Ondeges strode over to where I was waiting with Saltlick and Malekrin. "I'm sorry," he said, without preamble, "but there isn't room for you three on board ship."

I looked at him with vague horror, and a pained sense of inevitability. So much for Estrada's truce and my good impressions of Ondeges; here was where the truth came out.

We were to be stranded, a handful of discarded pieces in whatever malevolent game the man was playing.

But what Ondeges actually said was, "I suggest you take the giant in that rowboat of yours. We've rope enough spare to tow you behind us."

Malekrin gave him a foul look. "That 'rowboat' is..."

I dug an elbow hard into his ribs and, in the moment that bought me, finished, "...just the right size, as it turns out, for the giant, the boy and I."

Because given a choice between three more days of cramped discomfort and being abandoned on this miserable shore, I knew which option I found more appealing.

As it turned out, Ondeges was right. Unpleasant as it was to be crammed back into Malekrin's so-called *Seadagger*, I doubted we had it worse than anyone else. If our ship had been somewhat under-crewed on the journey here, its sister vessel was distinctly cramped with twice the number aboard.

At least our progress was unhindered. The powerful gales that had carried Malekrin's boat down from Kalyxis's camptown were blowing hard as ever, and even overloaded, the ship whipped through the foam-capped water. On the rare occasions that the wind slackened, there was no lack of oarsmen to help pick up the pace. From what little I could discern of life on board, I suspected everyone was glad of whatever work they could get, just to relieve the tension. Even before war had broken out, relationships had never been exactly amicable between city and palace guards, and I almost felt sorry for Mounteban's freebooters, stuck between the two.

Aboard *Seadagger*, meanwhile, relationships were only a little less strained. Malekrin had been sulking ever since we'd landed on the beach, and nothing I said relieved his mood – not that I had much interest in trying. As for Saltlick, though I'd spent half an hour in rebandaging his wound as best I could, I could tell he was still in discomfort, perhaps even in constant pain. Given how minimal his conversation was at the best of times, I soon gave up making an effort there as well.

With so little to relieve my boredom and with the confines of my world drawn so small, perhaps it was strange that I didn't give more thought to the threats closing around me. I hardly seemed to be thinking much at all – but when I did, it certainly wasn't of what fate awaited us in Altapasaeda, what that snake Mounteban had been up to in our absence, or even of what Kalyxis's response might have been to finding both her prisoners and her saviour-in-waiting vanished.

Given my unmindfulness, then, it was probably appropriate that it was Malekrin who saw them first.

It was late in the afternoon of our first day. Out of nowhere, stirring me from half-sleep, he pointed towards the northern horizon and said, "So, Grandmother noticed I was missing after all."

Irritated more than curious, I followed the line of his finger. I could make out the tiniest of black marks against the soft blue of the afternoon sky. Then, having seen one, I realised there was a second, a third, a fourth... and surely more, but the distance made it impossible to count.

"That's a *fleet*," I said. It wouldn't have surprised me if every boat I'd seen moored to that far northern harbour were upon the waves behind us.

Malekrin smiled unpleasantly. "What exactly did you expect for kidnapping a Shoanish prince?"

My first thought was to warn Estrada, but even as I considered it a shout went up from the ship, and I knew they'd seen what we'd seen. Estrada wouldn't need me to tell her who our pursuers were. I wondered, though, what explanation she'd offer Ondeges as to why a fleet of Shoanish war boats were suddenly on his tail.

After a while, as much to diffuse his smugness as anything, I said to Malekrin, "I wouldn't worry. I'm sure Ondeges can keep our lead until Altapasaeda."

"In that whale? I could catch it in *Seadagger*," Malekrin replied with dripping contempt. "No Shoanish boat would lumber in the water like that. How far is it to this Altapasaeda?"

"A couple more days," I said. "If this wind holds, that is."

"They'll be on us by then," he said, with certainty.

I avoided the subject after that – for no other reason than that it seemed more and more likely he was right. With nothing useful to do, I passed most of those two days in sleeping, or trying to at least. Whenever I opened my eyes, the black specks on the horizon had drawn closer – and by the third morning out, they could hardly be called specks at all. They were gaining inexorably, and whatever efforts Ondeges was making to outrace them were obviously not working.

Still, I could hardly believe they would really catch up with us. How could one boat be so much quicker than another? And my disbelief only made it all the more frightening to realise that, whatever my opinion of the matter, they really *were* faster than us. By late afternoon of that third day, I could clearly discern details of sails and rigging, could make out figures labouring on board the nearest vessels. By the time the sun started to dip, I might have shouted to them and been heard if it weren't for the incessant clamour of the waves.

But we were nearly home; I knew we must be. All that was left was to find that subterranean harbour, make land and get into the tunnel and there'd be no catching us. Striving to keep a tremble from my voice, I said to Malekrin, "At least *we're* safe enough. They'll never attack so long as they know you're here."

Malekrin turned me a look of disgust. "Is that what you think?"

Something in the way he said it sent a chill through my spine. "Don't you?"

"You have no idea. This place we're heading to, Altapasaeda… you said it's about to be attacked by the King, and the fact

that you were begging for help means you don't think you can
defend yourselves. Do you imagine Grandmother would let
me fall into that bastard's hands? Let him use me as a hostage
and watch all her plans unravel?"

I stared at him, aghast. "You don't really believe your
grandmother would let you die here just to keep you away
from Panchessa?"

But Malekrin had no time to answer – and as it turned out,
I didn't need him to. A resonant *thunk* made us both turn in
place. And whatever sense I might have got out of him, the
arrow sunk into the ship before us, not to mention the flames
licking up from it, were a hundred times more eloquent than
anything he could have said.

CHAPTER TEN

I'd never seen anything burn like that arrow did – nor the one that immediately followed it, nor the one after that, for in moments there was a neat and expanding line of fire etched across the boat's stern. It blazed with a heart of brilliant blue that melted into rich yellows and then thick, oily smoke.

"This is madness!" I bawled at Malekrin. "Are you saying they won't even try to rescue you? That your grandmother would be this quick to get rid of you?" Of course, I'd only known him for a few days and I wouldn't have thought twice about it – but surely, even amongst barbarians, blood ties must count for something.

"You notice they're not shooting at *us*," Malekrin replied, with no great interest. "This might be Grandmother's idea of a rescue."

I had noticed, but I'd put it down to settling for the larger target rather than any preferential treatment. It was miraculous they were hitting anything at such a distance; I doubted they could even know that Malekrin wasn't in the ship they were busy turning into a flaming pincushion.

"Anyway," added Malekrin, "it isn't just me she won't risk losing."

Then I saw what he was cradling in his lap, atop the pack he'd had stashed in the bows: a circle of gold shaped with consummate care, studded with stones that spat back the crackling firelight. It was an object I knew all too well, for hadn't I once stolen it? Hadn't I carried it with me for days? Hadn't I gifted it to Saltlick, as a replacement for his tribe's lost chief-stone?

I'd been right. Seamanship wasn't Malekrin's only talent – and he'd been busy indeed on the night of our escape. "You stole the crown," I said. "The crown of Altapasaeda."

He glared. "Stole? It's mine. Mine by right. Why should my grandmother have it?"

I let that doubtful bit of logic go. "You really think she's guessed you took it?" There was more than just a note of panic in my voice by then; the whole right side of the boat ahead was swathed in flame and the arrows were still flying, close enough that I could hear the thrum of their passage through the air.

"I told you," Malekrin said, "perhaps this is her idea of a rescue. Grandmother's never been one to do things easily." His attention was still on the glinting circlet in his lap. "If not, at least I got to be a real prince for a few days. Maybe she'd even have been proud."

When he looked at me, his eyes were ferocious – and for a moment I could picture all too well what his life must have been like, born and raised for a destiny he didn't want, desired only for the part he'd play and not for the person he was or might be. Didn't I know what it was like to grow up mattering to no one?

Then again, it was hardly the time for character insights, into Malekrin or myself. Ahead, the flames were building, casting garish light on the grey waves. I could hear rather than see Ondeges's measures to defend against the fire, some sort of hastily-ordered bucket chain. Yet the boat was overloaded, the sounds more of men tripping over each other and cursing than working for a common goal – and this was no normal fire. It coated almost the entirely of the craft's starboard side now, a rippling sheet, hissing swarms of yellow and blue sparks that at any moment were bound to catch the sail.

Small comfort, then, that our destination was finally in sight. We were close in to the cliffs by then, and as the ship swung past a buttress of stone I saw before us the low cave mouth opening, its innards thick with darkness. But what chance of reaching the docks inside? I could hardly imagine how Ondeges and his crew were keeping their craft afloat, or even be sure that they were; for the shouting from on deck had vanished, sucked into the roar of the conflagration. I thought just for a moment of Estrada, Navare and the others, of what might be happening to them – and then forced the question from my mind. They were alive or they weren't, and there was nothing I could do to help them.

My own life, though, and Saltlick's, maybe those I had a chance of saving. "We have to cut loose!" I cried.

What I'd failed to consider was that rope burned just as well as wood. The words were barely out of my mouth before our charred guideline flopped hissing into the sea. We had our freedom – except that freedom meant a burning ship ahead, vicious northerners behind and little say in whether we floated towards the one or the other...

Just at that moment, we broke through the periphery of the cavern, and it was as though a roof of night had descended on the last glimmers of evening. Amidst that nocturnal darkness, the fiery horror before us was like a second sun about to plunge under the waves. I shielded my eyes, and when that didn't help, looked down instead.

Only then did I realise that, against all reason, Malekrin still sat calmly staring at the crown. When my outraged gaze didn't draw his attention, I did the one sensible thing I could think of.

"Ow! You hit me!" He sounded more surprised than aggrieved.

"Damn right I hit you." I pointed into the gloom. "How do we make it to that pier in one piece?"

Malekrin glanced around, as though waking from a dream. "The wind's still more or less behind us," he said. "I think–"

"Save the thinking. If you can do it, do it."

Malekrin scowled as he shoved the crown back into his pack and scrambled to his feet. Yet just as before, his boat seemed the one thing he could find enthusiasm for. With my awkward help, he hauled the mast up, and snapped at me to hold it in place; that done, it took him mere seconds to hoist and rig the sail. Straight away, it whipped and billowed – for just as he'd tried to explain, the cave's mouth was open enough that the wind could find us even there. For the first time in days, we were setting our own course.

All well and good, except that now we were driving rather than drifting towards Ondeges's burning ship. It was impossible, inconceivable, that that craft, now more bonfire than boat, should be holding any kind of course. Yet there was no question Ondeges still had her prow pointed towards the pier. I couldn't believe it was mere chance; someone on deck was steering that ruined vessel, even as it began to succumb to its unlucky part as plaything of two elements.

"Turn us, damn it!" I bellowed at Malekrin, raising my voice over the nearing clamour of flames. He took a moment to throw me an aggrieved look and then hurried to adjust the sail, before throwing himself against the tiller, cursing Saltlick when he failed to crawl aside quickly enough. Our nose began to swing, and though we were close enough that I could feel the prickle of heat on my face, we drew alongside the burning ship rather than ploughing into it.

By then, though, another threat had occurred to me. The pier was drawing close, and I didn't like to think what would happen when we struck it. No, I knew a lost cause when I saw one, and *Seadagger*'s usefulness had run its course.

There was one thing still to do, however. "Saltlick!" I shouted. "Listen to me!"

He was rigid with horror, staring towards the ship blazing merrily behind us. I thought he'd ignore me, knew it with terrible certainty – for Estrada was still aboard that doomed vessel, and Saltlick was all but incapable of thinking of himself when a friend was in peril.

Then the first figure broke from the port side of the ship. They were followed by another and another – and in no time at all, bodies were plunging like rain into the sea, dark shapes bobbed on its surface, and the frontrunners were already hauling themselves with desperate thrusts towards the pier.

Was one of them Estrada? I couldn't say. But the possibility was enough to free Saltlick's attention. He looked at me, eyes huge.

"We have to swim," I cried. "Can you do that?"

Saltlick nodded – but beside him, Malekrin glowered at me with disgust. "I'm not leaving *Seadagger*!"

I could have told him what I thought of him, of his stupid *Seadagger*, of his murderous savage of a grandmother – but all of that would have taken time. Quicker by far to grab the folds of his cloak and push with all my strength. To his credit, he almost kept his footing; had he not stumbled against his precious boat's side, he might even have managed it.

Well, anyone who'd spent so much time on water must surely be able to swim – and if not, I doubted I'd lose sleep over it. I sucked down a deep breath and leapt after.

I went straight under, kicked hard, and had just time to register how far beyond cold the water was as I broke the surface. Then Saltlick tumbled after me, and it was as though the rock ceiling had abruptly caved in. The cascade of water he flung up caught me like a twig in a flood, lifted me and hurled me helpless towards the pier.

The fact that it was where I'd been heading for was small comfort – for there was a world of difference between swimming and being carried like a rag doll. When I reached the pier, it was with a crunching impact, and a great backlash of seawater that tumbled over me and sucked me down. I wondered briefly where Saltlick was, whether it was too much to hope that he'd save my life again. Then I was crashing against a strut, rough timber rasping my arms and face, and for all that it hurt I hung on and thrust an arm up and managed to clutch something that *wasn't* underwater. From there, it was only hugely difficult to get the other hand up and haul myself free of the dragging ocean. I vomited brine over the dark wood and rolled, spluttering, onto my back.

At least I'd been right about one thing. For there, staring down at me, was Malekrin, bedraggled but undeniably alive. "You might want to move," he said.

I didn't want to move. Yet there was a definite urgency to his words, and since he'd never sounded very excited by anything before, I couldn't but think that was a bad sign. I crawled to my knees and from there to my feet, choked up a last lungful of brine and turned to follow his gaze.

I had time enough to take in the basics of the scene, time enough to consider following Malekrin's advice. Time to consider, but no time to act – for by then, the burning ship was hammering its way into the tip of the pier.

Every plank quivered, every post shook, as though the wood had come to sudden, violent life. Flames erupted, washed outward beneath a fog of sparks, and the ship became to crumple, even as the pier itself moaned and broke apart. I took five rolling steps, just missing Malekrin, barely keeping to my feet, before the heat fell like an iron upon my back.

Ahead I saw Saltlick hauling his great bulk out of the water, inflicting yet more damage on the fractured wharf. I managed to stop in front of him and clutched for his arm; alone of everything, he seemed immune to the chaos, stable as a monolith amidst that world of churning motion. He was staring back towards the ruined ship and the blaze consuming it, and as much as I'd have preferred not to, I did the same.

The crew were just starting to drag themselves onto the pier, a task made alternately easier and harder by the fact that its last third was smashed into pieces. The boat was finally losing its battle to stay afloat; flames were giving way to great billows and coils of smoke. As I watched, the first survivor began to lurch towards us, his shape made weird by the filthy, thickened air.

It was one of Mounteban's buccaneers, and he looked barely perturbed by his ordeal, as though this weren't the first time he'd been aboard a burning ship and probably wouldn't be the last. The next to emerge was a palace guardsman – or so I assumed from his soot-stained uniform, for I didn't recognise him.

The third, however, I knew quite well. "Estrada! You're alive?"

It wasn't the most intelligent question I'd ever asked. Fortunately, rather than waste time in answering, Estrada merely cried out, "Hurry, Damasco," and pointed towards the cavern mouth.

In everything that had happened, I'd almost forgotten the cause of all this pandemonium – almost let the Shoanish fleet slip from my mind. The vessel that stood out stark against the last dregs of sunlight, peeling away from its brethren to drift towards us, was a harsh enough reminder. Was Kalyxis coming to finish us off? Or had her attack really been meant as a lunatic attempt to rescue Malekrin?

Whatever the case, I had no desire to renew my acquaintance with the woman, and certainly not on that half-demolished, smouldering pier. As Estrada rushed past, I fell in beside her, still teetering a little on the disintegrating boards. Behind us, Saltlick looked as if he'd have liked to pick Estrada up and carry her with him, like some precious object already come far too close to breaking. Instead, he also matched his pace to hers, sending the fragile planks into further convulsions.

A narrow crescent of gravel clung to the tunnel mouth. There, we regrouped. I was incapable of counting by that point, but it seemed Ondeges had managed to save not only himself but most of those in his charge as well – a truly remarkable feat. I could see Navare off to one side amidst a group of his guardsmen, and the buccaneers keeping close but apart. Whether everyone was there, though, I had no way to judge; for every face and every garment was black with soot, as though they were thieves about to set out on some night-time mission.

Ondeges was staring across the dark subterranean waters, watching the Shoanish ship draw nearer. He gave it a few moments, let everyone catch at least a little of their breath, and then said, "We'll hold them here."

If the words were intended for his men, who were already drawing their weapons, it was Estrada that Ondeges was looking at. Even as she began to protest, he stepped closer and said, "The boy's the important thing now. Once we've bought you some time, we'll try and rejoin you." Then, moving even closer, lowering his voice even further – *"but if we don't... remember our arrangement."*

So Ondeges knew about Malekrin. The boy in question was trailing behind us, and nothing in his face told me he'd heard those last, whispered words. If he had, though, he must surely be wondering – just as I was – what deal had been struck on his behalf. Were Ondeges and Estrada planning to trade his life to Panchessa for the safety of Altapasaeda? If so, I could hardly blame them, yet suddenly I felt a faint stab of guilt at the thought. I'd no reason to like Malekrin, no reason to help him, no reason even to care if he lived or died. But the pang was there, and rationalising didn't make it go away.

It was something I'd have to watch. Hadn't my irregular, irrational conscience got me into enough trouble already? Just then, however, it was hardly my most immediate concern –

for Estrada and Navare were already herding their people into the black mouth of the passage. I was surprised to see that this time Estrada had made Saltlick go first; didn't she realise he was bound to slow us down, now more than ever thanks to his injured leg? Then again, perhaps that was exactly why she'd done it, for so long as he was leading there was no chance of him being left behind.

As for me, I found myself towards the very rear, with Malekrin taking final place. With most of our own equipment lost in the wreck, it was fortunate Ondeges had thought to stow a couple of lanterns in the tunnel mouth for his own return journey. That meant one for each group and little enough light, but near darkness was a great deal better than total darkness. I could just make out the lambent glimmer ahead, masked by a snaking trail of bodies.

As I began to follow, I spared one last glance behind me, for Ondeges and his men. They were forming up around the mouth of the passage, ready to fall back into its confines the moment the need arose. Beyond them, out in the harbour, the Shoanish ship – still nothing but a sinister silhouette cast by the dying glow of the fire – was close now, manoeuvring through the debris-thick waters.

I looked away. Ondeges could take care of himself, which was more than I could claim if the Shoanish should come out on top of the impending fight. As I turned back, however, I caught Malekrin's eye, and I couldn't help wondering if he was having similar thoughts. It was hard to say who he had more to worry about just then, Ondeges or his own mad grandmother. Yet, hurrying with measured strides, he was all surface fearlessness; in fact, something in his posture reminded me distantly of his father, of Moaradrid's ferocious confidence. In Malekrin, though, it was undermined by a constant hint of awkwardness, as though it were a pretence he could never quite perfect.

Well, the boy could look after himself too; he was enough his father's son for that. I wasn't about to waste my time worrying about him, not when he might be the only one to survive should his barbarian friends make their way past Ondeges.

Our light was no more than a trembling glow in the deep dark of the passage; it gave the man ahead the barest definition. Without my noticing, I'd already fallen some distance behind. I realised I'd have to concentrate on keeping pace – for our column was moving swiftly enough that I could easily find myself abandoned in the blackness.

I wondered about Saltlick. How was he managing to move so fast, bent double and dragging an injured leg? I could hardly imagine how he was bearing up, but at least the trying diverted me somewhat from my own exertions.

For all that, however, it wasn't long before real tiredness began to set in. I wasn't about to slow, of course; at first the sounds of battle echoing down the passage saw to that, and after they'd finally faded to nothing, the fear of who might be coming after us in their absence.

No, I'd hurry until I dropped if need be – because if Kalyxis had been aboard that approaching ship, she was going to have questions that I knew I'd struggle to answer. They would involve crowns and princes, and I didn't think they'd be asked gently.

I couldn't tell how many hours had passed or what distance we'd travelled, had long since ceased to notice anything but the ache that ran bone-deep through every limb, when I recognised the pound of feet approaching. Only then did I realise I'd been hearing it for a long while, but failing to tell it apart from our own hurried steps. Unbeknownst to me, whoever was approaching had already drawn close.

I nearly called out a warning. But if I'd heard those hurrying feet, so had everyone else, and I wasn't certain I had the breath to spare. Anyway, what difference would it make? We were going as fast as we could go, and it was clear from the pace of those nearing footfalls that we had no hope of outrunning them. All I could do was continue as quickly as I could bear, knowing it wasn't enough, glancing again and again past Malekrin, who stared imperturbably ahead – until the first of them broke from the shadows.

Then, I was so relieved to recognise Ondeges that I could have hugged him – at least until I saw his expression, and the gore spattered across his jacket.

"Where's Estrada?" he snapped.

My brief affection turned to annoyance. If my lungs hadn't been two sacks of fire, I might have pointed out that it was hardly my responsibility to keep track of her.

Fortunately, Estrada picked that moment to brush past me. "You made it," she said.

"We couldn't hold them," Ondeges replied grimly. "They're licking their wounds, but they'll be after us soon enough."

It was exactly what no one wanted to hear. Our pace had already been starting to lag, as the last strength drained from bodies that had been overexerted even before this subterranean marathon began.

With Ondeges and his men amongst us, however, we did somehow manage to pick up speed once more. Their tirelessness, even after the bloody battle they'd just endured, was something between inspiring and shaming. That they could carry on almost at a run while we, who hadn't just fought for our lives, were struggling to even walk, implied that somewhere we must have reserves yet untapped.

If that were the case, though, I hardly felt it, for while I'd somehow managed not to fall behind, all it had earned me was new heights of fatigue. I *did* begin to rouse a little when we reached the junction between palace and barracks, however; even if the nearer exit was closed by the detritus of an entire collapsed building, the fact that we'd reached so far meant an end was in sight. I gritted my teeth, marched on.

By the time we reached the portal that led into the palace basements, I had no more enthusiasm left to muster. I was too dead on my feet even to wonder how close Kalyxis' barbarians were behind us. I noted with the barest interest that the door had been hacked from its hinges; so Mounteban had laid his greasy paws upon the only copy of the key after all. With no furniture in the corridor beyond, that meant no way to bar the passage behind us – but even that only bothered me a little.

It was only as we hurried through the dank cellars beyond that something finally managed to penetrate the murk of my languor. By the time we were halfway to the ground floor, it was obvious that things was very wrong ahead. Perhaps that wasn't surprising; what could be expected of a palace without its prince, entrenched in a city about to be assaulted by its own king? Whatever I might have expected, however, I wouldn't have guessed it would be quite so *noisy*.

To my ears, which were admittedly working no better than the rest of me, it was only a great commotion, mingled and incomprehensible. The best I could manage was to follow the man ahead and do my best to keep up; the prospect of considering what we might be rushing into was beyond me. Even as we entered the palace itself and the noise became overwhelming, I couldn't bring myself to try and analyse it. I glanced at the faces of those around me, palace soldiers and city guardsmen and Mounteban's swarthy buccaneers, and I wondered if they understood something I was missing.

We were heading for the main gates. Whose idea was that? It struck me that there was more than one agenda at work now – that Estrada and Ondeges might have different ideas about what came next and that, once again, we were two separate groups with two very separate intentions.

Yet, as if we'd been forged together by our long spell underground, we seemed incapable of separating. Palace and city guardsmen rushed side by side through the pristine corridors, along halls and through archways and past bubbling fountains – and against all reason, we were all hurrying together towards the din that reverberated through every wall.

Then, finally, we were plunging through the palace's main doors, and before us was the courtyard, beyond that the main gatehouse. The sight that met my eyes was the last I'd have hoped to see, the worst I might reasonably have imagined – but at least it explained what all the noise was about.

There in the courtyard, men were fighting, men of a similar mix to our own little party: palace soldiers lined against city guardsmen and Mounteban's ruffians, barbarians and swords-for-hire.

We'd arrived in the middle of a war.

CHAPTER ELEVEN

Making our appearance amidst a raging battle had one benefit: no one was paying us much attention. So preoccupied were they with hacking, slashing and bludgeoning each other that even the arrival of thirty and more men, a woman, one giant and a long-suffering thief had hardly turned a head.

Less advantageous was the fact that whatever fragile accord had developed amongst our party was fast dissolving. Ondeges had already split off his men, and all had their weapons drawn, even if they hadn't put them to use as yet; the same went for Navare and his guardsmen, who were manoeuvring, swords out, for a place to make their stand amidst the chaos. Lastly, the buccaneers were retreating in a ragtag pack around the inner wall, having evidently decided that this was a test too far of their tenuous loyalties.

That left only Estrada, Saltlick and I upon the steps leading from the palace entrance. Saltlick was deathly pale and still hunched over, as though his time underground had warped his spine forever. Staring at the fighting, his eyes held the panicked glint of someone who'd woken from nightmares into the most furious of storms.

Estrada, too, was gazing around wild-eyed – though her focus was solely upon Ondeges, Navare and their respective factions. "No... damn it! The truce–"

"What truce?" I yelled at her. "You can't believe Ondeges meant that!"

"Of course he meant it. Do you really think that..." The sentence broke off, as Estrada glanced about her. "Where *is* he?"

I was rapidly losing my grip on the conversation, not to mention any ability to care when nearby people were enthusiastically trying to kill each other. "Where's *who*, damn it?"

"Malekrin," she said. "Where's Malekrin?"

At that name, something cold sunk inside me, like a plumb line dropped into my inmost depths. Because Estrada was right, Malekrin was nowhere to be seen – and as my own eyes sought frantically over the space between palace steps and gatehouse, over the knots of fighting men, I realised I couldn't even say when I'd last seen him.

The Bastard Prince: the single concrete advantage we'd gained from our disastrous expedition, our bargaining chip with the King and for that matter with the Shoanish, if and when they arrived; in short, our one and only scant hope. I'd let him slip through my fingers and, as if that weren't bad enough, he'd taken the crown of Altapasaeda with him.

All told, this was one calamity I didn't want laid at my feet. "What do you mean?" I shouted, with all the innocence I could muster, "weren't *you* watching him?"

I'd expected a scathing reply. When it didn't come, I looked where Estrada was looking – and was startled to see Alvantes, sword in hand, staring back from the gatehouse. So he'd managed to escape the palace all those days ago, and now here he was again, once more deep in the thick of battle. Even as I saw him, he pointed in our direction and bellowed, "Protect Marina Estrada! Protect our men!"

Then he was moving – and when the mood took him, no one moved like Alvantes did. Though his clothes were torn and bloody, the chainmail beneath rent by two long gashes, he pushed forward with all the ferocity of a wild boar suddenly cut loose. When a half dozen paces placed a palace soldier in his path, Alvantes swatted the man's blade aside with his own and barged forward, sending his opponent tumbling. A second soldier he side-stepped past, before slamming an elbow like a hammer blow into his neck. Already Alvantes was halfway to us, and a channel was opening ahead of him that his men strove to fill, before their enemies could appreciate what was happening.

Meanwhile, Navare and his guardsmen had folded into a tight semicircle in front of us. "Ready?" he asked Estrada. She drew her own sword, gave a terse nod – and we were off.

There had to be some order to the fighting, some strategy or logic, but for the life of me I couldn't see it. To watch, it was hard to believe there were even sides, that it wasn't every man for himself. Yet with Alvantes making his push to rescue us and Navare forcing his own way through the turmoil, it was clear even to me that, whatever the nature of the battle had been, it was now changing abruptly.

Over on the left flank, I glimpsed another familiar face, though one I could happily have never seen again: Ludovoco was fencing simultaneously with two men in unfamiliar uniforms, who I took to be part of Mounteban's faction. It was clear he was barely testing himself – and even as he registered Alvantes's gambit, he dispatched one with such casual ease that the other almost tripped over his own feet in surprise. The man was so busy trying to retreat that he hardly even saw Ludovoco's sword go into his belly; he only flinched and crumpled round it, until Ludovoco tipped his arm up and let him slide to the cobbles.

Then Ludovoco raised the bloodied blade to point and said – not loudly, but distinct enough that I heard it even at such a distance – "Kill them!"

It was more than a command; it was an imperative. If I hadn't been so busy hurrying, hustled along by the guardsmen around me, I'd have struggled not to try and follow it myself. Our only slender advantage was that so few of his men were in any position to listen, and fewer in a position to respond.

But that was enough – thanks to Alvantes. Before we were even a third of the way across the courtyard he'd bridged the gap between our two groups, and the passage he'd left in his wake, cobbled with a dozen broken, bleeding men, was rapidly shored up by his troop. Navare's guardsmen fell in to join them – and suddenly there was an avenue through the turmoil opened before us.

Even as I broke into a run, Ludovoco's forces were starting to coordinate, trying to carve their way to us. Again, they'd have stood a better chance if it weren't for Alvantes, now fighting a frantic rearguard alongside Navare. In the instant I spared to glance his way, he was somehow fending off two palace soldiers at once, each a head taller than him and clearly baffled at how their blows failed to land upon a one-handed man.

Then we were into the gatehouse and through, and the guardsmen were collapsing back around us, those that could still move at all, as they threw whatever stamina they had left into covering our escape. Reaching the grand plaza that ringed the palace, I blinked against the bright morning sun and at the statued fronts of the temples. Still reeling from the shock of finding myself in the midst of battle for no clear reason, my head was awhirl.

I turned to see Alvantes and Navare now in the midst of organising a defence of the gatehouse, their two squads already merged back into a single force, as though none of the last week's events had ever occurred. Those at the forefront sallied to recover the wounded, to help or haul them back to relative safety. They were met with scant resistance, for beyond our lines Ondeges and Ludovoco's forces were doing the same, their two factions flowing together to secure the courtyard.

Seeing them apart, lined opposite each other for the first time, I could tell that the two sides were more or less evenly matched. Whatever we'd stumbled into, then, it was a very different conflict to the one I'd left all those days ago – and I could only assume that this time it was Alvantes who'd struck the first blow. But having once escaped the palace, why would he have returned? If he'd been set on rousting Ludovoco, why wait until now? There was more to this than I could see, more than this small, desperate tussle.

With the injured out from underfoot, it was apparent that the brief armistice was drawing to a close. Given how temperamentally unsuited I was to violence, I felt it was time I started seeking an alternative. Though it was all I could do to stand upright, I knew I'd find strength to run if I had to. But where to? Without knowing the context of this brawl, it was possible I'd be charging into even greater danger.

I'd have to decide soon, or else the decision would be out of my hands. Ludovoco had finished marshalling his troops; Alvantes and his men stood ready to meet them. Now that the combat had taken on more formal outlines, Ludovoco looked coldly self-assured, as though the rest were a mere formality. Given the efficiency with which his soldiers had taken their formation, compared with the ragtag performance of Alvantes's guardsmen, I couldn't help thinking that he had every right to his confidence.

But I was wrong, and so was Ludovoco, and he began to realise it at exactly as I did.

Then again, how was he supposed to have known that – even as he'd fenced with such cruel efficiency, as he'd calmly organised his forces for the next round of violence – a mob of furious barbarians had been working their way through the palace? Ludovoco registered the approach of running feet with only the slightest hint of puzzlement; but as they drew nearer, his icy calm began to slip.

If I'd found something satisfying in watching the vicious bastard's confidence waver, however, it was nothing to the look on his face when fifty scimitar-waving Shoanish poured from the palace entrance, with Kalyxis standing tall in their midst. I wished I could burn that image into my memory and keep it with me forever. It was the expression of a man whose plans had just been demolished in a fashion he couldn't even begin to make sense of, and it was beautiful.

Sadly, I didn't have long to enjoy it. Because whatever Kalyxis had been expecting, it wasn't this either, not a company of armed and already bloodied soldiers formed in perfect battle order. I didn't hear what she called to her followers, but I was willing to guess the word *ambush* figured in there somewhere. When Ludovoco's thin lips moved just slightly, I'd no doubt he was expressing a similar thought.

Either way, they were on each other quickly enough.

"You really did it?" cried Alvantes. "You brought help?"

"They're not here to *save* us, Lunto," called back Estrada.

Alvantes gave that news a moment's consideration. Then, "Navare," he shouted, "stay here with half the men and do whatever you can. Ludovoco mustn't leave, do you hear me? He's the target. If you have to take a side, make it the Shoanish."

Though Navare must have been every bit as shattered as I was, I'd have never guessed it as he began to organise the guardsmen closest to him. The rest fell into step behind Alvantes and Estrada, who were already pacing across the square. I tried a quick mental reckoning as to whether following was more or less risky than running as fast my legs would carry me in the other direction; but I had no more evidence than before, and at least with Alvantes there would be armed men between me and any threats. I hurried to catch up, and Saltlick – who had been hovering close, still looking frail and stunned – limped along after me.

A number of horses were tied before one of the larger temples, a blasphemy Alvantes had presumably chosen to overlook – though it was hard to imagine whichever god was represented by the fish-headed statue glaring down at us agreeing, given the still-steaming offerings a couple of the beasts had deposited on his doorstep.

We mounted hurriedly, and I barely had time to wonder what Alvantes had in mind before we were off. He was leading us north, I noted; the main road we joined would eventually end at the northwestern gate, the one recently pulverised by the giants in our bid to rescue the city from Mounteban.

Speaking of giants: "Slow down!" I bawled at Alvantes. "Don't you see he can't keep up?"

I was referring, of course, to Saltlick, who was trying his best to keep pace with the horses despite his recent injuries and failing hopelessly. Seeing how far he'd already fallen behind us, Alvantes threw a questioning glance at Estrada, and then said, "All right, damn it... slower, everyone."

He didn't sound at all happy about it, and it was perhaps as much to divert his thoughts as from genuine curiosity that Estrada chose that moment to ask, "What's been happening, Lunto? Why were you fighting?"

Alvantes's face somehow became a shade grimmer. "The King's at the gates. Or through them by now, who knows? Mounteban's covering that end, damn him."

"But the palace...?"

"We had to keep Ludovoco where he is. He knows too much about what's been going on inside the city; I couldn't let him take that knowledge to Panchessa."

So that was it. Altapasaeda was defending itself on two fronts – and that wasn't even to mention Kalyxis and her Shoanish, or for that matter, Mounteban's inevitable next betrayal. Perhaps I'd made the wrong call in trailing after Alvantes. Then again, it was hard to imagine where I'd possibly be safe with so many enemies around, every one of them after my blood for their own reasons.

"And now you're hoping Kalyxis and Ludovoco will keep each other occupied?" Estrada asked.

"Exactly," agreed Alvantes. "Anyway, I can't trust Mounteban to hold the walls. What does containing Ludovoco matter if the whole city's overrun?" He drew up abruptly at a junction, where an easterly road cut towards the Market District and eventually the docks. "Before that, though, we have to get you to safety."

"What?" Estrada's tone hardened. "Don't be absurd, Lunto. If we can't hold off Panchessa, here and now, there'll be no safety anywhere."

It was a sentiment uncomfortably close to my own thoughts. However, I recognised that look in Alvantes's eye, that certainty beyond doubt that he was right.

Then again, I'd seen the stubborn set of Estrada's jaw often enough as well. "What hiding place is going to last once the King's inside the walls?" she added, a shade more gently.

"There are still boats in the harbour..." Alvantes began.

"No. Lunto, *no*. Even if they haven't blockaded the river, which they most probably have, I'm not leaving. Now, stop wasting time that peoples' lives depend on."

"She's right," I told Alvantes, "and you know it. For once, why don't you save yourself the trouble of losing an argument?"

Though he glowered – at me, of course, rather than Estrada – Alvantes didn't try to disagree again. Instead, he tapped his heels against his horse's flank, and we were off once more.

I gritted my teeth. I had a fair idea of what we were riding towards; the noise was a sure portent. It had been audible since we'd left the palace, and building ever since – though proximity only made it harder to pick individual sounds from the roar of shouts and thrash of weapons. It was the cacophony of violence on a grand scale, and it was becoming all too familiar.

If it was making me jumpy, it was terrifying the horses. Guard animals they might be, but they'd never had to experience

PRINCE THIEF

a war, and panic was spreading rapidly through their ranks. Approaching a bend, Alvantes signalled us to halt and called, "We'll dismount here."

We hurried to alight and I cautiously tethered my steed, for the expression in his large and too-white eyes told me he'd much rather be galloping in the other direction. "You and me both," I muttered, as I tied off a last knot.

By the time I had him secured to my satisfaction, the others were already hurrying on. I dashed to catch up. As we careened around the bend, the northwestern gate came into view – and for all that I thought I knew what to expect, my jaw still fell open.

The gates were wide open, their inner edges broken and splintered. Perhaps that was small wonder, for there was only so much that could be done to repair a portal so recently smashed, especially in a city that was coming apart at the seams. And just as at the palace, the gatehouse had become a focal point for the fighting, its narrow confines going some way to levelling the odds between the city's defenders and the purple-clad soldiers pressing from outside.

All of that was shocking, without doubt. I'd never truly believed Altapasaeda could be vulnerable to any army; compared with the rest of the Castoval, it had always seemed indomitable. Yet, strange as it was to see the city under attack, it wasn't unexpected. No, what defied my belief wasn't the fighting already inside the walls – it was just who was fighting.

Giants. There were giants massed alongside the defenders. And in case I tried to convince myself it was a trick, a scam like the one I'd once conceived myself, they were wearing armour made ready to their scale and bearing weapons, great spiked hammers each as tall as a small tree, and they were using those weapons, sweeping bloody swathes through the men crowding into the breach.

I realised too late what was about to happen, what was *bound* to happen, and I was already asking myself what I could possibly do to stop Saltlick when he thundered past me. He was roaring a word in giantish, over and over and over – and though I couldn't understand, though it was reduced to sheer noise by rage and grief and buried in the crash of his feet, I was sure I knew exactly what he was saying.

No! No! No!

Then Saltlick was amidst the fighting, men diving and stumbling to get out of his way, and he was forcing himself into the very heart of the violence, like a surgeon's knife plunged into a canker. His brethren looked astonished to see him, and cowed. He snatched a hammer from one and hurled it as if it were a twig; it struck the wall and lodged there, its head a hand deep in the spider-webbed stone. Another followed after, scattering cobbles, a dozen men tumbling to avoid its impact.

It was clear now that most of those pressed in the gatehouse were Pasaedans, and that the giants had been the only thing keeping them out of the city. With our attackers' initial alarm beginning to pass, they seemed more unsure than afraid. It must be dawning on them that Saltlick, still busy plucking and discarding hammers, wasn't simply another foe. In fact, wasn't he aiding rather than hindering their assault? He'd disarmed most of the other giants by then, meeting no resistance – for they stood like sleepwalkers as he tore the weapons from their hands. Not only that but, unlike those others, Saltlick wore no armour. And while he might be doing the Pasaedans a favour, he still stood between them and their goal...

The first blow was hesitant, barely a prick. A soldier poked his sword at Saltlick's calf, as if he expected the weapon to burst into flames the moment it made contact. When it didn't, he looked more amazed than he had already. But that didn't stop him from trying again, less delicately this time – and that was all the encouragement it took for those nearby to mimic his example.

Saltlick staggered. He glanced around him, as if dazed. The other giants were all unarmed now, but they weren't backing off, were making no effort to disengage from the fighting – and I realised that nothing else would make Saltlick retreat.

I wanted to scream at them, but it was as though my tongue had swollen and clogged my throat. Anyway, by then it was already too late.

Because in that moment, Saltlick went down.

CHAPTER TWELVE

I watched it happen. I didn't believe it.

Not one man there reached past Saltlick's waist. They were mere men and he was a giant, and even as their swords fell against his flesh, it was impossible to imagine they could hurt him – really *hurt* him. And maybe if he hadn't been wounded, half crippled by his spell underground and far past the point of exhaustion, they never could have. But Saltlick was all of those things – and as much as I refused to believe, still, I watched him fall.

Once he was on his knees, that made things easier for his attackers – though, more concerned with avoiding being crushed by his bulk, they were slow to appreciate the fact at first. It was only a brief reprieve, however; just as long as it took them to realise that a defenceless giant on all fours was even less of a threat than one standing.

By then, the Pasaedans could have simply gone around Saltlick, could have charged past all the giants had they wished to. It would have been the sensible, the tactical thing to do, and surely the fact that they didn't had much to do with the brutal losses they'd just endured. In a mass, they closed upon Saltlick.

There was only one thing I could think to do. I grabbed Alvantes by a bunch of his shirt, shook him hard as I could, and – though I couldn't quite believe what I was doing, though a part of me was already curling up in terror – I screamed in his face, "Damn you, get him out of there, you bastard! Do it now! You won't let him die, you son of a bitch..."

That was as far as I got before Alvantes wrenched free and pushed me to the ground, none too gently. I fully expected his sword to follow – and in that moment, I didn't care. Because behind me they were killing Saltlick, and I couldn't let that happen.

I was on my feet before Alvantes knew it and went to grab him again, which was a mistake. All it earned me was a fist slammed hard into my jaw. It felt like he'd struck me with a sledgehammer, and I was sure I'd fall and never get up; but something inside me pushed back and, driven by I knew not what, I only teetered and lurched once more towards him. "You save him," I hissed, "or so help me, you'll have to kill me here and now."

"I *can't*, Damasco." I was brought up short by the grief in his voice. "Look around you. Will you just look?"

I didn't want to look. I knew too well what was happening. Worse, I could hear it. Yet to not look was to give up, and I couldn't do that either. Starting to turn, I saw Estrada first, staring past my shoulder. Tears were streaming down her face. "Saltlick," she was saying, her voice on the edge of breaking. "Saltlick, Saltlick..."

Where Saltlick had been, there were now only Pasaedan soldiers. The only clue to where he'd fallen was that their blows were all landing in one place. The Pasaedans were everywhere now, well past the border of the gatehouse. All that kept them from overrunning us was the effort of ending Saltlick's life.

I understood what Alvantes had said – and as I looked back, I understood too the helplessness in his eyes.

Perhaps he misread my own expression though, saw condemnation where there was only despair. "What can I do, Damasco?" he shouted. "We can't save him!"

I understood. But I couldn't accept it. Saltlick was the only true friend I'd ever had, the only one who'd ever shown me real decency and asked for no recompense. I had to do something, and there was nothing at all I could do. My knees were weak, so I sank onto them.

Then over the tumult, came a voice – a voice I knew and hated.

"Maybe you can't," cried Castilio Mounteban. "But I'm damned if I won't."

Had I not been so absorbed with Saltlick, I'd have seen him coming; for Mounteban was close enough by then to have heard Alvantes, close enough that I'd have made out his horse's thundering approach upon the east-west road if I'd only thought to listen. And confident as he sounded, it wasn't his words that gave me hope; it was the crowd of armed men he was leading.

It took a single moment for that hope to sour. I couldn't count their numbers, but they were a ragged enough bunch. Though a few were mounted, most were on foot, and it was obvious they'd been running hard. They all wore the Altapasaedan uniform Mounteban had thrown together, leather armour under cloaks the colour of old blood – but the gore that marred their clothing was fresh enough. Wherever they'd come from, they'd already seen more than their share of fighting.

At their head, Mounteban rode upon a hulking black charger that looked every bit as foul-natured as its rider. His face was slick with sweat; the tunic he wore beneath a shirt of chain mail was stained dark at the underarms. Still, there was ferocity in his expression, a rawness of passion I'd never have expected, as though the presence of enemies within the city walls were an indignity aimed just at him. As he drew his scimitar, as he pointed it in wordless order at the Pasaedan troops, he almost looked heroic.

The impression lasted only as long as it took him to crash into the hurriedly reforming cluster of men in the gateway – for there was nothing noble in the fury with which he flung his sword about. I couldn't say what he meant to achieve, if he was trying to rescue Saltlick or to single-handedly push the Pasaedans back, or whether he had any plan at all. As he flailed at any head within reach, it was easy to believe that he just wanted to inflict as much injury as possible.

Then again, maybe Mounteban's charge stemmed from more than mere bloodlust. His frantic assault had made time enough for his motley pack to catch up, for them to join with the existing defenders and hurl themselves into the fray. For all their matching uniforms and surface unity, they attacked with no hint of order or battle plan; no two men standing shoulder to shoulder fought the same way. Suddenly, the combat looked less like two armies clashing, more like a street fight grown wildly out of control.

Just then, however, perhaps chaos was what was needed. The Pasaedans had come expecting a war, had faced monsters instead, and now these men who looked like soldiers but battled like the dirtiest bar brawlers. And it did nothing for our enemies' discipline when, with a ferocious roar, Alvantes chose to lead his small posse of guardsmen into their exposed flank.

That was the tipping point. Perhaps they had the weight of numbers, but with attacks from two sides and no room to manoeuvre, the Pasaedans had no option left except retreat. Even that they couldn't do in any orderly fashion, for every slight gap in their ranks was an opening for one of our side to jab his blade through. By the time they were halfway through the gatehouse, the Pasaedans were practically in disarray.

But I couldn't have cared less about that, or even the battle for the city. All that mattered was that the retreat had freed

Saltlick from the Pasaedan lines, like a boulder revealed by a receding tide. I couldn't tell if he was moving, if he was alive. All I could see was that the cobbles were drenched with blood enough to drown a man in, and his pale hide was a web of dripping crimson gashes. I wanted to run and help him, but what could I do? Even if I'd known the first thing about doctoring, I doubted there were bandages enough in the entire city to cover those wounds.

Fortunately for Saltlick, Estrada was less quick to admit defeat. She was already dashing across the intervening space and, even as I wondered what she meant to do, began to beat upon the leg of the nearest giant. She didn't lay off until he tilted his head to look down at her; then she pointed.

What Estrada had indicated was a horseless cart, drawn up in the lee of the walls. Perhaps it had been intended to shore up the gates, or left by some panicking merchant. Either way, the giant gave no indication that he'd understood. When Estrada took a step towards the stranded vehicle, however, he followed. Finally, when they were halfway to it, he blurted a couple of blunt syllables in giantish, and a second moved to join them.

Though Estrada had given up trying to communicate in gestures, it seemed the giants had grasped the fundamentals of her plan by then. Rather than try to drag the cart, they decided the easiest course was simply to hoist it upon their shoulders; they were moving with urgency now, as if they'd woken to the horrors of recent minutes at last. The two bore the cart as though it weighed nothing at all, dropped it with a crash that nearly shattered its every wheel upon the red-slicked cobbles.

"Careful!" Estrada hurried to bar their way, and when they looked confused, tried to indicate through gentle sweeping motions that Saltlick couldn't just be hoisted like a sack of potatoes.

Alvantes and Mounteban, meanwhile, had managed to not only drive out the Pasaedans but to slam the damaged gates

upon their backs. While Mounteban coordinated the effort
there, Alvantes turned to haranguing the remaining giants:
"Damn you," he bellowed, "do something useful! Barricade
those gates!"

They surely didn't understand his words, but the
accompanying gesticulations were easy enough to follow.
There were supplies close at hand, heaps of sturdy wood piled
not far from the gatehouse, no doubt intended for just such
a purpose. The giants began to prop beams in place, to pile
timber haphazardly against the weakened sections. If it was
clear that they didn't quite grasp the sense of what they did,
still they managed in mere minutes what would have taken
men the rest of the day.

By the time they'd finished a rudimentary barricade, the
other two giants had Saltlick into the back of the cart. A slug
trail of crimson led from where he'd fallen, and the cart's inside
was slicked with blood. I still couldn't tell if he was moving.

Finally, I managed to shift my legs. Maybe there was nothing
I could do, but I could only bear being useless for so long. Close
up, Saltlick looked even worse, like a slab of well-worked meat
on a butcher's stall. As I watched, though, one eyelid – the one
not caked shut with gore – fluttered ever so slightly.

"He's alive," confirmed Estrada. "But barely. Easie, I don't
know if even Saltlick can–"

I didn't want to hear the end of that sentence. "He has to,"
I said.

"If we can stop the bleeding–"

"We've a hospital set up in the Market District," put in
Alvantes, marching towards us. "You two," he summoned
the giants waiting patiently nearby, and pointed back the
way we'd come. "Carry him that way." Then, waving over a
guardsman I recognised as Gueverro, he added, "Sub-Captain,
accompany them. Find a good surgeon and make certain they
do whatever's needed."

But all of that I saw and heard as though through a haze. For the instant Alvantes had begun to speak, memories cold and clear as ice water had spilled into my mind – recollections of a conversation we'd had not so very long ago. With hardly a thought and for the second time that day, I grabbed Alvantes by the throat. "This was your doing, wasn't it?" I screamed. "You vicious bastard! You've been planning for weeks to drag the giants into your stupid wars. Are you happy now?"

I realised what would feel even better than shaking Alvantes – and almost before I knew it, my fist was crunching into his nose. It mightn't have been much of a punch, but it was more satisfying than anything I'd ever done – and the second was better. There was a roaring in my ears and my sight was a tunnel edged with red; but I could hear the smack of my knuckles against Alvantes's face well enough, I could see each blow landing, and it was easy as anything to just keep going.

I noted with distant satisfaction when scarlet spattered from his nostrils. Alone, however, that probably wouldn't have been enough to stop me – but at that point someone caught and gripped my wrist, and as I span around I was puzzled to see Mounteban, watching me from his one good eye.

Mounteban let go of my arm. "If you must know," he said, "it had nothing to do with Alvantes. I talked the giants into helping. And if it saved Altapasaeda, I'd do the same again. So if you want to hit someone, Damasco, you're welcome to try and hit me."

I was furious. I wasn't suicidal. If I threw a punch at Castilio Mounteban, it would be the last thing I ever threw at anyone.

Still, that didn't mean I had to let it go. I fixed him with my best stare, poured every drop of hatred I felt into it, and said, "I might not have lived a blameless life, Mounteban, but I'm no killer. If Saltlick dies, that's something I'll be looking to change."

Mounteban held my gaze – and I realised then how hopeless it was to try and intimidate him. You didn't lead the life Castilio

Mounteban had lived and let yourself be afraid, of anyone or anything. "One of these days," he said, "we'll have to have a talk about what happened to my man Synza."

Synza... the lunatic assassin Mounteban had sent after me during our recent conflict, and a subject I'd hoped might have slipped his mind. I really *hadn't* killed Synza, a misjudged step from a high cliff had taken care of that, but nor had I been entirely blameless in his death.

Then it occurred to me that Mounteban had played right into my hands. "All you need to know," I said, "is that it was messy, and that it could easily happen again."

However, I had to abandon our glaring contest then, for, with a grunt more of irritation than pain, Alvantes had climbed to his feet – and I could hardly keep looking at Mounteban when I was about to have my face pounded into blood porridge.

When Alvantes took a step towards me, Estrada put a restraining hand on his shoulder. "Don't worry," he said, brushing her fingers off with his own and then dabbing a smear of crimson from his nostrils. "I'm not going to hurt him. Anyway, he was right; I *did* want to make the giants fight for us." His eyes brushed across Mounteban. "And I see now that it's something only a monster would have done."

With my anger and excitement rapidly abating, I felt none too good about attacking Alvantes. We might be far from friends, but it was also true that a good part of our mutual animosity had dissolved in recent days – and now here I was, pummelling his face for no reason, after he'd just fought not one but two desperate battles. "Alvantes..." I began.

He looked at me for the first time. "Still," he said, "you might want to keep out of my way for a day or two, Damasco."

I nodded weakly. "I'm going to see if there's anything I can do for Saltlick," I mumbled, to no one in particular.

"I'll come with you," said Estrada. "Unless you need me here, Lunto?"

Alvantes looked once more to Mounteban, and this time there was nothing in his eyes; he spoke with the frank civility of one commander communing with another. "What's the situation, Mounteban? Is Altapasaeda falling?"

"I think not," replied Mounteban, in the same tone. "Not today. They played us well... made it look as though they were throwing their weight at the northeastern gate and then hit this one twice as hard. But we routed them on the other side of the city, and thanks to the giants, here too." He paused, looked thoughtful. "There are plenty in the city who didn't quite believe their noble king would really attack his own city. Now that he has, I suspect we'll have a few new recruits on our hands."

"Panchessa's tested our strength," Alvantes agreed. "I think he'll wait before trying anything else. Do whatever you need to do, Marina, and we'll reconvene this evening to discuss what happens next."

What happens next. Alvantes said it so calmly. Only listening to his conversation with Mounteban had it really sunk in that outside those walls, Panchessa and an army of Pasaedan soldiers had made their camp; that unless these two men found a way to keep them out, something uniquely terrible in Castovalian history was about to happen.

I shuddered. Every muscle in my body itched to be out of there, free of Altapasaeda once and for all. But damn him, there was no way I could go anywhere until I knew what was to become of Saltlick. Why had he put me in such a position? Why thrust himself into harm's way and then not even have the basic sense to defend himself? What creature could be so wilfully stupid?

A sob rose in my throat, and I had to cough hard to choke it down. I couldn't talk myself out of this one with anger. It had taken me long enough to distinguish Saltlick's unbending decency from a lack of sense, but now that I had, there was no going back. Nor was it so easy to return to being the self-serving thief who'd willingly put his own interests before those of others, whatever the cost.

No, that person had been dying slowly since the moment I'd met Saltlick, dissolving day on day. And maybe that was the one thing I had a real right to be angry with him for, but I couldn't find that in myself either. Perhaps there was nothing to keep me in Altapasaeda, no good I could do; yet there was no way I could leave either, not until I knew whether Saltlick would live.

"Hurry up if you're coming, will you?" I told Estrada, speaking as sharply as I could to hide how my voice was shaking.

I set a fast pace, for the cart and its giant attendants were long gone, I didn't know where they were headed and I could hardly ask Alvantes, leaving my only option to catch them before they left the main road. Then I remembered that our mounts were tied just around the first bend; on horseback, I'd be able to close the distance in no time. Rounding the turn, I saw the horses just as we'd left them, though a touch calmer now that the tumult had passed. There was no sign of the cart, however – and even if there had been, no possibility I'd be riding after it.

After everything I'd seen that day, after everything that had happened, I should have been past the point where anything could surprise me. Yet it still came as a shock to see Kalyxis and her barbarians stalking towards us, claiming the centre of the street as if they owned it.

"That's her?" Estrada asked. "That's..."

"Kalyxis," I said.

"What do you think she's...?"

"Keep quiet and I'm sure we'll find out soon enough."

It took me a moment to notice that Navare was with them, hurrying just behind Kalyxis herself. As they drew close, he picked up his pace so as to meet us first. "She called for a truce," he explained quickly, "and said she wants to parley with our leaders. Ludovoco had crawled back into the palace by then; I could hardly say no."

Then Kalyxis had caught up, leaving Navare no choice but to sidestep quickly out of her way. I was astonished by how undaunted she seemed to be there, in the heart of what could only be considered enemy territory. Indeed, her bearing was just as when I'd first met her; haughty and aloof, as though her status was something that travelled miasma-like about her.

Kalyxis's eyes roved over me, with first recognition and then distaste. "Dinascus, wasn't it?" she asked.

"Damasco," I corrected – and never had I found it so difficult to pronounce that beloved name.

"Ah. Yes. *Damasco*." Kalyxis nodded thoughtfully, as though this information were the last piece in a conundrum she'd been pondering. "Damasco," she said, "you have as long as it takes me to count to five to tell me where my grandson is, or else my men will flay you to death right here in the street."

CHAPTER THIRTEEN

"One," Kalyxis began.

A thousand thoughts coursed through my head, and nine in every ten involved running... run left, run right, hurl myself through the nearest open window, dash at Kalyxis screaming and hope she was too surprised to have her men slice me to ribbons.

"Two."

No, fleeing would only get me cut down in the street like a mad dog. So could I bluff? Should I plead innocence? Perhaps blame someone else? Hadn't I once pretended to be my own brother, and now that I considered it, hadn't it worked?

"Three..."

Of course, had I *really* been thinking, I'd have realised there was no way I'd get to do or say anything before the situation was taken from my hands. "My name is Marina Estrada," said Estrada, stepping forward, "Mayor elect of the town of Muena Palaiya. On behalf of myself and my associates, I welcome you to Altapasaeda."

If Estrada was staring down a force of heavily armed savages, if she had nothing except audacity and the shirt on her back to bargain with, if her eyes were locked with those of the most singularly dangerous woman she was ever likely to meet, you would never have guessed it from her tone. And if nothing else, she seemed to have Kalyxis's attention. As long as it was off me, I was willing to count that a success.

"You've arrived in the middle of a conflict between the King of Ans Pasaeda and the people of this city," continued Estrada, "here representing the rights of the Castoval entire. The events of today will have immeasurable consequences for both nations... and, as I'm sure you must realise, for your own land of Shoan as well."

Kalyxis had been watching her all the while – and just as when I'd first met her, her stare brought to mind images of a raptor scrutinising some distant prey. Might it be too big to carry off? Might it have teeth? Might it have claws? And I supposed that for Kalyxis there was one question that no eagle had ever had to worry about: might it be an ally, now that I've found myself far from home and in the middle of someone else's war?

However, if the possibility had so much as crossed her mind, the toneless chill of her voice hinted none of it. "My name is Kalyxis of Shoan. My grandson has been kidnapped and this degenerate knows where he is. The time he has left to convey that information to me is dwindling rapidly."

"I believe there's been a misunderstanding," replied Estrada, calm as ever. "I swear to you, if it's within my power, I'll make certain it's resolved to your satisfaction."

"Your word means nothing to me," said Kalyxis. "And neither do you. I've made my terms abundantly clear."

"You and your men must be tired and hungry. Come with us now, and we'll discuss this in more comfortable surroundings."

Estrada's poise in the face of provocation was astonishing; almost as remarkable was the fact that it seemed to be having no effect on Kalyxis whatsoever. "My men are warriors of Shoan," she said. "They've endured far worse with far less cause. We'll rest when we've left this barbarous land behind with my grandson in tow."

Had she really just called us barbarous? I was surprised by how much my blood rose at that, when all I'd felt until that point was fear.

Even Estrada seemed finally to be losing a little of her patience. "Kalyxis," she said, "through no misdoing of your own, you've placed yourself and your men in grave danger. I know you're no friend of the King, and he may well be marching through these streets before the day is out. When circumstances have made us allies, what can you hope to gain with threats?"

The way Estrada talked, you'd think she actually had something to bargain with; that it was she who had the entourage of armed men and not Kalyxis. More than anything she'd said, it was that inexplicable bravado that made me open my mouth when every shred of sense told me to keep it shut.

"The fact is," I said, before Kalyxis could deliver whatever scathing rebuttal was working towards her tongue, "that you asked Navare here for a truce. Well I'll tell you now, here in Altapasaeda, truces don't involve threatening to have people flayed. Like Estrada said, the best course of action here is that we get together, without quite so many swords on display, and have a civilised discussion about how we find your missing grandson."

Kalyxis turned her aquiline glare on me. "*Missing*?"

The way she pronounced that one word made my heart want to stop for sheer terror. Yet I knew that if I didn't press on now, I was done for, and Estrada and Navare too. "Exactly, missing. And not likely to get any less so unless we all calm down."

By *we* I'd meant *you*, but I assumed that years of politicking would have prepared her for such linguistic niceties. Which meant I'd effectively just told a terrifying barbarian queen to get a hold of herself; suddenly, keeping quiet seemed as if it would have been by far the better option.

Then again, wasn't reason on my side? However limited Kalyxis's knowledge of the Castoval might be, she had to realise that the chances of finding one wayward youth, in the middle of a war no less, were just below the odds of finding one lost eyelash in a brothel.

Still, the woman had failed to show much in the way of common sense so far. Her approach had been more along the lines of *execute now and work out what the question was later*. It would be a mistake to expect her to reach the same inescapably rational conclusion I had.

Thus, I was as surprised as I expected Kalyxis herself was when she said, "You have until sunset. Tell me by then how my grandson will be returned to me or, so help me, this city will find itself losing a war on two fronts."

Estrada had failed to take into account one thing: organising meetings, food, shelter or anything else in a city that had suddenly – and for the majority of its self-absorbed citizenry, unexpectedly – found itself under attack was a lot like trying to organise an archery contest aboard a sinking ship. No one was interested in the tasks Estrada wanted to set them; for some reason, they were far more eager to get distracted or fly into panics instead.

Estrada had decided to commandeer the Dancing Cat, the inn that had served as Mounteban's headquarters and afterwards his prison. Her reasoning was sound: there was food and drink there, ample space even for a force of irate Shoanish, and since the Cat had gained such significance lately in the city's affairs, it had become an unofficial meeting point for the remains of the guard and other factions in the defence effort.

As it turned out, however, it was for exactly that last reason that no one was willing to do what Estrada wanted them to. I watched and tried to find some amusement in the sight of her commandeering passing guardsmen and members of

Mounteban's hotchpotch army, who feigned attention only to rush off on their original errands the moment she let them out of her sight.

Throughout, I kept expecting Kalyxis to run out of whatever passed in the far north for patience. Yet as minutes turned to hours, she only waited with her rough companions, sometimes speaking in muted tones to them, more often observing the commotion unfolding around her as if it were the sort of entertainment always put on for visiting dignitaries. Innumerable as her other flaws of character might be, it appeared that once given, she kept her word.

All the while, I dithered over the prospect of getting out of there to try to find Saltlick. A dozen times I told myself I would, Kalyxis, Estrada and everyone else be damned; I wouldn't be kept hostage just because I'd had the misfortune of making Malekrin's acquaintance. Though I'd quickly realised that a couple of the Shoanish were always watching me, I had no doubt I could elude them once the right diversion presented itself.

Yet diversions came and went, one opportunity after another arose for me to duck out of sight, and all I did was stand there, lost in my thoughts. Each time it became harder to deny that what was keeping me in place wasn't a sense of responsibility, or any faith in Estrada's attempts at peacemaking. No, it was fear that rooted me, and not just of Kalyxis or her men. What terrified me was the prospect of succeeding, of managing to get away and track down Saltlick – and of what I'd find if I did.

I was disgusted to admit it, and I could see Estrada was even more dismayed, but it was only when Castilio Mounteban arrived late in the afternoon that the situation with Kalyxis began to improve. He never said what he'd come for, but he was quick enough to note the room full of Shoanish and the alarming figure standing tall in their midst, and to draw the correct conclusion.

Mounteban spoke a few muted words to Estrada, and then began to bark orders – orders that, unlike Estrada's, were actually followed. As much as I sympathised with her, it made sense; for all her strength of personality, she was mayor of a town half the land away, while Mounteban had spent days making this city his own and making damned sure everyone knew about it.

Only once he'd established to his satisfaction that food and wine were on the way, that rooms would be arranged in an even larger nearby hostelry and that a representative sample of city dignitaries would be on hand for the proposed conference did Mounteban turn his attention to Kalyxis. She had been patiently observing all the while from the far end of the taproom. When Mounteban approached, she nodded to her men, and their ranks opened.

"It's both a pleasure and an honour to make your acquaintance, my lady," he said. "My name is Castilio Mounteban."

"Mounteban?" Kalyxis replied, her tongue rolling round the word as though it were a cat playing with a dying bird. "Yes, I recognise that name. I remember a writer of implausible letters and a maker of dubious promises. I fear I owe you a messenger. The one you sent me was... ill-used."

"Accidents will happen," said Mounteban, with utter casualness. "A good envoy prepares accordingly. And I've never in my life made a promise I couldn't keep."

"I do seem to remember a certain trinket falling into my possession," Kalyxis observed, "albeit briefly. It was stolen, I think, by a thief standing not far from us at this very moment."

I flinched, at the word "thief" more than anything, for it took me a moment to realise she actually *was* referring to me. In sudden panic, I thought about protesting my innocence, about pointing out how her revolting grandson was the true culprit.

Perhaps fortunately, Mounteban was quicker on the uptake. "Nor would I give a gift and then allow it to be misappropriated," he said. "I assure you, anything taken by anyone here will be returned to you before the sun sets."

I'd also have liked to point out just how unlikely that was. But it was obvious I had no part in this conversation – and equally clear, though mystifying, that Mounteban was making progress with Kalyxis I might do better not to interrupt. I'd have expected her to see through such oily obsequiousness in a minute. Yet at that moment, a faint but undeniable smile was drawing upon her thin lips.

"You're a man of grand claims, Castilio Mounteban," she said, "and it's clear that you have a little power in this ugly, unclean city. I extend to you the same offer I made the woman there. Deliver my grandson to me, make good on your gift, and you won't have made yourself another enemy."

"On the contrary," said Mounteban, his smarm now so thick that I wondered how it wasn't dripping from the rafters, "I hope that by the end of the day you'll have learned to consider me a friend." He even finished with a bow; it should have looked absurd from a man of his size, but somehow he managed to pull it off with a measure of grace.

Then, while Kalyxis was still judging what to make of his performance, he turned and marched back towards our end of the room, pressing through the barrier of Shoanish as though they were a throng of irksome children. Drawing close, he whispered to Estrada, "That should hold her a while."

"Need I remind you," she hissed back, "that the crown of Altapasaeda is not yours to bargain with?"

Mounteban stopped. He looked vaguely surprised and, I thought, disappointed. "And need I remind you," he said, "that we're in the middle of a war? Assuming Kalyxis wasn't really stupid enough to come here with only this handful of men, don't you imagine that her support is worth the loss of some obsolete gewgaw?"

I remembered the fleet that had pursued us from Shoan. Did Mounteban have a point? Could those other boats be waiting, in the underground harbour perhaps, for some order from their queen? If so, and if we could hold the King off for long enough, her support might mean the difference between victory and defeat.

Yet just then, that was far from the most important question on my mind. "You tricked us!" I spat. "As far as Kalyxis was concerned, we were just more of your disposable messengers! You sent us hurrying into a trap."

Mounteban looked at me with contempt. "Would it have helped you to know I'd offered Kalyxis the crown?" His eyes roved back to Estrada. "Or would you have argued and wasted time we didn't have? As usual, it fell to me to do what needed to be done." And before she could respond, Mounteban had turned on his heel and was out the door.

I watched it slam shut behind him. The arrogance of the man was astounding, hypnotic even. Only in his absence could I properly appreciate how much I despised him. That was the problem with having so much to think about: important details, like who your real enemies were, tended to slip between the cracks.

Estrada and Alvantes had been quick enough to forget that the only reason we'd come back here was to make damned sure Mounteban never gave another order in his life. Now here he was, organising the city's defence and brokering his twisted alliance with Kalyxis, back to running Altapasaeda as if nothing had ever happened.

Well, they might not remember, but I did. And even if I had to do it alone, I was going to take Mounteban down, once and for all. I had no idea how, but I was absolutely clear on the why: after every other despicable deed he'd somehow got away with, he had hurt my friend, and apparently thought nothing of it. I wouldn't pretend I was doing it for Saltlick, who probably didn't even have a word in his language for "revenge"; but that didn't mean I couldn't do it *because* of him. Before this was over, I would see Castilio Mounteban pay.

In the meantime, however, I wasn't sure what I should do with myself. I very much wanted a drink, and to be out of that room cramped with ill-smelling barbarians. Since I was in an inn, there was a realistic hope of the former, but I suspected the latter remained a doubtful hope at best. Just to make certain, I asked Estrada, "I suppose my attendance is required at this momentous meeting?"

Estrada, whose eyes had been fixed on the door since Mounteban's abrupt departure, looked at me distractedly. "I think Kalyxis will expect to see you here."

"I'd hate to disappoint the lovely lady," I said sourly.

Then, spying a bottle behind the bar and no one watching, I started in that direction – but Estrada called me back. "Wait," she said, "I meant to tell you. I asked one of the guardsmen to check in on Saltlick, and he sent word just before Castilio arrived. Saltlick's alive, Easie... but they can't say for sure that he'll last the night. Apparently he was conscious for a little while; I'm sure he'd like to see you."

"I'll tell you what," I said, trying hard to keep the sudden quaver out of my voice, "if Kalyxis doesn't have my head for kidnapping her idiot grandson, I promise Saltlick's bedside will be my first port of call."

"And I promise I won't *let* her have your head," Estrada said. "No one's going to bargain with your life, Easie."

"But you'd rather I didn't wander too far in the meantime... just in case, I mean?"

Estrada sighed. "Just in case," she agreed.

The conversation having reached its logical end, I carried on to my bottle, which turned out to contain a sturdy if oversweet red wine. I dug out a cup from beneath the bar and filled it to the brim, heedless of the filthy looks some of the Shoanish turned my way. Probably they weren't following the current circumstances and took me for some self-indulging serving lad. Just in case, I presented them a broad grin before taking my first gulp.

I was two-thirds through the bottle by the time Mounteban returned. I'd half expected him to bring Alvantes, but I supposed that someone was needed to keep our other invading enemies on their side of the walls; it would be embarrassing for everyone if the King were to arrive mid-meeting. Then again, it was just as likely that Mounteban had deliberately withheld this latest news from his co-commander – a thought I filed away as a small first step in my vendetta against the fat filcher.

Mounteban did however have a couple of the local lords in tow, as well as representatives of the criminal types he liked to keep close at hand. I noted that the smallest faction in his conclave, the Shoanish warriors left over from Moaradrid's scattered army, were unrepresented; presumably Mounteban had felt it wise not to remind Kalyxis of her son's recent visit or of its final, fatal outcome.

Either way, there were now even less people in the room I wanted to be around. I settled towards the back and tried my best to look inconspicuous, while still keeping my bottle close at hand.

Mounteban had also brought a few assorted lackeys with him, and they hurried to construct a makeshift stage out of planks and crates brought in from the yard. That done, he clambered up and surveyed his nearest audience: the lords and crooks he'd brought along, Estrada, Kalyxis and two Shoanish I took for bodyguards.

"Gathered dignitaries of Altapasaeda," Mounteban began, "I know I express all our sentiments by declaring my honour in having Kalyxis of Shoan here today. My only regret is that the circumstances aren't more favourable – for surely there was never a better time for unity between Castoval and Shoan.

With that in mind, lady, will you take the stage and state the reasons for your presence, so that we may resolve your concerns without further delay."

As Kalyxis moved to take her place, I noticed Mounteban make a small nod in my direction. It certainly wasn't me he was signalling; more likely, I realised, it had been meant for the two burly thugs who'd materialised, one at each of my elbows. I could hardly say I was surprised, but I wished Estrada were closer. I'd have been intrigued to hear her explain just how she intended to protect me now.

I looked back to the stage, where Kalyxis now stood beside Mounteban. Though he dwarfed her by more than a head, she somehow managed to look every bit as tall as him – and certainly she was a dozen times more impressive. "Since I despise repeating myself," she said, "I will be brief. There is a thief here who came to me under a flag of truce, only to steal a valued possession and kidnap my grandson. Unless both are returned to me, I shall have no choice but to recover them by force."

"For those who don't know Easie Damasco," put in Mounteban quickly, "he's a lowbred guttersnipe who has somehow managed to play a disproportionate part in recent, significant events – primarily by stealing important items from some very important people. However, since Damasco was acting in concert with others of far nobler character," he added, with a conciliatory glance towards Estrada, "it may be that we should give him the benefit of the doubt on this occasion. Marina, do you have anything you'd like to contribute?"

It was obvious where this conversation was heading, and I wanted no part of it. Yet there was no escaping the fact that my fate was high on the list of topics – and hadn't I vowed mere minutes ago that I'd do anything I could to undermine Mounteban? Well, here was an opportunity I'd never have again.

So before Estrada could speak, I said loudly, "Hold on a moment," and in case that wasn't enough to draw all eyes in my direction, dramatically cleared my throat. "I'm sorry to interrupt, Castilio. But do you think I could take the floor, just briefly? I think I might have something constructive to add. I mean, if that's all right with you."

Mounteban gave me a look that was suspicious and murderous in equal parts. I'd never called him Castilio in his life and that if nothing else should have tipped him off. "Please be brief, Damasco," he said. "I'm sure we'd all hate to see you talk yourself onto an early funeral pyre."

"Ha!" I offered him my widest grin. "How kind of you to think of me. And truly, you made some interesting points there... I particularly liked 'lowbred guttersnipe'." I dropped his gaze and turned my attentions to Kalyxis, trying not to shudder as her pale eyes met mine. "But the fact is, neither of you know what you're talking about."

I'd hoped for an awed sigh from my audience, but the thick silence, which at least seemed to qualify as stunned, would have to suffice. In any case, it was what I said next that would really put the dog amongst the rats – because what I'd finally come to accept was that no lie was going to serve me quite as well as the truth.

"I *didn't* kidnap Malekrin – who, since he prefers it, I'll refer to as Mal henceforward. In fact it's truer to say that Mal kidnapped me. He told me he was sick of being a pawn in other people's battles; that he'd rather be a vagrant in the Castoval than a prince in Shoan. Which, come to think of it, is probably why he snuck away while you were chasing us. Oh, and lest I forget, if you were wondering how I could have stolen that object Mounteban had me smuggle into your hands when I was chained in a tent... well, you might want to give some thought to your light-fingered grandson on that count, too."

There it was, all of it out, like burning tinder dropped into a haystack. I could feel Kalyxis eyes burning into me, *through* me, cutting clean circles of fire through the back of my skull. "You seem to know a great deal about my grandson," she said.

I gulped, tried to steady my pummelling heart. Showing fear beneath that hawkish gaze could kill me just as surely as an arrow to the head. "Perhaps I came to know him a little better than you do," I said.

"In the space of a mere few days?"

"Unlikely, I know. Then again... do you even know what he calls his boat?"

A faint tremor tugged at Kalyxis's mouth then. It was the first sign of anything that might be construed as emotion I'd seen her show, and that made it almost more unnerving that her usual stern intensity. "Malekrin has no boat," she said.

"Mal," I told her. "As I mentioned, he likes to be called Mal. And, I suppose you're right... I very much doubt it survived you trying to kill us all. But before that, for reasons that undoubtedly have a lot to do with his age, he called his boat *Seadagger*."

"You seem to know my grandson... *Mal*... very well," Kalyxis said once more. "And to have struck up a friendship of sorts."

On that point, at least, I wasn't sure the truth would help matters. "That's fair to say," I replied.

"And you were with him when he disappeared."

"I suppose I must have been."

"So it only makes sense that you should be the one to find him."

"Well, if you mean that I'd stand a better chance than fifty armed men charging around the Castovalian countryside and... Wait, *what*?"

"Since you know this land," Kalyxis said, "and since you know Mal. Wouldn't you agree?"

I wouldn't. I didn't. But I could see now with perfect clarity the corner I'd backed myself into. "That, as it happens," I said, "is exactly what I was about to propose myself."

As had happened so often in recent weeks, my choices had dwindled to nothing; fate, ill-fortune and the malice of others had set me on a course not of my choosing, and what could I do but follow?

Well, there was one thing I had a say in, one thing I wouldn't be denied, whatever anyone else thought. With a little negotiation and with Mounteban's two thugs acting as both guides and guards, it was agreed that I could be allowed a couple more hours of freedom before my hopeless mission began.

It was sunset when I reached the temporary hospital that the defenders had set up in the Market District, and a light rain was falling from a sky of purple and smudged grey. Even outside, the smell was revolting: a stink of sickness and death, with undertones of tinny blood and the sharp rankness of vomit. Within, what had once been a small warehouse was now filled with an assortment of beds, all presumably requisitioned from nearby homes. Perhaps two-thirds were currently occupied; the majority of the bedridden wore what I'd come to think of as the Altapasaedan uniform, and all but a lucky few possessed injuries that turned my stomach just to look at them. I kept my eyes down as I traversed the room, manoeuvring to avoid the assortment of priests, healers and red-robed surgeons that were trying, inadequately, to divide their attentions amongst the wounded.

None of the beds had been large or sturdy enough to support Saltlick, so they'd built him a kind of nest from straw instead. From a distance he looked like a stillborn chick, still smeared with natal blood. His carers had bandaged his wounds as well as they could, but since they hadn't been able to move him, many gaping cuts and countless shallower gashes had been left undressed. I was used to him healing quickly, quicker than a man every could, but so far as I could judge he was in no better state than when I'd last seen him. It struck me that perhaps his powers of recuperation had simply been overwhelmed by the sheer volume of his injuries – and the thought made the pit of my stomach turn cold.

Saltlick's eyes were open. When they fixed on me, I thought for a moment that he smiled, ever so distantly. Then again, it could as easily have been a twitch, a convulsion of pain rather than recognition.

I knelt beside him, so as to bring my face closer to his eye level. "Saltlick... I'm going to have to go away for a while."

I hadn't expected a response, but it still stung me when none came – not even the flicker of an eyelid.

"When I get back," I continued, "I expect to see you on your feet. We can't have you lolling around like this in a crisis."

Saltlick blinked then, slowly and heavily, as though the effort was almost too great. For a moment, I wasn't sure he'd open his eyes again – but when he did, it was only to stare through me once more.

"I don't know how long I'll be. I wish I could stay here to help look after you... because frankly, I don't much trust anyone else to do it. But I'm sure Estrada will do her best. I suppose she's good at this sort of thing."

I sought out a patch on his arm that wasn't marred with blood or bandages and placed my hand on it. I thought he flinched when my skin touched his, but it was over in an instant, so I didn't move the hand away.

"Everything's going to be all right," I told him. "Do you hear me, Saltlick? Do you understand?"

But there was no reply – and whether that meant he didn't hear or that he couldn't answer or that things really *wouldn't* be all right this time, I had no way to tell.

CHAPTER FOURTEEN

It was dark when I left Saltlick and the hospital, darker than the city had any right to be at such an hour – as if no one was willing to light a torch or lamp for fear it would somehow draw the notice of the enemies outside their gates. The rain had picked up, too, turned from a drizzle into the cautious beginnings of a torrent, and the chill it had brought to the air was enough to make me huddle inside my cloak.

At least the gloom and the foul weather suited my disposition. I'd thought I'd prepared myself, thought I'd accepted the possibility that Saltlick might die; but I'd been wrong, and I knew now that nothing could have prepared me. Nor was fear for my friend the only thing poisoning my mood. Though Saltlick hovered constantly in the back of my mind, the foreground was filled entirely with worry for myself. Because one indirect consequence of Saltlick's injuries was that I couldn't possibly do what I might have under other circumstances, and take the opportunity I'd been gifted to flee Altapasaeda forever.

I couldn't care less about Kalyxis and her threats. Alvantes and Estrada could look after themselves, and wasn't it their poor judgement that had brought the accursed woman down on us in the first place? Whether I came back with or without Malekrin, it wasn't as if I could contribute to the city's defence, other than to be another victim when the gates were finally breached. No, I could see little reason to return, but for that one thing: if I left now, I'd never know whether Saltlick was alive or dead.

Which meant that, rather than use my mission as an opportunity to slip away, I'd have to take it seriously – no matter how futile it almost certainly was. And since my recent trip to the far north had left me with a definite distaste towards blundering in unprepared, that in turn meant one more visit before I even considered leaving Altapasaeda.

I'd vaguely hoped Mounteban's thugs would consider their duty done and leave me to my business. But I'd recognised it for the vain wish it was, and I wasn't surprised when, as I turned not back towards the Dancing Cat but eastward in the direction of the docks, one of them caught my shoulder and said, "This isn't the way."

"This is *my* way," I told him.

"Not likely. You got a job to do, the boss says."

"I have, and I'm doing it. If there's a problem, feel free to run along to Mounteban and ask him what you should do."

"Or I could break your knees," the thug said thoughtfully, as though he were merely contributing to a philosophical debate.

"Why not?" I agreed. "I'm sure I won't need to be able to walk or ride for that job you're supposed to be making sure I do." Then it occurred to me that sarcasm was a risky proposition when a misunderstanding had the potential to end so badly. "This is a *part* of the job, all right? So just tag along and keep quiet."

I could see he didn't like it, but since Mounteban obviously hadn't filled him in on even the most basic details of why he was here, he didn't have much choice. He shrugged bulky shoulders at his companion, and the two of them retook their positions at my elbows.

Just then, that actually suited me. The avenues I wove my way through were a little too quiet, and it struck me that even in the driving rain there were bound to be a few disreputable types out, those who hadn't given themselves over to Mounteban's cause and who would consider a burgeoning siege the perfect opportunity to go about their business undisturbed. Given the scanty illumination, I could have made my way across the city unseen without much effort, but it was quicker and easier to be escorted by two such off-putting companions.

Sure enough, no one bothered me in the time it took me to find the one narrow, dead-end street I sought; in fact, everyone we saw was quick to change their route. I hurried to the door I was after, a portal that only revealed itself as different from its neighbours on careful inspection: for where those were cheap and rickety, this was reinforced within by sturdy beams and metal bands, and probably only a little less solid than the city's own gates.

Behind that unusual door was the home and business of a man named Franco, dealer of weapons, outfits and more outlandish merchandise for the criminal of discerning tastes. The last time I'd visited he'd made it quite clear that I wasn't forgiven for embroiling him, however indirectly, in our conflict with Castilio Mounteban; but if there was one thing that could be said for Franco it was that he'd never turn away paying business.

I hammered on the door, and after a few seconds a panel in its upper half slid aside, revealing narrow eyes set in crinkled, leathered skin. Franco squinted suspiciously, first at me and then at Mounteban's thugs. "Damasco," he said. "I didn't expect to see you again so soon. Who are your new friends?"

"These are Pug and Lug, my bodyguards. Careful what you say around them, they might just take offence at your tone and come in there to twist your arms off."

"Hah! You're in trouble again, aren't you? Well, of course you are. If there's a sun or a moon in the sky, it's a safe bet that Easie Damasco's in trouble."

From the far side of the door I heard the rattle of chains, the clunk of locks and the heavy thud of a bar being drawn aside; it sounded as though Franco had added to his already considerable security since my last visit. Eventually the door swung open, to reveal the ancient and eccentrically garbed figure of Franco himself, dressed as always in his scruffy poncho and hopelessly outsized hat.

"I'm surprised you're still here, Franco," I told him. "Has no one told you there's a war on? Isn't it time you thought about retiring to some place a little safer?"

"Are you mad?" he asked me, with genuine surprise. "I've sold two-thirds of my stock to Mounteban and his brigands."

"What? Are they planning to rob the King's army to death?"

"They took most of the specialist weapons, the crossbows, the concealed knifes... and I hate to think what anyone could want with that many caltrops. Know what happens when you recruit thieves and cutthroats into an army, Damasco? You get an army that likes to fight *dirty*. And whichever way it goes, long, drawn-out siege or desperate resistance effort against the northern oppressors, I expect to shift the rest of my stock before the month is out."

"Aren't you forgetting the third possibility?" I asked. "The one where Panchessa marches in and slaughters everyone he sets eyes on?"

"Hah! Don't worry about me, Damasco. Maybe Mounteban, the Boar and a few of their lackeys will lose their heads in Red Carnation Square, but no king ever cared about one harmless old man. Now what is it you want? I can't stand around talking to the likes of you when there's good commerce to be done."

"I'm going on a small expedition," I said, "and I think it's time I refreshed my wardrobe."

"All to the good," replied Franco, "but you can leave your little bodyguards out here. One customer at a time's the rule."

"That's not going to happen," put in the brute I'd just christened Lug. "Where he goes, we go."

I was about to point out that there was only one way in or out, and that the worst I could do would be to never leave – but before I could say a word, Lug's companion elbowed him ungently in the ribs. "Are you stupid?" he hissed. "That's bloody *Franco*."

They shared a look, and then Lug waved me on, with a scowl.

It never ceased to amaze me what a reputation Franco had accrued amongst the city's seamy underclass. Perhaps it was simply that he'd survived for so very long in an industry not known for its long lifespans. He led me through a hallway, drew up a hatch in the room beyond and continued down the stairs it revealed, into a dimly illuminated cellar. Franco had told the truth, his stock had been severely depleted since I'd last seen it; still, by any normal standards, the display was staggering. Anything the professional criminal could conceivably want to wear, use or injure someone with was in there somewhere.

My funds were hardly in a healthy state, but it was difficult to imagine an outcome where I lived to spend my money, so I might as well be extravagant while I could. "I'll take a cloak, shirt and trousers in the darkest grey, a good belt, an undershirt of fine chain link, a dagger I can wear out of the way – actually, make that two – and now that I think, a cosh as well. Do you have any of those famous knockout drops of yours? A bottle of those too then. I'll need a new backpack, another length of rope wouldn't go amiss... and some lockpicks, of course."

Franco smirked at me from beneath his outrageous hat. "Quiet day in the countryside, is it? A little camping trip to clear the vapours?"

I grinned. "A family visit, actually... but you can never be too careful."

Of course, that wasn't entirely divorced from the truth; it just wasn't any relative of mine I'd be seeking out. I settled up with Franco, wincing to see how few coins were left in my purse by the time I'd finished. Then I changed quickly, strapped on the belt and daggers, stashed the cosh in a pocket of the cloak and crammed everything else into the backpack. When I looked in Franco's grimy mirror and saw a well-dressed thief staring back, I felt like myself for the first time in days. How hard could tracking down one headstrong prince be anyway?

Franco escorted me back to his front door, where my two handlers were waiting impatiently. "Listen, Franco," I told him, "take care, all right? If it gets too hot, keep your head down, will you?"

"Of the two of us," Franco said, "we both know damn well you're not the one who should be worrying about me. And believe me when I say that I won't be losing a minute's sleep wondering what's become of you."

"Pah!" I scoffed. "Why would you need to? I can take perfectly good care of myself."

As I said it, I even believed it – and it was only a shame that the sound of Pug and Lug's sniggering completely ruined my moment.

By the time I made it back to the Dancing Cat, Kalyxis and her barbarians were gone, presumably to somewhere they could be fed and lodged without getting in the way of the war effort. Mounteban was holding court in the taproom, he, Estrada and his inner circle of crooks and the crookedly wealthy gathered round a cluster of tables spread with maps of the city. If I hadn't already been feeling frustrated and miserable, that glaring reminder of how completely we'd failed to roust the vile filcher from power would certainly have done it.

"I'm ready," I told him. "But I'll need a horse, and a way out of the city."

Mounteban nodded to Pug and Lug, tipped his head in the direction of the rear of the inn, and said, "Tell them to let him through the western gate." At no point had he even looked at me.

That's fine, I thought. Because the sooner I get this done, the sooner I can come back here and make you suffer, you blubbery, conniving weasel.

Estrada, at least, glanced up. Her eyes were haggard. "Be careful, Damasco," she said. "You know how important this is, don't you?"

"I have some idea," I told her.

"Then don't go because Kalyxis thinks you should. Malekrin's our best chance of ending this without more bloodshed, and *you're* our best chance of getting him back here in one piece."

Estrada's faith in me, no matter the accumulation of evidence to the contrary, never failed to perplex me. I'd have pointed out how minute the odds were of me finding one lost youth who didn't want to be found in a land the size of the Castoval, but Estrada had returned her attention to the plan of the dockside spread before her, and one of my escorts tapped me hard on the shoulder and pointed towards the door that led through to the kitchens. Seeing no point in resisting, I led the way instead, and carried on through the room beyond into the coach yard.

There, I was surprised to see a horse already saddled and waiting. However low my mission might be in Mounteban's priorities, it appeared I was at least in there somewhere. The horse was a placid mare, who eyed my hands hopefully when I went to pat her nose. Though obviously disappointed when no food materialised, she made no complaint when I climbed into the saddle.

We set off at a walk, Pug and Lug to either side of me, Lug lighting our way with a lantern he'd found in the stables. It didn't take us long to reach the western gate, the entrance that until recently had been reserved for the City Guard. It was both small and sturdy, and those virtues had evidently reduced it to a minor concern in the city's defence, for there were only two men standing sentry, both of them dressed in Altapasaedan uniform and leaning disinterestedly against the wall.

"This one's called Ducascos," Lug explained, holding up the lantern so that they could see my face. "Mounteban says open up for him. If he ever comes back, I suppose you should let him in again too."

I was surprised when he passed the lantern up to me, and even more so when he tipped me a nod goodbye. Returning the gesture, I rode into the narrow gatehouse, grateful for the waft of wet dirt and foliage smell that met my nostrils. There was only so much of city living I could stand, and I'd been spending far more time in Altapasaeda lately than I'd have liked.

I'd half expected to find Pasaedan soldiers camped outside, but the road was clear as far as I could see in either direction; the King must be focusing his efforts upon the northern walls for the time being. I turned left, glad that my way lay inevitably southward – for there was only one place I could have lost Malekrin, and unlikely as it seemed that anyone could have squeezed through the door beneath the barracks, that skinny brat would have stood a better chance than most.

Then again, I was just as likely to find him still wedged there, or else buried beneath the rubble on the far side. Kalyxis hadn't specified, but it was safe to assume that she was expecting her grandson back alive. Dragging his crushed corpse back probably wasn't going to satisfy her.

Still, one way or the other, I had to know. I rode on through the night, clasped in a shell of pounding rain lit by the amber glow of my lantern. It was strange but, despite the cold and wet, despite everything that had happened so far that day, I actually felt quite at peace. For the moment at least, there was nothing I could do about anything. I couldn't help Saltlick, couldn't protect Altapasaeda, probably couldn't even save my own skin from Kalyxis. All I could do was see what was waiting for me at the barracks and follow where it led.

My calm lasted until I was nearing the last turn before the barracks, and the moment when something hissed past my eyes and shattered with a resounding crack upon a roadside rock.

"The next one goes through your neck," a voice said. "Who the hells are you and what do you want?"

"My name's Easie Damasco," I said. "Perhaps you know it?"

"Damasco? Of course." A cloaked figure materialised on the bank to my left and picked his way down to the road, all the while careful to keep his bow trained on me. Close enough that he couldn't possibly miss but still well out of my reach, he ordered, "Show me your face. No sudden moves."

I drew down my hood, careful to make no moves that might be interpreted as sudden.

He paused to inspect my features. Then, apparently satisfied, he pulled back his own hood. When I failed to show any recognition, he said, "It's Panchez. From the City Guard."

"Right... Panchez." I vaguely remembered Alvantes using the name for one of his handpicked elite of guardsmen, but they all looked more or less the same to me. "What are you doing here?"

"Oh, spying mostly," he said airily. "Keeping an eye out for trouble, you know? There are only a couple of us left here since the fighting broke out." Finally, he lowered his bow, slipping the arrow deftly into a quiver slung over one shoulder. "How about you, Damasco? Don't get me wrong, it's always nice to have a visitor, even at so late an hour, but they're not exactly common these days."

"Panchez, I need some help. I'm on a mission for..." I almost said Mounteban, realised at the last moment how it would sound. "For Alvantes. I need to have a look at the door that leads into the palace tunnel."

"You'll have a fine time getting in there," he said.

"I just need to see it. It's a long story."

Panchez shrugged. "Fair enough. If you're here on the Hammer's orders, that'll do for me. This way, Damasco."

The barracks had been burned almost to the ground under Mounteban's brief reign; however, there was one portion that had escaped the flames, and that was where Panchez led me. I tied the mare off to a stump of blackened timber and we brushed through the curtain that served as a door. Inside, a second guardsman sat beside a small campfire on which a hunk of meat was roasting; he looked up suspiciously and then, seeing Panchez, greeted me with a wave.

Panchez pressed on through a second doorway, into the central quadrangle that had once been the guard's training ground. He led the way to a section of building in the northwest corner – or what was left of it, for the fire had struck hard there, leaving little but rubble and charred wood in its wake. I could see how the floor had collapsed, depositing much of the upper room in the cellar below.

The last time I'd seen this place it had been from the other side and below, looking out through the gap in the hidden subterranean doorway. Holding my lantern high, I thought I could make out where that entrance must be, though it was impossible to say for sure with all the debris piled about it. There was certainly no sign of any princes, dead or otherwise – and I only realised then that I'd been half hoping to find Malekrin here, trapped and whimpering to be let free. No such luck; my mission wasn't going to be so easy.

"I don't suppose you've seen anyone leave this way?" I asked Panchez.

"We haven't seen anyone at all before you turned up," he said.

My heart sank. Could I have been wrong? If Malekrin hadn't escaped this way then he could only have left through the palace. He might even still be hiding there; if he wasn't, he could be anywhere in Altapasaeda. Not only had I come here for nothing, the chances of me finding him in the city's myriad nooks and crannies were beyond non-existent.

"But," said Panchez, "we lost a couple of things this morning. A travel cloak and some food. And now that I think, there was some trouble in the stables too. One of the horses kicking up a fuss."

"None of them missing though?"

"I think we'd have noticed a missing horse," he said.

So Malekrin *had* come this way. He'd stolen a fresh cloak, probably as a disguise, taken food for a journey, and he'd tried to take a horse, without success. Luck was on my side there, for if he'd managed it I wouldn't stand the faintest chance of catching him.

I guessed that he'd have headed south then, as soon as he'd realised that the city he was so keen to avoid lay to the north. If I was right, he was unlikely to have come across anything more rideable that a goat, for the stretch of land between here and the southern tip of the Castoval was sparsely populated.

"You think someone came through this way?" asked Panchez, breaking in on my thoughts. "Must be someone important, too, for you to be hunting around on a night like this."

I could think of no reason not to tell him. "Prince Malekrin of Shoan has decided to take a tour of the Castovalian countryside. His grandmother, being the fond, maternal sort, is concerned for his wellbeing and would like to see him back."

"Phew! Politics, eh? It'll be the death of all of us," said Panchez, as though it were a subject he'd given much consideration to.

"Right now," I said, "I'm expecting something sharp and pointed to be the death of me, when I have to go back without him."

"Why's that?" he asked. "It shouldn't be too hard."

"Oh no," I said exasperatedly, "there's no reason at all that finding one lone boy whose only goal is to stay undiscovered in a vast wilderness should be difficult."

"Well, that's it," replied Panchez, apparently un-concerned by my outburst. "If he's sleeping rough, you probably don't stand a chance. But if he wanted out of this rain and was willing to pay, there's really only one place he could be."

A sarcastic observation regarding Panchez's expertise in tracking lost princes was halfway to my lips before I realised that he had a point. Malekrin didn't know this country even slightly and there'd been rain enough by now that his heavy clothes would be soaking. For all he knew, there might be bandits, wolves or three-headed monsters lurking in the wilds. Ignorant of the local geography, he'd have had to rely on asking directions of anyone he met, and they would all have told him the same thing: there was only one inn nearby that he could hope to reach on foot.

"The tavern at Midendo," I said.

"It's worth a try," Panchez agreed.

"If you're right, I owe you a drink or seven," I told him.

"We've drink enough in the stores," Panchez said. "If you want to do me a favour, ask the Hammer to let me in on the fight against those bastards camped outside our gates."

I rode south, as fast as the mare, the darkness, the poor state of the road and the need to carry my lantern in one hand would allow me – which wasn't very fast at all. Still, I was confident that even the trot we managed would be enough to gain on Malekrin. He'd have been weary, confused, unsure of his direction. After our dramatic arrival in the subterranean harbour, the long flight through the tunnels under the mountain and then clambering through the wreckage beneath the barracks, he might even have had to waste a few hours in resting.

Which reminded me: when had I last slept? Certainly it hadn't been today, and before that my memories became blurry. Even the events of the morning seemed a great distance away. When, for that matter, had I eaten? I resolved that whatever else I did when I arrived in Midendo, I'd spend a little time addressing my own neglected bodily needs. For what good would it do me, Kalyxis or anyone if I should keel over from exhaustion?

Now that I was conscious of my tiredness, however, the distant prospect of rest was of little comfort. As the hours wore by, I found myself nodding more and more in the saddle – and on a couple of occasions, even waking with a frightened jolt to find the horse still trotting beneath me. I grew anxious that I'd miss the turning I sought, though there were few enough junctions on the road. But even fretfulness wasn't enough to keep me fully awake. I could hear the river murmuring a lullaby somewhere to my left, and the blustering rain made the trees sigh and the grass whisper beside me. In desperation, I began to sing to myself, and when the sound became too strange amidst the night-time quiet, to talk to my horse, narrating choice highlights of my recent adventures.

I was just detailing how I'd almost single-handedly defeated the deadliest assassins of two lands when I realised there was a track winding off from the main road ahead, and a finger post offering directions in black letters seared into the wood. Sure enough, under the lantern light I could read the ill-scrawled word *Midendo*.

As I took the turnoff, I wondered what portion of the night I'd ridden through. The moon was lagging in the eastern portion of the sky, as if it too had worn itself out. Though the darkness was thicker than ever beyond the circle of my lamplight, I guessed that dawn might not be too far off.

It wasn't long before I crested a ridge and saw Midendo before me, nestled cosily in the cleavage of two hills. Midendo was a nothing of a place; folks thereabout considered it a town, but it was hardly large enough to warrant the description, and far enough off the main road that no one was ever likely to stumble upon it by accident. I supposed it was left over from before the Sabre was built in Altapasaeda, when the only bridge had been the one that crossed the Casto Mara to the south and the highway had seen regular traffic. Now, from what I knew, Midendo served primarily as a hub for the nearby villages, with its small market and of course its tavern, the Nine Lights.

That was an ironic enough name from my point of view, for the tavern – and indeed the entire village – was sunk in darkness as I drew close. Deciding that I'd sooner not draw attention, I tied the mare off in a thicket beside the dirt road, extinguished my lantern and continued on foot.

I made it to the Nine Lights without difficulty, seeing no one and confident no one had seen me. I doubted there was anyone around in Midendo at such an hour, and I was certain it had no guard, for what was there here that anyone could possibly want to steal?

Then again, what I was about to do might well be deemed criminal – for the Nine Lights was locked up for the night, and I was hardly about to start hammering to be let in if there was a chance that Malekrin was asleep inside. A quick inspection revealed a small door at the back in addition to the main entrance; of the two, that seemed best suited to my needs. I'd hoped it might be unlocked in a place as quiet as Midendo, but a gentle push proved otherwise. Still, it might as well have been for the easy work I made of it with my picks. I had the lock sprung in seconds, and opened the door with a soft shove, slipping in through the gap.

There was a kitchen beyond, as I'd guessed there might be – and I was in luck. I'd had images of having to break into every room in the place, until I found either Malekrin or someone who could help me; but asleep before the fire, in a great rocking chair that creaked in time with her snores, was a plump, grey-haired woman I took for the tavern's proprietor.

There was no time for niceties. I tapped her roughly on the shoulder. Her eyes opened a slit – and then very wide. "Aagh! Thief! Va–"

I clapped my hand over her mouth and held it there, despite her wriggling and considerable strength. "Calm down," I hissed, "and listen. I'm not here to hurt you. If I was, wouldn't I have done it by now? I'm here on behalf of the Altapasaedan City Guard and there's good coin in it for you if you'll help me... but I need you to be *quiet*, all right?"

After a moment's thought, she nodded as well as she could; when I removed my hand, however, she gave me the filthiest of scowls. "What kind of guardsman breaks into a woman's tavern?" she asked, still louder than I'd have liked.

"Please, keep your voice down. I never said I was a guardsman; I'm just here on their behalf. I'm looking for someone who might be staying here. It's important, and I can't have them knowing I'm here."

"I've only the one guest," she said, "and he's a strange one. I can't think what you'd want with him."

My heart throbbed in my chest, as if my ribs had become a closing fist. I hardly dared ask, though I knew I had to. "Strange *how*, exactly?"

"In every way you can think of. He's almost too young to be wandering around on his own, and he hardly seems to know where he is. He's dressed up in skins and furs like a trapper, and he's dark enough to have been living outside all his life, but he talks like he's somebody and he's got good coin, though even that's not proper–"

"All right, all right," I said, breaking in upon her flow before her volume could escalate any further. "That's who I'm looking for." My mind was whirling, as I tried to figure out my next step through a haze of tiredness. I was close, but there was still ample scope for everything to go wrong if I wasn't careful. "Does his room have a lock?" I asked.

"Of course. This is a quality establishment. All my rooms have locks," she said. "To discourage *disreputable* types," she added pointedly.

Quality establishment or no, I didn't need her to tell me that those locks wouldn't be anything I could pick; more likely, the rooms would be secured with something as crude as a bolt or bar. Maybe I could kick Malekrin's door in if I paid her enough in advance, but just then I wasn't sure I'd have the strength – and if it took me more than a couple of attempts, he'd be out the window and gone.

No, there'd be no kicking in of doors. I had a better idea. "He's your only guest, you say? The only one staying upstairs?"

She nodded.

"Well then, here's what we're going to do..."

CHAPTER FIFTEEN

I was jolted awake by a vast noise of crashing and rattling – and even though I'd been expecting it, I couldn't but stare around in confusion for a moment.

The taproom of the Nine Lights was still lit by the glow from the fireplace at my back, but now there was also a little pale daylight seeping through the narrow windows. At the far end of the room, at the foot of the staircase, Malekrin lay sprawled.

I rose from the chair where I'd passed the last hours of the night, paced over and offered him my hand. "Prince Malekrin," I said. "What a surprise to find you here."

Ignoring my outstretched palm, Malekrin hopped to his feet and backed away from me, looking somewhat like a startled rabbit. "Surprise?" he spat; his eyes were on the remains of the tripwire I'd set above the third step and the bundle of pans and cups I'd hung from the other end, which were now spread over the tiled floor.

"All right, you've got me," I admitted. "The truth is I may have been hoping to run into you. And I'd have hated for you to leave without seeing me, after I'd come all this way."

Malekrin took another backwards step towards the door, placing a table between him and me. He looked tired and dishevelled; I suspected he'd slept in his clothes, and that they'd still been damp when he'd got into bed. There was less of the cocky bravado I'd come to expect from him in his expression, more a nervousness that he was trying hard to hide. "You've come to take me back," he said. "Well, I'm not going. You can't make me."

"You're right," I said, "I've come to take you back. Not through choice, mind you. Still... I'm not going to try and force you."

"You couldn't," he said.

"You're probably right," I agreed – and even as I said it, I fantasised briefly about the other, simpler plan I'd toyed with, the one that involved my cosh and the back of Malekrin's head. "So there's no hurry for you to leave, is there? Frankly, you look like a bucket of boiled shit, Mal. Why don't you join me for breakfast? If you want to keep running, you'd do better on a full stomach."

He eyed me suspiciously. "I told you," he said, "I'm damned if I'm going back."

"Yes, you told me," I agreed, pulling up a chair at the nearest table. "Ho, Marga," I bellowed, "what are the chances of getting a little service in here?"

Marga, the innkeeper whose acquaintance I'd made during the night, bustled into the room. It was a safe bet that she'd been woken by my little booby-trap, just as I had, and that she'd been listening at the door ever since. "I can make porridge," she told me grudgingly.

With the money I'd given her last night to light the taproom fire and let me misuse her culinary implements, it wouldn't have been unreasonable to expect a fresh lobster flown in from the coast by a squadron of trained eagles. Still, I had no desire for an argument on two fronts. "Porridge will suffice, so long as it's hot," I agreed, "and so long as you warm two cups of good red wine to serve along with it."

"This isn't Altapasaeda," she said, "I can't promise you better than mediocre wine," and she disappeared back into the kitchen.

Malekrin stayed on his feet until the smell of cooking porridge began to waft in through the doorway; then, grudgingly, he sat, at the farthest corner to me. "I'll eat with you," he said. "And then I'll leave."

"Fine, you do that. At least I can tell your grandmother I got a meal inside you. Maybe she'll give me a blindfold when they chop my head off."

He let that one go, and I didn't press the point. The scanty hours I'd spent asleep before the fire had done nothing but emphasise how exhausted I was, and my stomach was growling as fiercely as any angry mother bear. I couldn't deny that this plan had as much to do with serving my own bodily needs as it did keeping Malekrin in place.

So we sat in stubborn silence, neither of us looking at the other, as the odours drifting from the kitchen became almost too much to stand. Just as I was beginning to wonder deliriously if starting breakfast with my own fingers might not be the worst idea I'd ever had, Marga flurried in with a broad platter in her arms and crashed it down upon the table. There were two deep bowls and two brimming cups, each now sitting in its own ruby puddle.

The final result was a considerable improvement on what I'd been expecting. There was dried apple and raisins in the porridge, and a swirl of honey and milk floating upon its surface. Just then, I thought it was the most enticing thing I'd ever laid eyes on. A glance at Malekrin told me that he was just as captivated, however hard he was trying not to show it; the drool working unnoticed down his jaw was a sure giveaway.

First things first, though: I caught up my cup and tipped half its contents down my throat, almost groaning with pleasure as its rousing warmth worked into my veins. Marga had been too hard on the local vintners, the wine was at least decent, and in my present state of mind I was willing to believe it might even be quite good. Slamming my cup down, I nodded to Malekrin, and with some reluctance he picked up his own – reluctance, at least, until the first drops ran into his gullet. When he finally managed to tear the cup from his lips, there was barely a finger's breadth of fluid left swirling in its base. He gave a trembling sigh. For a moment, I thought he might even smile.

"Better?" I asked.

Malekrin frowned. "Your southern wine tastes like horse piss."

"I wouldn't know," I said, "I've never drunk horse piss. I hear you wean babies on it up in Shoan?"

Malekrin leaped to his feet, his face flushing.

"Sit down," I said, "and don't insult your hostess. Manners are manners wherever you go; the wine's fine and you know it." I dipped a spoon into my bowl, shovelled a mound of grey sludge into my mouth and chewed. "So's the porridge," I added. "You should try it."

Reluctantly, Malekrin sat down again. He stared hungrily at his bowl, but although his fingers twitched near his spoon, he didn't pick it up. "How do I know this isn't a trap?" he said.

"A trap?" I asked. "Does it really look like a trap?"

Malekrin pointedly turned his eyes to the tangle of kitchenware near the base of the stairs.

"I've already explained that," I reminded him. Then, when he still made no move to claim his spoon, I shoved my bowl across to him and dragged his untouched one to me. "There. If it's a trap, we're both in it now."

Perhaps that was enough to satisfy him; from the longing in his eyes and the way his jaw had been slowly working at nothing, however, I thought it was more likely that ravenousness had simply won out. He clutched the spoon as if it was a timber thrown a drowning man, and ten quick mouthfuls had vanished before he even paused to breath.

"Careful," I said. "You're no use to anyone if you choke."

Malekrin managed to tear his eyes from the bowl long enough to spare me one of his characteristic frowns. "I don't *want* to be any use to anyone. Not you, not my grandmother, not the people of Shoan. I don't want to be my father. I don't want to be a hero."

I doubted he was in much danger on those last two points; certainly, the only similarity I could see just then between the tired, dishevelled boy before me and the ferocious warlord who'd so dramatically upended my life was that they were both colossal pains in the arse.

"So what then?" I asked. "You're going to roam the Castoval like a vagabond?"

"I have money," he said. "And I've got skills. Maybe I'll become a fisherman."

"Or a cutpurse. You still have the crown, I suppose? Any thoughts on what you're going to do with it?"

Malekrin looked wary. "That's my problem, isn't it?"

"The only possible heir to the throne," I said, "wandering around with the crown of the Castoval. They'll never stop looking for you, you know. If it isn't your grandmother, it'll be the King. Or someone else... someone even worse, maybe."

"They won't find me."

"Oh? Because I had so much trouble."

Malekrin gave me another filthy look and returned aggressively to his porridge. I left him to it for a minute and then said, "There are other possibilities, you know. Other than becoming the next top warlord of Shoan or getting your head lopped off by your grandfather, I mean. If you're so smart and capable, why not put all that ability towards something useful? Like trying to stop a war?"

"Because it's not my war," he muttered, through a thick mouthful of gruel.

"I'm sure most of the people who'll die in it could say the same," I said. "But I doubt anyone will listen to them." Suddenly remembering, I added, "It certainly wasn't Saltlick's war, and that didn't do *him* any good."

Malekrin looked up again at that. "The monster?" he asked – and I was surprised by the note of genuine concern in his voice.

"He tried to stop the fighting," I said, "and got cut down in the street for his troubles. Come to think of it, maybe he isn't such a good argument for peace-brokering after all."

Malekrin dropped his gaze once more; but this time he didn't go back to eating. I'd almost given up expecting a response when he said, "I won't pretend to be something I'm not."

"I can see how that wouldn't appeal," I agreed.

"I never wanted any of this," Malekrin continued, as though he hadn't heard. "My father, my grandmother... it's always been about what *they* wanted. A unified Shoan. No more tithes to the King. But what does any of it have to do with me?"

I picked up my spoon, ran it around the rim of my bowl and looked regretfully at my now-cooling, untouched porridge. "Tell you the truth, Mal, I know how you feel. After all, I've been through exactly the same these last weeks. It's all, 'Damasco do this', 'Damasco do that', 'Damasco, why aren't you behaving more like a hero and less like the gutter thief you are?'... but whatever I do, however hard or often I try, it's never enough. I saved Altapasaeda, I've hardly stolen a thing in days, and still they treat me like something stinking and sticky they trod in."

Now there was clear confusion on Malekrin's face. "What are you saying?"

"I'm saying, maybe you're right. You should look after yourself, and damn the rest. They'd do the same to you if you gave them half a chance. In fact, they already have."

Malekrin put down his own spoon. He was aiming for the patch of table beside his bowl, but he misjudged, and the utensil slipped from the table's edge and clunked onto the tiles. Though Malekrin considered it with puzzlement, he made no effort to retrieve it. "Is this how you try and convince me to come back?" he asked. "Are you really the best they could send?"

"Well that's just it, isn't it? I'm all they could *spare*. Apparently, stopping the King and his army smashing their way into Altapasaeda and burning everyone in their beds is more important that wandering around the countryside looking for you. I tell you, they couldn't value either of us much less if they tried."

Malekrin knotted the fingers of his right hand in his dark hair and propped his elbow on the table, nearly tipping the bowl and the last dregs of his wine. Despite the much-needed meal, he was looking distinctly queasy. "If I go back," he said, "Grandmother will force me to lead her stupid army to their deaths; or else, your people will hand me over to the King. Either way, I end up dead."

"You probably will. In fact, there's no reason either of us should go back to that sewer of a city. I know we haven't exactly seen eye to eye so far, Mal, but if you'd tolerate a little company then I'm about ready to walk away from this whole damn mess."

Malekrin fixed his gaze on me, though he was wavering slightly on his crooked arm. "You know," he said, "you're terrible at this. No one could have done a worse job of trying to convince me."

I grinned. "You're Malekrin, son of Moaradrid and grandson of Kalyxis and King Panchessa. You've just run the length of three countries to avoid doing what other people thought you should do. I doubt anyone's ever going to talk you into anything you don't want, are they?"

Hesitantly, Malekrin returned a thin smile. "All right," he said. "I'll come with you. I'll try to stop this stupid war. But I'm not going back to my grandmother."

"I don't blame you," I said. "Frankly, the woman's terrifying."

"That's right. Terfiriying." Malekrin stared intently at the table's surface, like a baby entranced by the dance of motes in a sunbeam. "You know, Dasmacco, it's been... been..." His chin jolted forward on his fist, and with an effort he drew it back. "Whu... when?" he whispered, even as his eyes began to glaze.

"The sleeping draught? When I swapped the bowls," I explained conversationally. "Frankly, I'm surprised it took this long to kick in; you must have the constitution of a bull. I'm sorry, Mal, but I didn't want to rely on my powers of persuasion or your good nature. Well, who would?"

"I was... I was going to... come back..."

"I know that now," I agreed, as he toppled face first into the remains of his porridge, with a definite splash that showered gobs of grey across the table top. "However, as I just pointed out, I didn't want to take any chances. I hate to be the one to say it, but this thing's bigger than you and I – and I've a friend in Altapasaeda I promised I'd be back for."

To judge by the spluttering snores issuing from his porridge bowl, Malekrin wasn't paying me much attention anymore. I walked round and hauled him up by the shoulders, then wiped the worst of the gruel mess from his chin using the hood of his cloak.

If I remembered rightly, Franco's number twelve knock-out drops lasted for something in the region of six hours. Given Malekrin's youth and constitution, that might be reduced by an hour or so. Still, I had a fair while yet.

I sat gratefully back in my chair. If there was no hurry, I at least might as well finish my breakfast.

Having made the most of my cold porridge, I set out into Midendo. It soon became apparent that the chances of finding a second horse for purchase were up there with those of being offered a giant, saddle-trained rabbit; an hour's questioning, however, did lead me to an ancient cobbler willing to part with his equally venerable ass.

"He'll be dead soon enough," he pointed out, "and I will be too. At least now I can afford a proper pyre."

I handed over an onyx, hardly thinking about how grossly I was overpaying or how little I had left; having squandered a fortune, what difference could one more coin make? The ass was vicious and curmudgeonly, but since it would be Malekrin he'd be carrying rather than me, that seemed both appropriate and fair.

Back at the Nine Lights, it was frustrating to realise that all drugging Malekrin had left me with was an unconscious barbarian prince to transport back to Altapasaeda. Had I been able to trust him to make the right decision on his own I'd have saved myself the effort of hauling him onto the protesting beast and tying him in place.

At least Marga, who seemed to have more or less accepted my story that all this strange behaviour was in some way serving the Altapasaedan City Guard, came out to help me. "Who is he anyway?" she asked, as I pulled the last knot tight. "He certainly has funny clothes on under that cloak. Not one of that fiend Moaradrid's lot, is he?"

I was a little impressed that she'd even heard of Moaradrid all the way out there. "He's his son, in fact. Malekrin, the bastard Prince of Shoan, one possibly true heir to the thrones of the Castoval and Ans Pasaeda."

She glared at me. "All right," she said, "You could have just told me it was none of my business."

I gave her my most courteous bow. "Thank you, madam, for your kind hospitality, and for the excellent porridge. If I'm ever back this way, I'll be sure to call again."

"If you're ever back this way," Marga said, "you can sleep in the stables." And before I could even consider a suitable retort, she'd marched back inside and slammed the door on me.

••••

Malekrin woke some three hours later; perhaps three hours of being jolted on an uneven road while his extremities went steadily more numb had somehow accelerated the effect of Franco's soporific. When he began to struggle and curse, I was glad I'd taken the time to tie his knots tightly.

"Calm down," I told him. "I'll let you up once you stop thrashing. The ropes are only to stop you falling off. After all, you did say you were willing to come with me, didn't you?"

"I'll cut out your eyes for this, Damasco," he mumbled.

"No you won't. But if you're seriously considering it, perhaps I should leave you tied there a while longer."

Malekrin went silent for a while. Finally he said, a fraction more calmly, "Will you untie me?"

I was tempted to ask for a *please*, but the faint note of humility in his voice would have to do. I dismounted, stopped the ass in its tracks and with one of my knives severed a couple of the ropes that held Malekrin in place. When I was confident he wasn't about to tumble into the dirt, I cut another, so that he could sit up and massage his wrists; that done, I hacked away the cords holding his legs and ankles in place.

"Will you help me off?" he said. "I don't think I can stand."

I still wasn't quite convinced he wouldn't go for me at the first opportunity, but I lent him my shoulder, and with some difficulty Malekrin managed to half climb, half tumble down onto the road. I let him support himself against me for a minute, until he could stand alone.

"Do you have water?" he asked.

I'd picked up a skin of water, along with some food, before I left Midendo. I brought it over to him and he took a long swig, and then spat into the dust. "My mouth tastes like a dog threw up in it," he explained.

"That will be the knockout draught," I said. Then, feeling something more was called for, I added, "Look, Mal, perhaps

I should have given you the benefit of the doubt. Before I drugged you, I mean."

Malekrin shrugged, handed back the water skin. "I didn't give you much reason to."

"No," I agreed. "Still..."

"I think I can ride now," he said. "We should get moving."

We rode in silence after that. I didn't know what to make of Malekrin's mood, which seemed for once more introspective than hostile; nor was I interested enough to pay him much attention. It was a drizzly day, with a bite of autumn cold in the air, and as good as my new clothes were, they didn't quite keep me warm. Had the decrepit ass not been setting our pace then perhaps I could have ridden faster and warmed myself that way. As it was, trailing beside the miserable beast and its miserable rider only served to further spoil my humour.

I stopped around lunchtime and shared with Malekrin the food I'd bought: some stringy meat, corn bread and too-hard cheese. I sensed he'd have liked to refuse the meagre fare, but I could hear his stomach rumbling from where I was, and he was quick enough to wolf it down. Still, he said nothing beyond a curt thank you, and I felt no inclination to push for more.

When Altapasaeda came into view in the middle of the afternoon, it was exasperating to realise that my journey was still far from done. But I was certain the southern gates would be sealed and barricaded in case the King should move his attack, so rather than waste time in trying them I took the side road that wound off to the west, and Malekrin fell in behind me without comment or question.

I turned off again before I arrived back at the barracks, and we cut across to the half-derelict northern road, which threaded along the western flank of Altapasaeda. I thought about what might have been happening on the other side of those high walls while I'd been away, and the question was enough to make me wish I was heading anywhere but where I was.

By the time the western gate came into view, my worry had passed its peak and turned into a kind of numbed acceptance. A glance at Malekrin's pinched, vacant face made me wonder if he wasn't bearing his fate in similar fashion. Then again, maybe he was simply bored senseless from riding all day on the back of a slowly expiring ass.

I dismounted, looked up at the battlements. There was no one visible. I hammered on the gate and shouted, "Open up, it's Easie Damasco." Then, because that sounded less impressive than I'd hoped, I added, "I'm here with Prince Malekrin of Shoan."

I'd anticipated an interrogation, or perhaps nothing at all. For all I knew, the city had fallen and there was no one on the other side to care. But a mere few seconds had passed before the gate eased open. I recognised the guard on the other side from when I'd left that way. "Mounteban's expecting you," was all he said.

Expecting? A touch disappointed that I wouldn't be surprising anyone with my improbable success, I hauled myself back into the saddle and rode through the gap. I'd imagined the guard might accompany us, if our presence was so very important to Mounteban; however, he and his companion only ignored us in favour of forcing the gate shut in our wake.

I led the way up one street and then another, and five full minutes had passed before Malekrin said to me, "What now? Do you hand me over to this Mounteban? Do we find my grandmother, so I can explain I won't be going with her?"

I'd been asking myself a similar question – and I'd quickly realised that for me there was only one answer. Right then, for all I cared, Mounteban, Kalyxis and the whole damned city could go hang. "You can come along or not," I told Malekrin, "but before we do anything, I'm finding out if my friend's alive."

CHAPTER SIXTEEN

The hospital was noticeably fuller than when I'd last seen it.

Straw cots had been dragged in to fill the gaps between the existing beds, and all of those were occupied as well, so that the surgeons and priests had to tread carefully around and over the bodies of the wounded just to navigate the room. Their own numbers, however, hadn't increased; perhaps there were even fewer tending to the fallen than on my previous visit. I supposed that the influx of wounded hadn't been organised to take their endurance into account; certainly every one of those that remained looked ready to drop.

The air was noisome, a bitter-sweet odour of rot and sickness struggling to get out from beneath cloying layers of incense. A chorus of groans and sighs and the occasional, muted scream was undercut by the whine of the wind from outside, as it whipped the torch flames hovering around the walls. I hurried to push shut the door, and as I did so noticed the expression on Malekrin's face, the mingling of pity and disgust.

"So many?" he asked.

"Are you joking, boy?" grunted a red-robed surgeon as he brushed past. "They've filled two more warehouses since this one."

Looking round for Saltlick, I realised how much more varied the constituency of the injured had grown. Most, of course, were from Mounteban's improvised army, suspicious-eyed faces of hardened criminals beside professional soldiers staring stoically at the rafters, not to mention the occasional darker-skinned visage of a Shoanan far from his home. More surprising were the many in civilian garb, looking bewildered to have found themselves in such company; and most unexpected were the small group in what I recognised as Ans Pasaedan uniforms. These last were gathered in one corner, watched over by a couple of city guardsmen – though from what I could see of their wounds, the precaution was unlikely to prove necessary.

Finally I picked out Saltlick's bulk in the gloom. I hurried towards him whilst taking care not to accidentally plant my boot in a crumpled rib cage or stomp upon a shattered arm. The air was close and smoky, and it was only as I drew near that I realised he was sitting up. I couldn't resist the rush of hope that poured like bile up from my stomach into my throat – but it only took me a moment to understand that sitting was far from healed. Saltlick had been propped against the wall, his back supported by packed bundles of straw; however he was still bandaged from head to toe, his uncovered skin still latticed with cuts and gashes.

If my brief hope had been unjustified, though, perhaps so was the despair that had followed it. For the bandages were clean and mostly white, rather than reddened with seeping blood, just as most of his visible injuries were less shockingly raw than when I'd last seen him. Saltlick was alive, he was healing, and together that was more than I'd dared expect.

One other thing, too, went some way to assuaging my fears: Saltlick's eyes were open, and though his lids were heavy and drooping, he was looking at me. I bent down, bringing my head as close to his as I could manage. He smelled of straw and stale sweat, and very strongly of dried blood, a metal tang that I could taste on the roof of my mouth. "Saltlick? Can you hear me?"

After a pause so long that I'd all but given up on an answer, he nodded his head, just slightly.

"Stay still," I said. "It's all right. I just wanted to be sure you were really awake."

Saltlick tried to move his head once more, and this time I realised he meant to shake it.

"What? You're *not* awake?"

He made a noise, low in his throat. I felt sure it was meant to be a word, though whether in my own tongue or giantish, or nothing but nonsense, I couldn't tell.

"Stop it!" I said. "Saltlick, you're supposed to be resting."

Again he shook his head, and the effort made the ropes of muscle in his neck twitch and jump.

My visit wasn't going at all how I'd intended. Desperate to make him stay still, I shifted even closer, so that my head was tilted alongside his. "What is it?" I asked. "What are you trying to tell me?"

I felt his warm breath on my ear. Then he made another sound I couldn't understand. Perhaps he was just groaning; perhaps these noises were only broken-off fragments of whatever pains he was enduring. Then, just as I thought he must be delirious, I recognised the next whisper for a word – and the next, and the next. Three words: words I'd heard him say often enough, three words, indeed, that had made up the first full sentence he'd ever spoken to me.

No. More. Fight.

I knew he wasn't talking about himself; not even Mounteban would try and cajole him into violence in his current state. No, this time, I understood without doubt, Saltlick was asking for something far more than his own welfare.

"Saltlick, that's..." I was about to say, *too much responsibility.* I was about to explain that I was just one lowly, more or less former thief, that no one listened to me at the best of times and these were far from those, that there was probably no one in Altapasaeda less capable of influencing the giants' destiny than me. But before one more word could issue from my lips, I was brought up short by a hand upon my shoulder. Imagining that one of one of the wounded had risen from their deathbed to hiss some final vision in my ear, I choked off a scream and did my best not to tumble onto Saltlick.

"Calm down, Damasco! It's only me."

I span round, still not quite convinced that I wouldn't find myself face to face with some ghastly apparition. "Estrada? What are you doing here?"

Despite the faint amusement in her eyes, Estrada looked gaunt and weary; an expression not unlike those of the bustling surgeons and priests. "The guards on the western gate sent word that you'd entered the city," she said. "Mounteban is fuming, and Kalyxis is already claiming this was all some plot on his behalf. I told them I'd find you and bring you in."

"Oh," I said. The news was neither interesting nor surprising; probably it was only through the gate guards' negligence that Malekrin and I had stayed free for so long.

"I thought I might find you here," Estrada went on. "Anyway, it's been a few hours since I checked in on Saltlick."

Irritable for being treated like a downed hare to be dragged back and dumped at Mounteban's feet, I almost made some sharp reply. But even I could see that there was no way the desperately busy attendants had expended so much effort on Saltlick. It was surely Estrada I had to thank for the fact that he was alive and recuperating, and perhaps my anger was better saved for someone who deserved it.

"Fine," I said, "I'd hate for poor Mounteban to be worrying."

The crack of a sharp throat-clearing drew my attention, as it did Estrada's. Malekrin was observing us both with what I'd come to think of as his characteristic scowl. "Am I likely to be included in this conversation?" he asked, with what he probably intended as dignity.

"Prince Malekrin," said Estrada, "it's good to see you again. I hope you've found the Castoval to your liking?"

"The wilds of the Castoval are a hideous place compared to the flowing plains of Shoan," Malekrin said, "and their people uncouth and ignorant. I'd thought nothing could be worse until I came to this ugly, reeking city."

"You may find it grows on you," replied Estrada, her smile forced. "And I apologise if I excluded you. Was I wrong to assume you're here to reunite with your grandmother?"

"You were very wrong," said Malekrin. "I won't go anywhere with her. What I'm here to do, if you'll let me, is to help negotiate a peace." Malekrin glanced around the dark room then, and his eyes narrowed. "I think it would be a good alternative to this, don't you?"

"There's nothing I'd rather see you do than help stop this needless war," said Estrada, looking impressed almost despite herself. "And I promise you won't be made to do anything you don't want to."

Ah, Estrada, never one to shy away from a promise she had no means of keeping. Still, her earnestness seemed to satisfy Malekrin, and I was grateful for that – for just then I was finding his nobility almost as insufferable as his sulking.

"We should go now," Estrada added, speaking to me once more. "Delaying will only make a bad situation worse."

It struck me that I was more than ready to leave the grim confines of the hospital, even if it meant facing Mounteban and Kalyxis again. I glanced at Saltlick, thinking of our interrupted reunion for the first time since Estrada had arrived. His eyes were still open, and he was watching us. No, he was watching *me* – and while it was impossible to read anything from those glazed orbs, I couldn't but feel a sense of reproach. He'd asked for my help and I'd given him no assurance in return. After everything he'd done for me, all the times he'd saved my life, I hadn't even promised to try and help his people.

Yet what could I do? What promise could I make that wouldn't be empty? I had little enough idea how I was going to save myself, let alone an entire populace of giants trapped in a war-ravaged city. No, to say nothing would be less cruel in the long term than a comforting lie.

I tore my eyes from Saltlick's, with a feeling equal parts guilt and relief. "Let's go," I said, striving to keep both emotions from my voice. "If we hurry, the two of you might have this war settled before dinner."

Outside in the streets, night had fallen in earnest. Beyond the faint glow edging round the doors and shutters of the hospital, we were in thick darkness.

Ironic given her talk of haste, Estrada had arrived on foot, leaving Malekrin and I forced to lead our mounts; yet another irritation, given the aches I'd accumulated throughout the day. Malekrin, meanwhile, seemed grateful for the chance to preserve a little dignity, for he looked considerably less absurd leading the ass than riding it. Apparently the beast was determined to spend what life it had left in humiliating its new master, however, for we hadn't gone far before it began to protest in rasping brays.

I assumed it was that raucous noise that made Estrada hurry ahead, just as I had; but once she saw that we'd gained a few paces, she leaned closer and said, "It's good to see you back, Easie."

Still frustrated to be walking when I might be riding, I decided Estrada must be referring to the fact that she hadn't expected me to return. "Astonishing isn't it?" I said. "Who'd have guessed Mounteban wasn't the only lowlife who could sacrifice himself in the service of the Castoval."

Estrada ignored the jibe. "How did you convince him?" she asked, with a nod behind us.

"Oh, you know. Porridge, a sleeping draught, a few pots and pans... the usual. Also, and I know how absurd this sounds, but I think the boy actually *wants* to do the right thing."

"There's never been a better time for it," replied Estrada, with feeling.

"How have things been?" I asked. "With the war, I mean?"

"Truthfully, better than I'd dared hope. I don't think anyone really believed we could hold Panchessa out for even a day."

"But you have," I observed, redundantly.

"Half of Altapasaeda's up in arms now. After the first attack, they finally realised what was in store for them; our numbers had tripled by the second day. I think Panchessa had been expecting to just walk in by then, and it shook him when just the opposite happened. So far as I know, there's been no significant fighting since."

"Which means a siege," I suggested, a little irritated by her optimism.

"Not yet," she said, "So far, Panchessa's keeping his forces to the north wall. But if he can't win in a straight fight, there's every chance he'll try to starve us out."

I had no answer for that. It seemed self-evident to me that whether our ends came at the point of Ans Pasaedan blades or by slow starvation, we were every bit as doomed.

Then, as if countering an argument I hadn't bothered to make, Estrada continued, "I think Kalyxis and her Shoanish could be persuaded to join us, especially now that Malekrin's back. Either way, I can't shake the feeling that she's up to something. If I'm right and it involves Panchessa, there's a chance it might work to our benefit."

"That's wonderful," I said. "How can we lose with that mad witch on our side?"

Estrada gave me a look that, though it was difficult to read in the darkness, almost certainly meant *keep your voice down*. I darted a glance back at Malekrin, but he didn't seem to paying us any notice; all his concentration was on dragging the clamorous ass.

Obnoxious as he unquestionably was, it occurred to me that he was being remarkably rational for someone who had Kalyxis for a grandmother and Moaradrid for a father. Taking that lineage of evil and insanity into account, it was to his credit that he could even hold a conversation without frothing at the mouth. Perhaps there was an argument for cutting him more slack than I had so far.

Then again, he really *was* obnoxious.

Despite the lightless streets, I had a fair idea where we were. I knew we were drawing close to the Dancing Cat and I couldn't escape the sense, like a cord tightening around my neck, that whatever happened in the next few minutes would decide all of our fates. What would happen when Malekrin rebuffed Kalyxis? How would she react, and what would Mounteban do about it? Perhaps it might have been better for Altapasaeda if I'd left Malekrin wandering in the wilderness.

Rounding a corner, I saw a building not only lit up but bright amidst the surrounding blackness, as though its very existence was a remonstration with the night-shrouded city. Not only was torchlight seeping from every gap, a dozen lamps had been hung outside from ornate hooks that jutted from its beams.

On impulse, I dropped back to where Malekrin was trailing behind us. "We're nearly there," I said. "Are you ready?"

His only reply was a terse nod. Beneath the Dancing Cat's extravagant lighting, I could see that his mouth was set in a tight line, that his eyes were narrowed, like wounds cut into the dark skin. How long had Malekrin been preparing what he was about to say to Kalyxis?

Inevitably, there were armed men on the door of the Cat. They were quick to recognise Estrada, and made no argument when she asked them to take our mounts round to the stables.

I gave my horse a goodbye pat, and Malekrin and his ill-tempered ass parted with a look of mutual disgust.

As Estrada led the way inside, we were met by a rush of warm air, turbid with smoke and redolent with the odour of cooking food. The majority of the furnishings had been drawn together into one long table, which reached the length of the room. Around its far end, sat before heaps of maps and charts, were a great many people I recognised. There was Mounteban and a few of his hangers-on, Kalyxis and a couple of her Shoanish, and Alvantes, along with his sub-captains Gueverro and Navare.

All eyes turned at the creak of the door – and as Malekrin entered behind me, Kalyxis rose to her feet, though not hurriedly. "Malekrin," she said. From the indifference with which she spoke his name, no one could ever have guessed that she was reuniting with a lost relative she'd had every reason to fear she'd never see again.

"Grandmother," replied Malekrin. If anything, there was even less affection in his lifeless monotone.

"It's good that you're back," she said. "I don't know why you ran away and I don't care, so long as it never happens again."

"Grandmother," said Malekrin once more.

"What matters," Kalyxis went on, "is that you saw reason; that you realised your responsibility to your people is something you can't outrun."

"Grandmother..." repeated Malekrin yet again, and this time there was definite heat in his voice – though no one but me and perhaps Estrada appeared to notice. I realised I was holding my breath, for there was something in Malekrin's face that made me think of a storm that had been building for far too long.

Then there came a hammering upon the tavern door, and I started so violently that I nearly tumbled over a nearby chair. My held breath flooded out in a great whoosh.

"What is it?" roared Mounteban.

The door sprung open, and one of the men who'd been on guard outside hurried in. "Sir, you said you weren't to be disturbed once these three arrived–."

"And yet here you are," said Mounteban, "clearly disturbing us."

The guard blanched, nodded. "Only," he said, "there's a runner out here from the barricade on the Sabre. The bridge..."

"What *about* the bridge?" Mounteban asked. This time there was genuine enquiry in his voice.

"Sir," said the guard, "I think this is something you'll want to see. Some men have arrived over the Sabre, and they're asking for Captains Ondeges and Alvantes."

I couldn't but be impressed by the fortifications prepared for the great river-spanning arch of the Sabre. With no gate to protect it, the bridge was theoretically a weak point in the city's defences; though in truth its narrow, unsheltered span favoured its defenders over any attacker. Now, however, it was every bit as impenetrable as the city walls – for a barricade had been built along its Altapasaedan edge, not only of thick timbers but of great stone blocks, piled higher than a man's height in places.

It had probably never occurred to anyone to expect visitors from that direction. As we drew near, I could see – by the light of torches set upon tripods – that the men there were only just now drawing close to clearing an entrance for the mysterious arrivals.

Since everyone had been curious to accompany Alvantes, since Mounteban had insisted on bringing ample security in case this was some underhand attack, and since the swelling of our numbers had required him to requisition every nearby coach and horse, we made quite a convoy as we approached along the upper dockside. Our arrival had apparently spurred on the barricade-dismantling party, and by the time I climbed from the coach I'd managed to hitch a lift on, they were just levering a last beam out of the way. Even as I watched, one signalled towards the gap, and a man rode into the crescent of flickering torchlight.

Though he was elderly, it was clear that whatever vexations of age he'd suffered had been amply cushioned by wealth and the comforts of high living. He rode stiff-backed, with his chin tilted back, as though intent on something occurring just above our heads. Ignoring the traveller's usual discretion, his riding cloak was of a bright crocus yellow that seemed almost luminous beneath the amber light; the four companions following behind him, burly types with swords conspicuous at their sides, wore a similar though less dazzling shade.

His appearance, there upon the barricaded bridge, riding with all the studied casualness of a guest arriving at a banquet, was startling enough in itself. Yet it wasn't that that held my attention. Rather, it was the realisation that I'd met this man before.

"Senator Gailus," cried Alvantes from behind me. "This is a genuinely unexpected pleasure."

Yes, that was it, *Gailus*. I'd met him during my and Alvantes's ill-fortuned trip to Pasaeda; indeed, it was thanks to his assistance that we'd left with our heads. Gailus was an acquaintance of Alvantes's father – or had been, rather, until Alvantes Senior's brutal murder at the hands of the King's assassins.

"Lunto Alvantes," called back Gailus, his voice firm despite its fluty, birdcall pitch. "It's good to see you again, my boy. I offer my deepest condolences as to the death of your father. I hope you'll believe me when I say that it's shaken us all to our very cores."

"Thank you," replied Alvantes, and the emotion tugging at the edges of his voice was unmistakable.

"But what of Captain Ondeges?" asked Gailus, over the tap of his horse's hooves upon the cobbles. "Is he not here with you?"

"As far as we know," replied Alvantes, "he's left the city to side with the King."

"That's disappointing," said Gailus, with a shake of his frail head. "Still, it may be that his motives are better than you give him credit for."

He drew his horse up before us, and his men fanned into a semicircle behind him. "I wish there were time for pleasantries," he continued, "however you know better than I that time is short." Looking around, he took in the considerable crowd gathered beyond the bridge. "You represent the defenders of this city, yes? Then what I have to say concerns all of you... and may even provide a little comfort. Do I have your permission to disclose my news, Lunto?"

Alvantes glanced at Estrada and, to my surprise, at Mounteban as well. When neither offered any comment, he said to Gailus, "Of course. If you've come so far to tell it, I've no doubt it must be important."

"Oh, imperative," Gailus agreed, "vital beyond measure." Glancing around once more, Gailus raised his voice to a more oratory volume. "This war is being fought without the backing of the Pasaedan Senate," he exclaimed, "and so is unconstitutional. In fact, since the assassination of Senator Alvantes, the Senate has temporarily withdrawn its support from the Crown. The King is here, in short, against the laws of his own land and against the will of his people."

It took a long moment for that to sink into the crowd, no doubt because most of them were unfamiliar with the intricacies of Ans Pasaedan politics. I hadn't quite followed what Gailus had said either, but I'd gathered enough during my time in Pasaeda to understand the point: the King wasn't supposed to go running around making wild decisions and picking fights without the say of the Senate, and the Senate had had enough.

As everyone at last reached the same conclusion as I had, there arose a ragged cheer. I didn't join in. Whatever the Senate might think, their disapproval hadn't stopped Panchessa bringing his armies to the walls of Altapasaeda, so what good could it do now?

"I've come here to negotiate with his highness," said Gailus, once the applause had subsided. "And to tell him that if he continues with this course of action, he will not be welcomed into Pasaeda upon his return."

A coup, then, was it? Well that was more interesting – but would it be enough to distract Panchessa, when he'd already come this far? Most of those listening seemed to think so, for there came a second cheer, more certain than the first.

As silence once more descended, Alvantes moved closer to Gailus. "You've brought good news indeed," he said, "and we're grateful. But you should rest now. You must be exhausted."

"And what if Panchessa should attack at dawn?" replied Gailus. "No, I must see him as soon as possible. He must know that his people won't tolerate this scandalous war. Only brief me on what I need to know and I'll be gone."

"Then at least take a coach the last distance," suggested Estrada.

Gailus nodded. "Gracious of you, my lady. I think that's a luxury I can afford myself, at least."

He dismounted, and Alvantes nodded to one of his own men to take the senator's horse. I was annoyed when Alvantes picked out the coach I'd arrived in, the one I was still waiting beside, apparently unnoticed in the darkness beyond the torchlight.

Then, as Gailus was stepping towards the door Alvantes held for him, he said softly, "There's something else... something I didn't want to say in front of your troops."

Alvantes paused. "Go on."

"There have been rumours for months now that the King's health was poor. After he left, we finally managed to convince one of his physicians to speak."

"It's serious, I take it?"

"More than serious. The King is dying, and has been for months now. Who knows how long he has left?"

"Hence his recklessness," said Alvantes, thoughtfully.

"Panchessa has *always* been reckless," observed Gailus. "But yes, I can't believe he'd have gone this far if he was in his right mind. In any case, that was the weight that tipped the Senate's decision. The question of succession is paramount now. The King must be made to see reason, while there's still time."

Gailus looked up then, smiled and nodded as if they'd been discussing some trivial matter, and beckoned to his four escorts, who had already dismounted. "Well," he said, "whether or not his highness is expecting me, it never does to keep your king waiting."

A few moments later and the coach was trundling from view towards the Market District, with Alvantes and a couple of his guardsmen riding escort. As I watched them go, I wondered what all of these new revelations added up to. Could it really be that the war might be almost over, when to all intents and purposes it had barely started?

I didn't want to put too much faith in Gailus; it wasn't as if things had ended particularly well the last time we'd met. Nevertheless, I couldn't shake the thought, the dim possibility wheedling at the back of my brain, that for the first time since I'd heard the King was marching upon Altapasaeda, we had a genuine chance.

Maybe I'd ducked my unlucky fate yet again. Maybe I could keep the promise I hadn't dared make to Saltlick. And maybe, just maybe, this whole horrible mess would end without more bloodshed.

CHAPTER SEVENTEEN

By the cold light of the next day, my optimism regarding Gailus had dimmed and my doubts had hardened to a certainty. When armies were facing off, when mad kings were on the loose and the fates of entire lands hung in the balance, what difference could one elderly senator make to anything?

Not much, it seemed, for the morning brought no word from Gailus. That it brought no further attacks either might have been considered a good sign; however, the quiet beyond the walls might as easily mean the King had concluded that a few weeks of siege would make his final victory all the more effortless. Likely, Gailus was now in chains somewhere, or else his head was atop a pole before Panchessa's tent, as a cautionary message to anyone else who might think they knew the King's affairs better than he.

With the excitement of the previous night vanished like some hobgoblin, all I could feel was disgust at myself for daring to get my hopes up. If not everyone was quite as despondent as I, nevertheless the general mood was dour. There was much hushed discussion amongst Alvantes, Estrada, Mounteban, Kalyxis and the many lesser players of note in Altapasaeda's convoluted drama. From what little I could catch, no one had any more idea of what might be occurring outside the walls than I did. The men posted upon the ramparts had reported nothing, and nobody could agree how long Gailus's negotiations might be expected to take, assuming they were taking place at all.

At least, having risen late from a makeshift bed in the Dancing Cat's stables, I managed to wrangle a decent breakfast, the staff there apparently accepting that I was connected with Mounteban while thankfully failing to consider just what that connection entailed. And at least, with my breakfast over, I had time to look in on Saltlick once more. For once, no one seemed interested in my affairs, and with Malekrin delivered as promised, it appeared I was once again a free agent.

If it seemed redundant to check on Saltlick so soon after my last visit, I could think of no more useful way to pass my time, and at least it might set my mind at rest for another day. Perhaps, too, I'd have the opportunity to explain why I was so ill-suited to the responsibility he'd tried to foist on me the night before.

I considered inviting some company, but Estrada was busy and Malekrin nowhere to be seen. I set out to find the weather warmer than it had been for the last couple of days, the sky clear of cloud or drizzle. Feeling livelier wandering the streets than I had cooped up in the Dancing Cat, I found that by the time I drew near the hospital, my attitude had grown more pessimistic than outright gloomy.

It was a good thing, too, for a strange sight awaited me as I turned onto the street: four giants stood upon the cobbles, a litter of split timbers and sail cloth hoisted between them, and upon that makeshift stretcher lay Saltlick. The giants were talking amongst themselves in their own language, but from the way they shuffled about, swapped hands and such, I guessed they were debating how best to carry their fragile charge without tripping over each other's feet. There was a surgeon with them, too, recognisable by his ambiguously red robes and currently glaring at the ensemble as though they'd gathered there purely to tax his patience.

"What's going on?" I asked him. "Where are they taking Saltlick?"

"Oh, how should I know?" he growled. "Do you think I understand a word of that nonsense they're spouting? Back wherever they came from, I suppose."

I decided to try a different tack. "But why?" I said. "Why are they moving Saltlick at all?"

At that, the surgeon finally looked round at me. "You're the one who was here last night," he observed bitterly. Then, perhaps realising I hadn't actually done anything to annoy him, he began again, "One of the priests complained to that man Mounteban, you see, about how much space the giant was taking up; space that could be used for wounded... you know... *people*."

"Castilio Mounteban? He's been here?"

"At the crack of dawn, damn him. He asked if the giant was fit to be moved and we told him yes. The next we knew..." He waved towards the giants. "The next we knew, this."

I felt that there was some detail I must be overlooking. "Isn't that what you wanted?"

The surgeon looked at me with new focus, as if unwilling to waste more words until he was certain of exactly how stupid I was. "You've seen what it's like in there," he said. "It's been chaos for an hour and more, while we tried to work out a way to get them in so we could get *him* out. I'm only wasting more time now because I want to be damn certain they're leaving."

We both glanced aside then at the sound of heavy footfalls. I saw that the four attendants, having successfully lifted Saltlick between them in such a way that no thumbs were squashed or giant toes stubbed, were now moving off down the street.

"That's it!" the surgeon declared, starting towards the open hospital doors. "Thank all the gods. Can you even imagine what it was like moving a thing that size through a hospital?"

"He's not a thing," I called at his disappearing back. "He's the hero who saved this city." Then, as it struck me that perhaps I shouldn't be lecturing about heroism to someone who'd been on their feet for days tending the wounded, I turned quickly away and hurried after the retreating party of giants.

So far as I could judge, they were heading towards the former tannery that had become their home. With Saltlick raised above my head height, I could only see a portion of his nearer side; but even that limited view was enough to make my breath catch in my throat. Though Saltlick's powers of recuperation had always amazed me, the wounds I'd seen him recover from before were nothing to what he'd sustained in the recent fighting. It seemed, however, that his remarkable constitution was finally rising to the challenge. Saltlick looked noticeably better than he had the night before, his deeper cuts appeared to be knitting – and best of all, he was sitting up, propped on one knobbly elbow.

"Saltlick!" I called.

I'd managed to almost catch up, though I'd had to sprint to match the giants' strides. Saltlick's gaze drifted down to me and he smiled.

"I won't keep you," I said, rather foolishly, for there was little I could have done to stop the marching giants except throw myself beneath their feet. "I just wanted to see how you are."

"Better," Saltlick agreed. His voice was rasping, but clearer.

"And you're going to be with your people?"

Saltlick nodded, though the gesture made little sense when delivered from the bobbing surface of the stretcher.

"That's wonderful," I panted – for by then, the giants having failed to slow to accommodate me, I was starting to severely lose my breath. "So... you can keep them safe. You won't need me... after all. Well, I'm sure... I'll see you soon..."

If Saltlick answered I didn't hear, for at that point a stitch dug hard into my side and I had to slow to a hobble. I watched, panting, as the bizarre spectacle of the giant stretcher-bearers vanished around the next corner.

Even ignoring the pain jabbing at my ribs, the encounter had left me deflated. Perhaps it was just that Saltlick hadn't thought to ask his bearers to slow for me; such inconsiderateness wasn't like him. Had it been that he didn't want to speak to me? After what he'd endured, maybe I had no right to blame him. However good my intentions, I was the one who'd brought the giants to Altapasaeda, the one who'd first put weapons into their hands; then, when Saltlick had asked me to try and repair the harm I'd unwittingly done, I'd let him down.

Not knowing what else to do with myself and hoping there might have been some report regarding Gailus, I trudged reluctantly back to the Dancing Cat. Even the news that the King was cooking him on a spit outside our gates would have cheered me up just then. However, the taproom was all but empty, with three men in Altapasaedan uniform talking beside the bar and a couple of Kalyxis's barbarians hovering close to the doorway. There was also one person sitting conspicuously on their own: Malekrin was moping near the fireplace with his chin planted firmly upon his fist and his hood drawn over his face.

"What are you doing here?" I asked, keeping my voice low enough that the Shoanish by the door wouldn't overhear. "Don't tell me Mounteban's letting you stay after you had things out with your grandmother?"

Malekrin's mouth turned down even further. "I couldn't get a word in to argue with her," he muttered. "She wouldn't even listen long enough to hear how I can't stand her."

I pulled up a stool opposite his. "So why sit here sulking?" I asked. "Go talk to her now."

Malekrin shook his head inside the cowl. "She says she's too busy to see me. Just like she's always been! A straw doll with my name would be every bit as much use to her."

And it would complain less too, I thought, and then immediately felt uncharitable. Despite myself, I did feel a little sorry for Malekrin this time. Not only had his planned reckoning with his grandmother come to nothing, his role as potential saviour and ender of wars had been effortlessly supplanted by Gailus. Now here he was, trapped alone in an unwelcoming city, with nowhere to go and nothing useful to occupy his time.

"Look Mal," I said, "why don't I show you a little of Altapasaeda? Better than sitting here moping."

Malekrin looked at me with disgust. "I've seen more than enough of this loathsome place," he said.

With little personal affection for Altapasaeda, I merely grinned at him. "It's a little better by daylight, but not much. I'll leave you to your woeful thoughts then."

I stood up and started back towards the door, drawing a hostile glance from the two Shoanish there.

Then, just I was about to leave, Malekrin called after me. "Damasco..."

I paused.

"Another time, maybe?"

It was the first occasion I could remember that he'd sounded at all contrite. "Why not?" I said. "It isn't as if either of us has anything better to do."

I didn't see Malekrin again that day, however, or anyone else I was familiar with for that matter. There was a part of me that was eager for company, or at least a little conversation, and at one point I even found my feet drawing me towards Franco's deceptively tumbledown home. But that was a level of desperation too far; if I was even considering passing my time with that antique swindler then I was better off on my own.

Instead, I wandered to a small inn near the Temple District that I had fond memories of from my time in the city. The place had apparently changed hands since then, for I didn't recognise the woman unhurriedly cleaning tables with a rag, but the smell of food from the back rooms was enticing and there were tables out front where I could enjoy the day's warmth.

Moreover, I practically had the place to myself. I'd have imagined that taverns would do good business in times of war, but it seemed the opposite was true. Could it be that all the able-bodied drinking men were atop the walls instead, pulling faces and rattling sabres at Panchessa's army? Knowing Altapasaedans, they were more likely to be hiding in their cellars. I ordered my lunch, a well-spiced dish of rice and vegetables with a few thin slices of sausage mixed in, and it turned out to taste every bit as good as it smelled. I ordered a glass of wine to go with it, and immediately corrected myself; a bottle would be more suited to my plans for the day.

As it transpired, however, one bottle turned into two, and by then it was late afternoon and a few other patrons had arrived, and the second bottle didn't last very long at all; fortunately a third soon materialised in its place, and at around the same time I found myself singing an old village tune regarding the many and varied loves of a certain wheelwright's daughter, which others were eager enough to join in with, and from there we somehow managed to begin a round of Lost Chicken with a pack of greasy and well-thumbed cards...

After that, unfortunately, my perceptions grew unreliable. I only knew that it was dark when I staggered back towards the Dancing Cat and tumbled into my bed in the stables.

I was pleased in the morning to discover that I'd ended the previous day slightly richer than I'd begun it, a tremendous feat considering how drunk I'd been and that I'd hardly even been cheating; the gain was more than balanced out, though, by the pain steadily erupting throughout my head.

When the discomfort of lying in agony and scrunching my eyes against the light from the part-open doorway became too much, I hauled myself to me feet and staggered through to the kitchens, where I explained more through gestures than words that I'd need breakfast and a great quantity of water. The cook, having presumably grown used to unreasonable demands under Mounteban's patronage, managed to slop a dish of stewed apples before me, along with a cup and a pitcher of water. I did my best to grin at him in thanks, and he hurried away, looking disgusted.

Breakfast and three brimming cups of water having gone some way to relieving my head, I wandered on through to the taproom. Just as yesterday, there was no one of any importance around; Malekrin, however, was back in his corner, or perhaps had never left. This time he'd found a small flute from somewhere, and was playing a doleful tune to himself.

"Stop that," I said, "I won't be hung over and miserable as well. I need to clear my head and you need to get out of this place for a couple of hours. I won't take no for an answer."

The look on Malekrin's face told me that *no* was precisely the answer I should expect, regardless of my feelings on the matter, yet at the last moment, he stood up and said, "Maybe you're right."

"I'm always right," I said. Then a particularly violent pang threatened to split my head in two, and I amended, "Well, mostly I am. But this time, definitely..."

I came up with a route that took in the dockside, the Temple District and the mansions of the South Bank, but which carefully avoided the palace; I doubted it would do anything for Malekrin's mood to see what luxury his uncle Panchetto had grown up in while he was languishing in the wastelands of Shoan.

All told, however, Malekrin proved to be more tolerable company than I'd come to expect. As our walk wore on and as my aching head began to clear, I pointed out particular buildings and shared what anecdotes I could remember: "that's the home of Lord Alfunsco who married both of his own sisters", "that's where Lord Eldunzi lives, I hear he was recently flogged in the streets by the good people of Muena Delorca", and so on.

I could tell Malekrin was more impressed than he was willing to admit. It was there in his eyes as he stared up at the magnificent buildings that housed the Altapasaedan rich and their innumerable deities. More and more as the day wore on, he inserted his own observations, drawing comparisons – mostly negative – with his life in Shoan and even beginning to share his own tales. I was astonished to discover that when he wasn't sulking, Malekrin could be both amicable and moderately interesting.

Finally, as we started back in the direction of the Dancing Cat, I felt the time was right to ask a question that had been nagging at me all through the last few hours. "So... you gave the crown back to Kalyxis then, I imagine?"

Malekrin looked at me, surprised. "No. I told her I lost it."

"That you *lost* it? I can't imagine that went down well."

"I told her I dropped my pack when I was climbing out from the tunnel," he said.

"And you're still alive? You're even still walking straight. Surely she must have done *something* to you?"

"She shouted. Then, when she'd calmed down, she told me, 'It won't matter in the end. A crown's just a crown.'"

That didn't sound anything like the Kalyxis I knew. What could she be up to that she would dismiss the most valuable object in the land so casually? "Do you know what she meant?" I asked.

"No," replied Malekrin – and yet something in the way he pronounced that one syllable, some subtle hint, made me suspect he knew full well. But I could also tell that he had no intention of sharing his knowledge with me, and I was still far too hungover to press him. "So that was the end of it?" I asked instead.

"Oh, she sent men to search," he said.

"I'm guessing they won't find anything."

"No," agreed Malekrin, sounding both proud and a touch bashful. "They'll never find it. She'll never give it to that fat jackal of a man Mounteban. There won't ever be another prince crowned in Altapasaeda. It seemed the least I could do."

Only then did I realise why I'd been wondering so much about the crown, and why I'd raised the question of its whereabouts. "What if it could be put to a good purpose, though?" I asked. "What if it could help someone who really needed it? Who would never misuse it?"

Malekrin eyed me quizzically. "I hope you're not talking about yourself," he said.

"Hardly!" I scoffed. "I had the thing once and I gave it away."

"Then, if there really was such a person... I think I'd be glad to be rid of it."

I presented Malekrin with my finest and most carefully composed grin. "In that case, Mal, I have a proposition for you..."

The building that had been given over to the giants was in a region of the city I'd never been familiar with, and it took me nearly an hour to find it. Yet once I did, I knew I could never have missed it, for the smell thereabouts remained distinctively loathsome, and now two giants stood sentry, one to either side of the doors. Unmoving, they looked more like carved colossi than living beings.

"I'm here to see Saltlick," I told them cheerfully.

When no response came, I started towards the doors. Before I was halfway there, the two giants had sidestepped to block my way. It wasn't a threatening motion exactly, no more than creatures twice as tall and broad as me were threatening by their very nature. Yet there was no way I could get past them unless they let me.

"Perhaps you didn't understand," I told them – and then realised that, given the language difference, that was almost certainly the case. I tried again, more slowly. "I'm here to see Saltlick. He's my friend. Can you tell him Easie Damasco is waiting outside to see him?"

The two looked at each other. Then the one to the left crouched and ducked through the entrance. Confident that the remaining giant wouldn't do anything to harm me, I thought about hurrying after – but before I could do more than consider it, he'd moved to cover the entrance.

I waited impatiently. The former tannery reeked every bit as much as it had the first time I'd been there, and it didn't help that it was a warm day. Eventually, just as my head was beginning to throb once more, the first giant returned.

"You've spoken to Saltlick? I can come in?" I asked.

The giant shook his head.

"What? There must be some mistake."

He shook his head again. I had no idea if he even understood a word I was saying.

I couldn't believe Saltlick would turn me away, and while it was both possible and likely that the giant sentry had failed to convey who I was, I was sure he could have guessed. Taking those assumptions into account, I was at a loss; not even I could talk my way past guards who spoke a different language. Of course, now that I considered, there were valid reasons why Saltlick might not want to see me. Maybe his condition had taken a turn for the worse, maybe his extraordinary constitution had finally passed its limits. But there was no comfort to be found in thoughts like that.

Whatever the truth, I now had a dilemma. I stood for what felt like minutes, completely ignored by the two giants, as I stared at the bundle in my hands. Only after a seeming age did it occur to me that whatever was the *right* thing to do with the object wrapped within, it wasn't something I felt comfortable or sensible in holding onto any longer than I had to. I proffered it to the giant I'd spoken to before, and said, "Will you at least give him this? Tell him, 'With the compliments of Easie Damasco and Prince Malekrin'."

The sentry ducked inside once more. When he returned, his hands were empty. I could only hope he'd done as I asked, and not just dropped the crown of Altapasaeda into the nearest giant privy. I nodded a curt goodbye to the two guards, which both ignored, and started back up the street in the direction I'd come from.

As I neared the corner, I found my feet dragging. I had nowhere to go, nothing to do. I was depressed to have to admit to myself that I missed Saltlick, that my visit had been as much for my benefit as his. I'd grown too used to his presence. In some indefinable way, I'd come to rely on it. Now, without him around, I felt adrift.

I stopped at the first junction and wondered what I could possibly do with myself. Yet a mere few seconds had passed before my contemplation was disturbed, by the rumble of approaching wheels. Moments later, a coach swung around the next corner, covered the distance to the giants' building at speed and pulled up outside. Just as with my own visit, the sentries hardly acknowledged its presence. Nor did they respond when a figure pushed through the double doors and stepped quickly into the carriage.

But I did – with a sharp gasp of disbelief. For though I'd only caught a fleeting glimpse, I was certain the man I'd seen had been Castilio Mounteban.

A thousand questions sprang up altogether, and proceeded to row at each other across the narrow space of my skull. What did Mounteban want with the giants? Could he really have the temerity to try and talk them into fighting again? If so, pacifists or no, how had they refrained from smashing his head like a week-old egg?

But under all that, a barb hidden almost beneath the level of my conscious thoughts, was one last, whispered doubt:

Was Mounteban's presence the reason Saltlick had refused to see me?

Back at the Dancing Cat, there wasn't anyone around, not even Malekrin. I moved on to another nearby inn and ate there, a greasy meal of dried fish and overcooked vegetables. I barely had the energy to finish a bottle of wine, and I certainly wasn't ready for a repeat of the last night's revelry. Instead, I went early to my bed in the stables and did my best to sleep.

The next morning I was woken by someone hammering at the door. When I staggered bleary-eyed to the opening, I was surprised to see Malekrin, framed against the dull grey of a sky that still belonged more to night than day.

"Hurry up," he said, as excited as I could remember ever seeing him, "they're saying Gailus is back."

Even as he spoke, half a dozen men in Altapasaedan uniform shoved past me into the stable. "Clear the way!" one barked.

I considered a pithy retort, but it was obvious they only wanted to saddle the horses and hitch the coach kept there. I stepped into the yard and asked Malekrin, "So Gailus is still alive, eh? Any idea what news he's brought?"

Malekrin shook his head. "There are more coaches waiting out front," he said. "My grandmother, Mounteban and the others are going to meet with him. If you hurry, there's a place for you."

After so much time, I was curious to hear what Gailus had to say for himself. I followed Malekrin through the Dancing Cat and outside. The place he'd been referring to turned out to be on the back board of the third carriage in line, but I decided

I could tolerate a little discomfort for so short a journey. I clambered up, Malekrin vanished inside, and we were off.

It only took a few minutes to reach the northwestern gate. There were coaches and riders everywhere; word must have travelled quickly about Gailus's return. Gailus himself was sat upon a chair that someone had brought out for him, practically in the middle of the street. It would have been a comical sight if the man had only been in a better state. Gailus had looked tired the last time I saw him, but it had been the simple weariness of an old man who'd endured too much hard travel. Now, I could readily have believed that he hadn't slept a moment since.

When Alvantes and Estrada debussed from another of the coaches, Gailus managed to put on a weak smile. "Ah, Lunto. Lady Estrada. How good to see you both again," he said.

"And you," replied Estrada. "We were worried for your safety."

"Rightly so, I'm afraid," agreed Gailus. "I can't honestly say that the last two days have been agreeably spent." He sighed, as though at a particularly troublesome memory. "I dare say however, that they've been productive."

"The King is willing to talk truce?" asked Mounteban, climbing down from inside the same coach that had brought Alvantes and Estrada.

"He is," said Gailus. "With the three of you, as I'd hoped."

"Thank you," Alvantes said. "Your efforts may well have saved this city and its people."

"I can only take so much credit," replied Gailus. "You will be glad to hear that you have other advocates in the King's camp, not least of them Commander Ondeges, who has argued tirelessly for peace, at great risk to himself." A shadow of worry passed across Gailus's brow. "Also, you might not wish to talk about salvation just yet. The King is willing to talk, but that isn't to say he's willing to listen."

"Could this be a trap?" asked Mounteban.

Gailus shook his head. "I don't believe so. I'm convinced Panchessa is earnest in his desire to bring this matter to a peaceable conclusion, or I'd never have returned. He's sworn you safe passage, and in front of his generals. It would go badly for him if he were to break his word. However, his highness *did* impose conditions." Gailus glanced in my direction then, but I quickly realised he was looking past me. "Foremost among them, that the boy Malekrin also be present."

I looked back, was alarmed to see Kalyxis standing close behind me. I assumed she'd refuse or argue, for if it was obvious to me that regardless of Gailus's opinion this could easily be a trap, it must be doubly clear to her. Yet she hardly hesitated in answering: "I will accompany my grandson," she said.

I glanced at Malekrin, where he stood a pace behind his grandmother, once again expecting some words of protest. Now that he had his opportunity to try and win peace, would he really have the nerve to go through with it? Perhaps I'd seen a different side of him recently, but it was hard to believe he'd put his neck on the line with so little to gain.

Yet, as surprising as noble self-sacrifice would have been, it was something a little different that Malekrin had in mind. "I'll go," he said, "if Damasco comes with me."

"What? Are you insane?" Then, realising that might not be the appropriate tone to take, I added, "What I mean to say is, given my... shall we say, *spotted* history... and considering that the last time I saw the King he was ordering my death... well, I'm not sure it would be entirely appropriate."

Malekrin glowered at me. "It's your fault I'm here, isn't it? Then I don't see why you should get to avoid this."

Of course not. Why would there be a danger under the Castovalian skies that Easie Damasco should avoid being dragged into? No matter than it was none of my business, no matter that it made as much sense as asking a fox to a chicken market. Well, not this time. Prince or no, Malekrin was the only person I knew whose opinion counted for less than mine; for once, I wasn't obliged to be led by the nose into certain peril.

"I agree," said Kalyxis. "The thief should come with us."

Oh no was what I thought. What I actually said, sounding only marginally more aggrieved than I felt, was, "*The thief?*"

Kalyxis looked at me, with eyes like shards of black ice. "I'm sorry," she said. "Is that not your job title?"

I'd have liked to argue, but I supposed she had a point. "All right. But I don't see what I have to offer in such esteemed company. You don't *really* want me to steal from the King, do you?" I'd meant it to sound jovial, but just then nothing would have surprised me.

"You will accompany my grandson," Kalyxis said, "and advise him on local customs he might, through ignorance of this beleaguered backwater, fail to comprehend."

Ah, so I was to be the wet-nurse. I looked to Estrada for support, but she chose not to catch my eye; no one else there even seemed worth the effort of trying. "Well," I replied, "I'm sure that if the royal conversation should turn to matters of drinking, card play or larceny, I'll prove an invaluable asset."

The instructions Gailus conveyed were clear: No horses; no carriages; an escort allowed, but numbering no more than fifty; we could keep our swords, except in the royal presence, but could carry no bows. Sensible precautions all – but whether for a conference or an ambush, who could say?

Thus it was that I found myself in the front line of a great throng of men and women packed before the northwestern gate. Behind us were a mixed crowd of Alvantes's hardier guardsmen, Kalyxis's bodyguards and a number of Altapasaedan soldiers, in their new and yet already well-worn uniforms. As the last remnants of the barricades were dragged away, as the gates began to part and I found myself edged forward by a sudden press of bodies from behind, I tried to imagine what a real army would look like by comparison.

The gates opened wider, the pressure against my back increased – and suddenly I was stumbling into the gloom of the gatehouse. I was vaguely aware of Malekrin to my left, and another man – Alvantes? – to my right.

Then we were through, into the light, into the slum known as the Suburbs – and into the territory that was now our enemy's.

CHAPTER EIGHTEEN

It had been one thing to know that an army was camped on the city's doorstep, that nothing but stones and mortar separated me from thousands of bloodthirsty enemies. It was another thing entirely to see that horde with my own eyes.

The Suburbs had been evacuated days before: at first according to personal discretion, as its inhabitants came to realise that being between the King and the city had the potential to be bad for their health; then later, in the case of those too foolhardy or desperate to reach the obvious conclusion, with the encouragement of Mounteban's soldiers. Some refugees had been allowed into the city, on the condition that they earned their keep by aiding in its defence. Others had decamped for who knew where, fleeing into the hills, or across the river in their shabby rowboats and coracles.

By the time the King had arrived, there would have been no one left but a few stragglers and strays: the mad, the lost and the severely unlucky. I didn't want to think about what might have happened to them – for the Suburbs as I'd known it was no more.

Faced with the question of how to camp an army in the middle of a slum, the King and his generals had come to the obvious conclusion: use what they could and obliterate whatever they couldn't. The buildings nearest the walls had been left alone, for they provided good cover. Beyond the reach of bowshot, however, the flimsy structures were simply gone, as though some monumental storm had swept through and carried its debris with it.

At first we'd marched through the remnants of the Suburbs, and aside from the sentries watching our passage from each shadowed doorway and alley, it had almost been possible to pretend the place was as it always had been. Then we came to the end of a crooked street between ramshackle walls and, abrupt as if a line had been carved into the ground, the remnants of the Suburbs ended and the camp of our enemy began.

Beyond that point, there was nothing to see but tents and fighting men. Everyone had come out to see the ambassadors of their foes, and to mock, perhaps, at how paltry our strength was; or else, more likely, the King's first gambit was to show us how hopelessly outmatched we were, how badly a failure at the discussion table would cost us. For entering the enemy's territory was like stepping into a sea: no sooner had the last of our number passed the edge of the camp then their lines closed around us and we were submerged.

Those around me, however, were showing no signs of fear: not Estrada, not Malekrin, and certainly not Alvantes or Mounteban. It was as though they were unaware of the hostile soldiery clustered so close to either side. And I was surprised to find that there was something infectious about their bravery; that despite my terror I was keeping my head up, my eyes fixed stubbornly ahead.

It helped that our destination was both clear and magnificent; it almost made it easy to focus upon that instead of the walls of meat and metal hemming us in. The King's tent, dominating the centre of the camp, could only be described as palatial. It was impossible to conceive that it had been brought here and erected;

for though its walls were of cloth, it looked as though it could only have been constructed through the months-long labour of architects and builders. It had wings. It had towers. Pennants flew from a dozen poles. Many a lord or lady in the South Bank would have traded their mansion for it without a second thought.

There were six guards on the entrance, an outstretched pavilion itself as large as a good-sized cottage, and as we approached they hoisted their pikes to their shoulders, in what might as easily have been a threat or a salute. "You'll leave your escort here," one said, "and your weapons too."

We'd been expecting that, of course, and no one commented as they piled their swords, Alvantes, Estrada and Mounteban going first and then their followers in a long line afterwards – no one, that was, until it came to the turn of Kalyxis and her bodyguards. The beauty of the short, curved scabbard at her hip, all set with ebony and polished bone, did nothing to make me think that the blade within wasn't sharp as any razor. Her men's weapons were plainer and larger, altogether less subtle instruments; but not one of them made any move to discard their armaments with the others.

"I trust you'll be disarming also?" Kalyxis asked the sentry who'd give the order.

Though he scowled at her convincingly, I could tell he was thrown by the question. "We are protecting his highness King Panchessa."

"I am a queen of Shoan," Kalyxis replied, "and these men are *my* protectors."

"I have my orders," the sentry told her. He clearly didn't like the way she was looking at him, for his eyes kept trying to dart from under her gaze. "No one goes before his highness armed."

"My men have their orders also. It's their duty to keep me safe."

The sentry's calm was rapidly disintegrating; I didn't like to think what might have happened if Alvantes hadn't stepped between them. "Kalyxis, give up your weapon now or my men will escort you back to the city," he said roughly. "This meeting is for the sake of Altapasaeda and you're here on my sufferance."

Kalyxis gave Alvantes a smile that would have frozen fire. "Your sufferance?" she asked.

But Alvantes wasn't as easily cowed as the sentry. "Precisely," he said. "So choose quickly."

The smile twisted a fraction. "Of course," Kalyxis said. "I was merely seeking clarification."

She drew her short scimitar, held it long enough that its wicked edge caught the morning light, and then dropped it upon the pile. Her men unstrapped both scabbards and swords, as everyone else had done, and added them to the summit of the heap.

By then the sentry had recovered his composure. He pulled on a silken cord hanging near to his hand, and via some hidden mechanism the nearer flap of the entrance furled up. Stepping in first he said, "This way," as if this really was a palace and without his guidance we might have blundered off in the wrong direction.

Though no one seemed to have noticed I had it, I dropped my knife belt onto the weapons pile anyway, before slipping into line. The party that followed the sentry was significantly smaller than the one that had just traversed the Pasaedan camp, for Alvantes and Mounteban had both signalled their escorts to wait outside as instructed; it surprised me not at all that only Kalyxis had chosen to keep her personal guard with her. For my part, I stayed close to Malekrin; he might be the notorious Bastard Prince, son of Moaradrid and grandson of the formidable woman pacing before us, but I couldn't help feeling that he was almost as out of place there as I was.

We passed through two rooms: first the entrance, decorated with shields and armour mounted upon frames, and then a sort of conference hall, with long tables and shelves lined with neatly piled scrolls. It took an effort of concentration to remember that I was still inside a tent, and that tent lay within what had been the Altapasaedan suburbs less than a week ago. The third room dwarfed the first two – but it wasn't that that made me stare. Rather, it was the shock of familiarity. For the space we'd arrived in was clearly modelled on the audience chamber from the palace in Pasaeda, where I'd first encountered Panchessa. It was hexagonal, with curtained apertures in every wall, and though the central plinth from its sister-room in the Ans Pasaedan capital was missing, there *was* a throne – perhaps even the same throne, and my mind boggled at the thought of how it might have been dragged all the way here.

On the throne sat King Panchessa. If I'd been hoping he'd look pleased to see us, I was disappointed.

Everyone around me was falling to their knees, so I followed suit. Expecting a hard earth floor, I was startled when my forehead met a giving surface. With my view reduced to ground level, I saw that every speck of dirt had been hidden beneath luxuriant rugs, each as lovely as any I'd seen. You could say what you liked about Panchessa, but the man knew how to travel in style.

Then Panchessa said, in a voice both deeper and harsher than I remembered, "Rise all, and face your king."

Grateful to stop staring at the mazy design of red and gold beneath my nose, I stumbled to my feet. Malekrin and I were over on the right side of the gathering, and Panchessa was facing ahead, to where Alvantes, Estrada, Mounteban and Kalyxis stood close together. While his attention was elsewhere, I studied the King's face for signs of the sickness Gailus had spoken of. Might it be that traits I'd taken for evidence of bad character the first time I'd encountered Panchessa were in fact the symptoms of a more transient corruption? Could it be that the reason his deep-set eyes glittered so unnervingly, that his thick lips were set so grimly above his bloated chin, was that he wrestled with torments his position forced him always to hide?

Or perhaps both were true. Perhaps the King was a cruel, selfish man whose flaws were aggravated now by distemper eating at him from the inside. That was what my instinct told me, that and to not trust Panchessa – for I was certain beyond doubt that whatever he'd said, whatever agreement had been made, we were in dreadful danger. A man like him might have good intentions one moment, might even intend peace, but he could be relied on for exactly as long as it took some stab of pain or whim of vindictiveness to change his mind.

While I'd studied him, Panchessa's own gaze had been roving over the assembly beside me. Abruptly, as if we'd arrived in the middle of a conversation, he said, "Some of you I know," (and I couldn't but notice how his eyes snared on Kalyxis,) "and some of you are unfamiliar to me. But all of you are my citizens, under my law. Thus it follows that by raising your hands against me, all of you are traitors. The city of Altapasaeda is mine and you have barred its doors to me."

Only then did I wonder if our delegation had decided in advance just who would do the talking – for it occurred to me, far too late, that the wrong choice of speaker would doom us all. I was relieved when it was Estrada who stepped forward and not Alvantes or Mounteban. "Your highness," she said, "there's been a terrible misunderstanding here."

"A king does not misunderstand," said Panchessa. Now that I knew he was Moaradrid's father, the similarities between them were unmistakeable; and it was hard to say whether Panchessa's aloof indifference was less daunting than his son's barely checked madness had been.

Before Estrada could reply, to my horror, Mounteban had pushed forward. "What the lady Estrada means to say is that the only traitor here is me. I was the one who dared to think that Altapasaeda could stand alone. It was Mayor Estrada and Captain Alvantes who stood against me, and in your name rather than their own. They have shown me how wrong I was, so if my death is the price of peace, I willingly accept it. I brought this crisis on Altapasaeda. Let me be the one to end it."

"No!" Estrada clutched Mounteban's arm, hard enough to turn him towards her. "Absolutely not, Castilio. Your highness, Castilio Mounteban has no right to speak for our party, or to make offers without consulting us."

My attention had been so taken up with Panchessa that I'd hardly noticed there were other figures standing in the shadows behind him. I'd taken them for guards, and it was only when a familiar voice burst from the gloom that I realised how mistaken I'd been. "Rights? Offers? Is this how you dare speak to your king?"

It was Ludovoco – who I'd last seen as we fled the palace, who had felt the need to deliver the King's declaration of war with his own hands all those days ago. And it was only then, seeing how very close he stood behind Panchessa's shoulder, exactly as he had at the royal court in Pasaeda, that it occurred to me to wonder what part one militant commander of the Crown Guard might have played in the events of recent weeks.

Could Ludovoco have taken the notion of defending the Crown a leap too far? Or have forgotten his duties altogether in favour of a personal agenda? If Panchessa was ill, unstable, distressed by the death of one son and by the other raising an army against him, it wouldn't have been difficult to manipulate him.

As the toll of Ludovoco's words died away, I recognised someone else amongst the shadowed figures who I now realised must be the King's generals and advisors. Near Ludovoco stood Ondeges, captain of Altapasaeda's Palace Guard – and unlike Ludovoco, he didn't look happy to be there. In fact, he seemed every bit as discomforted by his

colleague's words as Mounteban and Estrada did. I thought
of what Gailus had said, that Ondeges had been our advocate
in the royal camp, and seeing the anxiety in his face I could
readily believe it.

But it was Ludovoco who stood at the King's side. It was
Ludovoco who had the gall to pronounce in his place. And
even as I thought it, Panchessa raised a hand to silence his
errant commander – but that was all he did. Ludovoco had
dared to speak on behalf of his king, and his punishment was
not flogging but hand-waving.

"Castilio Mounteban," Panchessa said, "we have heard of
you. A felon with notions of grandeur."

I'd never known Mounteban to let an insult go, not from
anyone. Yet it was with perfect serenity that he replied, "Just
so, your highness. Whatever has happened in Altapasaeda,
whatever has been done, it was my crime, committed for my
own ends. Being a simple thief, I thought I could steal a city
from under a king's nose and get away with it."

Had Mounteban really just described himself as a *simple
thief*? It was like hearing a mountain lion claim to be a toothless
old mouser. What was his angle here? I couldn't believe
that Mounteban would do anything without one, but I was
struggling to see what he imagined he could gain here.

"And now," said Panchessa, "with my armies at the gates,
you see the error of your ways?"

"Exactly," said Mounteban. "I was a fool."

To Mounteban's and my surprise both, Panchessa stood up
then, started with slow steps to cross the space between them.
Was it my imagination or did he limp a little? He was dressed
in a heavy robe, but within its loose, concealing folds I felt sure
he was carrying his weight wrongly.

Panchessa stopped halfway, just far enough away that
Mounteban couldn't possibly reach him before Ludovoco or
someone else from the King's faction intervened. "A fool?" he

said. "Is that what you are, Castilio Mounteban? Or, better yet, tell me this: do you also take me for an imbecile?"

Mounteban flinched as if stung. "I don't understand, your highness."

"I saw how you looked at the woman there," said Panchessa, pointing towards Estrada. "I saw it from the moment you entered this room. Do you think you're the first man to try and throw his life away over love?"

Mounteban's face purpled. His obsession with Estrada was old news to me, but I'd never heard it phrased quite so bluntly. For a moment, I thought he really would try to charge the King and strangle him with his bare hands. Ludovoco, tensed in the background, already had his sword half free of its scabbard.

Perhaps Mounteban really might have lunged then; maybe Ludovoco would have cut him down just on the off-chance. I never got to find out. For there came a sound from my left that froze both of them in place. I couldn't identify it first, except to say that it was chilling as the blackest winter's night, knife-sharp, and from its first note it made me shudder down to my boots.

I realised, finally, what I was hearing. Kalyxis was laughing.

All eyes were on her now, and Panchessa's in particular were snagged upon her face as though by invisible chains. Kalyxis's laughter choked away to nothing, like poison bubbling into a drain. "Love?" she said. "What could you possibly understand of love?"

"Kalyxis," said Panchessa, pronouncing the word as if it were the name of some particularly malignant disease, "you have no part in these proceedings; you were allowed here because I wish to talk with your grandson. If you dare to speak before your king, it had best be with good reason."

Kalyxis offered him the peculiar smile that I'd come to associate with her, the one that wouldn't have looked out of place on the slit lips of a snake. "Oh, you're right," she said, "I care nothing for Altapasaeda, nothing for your petty squabbling. Let me tell you, Panchessa, before these gathered witnesses, why I'm here."

She paused – and it struck me, as it should have from the first note of that terrible laughter, that whatever she was about to say, it meant trouble for every one of us.

As usual, my ability to spot approaching danger was only exceeded by my knack for underestimating it.

"Panchessa," Kalyxis said, "when I was a young girl, freshly married to a man of good and upstanding birth, you came to my land and you raped me."

The room went silent – deathly silent, as though all the air had been sucked from it. Certainly, I found I could no longer breathe at all. Panchessa took a step towards Kalyxis, another – and from the shadows at the back of the chamber, I heard a soft hiss, as Ludovoco's sword finally left its scabbard.

Mounteban, realising himself caught now between Panchessa and Kalyxis and his own anger suddenly irrelevant to the proceedings, hurriedly stepped aside. Kalyxis moved to fill the gap and glared at Panchessa defiantly. She was almost his equal in height, but seeing them so close together she seemed taller, as though her presence detracted from his.

"It was no rape," said Panchessa darkly.

Kalyxis paid him not the slightest notice. "By the time I realised I was with child," she continued, "it was too late. I begged the wise-woman of my husband's tribe to help me, but it had gone too far. The herbs she gave me made me sick for a week, but in the end my belly was still swelling. I couldn't hide the truth from my husband anymore; he spat on me, called me a whore and sent me back to my own tribe. So my child was born there... born a bastard. I named him Moaradrid, which means 'birthed in hate' in the old tongue of Shoan." Kalyxis's smile had vanished as she spoke; now it returned, more pitiless than ever: "I'm sure you've heard the name," she said.

Even from a distance, I could see that Panchessa was shaking; faint tremors ran up his arms and legs. Was it anger? Was it palsy? His fingers twitched spasmodically, perhaps imagining themselves around Kalyxis's throat. "You birthed a mad dog," he said. "Or if he wasn't born mad, you made him that way, spitting your venom in his ear."

"My son was a good and a brave man, who fought to free his land from tyranny. But he was born from bad blood, under bad stars. It should be you dead now and not him."

"If he'd been any true son of mine," Panchessa said, "I *would* be dead, and he'd be sitting on my throne... not feeding fish with his marrow at the bottom of the sea."

For the first time I could see that something had barbed beneath Kalyxis's surface calm. There'd been hate in her face from the moment she'd set eyes on Panchessa, but it had been controlled, like a serpent kept in a basket. Now it was free, and in control of every muscle of her face. "You wish to negotiate, do you, King Panchessa? Well, here are *my* conditions. You'll declare the land of Shoan a free territory, to be ruled by its own people, and never again pillaged under the name of taxation. And you'll agree for this boy, Malekrin, who is your grandson and the blood of your blood, to rule in your stead when the time comes."

It was Panchessa's turn to laugh then – though the sound was every bit as far from humour as Kalyxis's acid cackle had been. "You're as mad as your damned son was. What makes you dream you can make demands of me?"

"The fact," said Kalyxis, "that without an order from me, the fleet of Shoanish warriors that have navigated their way around the Castovalian mountains, who are presently sailing up the Mar Paraedra and will soon be occupying your great capital while your army wastes its time here, will never let you enter Pasaeda again."

The fleet. How could I have forgotten the fleet? How many boats had chased us from that barren Pasaedan shore; how many men? Under normal circumstances, I couldn't believe they numbered enough to take so vast and well-defended a city as Pasaeda. If its defences were severely depleted by the King's hurried march south, however...

"You lie," said Panchessa. "I don't know what you hope to achieve, but you lie."

"Oh, don't take my word. I'm sure a messenger will be along presently. And *you* saw it, didn't you?" asked Kalyxis, rounding upon Estrada. "You had the good fortune to witness the glory of Shoan."

Estrada's pursed lips told me she recognised a question with no right answer. "There were ships," she agreed. "They chased us from a beach off the coast of Pasaeda."

For all Panchessa turned the full force of his rage on her, Estrada might as well have admitted to single-handedly building the Shoanish fleet. "So you knew about this all along, did you?" he roared.

"That's ridiculous! We didn't... I mean, we thought..."

Alvantes put his hand on Estrada's arm. "We'd assumed that Kalyxis's forces were waiting at anchor," he said. "We believed she'd come here to recover her grandson."

"Ah yes," said Panchessa. "The boy." I realised just too late that his gaze was about to turn in our direction, so that his first sight was of me trying discreetly to cower behind Malekrin. I supposed I should count myself fortunate that, amidst all the dire rhetoric and decades-long vendettas, my past indiscretions were suddenly looking very insignificant. "The boy," Panchessa repeated. "The skinny little abortion who thinks he should be king."

I couldn't see Malekrin's face of course, so I had no idea how well he was holding up before the contempt in his new-met grandfather's eyes; but his voice was steady as he replied, "King Panchessa, I have no interest in your or any other throne."

"No?" Panchessa chuckled, a horrible, rattling sound.

"No," said Malekrin. "My grandmother doesn't speak for me."

"Malekrin..." Kalyxis's tone was rich with threat. However, when Panchessa held up a hand to quiet her, I was amazed that she did in fact drop silent.

"Whatever my grandmother has said," continued Malekrin, "whatever she's done, it has nothing to do with Altapasaeda. Whatever mistakes their leaders may have made, they have nothing to do with the people of Altapasaeda. That's all I came to say. I have no quarrel with you. Neither do the men and women behind those walls. Can't they be left in peace?"

Panchessa nodded thoughtfully. "An interesting idea, boy." For one ever so brief moment, I wondered if Malekrin might really have got through to him. Then Panchessa said, "Remind me, what is it they call you?"

"My name is Malekrin, sire."

"No. Not that. The *other* name."

Malekrin tensed. "I've heard they call me the Bastard Prince."

"And tell me this, bastard," said Panchessa, "what makes you dare to dictate to me?"

Finally, Malekrin faltered. "I came..." he began. "I just wanted..."

Fortunately, hiding behind Malekrin had placed my mouth close to his ear. "Let it go," I hissed. "*Let it go!*"

The half-finished words in Malekrin's mouth dissolved to nothing, but I was certain it was too late, that Malekrin had just damned himself to unspeakable tortures, and me along with him...

However, Panchessa merely returned his attention to the others, seeming in an instant to forget Malekrin and their entire conversation. "This meeting is over," he said. "You should never have brought that... *woman* here. Because I'm a man of my word, I'll give you time enough to leave my camp, but once you're inside the walls of Altapasaeda, my armies will pick them apart brick by brick. Do you hear me? Fight hard, Castovalians. Because when we meet again, your deaths will not be quick."

Estrada and Alvantes led the way. I wanted to scream at them to hurry. Didn't they see how every eye was trained on us, how every Pasaedan hand hung close to a sword hilt or held an arrow ready to be nocked? That I kept my mouth firmly closed had nothing to do with faith in Alvantes or Estrada; it was simply the certainty that all of our lives hung on a knife's edge just then, that any noise would shatter the fragile armistice. Even our footsteps sounded too weighty.

Yet we were moving. The remnants of the Suburbs were drawing closer. Once we reached them, we had a chance. If we made a run for it in those close streets, maybe one man in ten might make it as far as the gates – and a thief of some small competence could surely find a shadowed cranny to hide himself in.

From all around, however, there came a sense of unrest, and though it seemed impossible that the Pasaedans could know what had taken place between us and their king, I was sure they were pressing nearer. Perhaps it was only that, like a dog held back from a bone, they saw what they wanted and were frustrated not to get it.

Nevertheless, we were *still* moving – still approaching the verge of the camp. So long as nothing stopped us, so long as nothing went...

I should have known I'd never finish the thought. For ahead of me, Kalyxis had come to a halt, had turned around, and her two bodyguards were looking nervously after her, hands already hovering near swords. I thought again about running. Maybe whatever was about to happen would be distraction enough for me to make it to that wretched line of shanties. But the Pasaedans were poised ready to close the gap; we were already trapped. I turned instead.

There, approaching rapidly, was Panchessa, ringed by half a dozen of his guards – who looked as though they'd willingly have dragged him back inside his tent like some errant child. Panchessa was pacing towards us in their midst and they were hurrying to keep up, whilst striving to maintain a fitting distance from the common soldiery nearby.

When Panchessa was nearly upon us, one of the guards finally snapped, and hurled himself in his king's path. He probably thought it would be the last thing he ever did, but Panchessa barely seemed to notice. I doubted he was aware of anything, just then – anything except for Kalyxis. His eyes bored into her remorselessly.

"I never raped you, woman," said Panchessa. His voice was a rasp, yet it carried as well as any crow's caw. "I barely even had to *ask* you. It wasn't enough for you to be the wife of a lord amongst savages. You dreamed of being a queen."

Kalyxis took a step towards him. I thought there was something almost longing in the way she did it. It was like the motion of a lover kept apart from their paramour for too long, or a warrior ready at last to confront their ancient foe – or perhaps it was both at once. "You are a pig of a man," Kalyxis said, "and I will spit on your corpse if it's the last thing I do."

She said it softly, almost affectionately – but so very clearly. I had no doubt that those words had reached to every corner of the camp.

I heard the first sword rasp from its scabbard.

But I couldn't say where it had come from, their side or ours, because in an instant the sound was everywhere, and the ring of metal scraping free from metal was all I could hear.

CHAPTER NINETEEN

The air was rich with tension. No one on either side seemed quite certain what had just happened. Were we fighting? No blow had been struck. Words had been exchanged, and they'd been sharp to be sure, but the Pasaedans were soldiers; they fought for orders, not insults.

Yet it was clear they could hardly let us go. Already the ranks ahead were drawing together, tightening like the neck of a drawstring bag. Behind, Panchessa had disappeared from view, shielded from our tiny band by row upon row of protectors. Ahead, the Suburbs seemed infinitely more distant than they had a minute before. Alvantes was still leading us forward, but his steps were halting. What would happen when someone finally tried to stop him?

There came a noise from behind me: a silvery chime that turned straight away into a metallic rasp, and ended viscous and wet. Any sound would have been shocking just then, but there was something particularly awful about this one.

The sight was worse. I turned to see one of Kalyxis's bodyguards flailing his enormous scimitar, sending Pasaedans tumbling aside; it would have been alarming enough even without the great gash in his side, which had all but opened him entirely. He had no right to be standing, let alone moving – and as I watched, he realised as much himself. Still swinging, he pitched forward. He chopped at chest height, at thighs and then at ankles, and managed one savage stroke towards the churned muck of the ground before the last strength left him.

Who had struck first? Had someone moved upon Kalyxis, or had her protector simply lost his fragile calm? I'd never know, and nobody else seemed certain either. Even as the barbarian twitched out the dregs of his life in the mud, a vestige of our tenuous peace held: a moment's sizing up of opponents, of calculating odds, considering positions.

This time it was Alvantes who broke the stillness – and for all that I thought I'd grown used to his unorthodox strategies, his command was still the last thing I expected. "Charge!" he roared.

I doubted the Pasaedans had seen it coming either. When Alvantes flung himself forward, a few even struggled to get out of the way. Immediately Mounteban was there to fill the briefly opened gap – and as he pressed forward, sword sweeping, I saw him draw something from his belt. When he put it to his lips, I recognised it for a horn, hardly bigger than his hand. The note it produced was shrill, improbably loud. Mounteban gave two more quick blasts and then let it slip from his fingers, as he dodged to counter a blow aimed at his off side. Even as he swept the opposing blade away, Alvantes had lashed to cut down the man wielding it.

"Push back! Keep close!" someone called to my right, and glancing back I recognised Gueverro, one of Alvantes's sub-captains. He had taken command of our small entourage, forming them into a tight-clustered oval.

Whatever outcome Alvantes had hoped for, he'd planned for the worst. Probably only half of those under Gueverro's command were guardsmen, but I could tell that the remainder had been carefully chosen. Men who until recently had been

on opposite sides of Altapasaedan law covered each others'
backs like seasoned soldiers, keeping pace despite the fact that
most were moving sideways or even backwards.

They'd drawn bucklers from under their cloaks, and were
already fending off a hail of blows. The small shields were
worthless against arrows, but just then our enemies' numbers
were working more to our benefit than theirs. Disorganised,
fighting without order or instruction, the Pasaedans were
pressing too close; any archer fool enough to fire was as likely
to skewer one of his own side.

The clamour was deafening. I felt as if I was at the centre of
the fiercest of storms, fenced in by lightning and hammered by
thunder. Panic was rising in my gullet, and I had no argument
to talk it down. The Pasaedans were so close; everywhere I
looked, hard faces glowered back. It was impossible to imagine
that our thin line of Altapasaedans could be holding them back.

I went for my knives, realised that in the excitement I'd
forgotten to recover them from outside Panchessa's tent. Well,
maybe it was for the best; I couldn't have hoped to defend
against a sword, so why attract attention? Then again, there
were fifty of us, hundreds of them. Attention was going to find
me soon, whether I was armed or not.

Even as I thought it, someone stumbled hard against me.
I caught a fragmentary look at his face, streaked in red, saw
enough of his uniform to recognise him for one of ours, before
he landed in a tangle at my feet. Backing up, I jarred the man
behind, heard him curse revoltingly. Ahead, our line had
already clenched to fill the gap – but only in time for another
Altapasaedan to be cut down, this one with blood coursing
prodigiously from his stomach.

I danced aside as well as I could, desperate to keep up
with Alvantes and our advancing front. Only now, we *weren't*
advancing; our momentum was lost, and not even Alvantes
could regain it. It was all he could do to hold the ground he'd

already made. In fact, it was probably all he could do to stay alive, for I'd never seen him fight so desperately. Alone, even that might not have been enough, but I was astonished to note how Mounteban was risking himself to shield Alvantes's left side, compensating for his old enemy's one-handedness.

Meanwhile, despite both their efforts to keep her back, Estrada had joined the front line. At that moment, she was fencing expertly with a soldier fully a head taller than her. Close by, Kalyxis had her peculiar long knife in hand. As I watched, she stepped to where her surviving bodyguard was clashing with three Pasaedans and dug it halfway to the hilt in the nearest man's side. He hardly had time to look at her with wide-eyed horror before her bodyguard had sheared his head from his body, sending his corpse tottering into the other two.

Was I the only one not fighting? But the question had hardly crossed my mind before a colossal Pasaedan smashed with a roar past the men ahead and charged straight for me. Giants aside, I'd never seen such a monster; his neck alone was wide as my waist. My only thought was to get out of the way. I ducked, drove my weight left, felt my ankle catch on something I only recognised for a corpse as I stumbled over it. The bullish Pasaedan struck my leg with such force that I thought he'd take it with him. What little balance I had vanished and I went flying, as he plunged on, to crash into his own side with another bellow and the force of an avalanche.

I was halfway back to my feet when a sword whistled close over my head. Giving up standing for a bad idea, I tried instead to roll into a ball, but someone's heel smashed hard into my ribs and I flopped with a sob onto my back. I had a moment's dizzying, inverted view of the battle raging: swords whirling and men clashing and everywhere very much blood, with the sky an incredible, untainted blue above.

Then a Pasaedan fell towards me, using both hands and his last breath to try to hold his own guts in place, and that was enough to get me back on my feet. However, there was little enough room left to stand in; I couldn't so much as edge in any direction without meeting someone's back. Our small circle was shrinking fast.

"Hold! Hold the line!" cried Gueverro, at once swiping his sword towards a Pasaedan and dashing first one strike and then another aside with his buckler. Then he jerked hard to the left, as though someone had yanked him by the hair. He just barely kept his balance and tried to look round, seemed puzzled that he couldn't.

I hadn't seen where the arrow had come from; only a lunatic would have fired in the midst of that dense combat. Yet there it was, jutting from Gueverro's neck, half of its length sunk inside him. I thought he was trying to say something, but of course there was no way he could. Understanding dawned in his eyes, as terrible a sight as I'd seen. Then Gueverro hurled himself forward, thrashing his sword about as though trying to beat out a fire. The Pasaedan lines opened for him, closed, and he was gone.

I'd already watched many strangers die that day, but Gueverro had been the first whose name I'd known. I'd spoken to him; in so much as I'd considered it, I'd liked him. And there came over me then something deeper than fear. It might have been resignation, or merely understanding. What it told me was that I was going to end up face down here, bleeding my life out in the mud. We weren't moving, we were being cut down, and the Suburbs were far too far away.

Only... wasn't there one slender hope? I'd already guessed that Mounteban's horn was a summons for aid, prearranged for just such an emergency as this. I hadn't expected it to help. Yet, though it was barely possible to make out anything over the tempest of shouts, metal chiming on metal, cries of pain and feet slopping in mud, I was aware that somewhere beyond those sounds was another, rising out of the distance. It *had* to be Mounteban's relief.

I was hardly keeping count, but I thought that at least half our number were gone, dead or curled in the muck nursing awful wounds. Probably they'd each taken their share of Pasaedans with them, for these men were the best Altapasaeda had to offer, but what difference did that make? If they each killed ten, or twenty, or fifty, it would never be enough. Even if our tiny troop were invulnerable, they could hack and slash all day and never reach an end of the Pasaedan numbers.

Yet the horses – as I felt sure now they must be – were getting closer. I could make out the pound of hooves, the rattle of gear, the scrape of metal on leather. Nor was I the only one listening; if the fighting hadn't stopped, its tempo had slowed, some of the savagery gone from it. Glimpsing Pasaedan faces, I could see that they were asking the same questions I was. What was coming? Was it a few reinforcements or the entire Altapasaedan strength? Was this a rescue attempt – or the beginning of the final battle for the city?

Then, as the approaching racket gained the precise tone and volume of a rockslide tumbling towards us, the fighting really did slow to a halt. The Pasaedans, without any sign of unanimity or instruction, backed off to create a perimeter around us.

Without the imminent threat of a sword through my innards, I dared to focus on the nearest exit from the Suburbs, a plank-lined way that seemed to be source for the greatest concentration of noise. Whatever happened in the next moments would decide our fate. If Mounteban had planned a paltry rescue force, they might buy us a few minutes before they were cut down, and we with them. If he'd summoned every man, woman and child in Altapasaeda capable of holding a sword, we'd probably still be dead before sunset – but at least we'd have a chance.

I stared at that skewed alleyway so hard that my eyes watered. How many men were making that cacophony? How many horses?

Then they plunged into view – and it wasn't horses. It was giants.

But I could easily see how I'd been mistaken, for they were dressed like no giants I'd seen. They wore makeshift armour, as during the fight for the northwestern gate. This time, however, the emphasis was different; their torsos were scantily defended, while their arms and legs were buried in a patchwork of metal and leather. The explanation for that lay in the final detail of their outfits: colossal rectangular shields lashed to their arms and each almost as high as its bearer, planks that must have exhausted entire trees bound together by bands of iron.

These giants were familiar, too – the same ones who'd defended the gate. Was this a resumption of that day's violence, or could it be some sort of penance? Because I couldn't help but recognise their leader as well: even if I hadn't learned those lumpish features by long acquaintance, I'd have known the glinting circlet hung once more around his neck.

I didn't want to believe it. It was one thing to accept that Saltlick was on his feet, even running in armour – and the raw cuts lacing his flesh, the bandages still tight around his arms and thighs and waist, and the way that he still favoured his good leg, all testified to what the exertion must be costing him. But I knew Saltlick was brave beyond reason; that he'd wade through fire to save his friends if need be. That he would fight, though, against his most ingrained beliefs? Even to save Estrada, let alone myself? No, I wouldn't accept that. In fact, I realised I'd sooner die myself than watch him draw blood in my defence.

Only – he *wasn't* fighting. He was drawing nothing but confused stares. All he was doing – in fact all any of the giants were doing – was moving. And that might not have meant much were it not for the fact that they were giants. They were armoured, they were shielded, and their strength was prodigious. Their gentlest effort was enough to drive the

Pasaedans back – for who was about to plant himself in their way, to try to halt their relentless progress? They might only be moving, but moving was enough.

Before them, the Pasaedan lines were in disarray. Yet at first it seemed that all Saltlick would achieve was to herd our enemies over us, so that I'd die in a stampede rather than at sword point. However, Alvantes had recognised the danger, drawn our survivors into a narrow wedge. The fleeing Pasaedans flurried around us, like gale-driven snow about a stubborn crag – and in their wake came the giants, visible now only as a solid, moving barrier of wood and iron.

For a terrifying moment, it seemed that we too would be swept before those colossal shields. Only at the last instant did the giants raise them, and we scrabbled hastily into the space they'd cleared. It was an outpost in the heart of enemy territory; through every chink, I could see the Pasaedans gathered beyond the shield wall. It was a fort – except that its ramparts were made as much from meat and muscle as from metal and timber.

Suddenly I wanted urgently to know what Saltlick was doing here. It had to have been Mounteban's doing, had to relate to their mysterious meeting – but how? "Saltlick," I bellowed. "Saltlick!"

But either he didn't hear me or he chose not to answer.

"All right," cried Mounteban. "Back, now... quick as you can."

A *moving* fort. I couldn't begin to guess how Mounteban had persuaded Saltlick to go along with this, to pitch himself and his fellow giants into such hopeless danger. Yet there was no denying it was a brilliant plan – and this time, Saltlick *did* respond. I heard him utter one harsh syllable of giantish and the giants were in motion again, edging back towards the border of the Suburbs with their shields ploughing before them.

A gap had already cleared around the giants, leaving a circle of ground churned into waves by the passage of so many feet.

Beyond it, however, the Pasaedans were regrouping. If the appearance of the giants had thrown them, it was a temporary disruption at best. They'd faced this threat before, after all, and I had no doubt that the story of how Saltlick had been cut down had been bandied round night after night over the campfires. Now, every man knew that the giants could be hurt by weight of numbers – and without risk of retribution.

I looked towards the Suburbs. There too we'd been cut off. The giant-sized shields were impressive, but what would a battering ram do to those hastily bound planks? How well could they stand up against catapults or ballistae? And even if the Pasaedans chose against such dramatic shows of force, there were other ways to halt our creeping progress.

"Archers!" someone roared; I thought I recognised the steel-edged voice as Ludovoco's. "Archers, forward. Make ready!"

It seemed I'd considered nothing our enemies hadn't. The giants' armour was piecemeal, concentrated towards their fronts; the Pasaedans need only fire over their heads. One arrow might be like a thorn prick to a giant, but a hundred at once?

I looked once more to the Suburbs. I could have run the remaining distance in less than a minute. At our current pace it might take ten times as long – and it was time we'd never be allowed. The enemy were clustered thickly in the gap now. No doubt they'd guessed what I knew for a fact, that Saltlick would order a halt before he'd risk hurting a single one of them.

"Archers..." I had just time to decide that it was definitely Ludovoco's voice before the next word came: "Fire!"

I flung myself forward, pressed into the gap between the nearest giant's feet and huddled close. I had no idea how it would protect me, but there was nowhere else to go. I scrunched myself small as I could, closed my eyes and hoped that death might at least be quick.

Perhaps it would have been better to look, though. To do nothing but hear – the relentless swish of arrows cutting the air, the dry *thunks* where they struck the earth, the wetter sounds where they found flesh and the occasional, horrible sobs and gasps of pain – was almost unbearable. It seemed as if it would never end, and through every moment I felt certain I'd be next.

But in the end, the rain did slacken – and, finally, did stop. While it might have been a concession to mercy, I thought it had more to do with the need to reload. In the silence, I could hear a gurgling sound, weird and unfamiliar. Though I knew my hiding place hadn't done a thing to protect me – the three arrows spaced haphazardly up the giant's leg were ample testament to that – I didn't want to leave it. Even an illusion of safety seemed better than none, and I was sure I was better off not knowing what made that odd, unsettling noise.

Then again, it was moving nearer. Maybe ignorance wasn't so beneficial after all. I untucked my head from beneath my arm and dared a glance.

There was no question of where to look. At least a dozen of our small troop had been hit, but where their wounds had left them alive, they were expressing their anguish with familiar and very human cries and groans. I had to turn my eyes higher – to where one of the giants had stepped back from the circle, barely avoiding the survivors he'd been trying to protect. He turned slowly around, and at the same time crumpled to his knees, a wheeze escaping his blubbery lips – as if there was nothing but air holding him up and it was all escaping now.

There were any number of arrows in him, embedded into his back and thighs and shoulders. But I was sure it was the one rooted up to the fletching in his eye that had done for him. When he had no lower to sink, he toppled forward, and with a last, tectonic twitch, lay still.

The remaining giants, perhaps too stunned to move, made no attempt to close the gap in their ranks. Therefore I could see the Pasaedan lines clearly beyond them, the rows upon rows of archers each readying another arrow. And there, towards their front, I recognised the man who'd given the order that had just killed a creature out of legend. The smile upon Ludovoco's lips was almost worse, in its smug cruelty, than the horror I'd just witnessed.

I wasn't the only one to have seen him. Stepping quickly into the breach, Alvantes barked at the very top of his lungs, "Ludovoco! Will you end this with a massacre? Have you no honour?"

The archers were almost ready for another volley. In unison, they were raising their bows, angling to fire once more over the giants' shields. They weren't hurrying – and why should they? They could keep this up all day, which was more than could be said for us.

When at the last moment Ludovoco raised his hand, I didn't believe the motion could possibly be enough to hold back the coming tempest. Yet as one, the archers dipped their bows – and all of them watched him a little curiously.

Ludovoco took a few casual steps towards Alvantes. By the time he came to a halt, he was almost as close to our side as his own. "What do you propose?" he asked, his tone amused. "That we let you leave now, and go through all the trouble of breaking down your gates to kill you later?"

"We began a duel, all those days ago," replied Alvantes. "Would you care to see how it would have ended?"

"I *know* how it would have ended," replied Ludovoco. "And I know how it would end now. You never stood a chance then; now, you can barely stand. Will you really be so obvious, Captain? A last, noble sacrifice to buy the lives of your friends?"

"A sacrifice?" Alvantes smiled – not a reassuring expression on his granite, blood-spattered face. "Why don't we find out?"

"So," said Ludovoco. "It's clear what you gain if you kill me. I promise to let you leave, yes? And our army has one less commander, of course. But what can you possibly offer me?"

Alvantes didn't hesitate. "Not a thing, Ludovoco. I'd promise you our surrender, but everyone in Altapasaeda knows what you'll do to them if you get inside those walls. All I can offer is the pleasure of killing me by your own hand, rather than standing by and watching like a coward."

I'd heard better offers. If I'd been in Ludovoco's place, I'd have ordered another volley without hesitation, and probably gone for a cup of wine, far enough away that I wouldn't be bothered by the sound of our dying screams.

But Ludovoco wasn't me, of course. And something told me that the possibility of getting his hands bloody might just be the best news he'd had all day. "Yes," he said. "I think that will do nicely."

CHAPTER TWENTY

I'd thought I had a fair idea of what Ludovoco's standing in the Pasaedan camp might be. Now I was sure. A quiet word from him had brought their entire army to rest; not only that, it had turned them into his audience, an expectant throng clustered round to witness his martial prowess. Too, there was the fact that no one had dared challenge him. I could see others who, from their elegant dress and decorated armour, were evidently officers of high rank; yet no one had thought to suggest that the war for a city shouldn't be reduced to a scrap between two men.

No, with the King vanished, presumably hustled off to some point far from danger, it was obvious who was running this show – which meant that while Alvantes's gesture was undoubtedly reckless, it at least wasn't stupid. Taking Ludovoco out of the picture might really buy us a chance at escape.

It was only a shame Alvantes hadn't the faintest hope of beating him.

If Alvantes had reached the same conclusion, however, it wasn't evident from his manner. He had his sword in hand and was wiping it busily with a fold of his cloak. I hadn't much experience of such matters, but I guessed it was bad manners

271

to fence with an opposing officer while your blade was soiled with the blood of their soldiery.

"A duel, then," he said finally, once the blade was glisteningly clean. "To the rules of the Crown Academy?"

"Of course," replied Ludovoco, with a none-too-pleasant smile. "What other rules are there?"

"But – to the death."

"Oh, certainly. I'd say this is sufficiently a matter of honour."

It was Alvantes's turn to smile. "Or the lack thereof, Commander Ludovoco."

Ludovoco failed to disguise the anger that flushed his narrow face. "But then," he said, "aren't such questions always decided by the winner? I assure you, Captain, that when they speak of your death, and of how you let your city fall, and of the things that happened there in the days that followed, not one of the words they use will be *honourable*."

Alvantes twirled his blade in a tight figure of eight, as if experimenting to see how well it carved the air. "Maybe," he said. "But fights aren't won by talking." He took a step forward, raised the sword in nonchalant salute.

Ludovoco mirrored the gesture. I could see his good cheer was returning now that the prospect of violence was near, for there was a lightness to his movements that hadn't been there an instant before.

"One moment, Commander!"

I looked to where the call had come from, recognised Ondeges. He had broken free of the surrounding circle of men and stood now just inside, watching Ludovoco and Alvantes intently. "I never trained in the Academy," Ondeges said. "But isn't it the case that there ought to be seconds? I mean, according to their rules?"

"I hardly think that..." Ludovoco began.

"That there's anyone suitable?" said Ondeges quickly. "I put myself forward, Commander. I'm far from your match, but since you're hardly likely to need me..."

Ludovoco gave his fellow officer a sullen glare. "Not likely at all," he agreed.

"Then again," said Ondeges, "it wouldn't do for anyone to misinterpret this as a mere brawl."

"No," Ludovoco said with heavy irony, "that wouldn't do at all." Then, louder, he continued, "I nominate Commander Ondeges of the Altapasaedan Palace Guard as my second in this combat. Should I be incapacitated and unable to fight on, he will take my part. As for yourself, Captain Alvantes?" Ludovoco looked with contempt towards our small band of survivors. "If you have nobody left who's up to the task, I'm sure we can offer someone from amongst our ranks."

Alvantes's gaze swung over the handful of survivors, settled on Navare, his surviving sub-captain – and there was no mistaking his disappointment. For Navare was sagging beneath a savage gash to the right shoulder; he was only on his feet because another guardsman supported him. Navare wouldn't be seconding anyone.

Estrada started forward then – but before she could speak, a palm on her shoulder held her back, and Castilio Mounteban moved to take her place. "I'll do it," he said. "No one else has the right."

"Castilio..." Estrada's tone was imploring.

Ludovoco held up his free hand, waved it in mocking exasperation. "That's settled then. Is there anything else, before we begin? Anything anyone wishes to contribute?"

"No," replied Alvantes, "I think we're done here," – and almost before the last word was free of his mouth, he was in motion.

If he'd thought to surprise Ludovoco, however, it was a wasted effort. The Pasaedan slipped smoothly into a guard stance, his footing perfect despite the spoiled ground. The defence lasted not even a split second, for in less time than that he'd whirled round and swung for Alvantes's head. It was all Alvantes could do to twist his upper body, jar up his arm to fend away the blow and trip back into space.

Vivid memories of the last time these two men had fought sprang to my mind. Then, Alvantes had only held his own by fighting dirty. Now, it was obvious that something – no, *everything* – had changed. Ludovoco was both more confident and more wary. As he adjusted his stance once more, I noted how he held his arm outstretched, keeping Alvantes at a distance. Even without Alvantes's disabling wound, Ludovoco had the advantage of height, the advantage of reach, the advantage of not having spent the last few minutes battling for his life. So far as I could see, all he had was advantages.

Alvantes readied to attack, a mere twitch of a muscle – but Ludovoco was faster, his blade whipping low. Alvantes was forced again to turn his own blow into a block, their blades ringing discordantly. Before, Ludovoco had fought with cruel persistence. Now he was pressing his offensive straight away, his sword point cavorting in a whirl. All Alvantes could do was to keep his own weapon up and retreat. Mere seconds in and sweat was already sheeting from beneath his grey-flecked hair; I could hear his laboured breathing even from where I was.

Then Ludovoco's blade snuck past Alvantes's guard to nick his arm. A thread of blood trailed in its wake. Just a scratch – but even as Alvantes recoiled, Ludovoco had scraped the tip of his sword in a neat line across his opponent's thigh.

Alvantes gasped, tripped back two full paces. Did he realise how close he was to the Pasaedan lines? Once he was forced against that immovable barrier of men, any shred of hope he might have was vanished.

But perhaps Alvantes *did* recognise the danger, for he tried to counterattack then. Even one-handed, he was the stronger man; he thrust wildly for Ludovoco's left side, and as soon as the Pasaedan countered, hacked at his right. Each blow Ludovoco slid aside was followed by another, another. It was clear what Alvantes was trying for: to wear down the lighter man, or at least to drive him away from his own lines.

Either goal was as futile as the other. Ludovoco parried almost carelessly; to see the way he tipped each blow aside, or else stepped smoothly to avoid it, it was hard to believe Alvantes was even trying to hurt him. In the meantime, attacking was costing Alvantes more in exertion than defending was Ludovoco. Even regaining ground was beyond him; Ludovoco was making sure that all Alvantes managed was to wade in helpless circles.

To see Alvantes lumbering, flailing, was like watching a blind bear try to wrestle an acrobat. This was play to Ludovoco. And it was clear from his face, from the glimmer in his dark eyes and the smile tugging always at his lips, that it was play he dearly loved. I knew then without a doubt that whatever had guided Ludovoco to his current position, whatever excuses he'd made, whatever gifts of birth had eased his way, it was *this* that drove him. As Alvantes had said back in the palace, the man was a killer – and this game would end the moment it bored him.

I didn't have long to wait. Alvantes's thrusts were growing cruder, more desperate; Ludovoco's defence had only grown more graceful, as if in direct proportion. He'd never been moving slowly, but this time, as Alvantes drove for his flank, the Pasaedan was almost quicker than my eyes could follow. One moment he was before Alvantes. The next their blades met, flashed – and their chime hadn't even begun to fade before Ludovoco was at Alvantes's back and raking his sword across it.

Maybe it was Alvantes's leather brigandine that saved him. I could see it through the slice in his cloak, despite the blood already darkening both garments. More likely, though, was that Ludovoco could have killed him then had he wanted to. For while Alvantes was panting, sweating, barely keeping his feet, the only effort I could see in Ludovoco's face was the strain of concealing the fullness of his pleasure.

Though Alvantes turned in time to fend off another blow, it was obvious Ludovoco had left him that moment's opening. It went likewise for their next few exchanges, Alvantes escaping each by only the slightest of margins. Ludovoco wasn't giving him a chance, or even a moment's breath – only whittling him down. This was no longer a fight, if it ever had been. It was simply a protracted murder.

Then – and I couldn't say what tipped me off, perhaps a change in Alvantes's posture or in the tempo of the fight – it struck me that maybe things weren't quite so simple. I'd seen him fight many a time now, known him for longer than I cared to think about, and I felt more than saw the change in how he was handling himself.

Finally I understood. Alvantes had used the same ploy when he'd fought against Mounteban. It was a move unexpected enough to win him an edge – the sort of edge he urgently needed.

Even as I realised it, Alvantes dropped back on his right foot, lowering his defence a fraction. He was luring Ludovoco in, drawing the Pasaedan's focus away from his left side – because the last thing Ludovoco would expect from an enemy with a stump in place of a hand was a punch to the face. It would hurt Alvantes far more than it would Ludovoco, but it would buy him a moment's surprise – and just then, any chance was better than none.

Alvantes stumbled. For all his obvious exhaustion, his acting was impressive. Even I couldn't be sure whether this was his final gambit or just the last of his strength failing. His sword dipped further. In a moment, helplessly propelled by his duellist's instincts, Ludovoco was thrusting for his opponent's right side. But the stumble became a pivot, as Alvantes rolled on his left foot, shifted all his strength into his left arm – and lashed out.

Ducking effortlessly beneath the clumsy swing, Ludovoco flicked his blade across Alvantes's calf. Alvantes didn't cry out, but as he staggered, he did moan through gritted teeth.

"Really, Captain?" asked Ludovoco, with a joyful chuckle. "A cheap trick for so *honourable* a fighter."

Alvantes dropped to his knees. He looked surprised – whether at Ludovoco seeing so easily through his ruse or because his body had finally refused to stay up, I couldn't guess.

When Ludovoco took a step closer, Alvantes flailed for his legs. Ludovoco blocked, forced Alvantes's blade down, and – so quickly I could hardly register it – sliced Alvantes's arm. As his sword slipped from his grasp, Alvantes cried out for the first time, a sob of hopeless rage. He made to cradle his bleeding right wrist with his left hand. Then, realising the impossibility, he pushed to his knees and tried instead to fling himself at Ludovoco.

Ludovoco sidestepped; his foot crashed into Alvantes's ribs, sent him tumbling sideways. An instant later, it was followed by the point of Ludovoco's sword.

Behind me, Estrada screamed – a sound so naked and pained that I couldn't believe it could come from a human throat. It was almost loud enough to muffle Alvantes's own choked cry.

Ludovoco stepped round, careful to avoid Alvantes's hand, which still grasped spasmodically for his ankles. He put his foot on Alvantes's shoulder; it seemed to take only the slightest pressure to drive him down into the mud. Ludovoco levelled his sword, adjusted its angle carefully.

"A last mercy, Guard-Captain," he said. "A quick death. Much more than you deserve." As he raised his blade, I saw where it would land: across Alvantes's bared throat.

"Stop, damn you!" Mounteban's roar was huge amidst the unnatural silence; it actually froze Ludovoco in place. "Captain Lunto Alvantes is incapacitated," Mounteban cried. "Your fight is with me now."

Ludovoco looked as if he had every intention of going through with his execution, regardless of what Mounteban or anyone else thought. But Mounteban already had his own sword in hand, had already halved the distance between them; in the time it would take to end Alvantes's life, Mounteban would be on him. Reaching a swift decision, Ludovoco stepped away and dropped easily into a defence.

Mounteban hit him like a bull charging – and Ludovoco actually staggered. He span away into clear space, a half dozen quick steps carrying him free of Mounteban's first furious assault. Caught off guard, Ludovoco seemed momentarily to forget just who he was fighting, for when he scythed a blow towards Mounteban's left side, his steel span off a buckler in place of Alvantes's missing hand. Mounteban shoved the almost-delicate stroke aside and continued to chop wildly, pressing Ludovoco back still further.

Did Mounteban really think he could beat a fighter of such calibre by chopping like a woodsman? But whatever else he'd achieved, he had managed to drive Ludovoco away from our fallen guard-captain. As the two fighters paced round each other like angry dogs, Estrada was already running to recover Alvantes. Without quite thinking about it, I fell in behind her. As we drew near, Alvantes managed to push himself up onto hands and knees. He was alive, then – for the moment, at least.

Meanwhile, Mounteban had barely paused in his attack. Nor had it become less clumsy; it was still more a charge than an assault. I couldn't see what he hoped to gain by so inelegant a tactic. Rather than trying to hit his foe, it was almost as though Mounteban were flinging himself at him – which meant that for Ludovoco, it could only be a matter of waiting for the right opening.

Yet, for all its inevitability, when the end came it still caught me by surprise. One moment, Mounteban was hurling another blow at Ludovoco's head. The next, Ludovoco had flicked his entire body sideways, stepped with feline grace inside his opponent's defence. His sword wove a sinuous pattern in the air; it danced from Mounteban's thigh to his arm, and ended in a leisurely swipe across his forehead.

If Ludovoco had expected to stop him, however, he was bound for disappointment – for all the injuries did was make Mounteban press on all the harder. Though he was limping, hardly holding his sword, half blinded by blood, Mounteban opened his mouth and bellowed mindlessly and ploughed forward. Ludovoco's eyes went wide with shock that edged straight away into fear. For an instant, I thought he might really be in trouble.

Then the fear vanished, composure returned, and Ludovoco ran his sword clean through Mounteban's stomach.

Mounteban let go of his sword, watched vaguely as it tumbled earthward. His gaze drifted on, to note the blade run cleanly through his prodigious gut. Still clutching the hilt, Ludovoco made no effort to withdraw his weapon; only held his enemy's eyes and smiled. This time, however, there was relief mingled with his usual cruel glee – and I tried to take some slight comfort from that. Mounteban might have thrown his life away and all of ours with it, but at least, for a moment, he had made the bastard doubt himself.

Then, rather than try to pull away, Mounteban threw his arm around Ludovoco. He drew the other man close.

"What...?" asked Ludovoco, in horrified surprise. He was already struggling to get free, but Mounteban was a great deal bigger than him, surely twice his weight, and there was barely a thing Ludovoco could do. Mounteban reached with his free hand inside the folds of his cloak and then flung that arm too around Ludovoco's back, dragging the Pasaedan even more fiercely into his embrace.

Ludovoco's eyes went wide. He tried once more to force his way free, twisted in Mounteban's arms – but without any great enthusiasm this time. Like drunken dancers, the two turned before us. I saw Mounteban's left hand first, tight-clenched, pressed against Ludovoco's back. Then his fingers opened, his hand dropped away.

Where it had been, amidst a spreading stain just visible against the black of Ludovoco's cloak, there stood out a hilt and a finger's breadth of blade.

In width, the knife was little more than a needle. But I had no doubt of where it had come from, or what it was doing right then to Ludovoco's insides. I knew enough to recognise one of Franco's speciality knives, a weapon for an assassin or a street brawler rather than any duellist. It would have cut through mail and meat like a hot axe through butter.

Mounteban let go of Ludovoco then and slid backwards, flopped into the mud with a sigh. Ludovoco, for his part, looked round at us with vague disgust. He reached for the hilt protruding from his back, but rather than try to remove it, he merely patted around it with his fingers, as if curious. Then, his eyes still holding us, still showing nothing but contempt, he crumpled face down in the mire.

By then, Mounteban was lying on his back, knees hunched. He too was looking in our direction – or rather, I realised, at Estrada. He tried to mouth something, coughed, and flecks of blood sputtered from between his lips.

Estrada ran to him, slid to her knees. "It's all right," she said. "It's all right, Castilio. Hold on, will you?"

"Marina," he said – and her name brought with it another splash of crimson.

"Shush. It can wait."

Mounteban tried to shake his head, found the effort too much. "Listen..."

"I *am* listening," murmured Estrada. "But *you* have to stop talking."

"For you. It was."

"You stupid, stupid man. Lay still, Castilio."

"Forgive..." he tried again.

But the sentence would have to stay unfinished; for there was no more blood seeping from between his lips, nothing behind his eyes. And perhaps it was a small kindness, because it meant he would never have to hear Estrada's reply. "Oh, I wish I could," she whispered.

Yet, despite what she'd said, she was the only one who seemed concerned by Mounteban's passing, perhaps the only one besides me who'd even noticed. Excepting Kalyxis, the remainder of our number were clustered around Alvantes; at that precise moment, Navare was striving ineffectually to convince his captain that he shouldn't be trying to stand.

"It's not over yet," Alvantes was saying. "Don't waste time with me." His voice was a growl, barely audible. Yet, despite the fact that half his blood must have leaked out by then, his gaze was clear and fixed ahead.

I looked to see what had so preoccupied him, when by all rights he should have passed out a dozen times, and understood immediately. It *wasn't* over; the fury in the faces of the Pasaedan front line was ample testament to that. That barrier of armed men was moving, not towards us exactly, but swelling and shifting like water tugging at a shore. From all around there came a mounting blare of raised and outraged voices.

Was it only that their commander was dead? Or was it worse that he'd been cut down in so underhand a way? It occurred to me that Mounteban had died imagining he'd saved us, when in all likelihood he'd achieved nothing but to have us torn apart by an angry mob. Even if that rabble might be convinced to honour Ludovoco's word, they had other officers, and what possible reason would any of them have to let us go? The noise from all around was a rising tide – and I had no doubt that at any moment it would drown us.

Someone broke ranks then, and he'd taken a dozen steps before I convinced my panicked brain that his advance wasn't the beginning of a massacre. For the man approaching us was Ondeges, and his appearance set my heart on edge between hope and fresh trepidation. From what Gailus had said, Ondeges was an ally, sympathetic to Altapasaeda's cause, but he was also Ludovoco's second, and if he chose to pursue his fellow officer's cause against Alvantes, it would be a short fight indeed.

Ondeges came to a smart halt before our ravaged group. His steady gaze took in us all and settled upon Estrada. Loud enough that the Pasaedan soldiers at his back could hear every bit as well as we could, he said, "The duel is over. One man is dead. The other lives." He paused to weather a ripple of protest from his own lines and then raised his voice to continue. "By the terms agreed by Commander Ludovoco and as his second, I declare you free to go."

Estrada hurried towards him, paused only when she saw Ondeges's look of warning. "Commander," she said softly, "*thank you*."

"Leave now," replied Ondeges, matching his volume to hers. "I'd find a stretcher for Alvantes, but if you wait I fear it would do him no good anyway. I'll make sure your dead are brought to the gates before nightfall. Hurry, before they realise how little they care for my word."

"Captain Ondeges," Estrada said, "this is..."

"Nothing!" Ondeges hissed. Then, more gently he added, "A gesture... nothing more." He looked inexpressibly weary. Though his uniform was fresh, unstained by battle, he seemed every bit as exhausted as the most haggard of our party.

And suddenly, I understood. Everything I could have wanted to know about Ondeges was written clear upon his face. I knew how he'd worked for peace, how he'd challenged Ludovoco and even the King himself; I knew he'd risked his own life in doing so. For a moment, his gaze fell upon Kalyxis, and the rage I saw there was the bitter hatred of a man whose every plan had been brought crashing down, without sense or reason.

Then Ondeges looked back to Estrada and said, with perfect calm, "Nothing will make Panchessa change his mind now. Go while you can, pass the night as well as you're able... because tomorrow this army will be inside your walls, and there won't be a damn thing you or I can do about it."

CHAPTER TWENTY-ONE

We trooped back through the suburbs of Altapasaeda, less than twenty men and women passing where fifty had set out less than three hours before. There was myself and Estrada, Kalyxis and Malekrin; the remaining few, survivors of our fighting escort, were led by Navare, and bore Alvantes in a sling made hastily from their cloaks. He had slipped from awareness as we left the battlefield, and now his soft, unconscious groans were the only sound anyone made beside the slap of boots in mud.

As for the giants, they kept their distance, Saltlick leading and the remaining four carrying their fallen brother hefted upon their shoulders. Moving together like that, faces void of expression, armoured legs rising and falling in step, they none of them looked alive. I was reminded of a mechanism, like the cranes upon the docks of Altapasaeda, its parts blank and smooth. When they paused, I could only think of some great table rock made formless by the passing of centuries.

We'd survived – a few of us. Ludovoco, foremost of our enemies besides the King himself, was dead. Yet so was Mounteban, who for all my hatred I couldn't deny had fought staunchly for the city these last days; so, perhaps, would Alvantes be before the day was done. Gueverro had been cut down, along with many of our best fighting men. Not to mention a giant – a creature out of history, out of myth, with no right even to be on a Castovalian battlefield.

I'd lived to see another dawn. But, as the gates of Altapasaeda came finally into view, all I could feel was despair. Thanks to Panchessa and Kalyxis and their decades-old hatred, our last chance of peace was lost.

All that was left, all tomorrow could bring, was war. And as Ondeges had been so good as to point out, it was a war we stood no hope of winning.

Within the city we were met by a small crowd, blank-faced folk of various trades who watched as we struggled through a narrow opening in the northwestern gates. They didn't react to our arrival, nor did they attempt to question us – and no one, not even Estrada, tried to meet their gaze. As the last wounded man was helped inside, they broke up and began to mill away.

They'd waited to see if there was any hope for Altapasaeda. Now they had their answer.

I might not have fought in any meaningful sense, but I didn't believe I could have been any wearier if I had. It felt as if someone had removed each of my bones and replaced them with bars of lead. Free of the Suburbs, back in the relative safety of Altapasaeda, my fear was dulling to torpor. We'd tried and we'd failed; now, for all I stood to gain, I might as well lie down in the street and steal a few blessed hours of sleep before the end came.

I didn't imagine anyone would have cared if I had. Yet, though every step was like hefting a sledgehammer, I kept the pace. On some level I knew it was the right thing, the only thing left to do. Those of us who remained had been through something that would be burned into my thoughts for whatever remained of my life. If I closed my eyes I saw blood and filth and the bodies of the dead and dying. It would be a disservice to their memory to collapse now, when there was so much worse still to come.

I didn't notice at first when Saltlick and his giants broke from our pathetic column. Though they could easily have outpaced us, they'd been trailing behind, keeping what for them must have been the slowest of paces. Some sound or instinct made me glance sluggishly over my shoulder and I realised Saltlick had already vanished, that the last two giants were trailing into a side street. Given everything that we'd seen and endured over the last hour, I was surprised by how much it stung me that he'd left without any goodbye.

Just then, however, it was only another dull pain amongst others, a drop in a brimming lake; I was quick enough to put it from my mind. I felt as if I was trudging through thick fog, a miasma that hung just on the edge of vision. I took nothing in, paid no attention to the buildings I could dimly discern to either side. I had no idea or interest in where we were going. It was impossible to imagine a reason it would matter, so why concern myself?

Thus, it came as a surprise when I looked up and discovered that Estrada had led us back to the Dancing Cat. As always, there were men on the door, two of Castilio Mounteban's prized thugs. One eyed us sceptically while the other stepped to block our way.

"Mounteban?" the first asked.

Estrada shook her head.

He looked as if he wanted to say something more – his mouth half formed around it. Instead, he caught his companion roughly by the shoulder and drew him aside, indicating by the barest tilt of his head that we could go inside if we so chose.

Inside, the taproom was almost as desolate as the streets had been. There were a couple more of Mounteban's heavies in there, and a small cluster of men near the fire dressed in Altapasaedan uniform. They looked up as we entered and then, seeing our wounded, hurried to help. One of them swept a table clear – sending day-old plates and half empty tankards to the floor with a clatter that cut briefly through the murk in my head – and together they laid Alvantes there. He didn't stir; I'd have taken him for dead if it weren't for the faint moan that trickled from his closed lips.

Our other wounded lowered themselves or were helped onto benches. To one of the group who'd been there when we arrived, Estrada said, "Will you heat some water and bring it in here? There should be fresh bandages and ointments in my room upstairs... it's the second on the left."

Once she was satisfied that her orders would be followed, she hurried to Alvantes's side. Two of the men had successfully removed his brigandine and one of them was now trying to hack through the shirt beneath with a stubby knife.

"Let me," Estrada said, holding her hand out.

The man looked at her curiously, took in her expression. He flipped the knife and placed it hilt first in her palm. "Of course, ma'am," he said.

"If you want to be useful," she told him, "find a surgeon. Make certain they understand who their patient is."

The man snapped a salute, was out of the door in a flash. I heard his running feet thrashing the cobbles outside.

Estrada finished cutting Alvantes's blood-stiffened shirt free, working with a speed and deftness that the soldier had entirely lacked. In moments, she'd pared a patch of the wine-dark cloth. She peeled it away and let it drop with a moist smack to the floor.

I only caught a glimpse of Alvantes's wound – but it was enough. I threw out a hand to hold myself against the wall and let out a strangled gasp. Perhaps it was strange after all I'd witnessed that day, perhaps it was just one horror piled upon too many others, but it took all my strength of will not to vomit.

When I managed to straighten, I realised Estrada was standing beside me, her hand on my shoulder. "Get out of here, Easie," she told me. "Go rest. You can use my room for a while if you like."

I looked at her uncertainly. "*I* should rest?" Her face was waxen; her clothes were spattered with blood, some of it surely hers. "Estrada..."

"I'm all right," she said. "With Mounteban..." She paused, breathed deep. "With Mounteban gone and Alvantes hurt, I'm needed more than ever. I'll sleep when I can."

"You should at least have a bath," I mumbled. "You smell like a week-old corpse."

Estrada managed the faint ghost of a smile. "Thank you, Easie," she said, "I'll bear that in mind."

I nodded, tried to return the smile, realised my face had contorted into some sort of painful grimace and gave up. Hunting for something sympathetic to say, I tried, "Good luck with Alvantes. I hope... well, you know..."

"I know. Go, Easie."

There was an edge to her voice that time, and I realised that from her point of view, I was wasting both time and space. I turned away without another word, tramped up the stairs, pushed open Estrada's door – and was a little impressed with myself that I managed to make it all the way to the bed before I fell over.

I would probably have slept until a Pasaedan came to drag me from my bed. In so much as I'd had a plan as I passed out, that had been it.

It wasn't to be. Somewhere far away, someone was calling my name. Distant though the sound was, it was insistent, and try as I might I couldn't ignore it. Bit by bit, it was hauling me back to wakefulness.

I understood then what it must be like for the fish that's hooked and dragged out of its native element. But no watery depths could have been as comforting as the fathomless gulf of my sleep, no fisherman's basket as terrible as opening my eyes to the dim afternoon sun that seeped around the shutters.

Estrada was standing beside my bed – or rather, I remembered, *her* bed. It occurred to me that she probably wanted it back, and I tried to ask her, but the words came out in an incomprehensible slur.

"Damasco?" Estrada asked.

"All right," I managed. "I'm awake. What is it?"

"It's Saltlick, Easie. He wants to talk to you. It's important, and I think you need to be there to hear it."

"Can't he come here?" I mumbled. Then, realising how unreasonable that was, I began again. "Alright. Just let me get dressed."

"You're already dressed," Estrada pointed out. "You didn't even take your boots off."

I looked down at myself. She was right, and a goodly portion of the sheets were now black with filth. "Oh. Sorry."

I rolled to the edge of the bed, plunged more than climbed off it. Estrada was already halfway out the door by the time I'd righted myself, and so I hurried after. She was in the street before I managed to catch up. "How's Alvantes?" I asked.

"Alive," she said. "He's sleeping."

The faint chill in the air was going some way to bringing me back to my senses. "That's good news," I said, and meant it. "Now will you tell me what this is about? You obviously know more than you're letting on."

Estrada slowed a fraction. "I'll tell you what I can," she said. "Before we set out this morning, Mounteban told me about a deal he'd made with the giants... with Saltlick. He told me how he'd had smiths and carpenters working for days to ready that armour they wore this morning, back when he thought they might be convinced to join our side."

"Then Saltlick came back and threw that plan right out the window," I put in.

"Exactly. There was no way Saltlick could be talked into letting the giants fight. So Mounteban made him a proposition. Only, Mounteban's gone now, and it falls to me to honour his promise."

"I can't believe Mounteban had anything to offer that would make Saltlick take the kind of risk he took out there today," I told her. "If it had only been his own life on the line than maybe..."

"Free passage," interrupted Estrada. "A way out of the city. That's what Mounteban offered. He would remove the barricades from one of the southern gates and let the giants leave."

"That's ridiculous!" I cried. "They should have been allowed to go days ago. Why didn't they just tear down the barricades and make their own way out?"

Estrada didn't bother to answer, merely waited for my brain to catch up with my mouth.

"Oh. Right," I said. "*Giants.*"

It would never have occurred to Saltlick to force his way out of the city. His mind simply didn't allow for solutions that relied on force of any kind. For that same reason, Mounteban had had to think of another way of using the giants; a way that would fit with their rigid morality. They couldn't be made into a weapon, but a rescue party was different – especially when there were people Saltlick cared for amongst those in need of rescuing. Though Mounteban couldn't have known at the time that such a situation would arise, it was at least a probability – and anyway, the deal had cost him nothing.

If only I'd helped Saltlick when he'd asked. If only I hadn't been so damned selfish. If I could have persuaded the giants to make their own way out of the city then... well, then I'd be dead, Estrada too, and Altapasaeda would surely be in the hands of Ludovoco and Panchessa by now. But a giant wouldn't have died, and Saltlick wouldn't be bearing that death on his conscience, as I knew he must be.

"So now you're letting them leave?" I said. "At least that's something."

"The thing is, Easie," Estrada said, "there's more to it than that. But I think Saltlick needs to tell you the rest himself."

We passed the rest of our journey in silence; Estrada seemed no more interested in further conversation than I was. Minutes had passed before I recognised the former tannery that now served as home for Altapasaeda's giant population. Just as when I'd last been there, a giant stood guard to either side of the entrance.

While the day's cool breeze might have unmuddied my thoughts, it did nothing to shift the stink that hung around the place. I was ready to point out that there was no way I could go inside and listen to what Saltlick had to say, since I never heard well while gagging and passing out – but fortunately Estrada was ahead of me. "We're here to see Saltlick," she said, "he's expecting us."

Estrada's credit with the giants was apparently better than mine, for there were no communication problems this time. One of the sentries ducked inside and less than a minute later he was back with Saltlick. Saltlick looked every bit as spent as I'd expected and more; his wounds were lurid and inflamed, his face haggard and shadowed.

"Hello, Saltlick," I said. "It's good to see you."

He strived for a smile, but the vague upturn of his mouth didn't make it very far.

"Estrada tells me you have something to say," I tried.

Saltlick nodded. Even then, however, it took him a few moments to reply – and when he did, he spoke slowly, hesitantly. "This..." he said, taking in Altapasaeda with a sweep of one plate-sized hand. "No good. No good for giants."

"It hasn't been all that much good for people lately either," I pointed out.

Saltlick's obvious frustration told me I'd misunderstood. I watched as the effort of pursuing the right words contorted his features. "No kill," he said. "No fight."

"He means," said Estrada, "that it's not *their* fight."

I scowled at her. "I knew that. But Saltlick," I said, "no one *expects* you to fight. All of that was Mounteban's doing."

Saltlick shook his head. "Done," he said. "Too late. Must leave now. Go home."

"Estrada told me," I agreed. I couldn't understand why he'd said it so mournfully, with such clear remorse. Did he imagine I'd expected him to stay and help us? As far as I was concerned, the giants had done everything that could be asked of them and more; if they wanted to leave instead of being slaughtered with the rest of us then no one could possibly blame them.

"Not come back," Saltlick added – and there was something in the way he mangled those particular syllables that gave me my first glimmer of comprehension.

"Wait," I said. "You mean, not ever? Not even... well... not even to *visit*?"

"Not come back," he repeated, solemnly.

"But... Easie friend, right?"

"Easie friend," he agreed.

"All right. So I'll come and see you, then. If I survive the next couple of days, that is, which is unlikely enough I know. But if we somehow get through this, I can visit you?"

Saltlick paused for so long that I thought he'd failed to understand – and I was about to start again, more slowly, when he shook his head once again. "No more," he said.

"You're saying..." But I didn't finish. I *knew* what he was saying. It wasn't Altapasaeda that Saltlick was turning his back on; it wasn't even the Castoval. It was the entire world of men

– the world that had brought such immeasurable harm to his people. And however I might not like it, however I wished it weren't true, I was a part of that.

My first urge was to shout at him. Did everything we'd been through mean nothing? All of our adventures, our last minute escapes, our victories large and small... could he really have forgotten?

Except, I knew I had no right to argue. I understood perfectly. Saltlick had had to make a choice, a choice inevitable since the moment Moaradrid had first turned up at the giants' door. The one way he could protect his people was to return them to their own world and make sure that ours never intruded on their solitude again. Otherwise, there would always be someone who saw their size, their strength, their power, and mistook them for weapons.

Saltlick crouched and held out his hand. I placed mine inside it, though it barely covered two of his fingers, and we shook awkwardly. He repeated the gesture with Estrada. Then, before I could say even one of the hundred things I suddenly, urgently felt the need to tell him, he had turned and ducked back inside. The doors swung shut. The sentries retook their posts. And a lump of raw pain swam from somewhere in my chest and lodged hard in my throat.

"Easie... I'm sorry, I know how hard this must be for you," said Estrada. "But I have to get back. Are you coming?"

"I'll catch up," I managed.

Estrada patted my arm. "I really *am* sorry," she told me. "But this is for the best. You wanted to save the giants, and this is the only way."

I nodded dumbly. I'd have liked to tell her that I knew she was right, but all I could feel was overwhelming sadness, and I suspected that if I kept talking it was going to come out. However unremittingly horrible that day had been, I wasn't ready to break down in front of Estrada.

I watched her leave. Once she was out of view, I started back the way we'd come, engulfed in my misery. I'd never entirely appreciated what a comfort it had been to have Saltlick around until he wasn't there, how much more tolerable his presence had made the trials of the last few weeks. Now, whatever was to come, I'd have to endure it alone – with none of his huge grins or monosyllabic wisdom or giant-sized acts of kindness to help me.

In the wake of my sadness, slowly but surely, came anger. Not at Saltlick this time; no, now my rancour fell upon Mounteban, on Alvantes and Moaradrid, all of those who'd tried to bend the giants to their own will. Only, it was a useless sort of anger, because Mounteban and Moaradrid were both dead now, and Alvantes might follow them soon enough. So my thoughts roved onwards: to Panchessa and Kalyxis and their lovers' tiff turned countries-spanning war. I replayed in my mind the fateful meeting in Panchessa's tent, and considered those who'd helped tip it towards catastrophe. And suddenly I remembered one other person who'd contributed more than their share to the events that had forever separated me from my friend.

Malekrin. How had I forgotten about Malekrin?

Of everyone I had a right to be angry with, the boy might not be the guiltiest, but he was certainly the most available – not to mention the least intimidating. Anyway, he was that bit more deserving for the fact that until this morning I'd been starting to warm to him a little. Yes, if I had to vent my temper on someone then Malekrin was as choice a candidate as any.

My pace picked up in proportion to my mounting ire, and by the time I reached the Dancing Cat I was veritably storming. I wasn't even sure what I intended, since for all I knew Malekrin was with his grandmother and the contingent from Shoan. Just that once, however, luck had favoured me – for there he was, sat near the fireplace, at the table he'd claimed for himself in recent days.

By then I was so wrought-up that I practically skidded to a halt. "You knew, didn't you?" I snapped without preamble. "You knew what your grandmother was planning."

Engrossed in his own thoughts, Malekrin had apparently missed my hurried entrance. He looked up at me with mingled annoyance and incomprehension. "What? That she was going to pick a fight with Panchessa? How would I have known that?"

"The fleet," I said. "I'm talking about the fleet."

Malekrin's face fell. "Oh."

"So you *did*."

"I had my suspicions," he said. "I mean, what did anyone think my grandmother would want with a fleet of warships?"

A small part of my brain observed that he had a point, but I wasn't about to listen to it. "You could have warned Alvantes and Estrada. If they'd known, they'd never have let Kalyxis into that tent. Didn't you say you wanted to help end this war? All you've done is make things worse."

I was expecting an indignant reply, or perhaps anger to match my own – so that when Malekrin only looked aside, it took some of the wind from my sails. I had just time to consider that I might have been a little hard on him when a noise from the doorway broke in on my thoughts. When I looked round, two Altapasaedan soldiers were standing awkwardly on the threshold.

"We're looking for somebody called Malekrin," said one.

I was about to point out that they'd not only found him but were welcome to him, when Gailus bustled in after them. Before I could think to wonder what he might want, someone else marched through the door behind him – someone who had no right to be in Gailus's company, who shouldn't even have been within the walls of Altapasaeda.

"This here's..." continued the soldier.

"I *know* who they are," I cut him off. "That's Senator Gailus from Pasaeda, and behind him is Commander Ondeges, currently a general in the army that's getting ready to slaughter us tomorrow."

"I'm not looking for trouble," said Ondeges. "I'm here as ambassador of the King."

"And that's supposed to make me feel better?" I asked. Then, remembering the soldier's opening enquiry, I added, "What do you want with Malekrin?"

"I don't want anything," Ondeges replied. "But his highness requests his presence, as a matter of urgency. And I think it would be in all our interests if the boy complies."

"Does Marina Estrada know about this?" I said.

"She doesn't," inserted Gailus, "and there isn't time to tell her. Anyway, the fewer people who know, the less likely word is to get back to Kalyxis."

"Maybe word *should* get to her," I told him. "You've already walked us into one massacre today. What makes you think we should trust either of you?"

"It's all right, Damasco." Brushing past me, Malekrin addressed himself to Gailus and Ondeges. "I'll go."

"What?" I said. "Don't be an idiot."

Malekrin turned me a look more pained and, in its way, more childish than any expression I'd yet seen on that obstinate face of his. "You were right," he said. "I wanted to help and all I've done is made things worse. The King wants to talk to me, and I have things I want to say to him, so where's the problem?"

I sighed heavily. So this was my fault now? "I didn't *mean* that. I was just angry. Look, I'm sure this will all work itself out without you making any stupid, noble gestures. I've spent most of the last two months with one person or another trying to kill me, and I'm still here to tell about it. Why should this be any different?"

"Malekrin," Gailus put in, with a glare aimed in my direction, "if you're to go, it needs to be now."

Malekrin nodded, and then let his head hang; the gesture made me think of a prisoner placing his neck on the block in Red Carnation Square. "I'm coming," he said. "But, Damasco... would you come with me? I mean, in case..."

"Of course not!" I cried. "In case *what*? In case you decide you want to rob the place on the way out? You've already dragged me into trouble once today."

"In case," Malekrin said quietly, "I'm too much of a coward to go through with it."

Now he really did look like a child, a child trying to keep his head up in waters much too deep for him. "You're not a coward," I told him, as certainly as I could.

"Well... I'll find out, won't I?"

I sighed once more – and even to my own ears, it seemed to go on forever, like the last stale air draining from a bellows. It was the sound, I realised, of a man grown so used to defeat that it hardly even registered anymore. Could it really be any worse for me to hand myself over to the King today, rather than waiting for him to tear down the gates tomorrow?

"All right," I said. "I'll come."

CHAPTER TWENTY-TWO

After a brief discussion between Gailus and the sentries, Ondeges led us out of Altapasaeda by the western gate, the one once reserved for the City Guard.

Ondeges had horses waiting for us in a copse a short way from the road. However, even on horseback and at the quick pace he set, working our way around the jutting corner of Altapasaeda took some time. Evening was already falling, the sky a blue-grey trimmed with purple in its heights, as we crossed into the Suburbs. Unlit and empty of inhabitants, the buildings seemed even more derelict and ominous than usual. It took an effort of will not to think of our journey in the other direction a mere few hours ago.

It was strange to find the Pasaedan camp almost cheerful-seeming after everything that had happened so recently within its bounds. There was no sign left of the morning's fighting; no bodies, and no blood that I could discern in the fading daylight. But there were campfires now, their orange light wavering merrily in the gloom, and from more than one side I could smell the odour of food cooking. It only occurred to me then that I hadn't eaten all day – and though the soldier's dinner was surely meagre fare, I found my mouth watering.

By contrast, the royal pavilion looked less impressive in the evening light. Its colours were faded, its outlines confused; it looked less like a transplanted palace now, more like an odd-shaped hill with flags stuck into it. As before, there were guards on the door – the same two as before, I realised. When both Malekrin and I claimed to have no weapons, they made a point of patting us down until they were satisfied we were telling the truth. Then one of them, looking at me but speaking to Ondeges, asked, "Who's this?"

The King's own guards, it seemed, didn't have to be polite even to commanders. Ondeges didn't seem concerned, however, as he replied, "The boy wants him along. He's harmless."

"You vouch for him?" asked the guard.

"I vouch that he's no threat," Ondeges said.

The guard nodded. "All right. But no one else."

An elaborate way of saying Ondeges wasn't allowed in; again, though, he seemed unperturbed. But as the guard moved to lead the way, Ondeges leaned close to me and hissed, "*Just keep your mouth shut.*"

I didn't contradict him. I had nothing to say to Panchessa besides some enthusiastic pleading, if and when things went how I expected them to go.

Our guard led us inside by the same route as before, and on into the great hexagonal chamber. Just as before, Panchessa was waiting sprawled upon his throne. This time, however, only two cloaked lanterns burned, sinking most of the space in ruddy obscurity, and there was no one else to be seen: no advisors, not even any guards. At a wave from the King, even the one who'd escorted us departed.

What a shame Malekrin had picked me for a companion. Anyone else might have thought to smuggle a weapon in, or else attacked Panchessa with their bare hands, and so ended this war once and for all. Then again, I wasn't sure that Panchessa would need more than a nudge to ease him out of life. Now that my eyes had adjusted to the scanty, red-tinged light, I could see that he looked more infirm than he had that morning; he was gently shivering, every so often twitching, and his face was drawn and waxen.

Panchessa looked Malekrin up and down, ignoring my presence entirely. In the shadows, I couldn't make out anything of his expression. Finally, he said, "Thank you for coming, boy. There were things I'd meant to tell you before, and instead I let my anger at your grandmother get the better of me."

"My name isn't boy," Malekrin said. "It's Malekrin."

I winced – but all Panchessa said was, "Yes, I remember. I was hard on you earlier, Malekrin."

"I suppose," said Malekrin, "that being king means you can talk to people however you choose."

"True," agreed Panchessa, ignoring Malekrin's obvious gibe. "Still. Of all the conversations I might have had with my only grandson on our first meeting, that wasn't the one I would have chosen."

Malekrin shrugged. "I'm not sure what else we'd have to talk about."

Panchessa gave that a moment's consideration; at least that was how I interpreted his silence. Eventually he said, "I didn't rape your grandmother, Malekrin."

"That's between you and my grandmother."

"I didn't force myself on her. She was willing as any woman ever was. But I knew what she wanted; and when I think back, perhaps I knew as well how fiercely she wanted it. Power. To be the consort of a king. I took her, and I knew I'd never give her what she sought."

While he'd spoken, Panchessa had been staring at the carpeted ground. Now, he looked up, as though expecting a response. Whatever he'd been seeking, he seemed not to find it in Malekrin's face.

"She was a beautiful woman, then," Panchessa continued. "And I was a handsome man. What need had I to worry about

what some chieftain's wife might covet? Or whether she'd
hate me for it afterwards?"

Again Panchessa's eyes roved across Malekrin's face. Again
he failed to find whatever he'd been seeking.

"But she *did* hate. And if I'd known what harm would come
from those nights, perhaps I'd have done differently. Then
again, perhaps I wouldn't have. I've told no one this, Malekrin,
no one ever... but it saddened me to think that my son, your
father, despised me. I never met him. They tell me he was a
brave man, though – those that did and lived to tell."

"I wouldn't know," said Malekrin. If he was in any way
moved by the King's unexpected openness, it didn't show in
his voice; in fact, he sounded more bored than anything. "My
father hardly spoke to me."

"Malekrin," said Panchessa, "I know you're angry. I know
you have your reasons. But you should try and hear me now.
I'm an old man, I'm dying, and I've come to realise – perhaps
too late – that the legacy I leave is not the one I might have
chosen. Whether or not you can understand that, boy, I suggest
you listen to what I have to tell you."

I nudged Malekrin hard in the ribs. "You *should* listen, for
both our sakes," I whispered. So far, every word to leave his
mouth had seemed a deliberate attempt to lose us our heads.

"I have a proposal for you," Panchessa said. "Come back to
Pasaeda with me and learn what I can teach you in whatever
time I have left. If and when I'm satisfied that you can bear
the responsibility, you may have your wish: you will be king
in my place."

"I told you before," said Malekrin, without the slightest
hesitation. "That's not my wish, it's my grandmother's. I don't
want to be king. I just want you to leave this city alone; this city
and Shoan. I don't want anyone else to have to die because of
you and my grandmother."

Panchessa's face darkened. Whatever conciliation had been

in his voice was altogether vanished as he said, softly but ever so clearly, "You dare compare me to that woman?"

"You both think people are tools for you to use," said Malekrin. "Or weapons. Or toys. But they're not. They have a right to live their lives without being sent off to die because of someone else's stupid squabbles."

"You understand nothing about..."

"No, *you* don't understand. You think you can make up for all the harm you've done like this? All my life has ever been is what other people thought it should be!" Malekrin's voice was quavering, close to tears – and yet there was a streak of iron in it I'd never heard before. "Well, I won't be king. Not because you or my grandmother or anyone else thinks it's right. Not for *any* reason."

"You... ungrateful, you..." Panchessa stood then, in a sudden jolt that seemed to cost more effort than standing ever reasonably should. "Go now," he said. His voice was thick, strangled. "Get out of my sight. Whatever happens now, it's on your head."

Ondeges was waiting outside Panchessa's tent. One look at our expressions told him everything he needed to know. "It's war then?" he said.

"To the bitter end," I told him cheerfully. For no reason I could make sense of, I felt oddly light – as though a weight had lifted from my shoulders. It was as close to real happiness as I'd been in days.

Ondeges made no answer. His face was harsh and closed beneath the dancing firelight. He led us as far as the edge of camp, ignoring the curious looks of the huddled fighting men we passed. When we drew near to the Suburbs, he handed me the lantern he carried and said, "You can make your own way from here. There's much I have to attend to before morning."

"I'd imagine so," I said. "Murdering armies don't just lead themselves."

The look Ondeges gave me was certainly murderous enough; but all he said was, "No, they don't."

When he was gone and we were deep enough into the tumbledown depths of the Suburbs that I felt confident we wouldn't be overheard, I said to Malekrin, "Well, that was it... the last possible chance for Altapasaeda. And may I say what a pleasure it was to accompany you while you provoked the most dangerous man in the land."

Malekrin looked at me. There was pain in his eyes, but also defiance. "That wasn't what I'd planned. I'd meant to go along with whatever he said. Only... I couldn't."

"And even if you had," I said, "what's to say Panchessa wouldn't go back on his word? Or that the Senate would accept you? Or the rest of Ans Pasaeda, for that matter? And how would your grandmother have reacted if she'd thought there was a risk of you becoming anything other than her puppet?"

Malekrin's sullenness turned to open astonishment. "You don't think I was wrong to refuse?"

"I wouldn't go that far!" I exclaimed. "Still, what you told him in there... maybe you weren't right to *say it*, but you were right in what you said." I offered Malekrin a weary grin. "What I mean is, you may have just got us all killed, but for what it's worth, I have to admit I'm impressed."

Malekrin returned a hesitant smile. "Thank you for coming with me, Damasco," he said. "And I'm sorry I dragged you into this. You've been a good friend to me."

Now it was my turn to be taken aback. To the best of my remembrance, I'd never done anything for Malekrin that could be considered being a friend, let alone a good one. Then again, given the solitary life he'd led, I supposed his standards for such things were very low.

Either way, I'd meant what I'd said; I *was* impressed that he'd defied Panchessa, that he'd cast away a chance at unimaginable wealth and power in an attempt – however stupid and misguided – to stand up for what he believed. Given my present circumstances and their probably violent conclusion on the morrow, I supposed I could do worse for a friend than this troublemaking barbarian brat.

"You're welcome," I said. "Although, if any other bloodthirsty kings want to talk to you in the near future then perhaps I could stay home next time. Now let's get back, shall we? If there's one thing I hate, it's being slaughtered on a bad night's sleep."

Gailus was waiting just inside the western gate. He had acquired a chair from somewhere and, astonishingly, a portable brazier; he was sat on the one and warming his hands before the other, wrapped in an enormous woollen cloak that made him look both smaller and older than he was.

As the sentries let us in, he gave us a measuring look and said, "You two seem merry enough. I trust that means good news?"

"Oh, the best," I told him. "Malekrin told his highness precisely where and how far up he could stick his offer."

To my surprise, Gailus gave a shrill chuckle. "I have to say, I wish I'd seen that."

"You seem very relaxed," I pointed out, "for someone who's discovered he's sitting in a city that's going to be razed to the ground in a few hours."

"Oh, it won't come to that," Gailus said. "A few token executions, perhaps a building or two burned to remind the people who's in charge. Panchessa's a tyrant, but he's not a monster. There'll be no more freedom for the Castoval, but then what did you ever really do with it?"

"Some of the people getting executed will probably be me and my friends," I said. "And I'd think the point of freedom is that you don't *have* to do anything with it."

Gailus barked out a laugh. "Ha! Damasco, isn't it? You have a political head on you, I see. Perhaps you should consider a change of career?"

"I might have the head," I told him sourly, "but I don't think I have the stomach."

I realised then with abrupt clarity that, whatever happened tomorrow, Gailus's neck wouldn't be one of those on the chopping block – and for a moment, seeing him sat before his brazier speaking blithely of politics and death, I felt an almost uncontainable revulsion. Even before it had passed, I'd turned on my heel and begun back in the direction of the Dancing Cat.

I parted from Malekrin in a side street close to the Cat. Only after we'd said our brief goodbyes did it occur to me to ask where he was staying.

For my part, I went back to my space in the barn, which had come to seem as much like home as anywhere in Altapasaeda. But the warm scent of hay only brought back memories I'd have rather left alone. Whenever I started to drift I recalled that Saltlick was nesting nearby and opened my eyes with a jolt, to be met by darkness and the truth. Saltlick was gone, or would be soon, and I would never see him again.

For all my restlessness, I must have fallen asleep at some point – for I woke, a little scared and not at all refreshed, to a commotion thundering from somewhere nearby. I struggled to judge its source, but it was only as the last dregs of sleep drained away that I realised the reason for my difficulty: the sound was all about me, shouts reverberating within the inn, loud footsteps and more raised voices from the street, and an impenetrable backdrop of noise from the direction of the northern walls.

I crawled from my makeshift bed, stretched cramped muscles. Already the sounds from nearby were starting to diminish. There was no question that the uproar was focused increasingly upon the city's north side, and that could only mean one thing – the attack had begun. I felt a sharp tug then, deep in my bones, which said, *Head south, Damasco! Run, damn you!* Except that every gate was locked tight. There was no way out of the city, and even if there had been, it was too late to take it. I might not be any kind of hero, but this was what my life had come to, and I'd no choice left but to see it through.

I stumbled into the courtyard, wasn't surprised to find it empty. White Corn Road was quiet too, though I thought I could still make out the distant beat of feet and hooves from somewhere to my right. I turned in that direction and picked up my pace.

It was a pleasant day, the sky cloudless and richly blue; it was hard not to be roused by the sun's soft warmth upon my face. I might have mixed feelings for Altapasaeda in general, but on such a morning I couldn't help feeling a little awed by its brash architecture, its broad, cobbled streets and the grandiosity and strangeness of the Temple District. If I had to die anywhere, if I had to die *for* anywhere, I supposed the Castoval's one and only city was as good a place as any.

Turning the corner that brought the northwestern gatehouse into view, it seemed everyone left in Altapasaeda must be up there on the walls. I saw men and women, young and old, and most of them armed and armoured; that was, if pitchforks, spades and swords so antique that only rust held them together could be considered weapons, if leather aprons, handmade helmets and scraps of metal strapped at shins and elbows could be deemed armour.

Estrada was there as well, near to the gatehouse, with a heavily bandaged Navare and a few others I recognised, most of them hangers-on from Mounteban's short term in power. Alvantes, of course, was conspicuous by his absence. Had he survived the night? It sent a shudder through me to think that he wouldn't be with us for the city's last defence. With Alvantes, it would still have been a hopeless fight, but I'd seen Alvantes triumph against impossible odds more than once before. Without him, I feared hopeless really did mean hopeless.

I hurried up the nearest steps and onto the wall walk. I had to shove a little to get a view over the battlements, drawing nervous scowls from an elderly couple armed respectively with a pick axe and a surprisingly hefty-looking ladle.

I'd have done better not to have looked. If the Pasaedan army had been impressive up close, from above it was awe-inspiring, their numbers made all the more daunting by being crammed into and around the remaining streets of the Suburbs. They stood still and silent, split into divisions that lapped and angled round the shanty buildings. It struck me that their forward lines were well within bowshot, a strategic misstep I wouldn't have expected. Then again, they had shields, I only counted a handful of bows along the wall walk, and it would take more than a tiny advantage like that to swing things in our favour. Even including the most ill-suited and inept amongst our ranks, the Pasaedans outnumbered us by five to one.

So what were they waiting for?

There was no point in my trying to guess; despite what I might have occasionally imagined to the contrary, I was no strategist. Instead, I decided I might as well catch up with Estrada. I edged along the wall walk, careful not to startle any of the heavily armed citizens I slipped past. Drawing closer, I noticed Malekrin behind Estrada and waved a greeting, which he returned with a terse nod and nervous smile. He had found Shoanish armour and a scimitar from somewhere, both a fraction too large, and the resulting combination was absurd, yet undeniably a little impressive. Did his presence mean Kalyxis was close? Yes, there she was – and despite the press upon the walls, her small troop had a portion entirely to themselves.

I looked away before she could notice me in return and said, "Good morning, Mayor Estrada. Or is it Commander Estrada today?"

"Hello Damasco," Estrada said. Her face was gaunt, her eyes dark; I had no doubt she'd spent every minute of the night at Alvantes's bedside. "Call me whatever you find easiest."

A tempting offer under better circumstances. Instead I asked, "How's Alvantes?"

"Better," she replied. "He's awake, and talking. I think he'd have been up here with a sword if only he could stand."

"I don't doubt it," I agreed. Then, hesitantly, I added, "And Saltlick? Is he..."

"Gone. The giants are gone, Easie. They left just after dawn."

"Oh." Some part of me hadn't quite believed he'd go through with it – that Saltlick would choose to end the journey we'd begun so long ago without me. "That's that, then. For the best, like you said. That they weren't here for this, I mean."

But Estrada's attention had moved on from me. She was leaning forward to stare down into the street beyond the walls – and though the act seemed risky when arrows were likely to be pouring from that direction at any minute, I realised others were doing the same.

There was something irresistible in the wave of murmured exclamations running back and forth along the walls. I pressed into a gap between Estrada and Navare and spied over the battlements. At first, I couldn't see much that I hadn't noticed before; only the desolate ruins of the Suburbs and far too many soldiers to number. "What *is* it?" I asked. "What's happening?"

"Be *quiet*, Damasco," Estrada said. "The King..."

I saw then where she was looking. Along one of the wider streets, one of the very few in the suburbs that were paved, a palanquin was approaching. It was borne on the shoulders of four men who, if I hadn't been witness to the real thing, I would probably have described as giants. In front and behind rode a dozen riders, their armour as ornate as any lady's finest jewellery.

The palanquin finished its slow journey in the street below us and its titanic bearers laid it down, without apparent strain. Two of the riders dismounted, one moving to open a door carved with the royal heron insignia while the other held their horses.

Estrada had been right. Out stepped Panchessa, dressed lavishly, and even wearing a sword at his hip. The riders that were still mounted hurried to shield their monarch from attack – not that anyone on our side was showing much interest in making one. This would be the first time the majority of Altapasaedans had ever seen their king, and despite what his arrival portended, the mood seemed more curious than fearful.

Panchessa waited until silence fell. It didn't take long, and when it came it was a hush deep as an ocean, in which a mouse's flatulence would have sounded like a house collapsing. Amidst that unnatural calm, Panchessa's voice sounded stronger and more commanding than it had the night before. "Altapasaedans," he said, "open your gates to me."

"The day the frozen hells catch fire," muttered Navare, close to my ear. Estrada said nothing.

And me? I was caught by a single, overpowering thought. It had seemingly come from nowhere – yet as soon as it had arrived, I'd realised it had been building for days. "This doesn't make sense," I whispered.

No one responded – but then I hadn't been speaking to anyone except myself. Now that it was out however, now that my brain was working, I felt as if I'd woken from a long stupor.

"We have to do what he says," I said, "we have to open the gates."

Estrada's head snapped round. Her expression was somewhere between surprise and infuriation. "We have to do nothing of the sort."

"Listen to me," I told her, and this time my voice was urgent. "Estrada, listen to me now, if it's the only time you ever do. There's one way left we can save this city – and it relies on you opening those gates right now."

CHAPTER TWENTY-THREE

"If we open the gates," Estrada said, "there may never be another chance to listen to anything you say, Damasco."

"No! Don't you see?" I was growing frantic; I strove to check myself. "Estrada, it's the only way."

I knew what I said was true. Because as I'd looked at Panchessa, there in the street with his vast army at his back, I had tried to see a terrifying despot, a bloody-handed warlord intend on tearing down our city brick by brick – yet all I'd actually seen was an ailing old man.

With that realisation, memories of the last night's conversation had come back clearly into my mind. Malekrin might not have been able to hear what Panchessa had said, but I had – and though I hadn't understood at the time, I did now. Panchessa could have levelled Altapasaeda a dozen times, had he wanted to; if he'd been determined enough, there was no punishment he couldn't have inflicted, no enemy he couldn't have revenged himself upon.

"Estrada," I said, "what were you plotting with Ondeges, back when we were fleeing from the Shoanish fleet? No... don't tell me, I know."

"But it wouldn't have worked," she said, exasperated. "Panchessa would never have agreed, let alone Kalyxis. And Malekrin?"

"They will now," I told her. "Because there's no other choice. It's the only thing Panchessa cares about anymore, don't you see? Estrada, please, trust me on this... Give the order or we're all going to die here."

For a long moment, her dark eyes held mine, and I could read every emotion there, clear as day. I saw trepidation, doubt, even fear – not for herself, but for those who had gathered here, the people who had placed their lives in her care. I could see what the gamble I was so glibly arguing for actually meant to her, the hideous burden of it. And with that, all my certainty vanished.

I was about to tell her I was wrong, that I was the last person she should be listening to – but I was too late. "Do what his highness says!" she cried ringingly. "Unbarricade the gates!"

There was surprisingly little resistance to our dramatic about-face from the gathered folk of Altapasaeda. No one commented on the fact that one minute Estrada had been ready to fight for this gate to the last man, woman or child, and now here she was opening it simply because Panchessa had asked her to. I put it down to the fact that none of them had much wanted to fight, and certainly not against their king; whatever was happening now, it at least offered the slim hope of an alternative.

With a crowd of Altapasaedans working in concert, it took mere minutes before the last scrap of barricade was wrenched away. Beneath, the heavily patched gates looked like a patchwork quilt of wood. They creaked in grating protest as they were hauled wide.

I'd assumed Panchessa would climb back into his palanquin, and enter accompanied by his full escort. Instead, he crossed the short distance on foot, with a mere dozen men at his back. It might not stop his army pouring after in his wake, but it seemed a small concession at least.

Estrada responded in kind. She'd called Malekrin over and, despite the resistance obvious in his face, he had hurried to join us. Though many of Mounteban's former cronies had made efforts to catch her eye, however, she had carefully overlooked them. Kalyxis, too, she'd studiedly ignored, and I couldn't but notice how Navare and his men had moved to discreetly bar her path.

Thus it was that the party waiting just beyond the gatehouse consisted of three people only: Estrada, Malekrin and me. I'd never felt so conspicuous in my life; the expectation of the nearby crowds was like a weight pressing from all sides.

"Good morning, your highness," said Estrada, as Panchessa stepped from the shadow of the gatehouse. She gave a deep bow that Malekrin and I hurried to emulate.

"Is this a fit delegation to welcome a king?" asked Panchessa. "A woman, a bastard and," – he eyed me – "some sort of street vagabond?"

"I felt," replied Estrada calmly, "that when we have so little to offer and even less to negotiate with, this was appropriate. A show of weakness, if you like."

"At least you appreciate your position," Panchessa observed.

"We do," Estrada agreed. "If you choose to pit your armies against ours, we can't hope to win. But this man, Easie Damasco, has an alternative to offer, and I hope for all our sakes that you'll hear it."

Before I could sputter that I'd never intended to do any talking, let alone alternative-offering, Panchessa's gaze had swung to consider me – and every thought froze in my head. "You were with my grandson last night," he noted. "And haven't I seen your face before that?"

Actually, it's not so long ago that you ordered my death, I managed to refrain from saying. "I seem to have a knack for finding myself in the wrong places at the wrong times," I pointed out instead.

Panchessa nodded. "I've known such men," he said. "Trouble, every one of them. Go on then, Easie Damasco, speak your proposal."

I gulped thickly. Everything that had seemed so clear a few minutes ago was now just a soup of half-formed ideas, each foolish in its own right. I tried to hone on in something definite, something I felt sure of. "King Panchessa," I said, "I don't believe you came here to punish the people of Altapasaeda."

"Is that right?" Panchessa asked. "Will you tell me, then, why I marched my armies across two lands, if not to put down a rebellion?"

"I think you came because you're afraid of what your legacy will be."

It wasn't what I'd meant to say, or how I'd meant to say it, but it was too late – and Panchessa's expression was blacker than thunderclouds. "*Afraid*?" he said.

"Your sons are dead; you have no heir," I told him, wincing at each word. "The Senate in Pasaeda is close to rebellion, Shoan is openly at arms, and now the Castoval is slipping away too. I think *that's* why you came here... to make sure you left a mark on the world, even if it was stamped in blood."

Panchessa's face was contorted with fury now. He raised a trembling hand, beckoned to one of his men. I heard an all-too-familiar hiss – the snake's breath of steel slipping free of a scabbard.

I was supposed to be stopping a massacre. All I'd done was hasten it. I would be first to die, and it might even be a relief – because for whatever brief time remained to me, the deaths of thousands would be on my conscience.

But if that was the case, shouldn't I die as I'd lived? My mother had always warned me I'd talk my way onto a funeral pyre; here was my opportunity to prove her right. "Then," I went on hurriedly, "you saw a better way – a chance to keep your line on the throne of Ans Pasaeda. Only, that didn't work out either. Because your grandson, frankly, is every bit as bloody-minded as his father and grandparents."

All my attention was caught up in searching Panchessa's face for something besides anger, but I could sense what was happening around us, as clearly as if I'd been watching it. One word from their king and his men would be hacking us to pieces. One cry from Estrada, and Navare would fling himself into the fray. And close on their heels would come the entire Pasaedan army and half the population of Altapasaeda.

"King Panchessa," I said, with a firmness I barely felt, "Malekrin won't ever agree to be some king in training. But Altapasaeda has a palace sitting empty, and he *might* agree to fill it... at least for a while. Say, what, five years? That's a mayoral term here in the Castoval. It's not long, I know. Then again, he may find he warms to the job. Maybe the people will want him to stay."

I'd spoken with all the passion I could muster. I'd presented my argument as clearly as my garbled thoughts would allow. Yet Panchessa still looked furious. Behind him, his men still had their swords drawn.

I had his attention, though; it felt as if his gaze should have been scorching cavities through my skull and on into the stones of the city beyond. And surely that counted for something, the undivided attention of a king?

I'd never been much of a thief. I'd failed at becoming a hero. But my tongue had scathed warlords and put down tyrants, had rattled guard captains and toyed with giants – and I couldn't let it fail me now.

I closed my eyes and opened them, held Panchessa's eye – and there the words were, waiting in my mouth. They weren't insults, or mockery, but they were the truth. "Malekrin's a good boy, your highness," I said. "He'd be a good prince. And having him watching over this city, watching over this land, would be a fine legacy... far better than the alternative."

By then, I was no longer expecting an answer – at least, not one that wasn't the order to cut me down where I stood. So I nearly jumped for shock when Panchessa said, "And what of Ans Pasaeda? You'd have me leave my land without a king?"

"That's for Ans Pasaeda to decide," I said. "You can't force Malekrin to be king in your place. But if you ask him, he might do this."

Panchessa looked at Malekrin then. "Will you? Is *this* what you want?"

"If Alvantes and I helped you?" put in Estrada quickly. "If Commander Ondeges were to resume his role? If between us we carried some of the burden, until you felt you were ready?"

By then, we were all looking at Malekrin – and I could see him shrinking from our gaze, could tell how badly he wanted to flee. Only then, far too late, did I realise how much better it would have been to convince him before I put my proposal to Panchessa; that there was every chance he'd refuse and condemn us all.

But perhaps I should have had more faith. Because, for all the half-buried panic in his eyes, Malekrin hardly hesitated as he said, "I'll do it. If it saves more bloodshed, if it keeps this city safe – I'll do it."

I couldn't be certain, for it was the briefest flicker, but I thought I saw something lift from Panchessa's face then: a layer of weariness and pain slipping free. "Then," he said, "I wish you luck, grandson."

"Thank you, your highness," replied Malekrin softly.

Panchessa nodded, once, as though acknowledging some sentiment that had passed unspoken between them. Then he said, "I will speak to my people now."

He didn't wait for a reply. Instead, he strode past us, to a point where he could be seen clearly from the walls. He looked around appraisingly, took in the gathered men, women and children, their hotchpotch weapons and their makeshift armour. He cleared his throat – and for a moment, I thought the short cough might turn into a choking fit, for he pressed a palm hard to his chest.

The moment passed. Panchessa took one more deep breath and cried, "People of Altapasaeda. It has been suggested to me, by a young man I have some measure of respect for, that your lives might be better spent than as fodder in a war not of your choosing. And if that fact might have meant little to me a week ago, now I find myself swayed. Therefore, I offer you peace... and to my grandson Malekrin, I grant the princeship of Altapasaeda. He may not want it, but a little responsibility will do him good. Let him see firsthand the trials of wielding power."

Panchessa paused, then, gathered himself – and once again, his face darkened with the threat of anger. "However, all of this rests upon one condition: the woman named Kalyxis must leave your city now, and reclaim the force she has let loose in my lands. This is not open to dispute. I will not have invaders marching upon Ans Pasaedan soil. I brought an army to your walls, Altapasaedans, and I can do so again."

For all his tough words, Panchessa's voice had been fading throughout, the threat an outburst of coughing threading his speech like worms through old wood. Lifting his gaze one last time, he said, more firmly, "That's it. You have been spared, Altapasaedans. Use your freedom wisely."

Then Panchessa turned and, without another word, walked back the way he had come.

Half an hour later and the Pasaedan army was undeniably in retreat. The last regiments were falling back through the far hem of the Suburbs, and the distant back lines had even begun to collapse their tents.

By unspoken agreement, we had returned to the walls to watch. Now, however, Estrada turned away, a look of determination hardening her features. I'd seen that expression many a time, and been on the receiving end of it often enough; there was no question that it spelled trouble for someone.

When Estrada started in Kalyxis's direction, I couldn't resist falling in behind her. I had a sure feeling that this would be something I didn't want to miss. Navare hurried to join us as well, though I suspected his motives were more well-intentioned than my own.

Rather than shove through the Altapasaedans still thronging the walk to watch their enemies depart, Estrada descended to the street and rejoined the wall by a second flight of stairs – so that when she came upon Kalyxis, the other woman was still staring down at the receding Ans Pasaedan lines.

"Kalyxis," said Estrada, "you have to leave Altapasaeda now."

Kalyxis looked round then. I'd never found her easy to read, but I couldn't escape the conviction that the glint in her eye, her reaction to watching Panchessa leave with his armies in tow, was one of disappointment more than relief. But she recovered herself quickly, and her face was blank as a mirror as she said, "Do I? And walk into a trap?"

"If it's a trap," replied Estrada, "then yes, that's exactly what you'll do. But it isn't – and I think you know that just as well as I do. If Panchessa truly wanted you dead then we'd *all* be dead by now."

"So he's a coward. So he would rather win through trickery than face his enemies in an honest fight."

"Don't be ridiculous."

"*Ridiculous*?" Kalyxis's emphasis was fearsome.

Estrada, however, wasn't cowed; in fact, her own tone only became more adamantine as she said, "Yes, ridiculous. Not to mention self-absorbed, egotistical and irrational. If you really care anything for your people, if you want to win their freedom, if you haven't cooked up this entire conflict of yours because of a slight you suffered years ago, then this is the best and only chance you'll ever have. Get out of here. Get word to the force you sent, before they do something you'll regret. Start behaving like the leader you're supposed to be."

I was certain Kalyxis would go for her then – and though I'd seen enough to know that Estrada could hold her own in a fair fight, I doubted she'd fare so well with a few dozen Shoanish thrown into the equation and only Navare and myself to back her up.

Then Kalyxis relaxed, ever so slightly, eased her fingers with forced casualness away from the hilt of her sword. "I care everything for the people of Shoan," she said, loud enough that any of her followers could hear. "There's no risk I wouldn't take for them... not even this." Returning her attention to Estrada she added, with chilly disdain, "Now perhaps you'd be good enough to furnish us with a guide to this godsforsaken land of yours?"

In the end, Kalyxis had left through the small western gate. If I didn't quite trust her to call off the attack on Pasaeda, there was some reassurance in the fact that Gailus departed with her as the requested guide, and more in the knowledge that with Panchessa's great army marching rapidly northward, any attack upon the Ans Pasaedan capital would be nothing more than a messy suicide. The woman might be terrifying and vindictive beyond reason, but I'd come to suspect that she wasn't quite as crazy as she might seem.

I saw that she said a few last words to Malekrin, though I wasn't close enough to overhear just what passed between them. Perhaps Panchessa had settled their differences more ably than either of them could, for she had to leave and he had to stay, and the price if either resisted would undoubtedly be war.

Afterwards, seeing Malekrin looking lost and aimless, I pressed my way through the crowd that had gathered to watch Kalyxis go and said, "You look like a man in need of a drink."

Malekrin turned, startled. Then his brow furrowed. "I still remember what happened the last time you bought me a drink."

I grinned, to hide my embarrassment; I'd practically forgotten about drugging him. "I promise that any passing out you do with be entirely your own fault," I said.

"You could have warned me, you know," Malekrin said.

He was no longer talking about that day in Midendo, I realised. "What, and miss your expression? I tell you, it made all of this worthwhile. Now will you come drink, or are you too royal now to mix with the likes of me?"

Malekrin made a show of considering. Then, with a perfectly straight face, he said, "I'm going to have to learn to mingle with the common folk, aren't I? I suppose you're as good a place to start as any."

As we wandered back through Altapasaeda, I left Malekrin to his own thoughts. For all his show of good cheer, it wasn't hard to see the apprehension bubbling beneath the surface. Anyway, I felt a little guilty at my duplicity – for in fact it had been Estrada who'd asked me to seek him out, and asked too that I bring him to the Dancing Cat once Kalyxis was safely gone. Still, I reasoned, the drinking part had been all my idea, and at least I'd meant it honestly.

The streets felt alive for the first time in days. There were carts and horses, and a great many people moving hither and thither on foot, all of them travelling at speed. It wasn't entirely clear what everyone was doing; most seemed to be hurrying purely for the sake of it. Perhaps it was simply a process of waking up, I thought – the whole of Altapasaeda stretching like a bear that had roused after a long, cruel winter.

Whatever the case, I sensed that the general mood was more shocked than jubilant. Altapasaedans had grown used to the threat of first Mounteban and then Panchessa, and surely it would be a while before normality – whatever that word now meant for the city – truly returned. At any rate, I was grateful no one recognised Malekrin, for I doubted he would be ready yet for the demands and questions that would soon be hurled his way. Tomorrow he would be Prince Malekrin of Altapasaeda, but maybe for tonight at least he could remain plain, ill-tempered Mal.

The Dancing Cat, when we arrived, was surprisingly empty. Probably the crowd that I'd come to think of as its regulars, that motley crew of ex-guardsmen and Mounteban's former lackeys who had become the heart of the Altapasaedan defence, were off doing whatever important things needed to be done in a city that had just so narrowly escaped disaster.

I took the opportunity to requisition a bottle of wine and two cups from beneath the bar. Mal was already at his table of choice by the time I returned; I filled our cups to brimming, pushed one beneath his nose and said, "So what do you plan to do with the palace then? You can't live in all of it, you know."

"I couldn't live in a hundredth of it," said Malekrin. "I doubt there's a single room small enough that my tent back home wouldn't fit into it. So, I don't know. In the short term, though, I think it would make a good hospital. Better than what they have now, at any rate," he added, with a shudder.

"Anyway," I said, "I think you'll make a good prince..."

Malekrin's face lit, just for an instant. "Really?"

"Wait, let me finish. I think you'll make a good prince, is what I'd *like* to tell you... but the truth is, I expect you'll be awful at it. Still, I'm sure you'll try your best, and with everything that's happened, it might do people good to have a prince again for a while. Maybe you can hold things together until Estrada comes up with a better solution, at any rate."

Malekrin grinned. "Thank you, Damasco... for everything you've done."

"What? I haven't done anything."

"Well then, thank you for that." He frowned. "Anyway, where will you go now?"

I hadn't given the question much thought; there hadn't seemed much point in considering the future when I didn't expect to have one. "I don't know," I said. "Maybe I'll head north." I thought of Huero and his family, who had helped me to get the giants moving from the hillside where Moaradrid had abandoned them. "I made a few friends there. I think I'd like to see how they're doing."

"But you won't leave straightaway?" Malekrin asked. There was a hint of concern in his voice.

"No," I said, "I may as well hang around for a few days... see how this all pans out."

We both looked round then at the creak of footsteps on old wood, to see Estrada appear from the direction of the stairs. "There you are," she said – and, as her gaze took in the bottle of wine and the two now almost empty cups, she added, "Why aren't I surprised?"

"Because," I told her, "you are a woman of rare, keen insight."

"That's true," Estrada replied, with a sage nod, "that's certainly true. But don't think you can talk your way out of getting our new prince drunk, Easie. Anyway, it's you I was hoping to find." To Malekrin she said, "Do you mind if I borrow your drinking partner, your highness?"

Malekrin smiled, bowed low in his seat. "You may. So long as you return him before I'm forced to empty this bottle on my own."

I got to my feet, not quite steadily – for I'd cleaned my cup a little quicker than was prudent – and threaded my way over to Estrada. As we began up the stairs, she said softly, "That poor boy. After everything he's been through, and now a responsibility like this to bear. I wish there was another way."

"He'll be fine," I whispered back. "He's tougher than he looks." Then louder, I continued, "Anyway, did I understand what you told him in front of Panchessa? You're staying here in Altapasaeda with your boyfriend?"

Estrada paused at the head of the stairs – and I'd have sworn she was blushing. "I've told you before," she said, "he's *not* my boyfriend. But he needs someone here while he heals, and after that... well, I might stay on." Suddenly all of the defensiveness fell from her face and she said, "I love him, Easie. I don't want to live my life without him anymore."

Now it was my turn for embarrassment. My overwhelming urge was to make some glib comment, but seeing the weight of old sadness relieved by the hope in Estrada's eyes, I knew I just couldn't get away with it. "He loves you too," I said. "I doubt he's any better at saying it than he is at showing it, but believe me... I've spent far too much time with the man, and he'd give everything he has for you."

Estrada's smile was so bashful, so girlish, that for a moment the years seemed to slew off her and I saw the young woman she must have been when she first met a certain Guard-Captain Lunto Alvantes. "I know," she said. "I do know." Then the moment passed, the Estrada I was familiar with returned quicker than I could register, and she added, "Anyway, you'll be glad to know that Lunto is awake and feeling much better. And he has something he'd like to say to you. In fact we both do."

She carried on up the hallway, knocked lightly on the door to her own room, paused a moment and then opened it. Following behind her, I was more surprised than I should have been to see Alvantes lying in her bed.

He was wearing a cotton night shirt, but most of the side and one arm had been trimmed away to expose thick layers of bandage. He looked pale and hollow-eyed; but as Estrada had said, he was certainly awake, and – with the aid of a great many pillows – sitting up.

Alvantes looked uneasy at my presence, all the more so when Estrada leaned to kiss his forehead, and I found myself uncomfortably reminded of the last time someone I knew had summoned me. The memory of my last talk with Saltlick sent a tremor of tension through my chest. Was this to be another goodbye?

However, once Estrada had seated herself in the chair beside the bed, Alvantes regain a little of his composure – and weak though his voice was, I could tell he was trying to be jovial as he said, "Marina tells me you singlehandedly talked Panchessa into marching his armies out of here."

"Actually," I replied, "Malekrin did most of the work, last night." Then I remembered that neither Estrada nor Alvantes even knew about our clandestine meeting with Panchessa. "It's a long story," I added lamely.

"Either way," said Alvantes, "I wanted to thank you. You did well, Damasco."

For a moment, I was so startled that I could hardly think to reply – not so much because he'd said it, I realised, but because of how my heart swelled to *hear* him say it. It reminded me of something I'd been wanting to tell him for some time now. "I'm sorry, Alvantes... sorry I attacked you, and sorry I doubted you."

"It's forgotten." Alvantes touched two fingers to the side of his jaw, where the flesh was still faintly purpled, and grimaced. "Just never do it again, all right?"

"Well," I said, "I can't promise anything."

There was an awkward pause then, each of us having exhausted whatever limited stocks of manly sympathy nature had gifted us with. I knew that Alvantes was trying to shift our conversation onto more comfortable ground when he asked, "So Marina's told you that she plans to stay here in Altapasaeda?"

"She has," I agreed.

"This is a real opportunity for the city," he said, "A new beginning."

An odd thought occurred to me. "I can't see Malekrin carrying on the way Panchetto did, charging taxes just to keep himself in banquets. In fact, I can't see him staying on as prince for any longer than he has to. Today might be the first step towards a free Altapasaeda... a free Castoval, even, in time. Wasn't that Mounteban's dream?"

Alvantes scowled. "Perhaps a better version of it," he said gruffly, "if we get it right."

"Anyway, Easie," put in Estrada, "this brings us to the reason we wanted to talk to you. If I'm going to stay here with Lunto, someone else will need to look after Muena Palaiya. The charter allows me to nominate a proxy to serve until the next election, but obviously it can't be just anyone. It would have to be someone who knows the town, who cares about it... someone I can rely on to do the right thing."

"Good luck with that," I said. "Just finding anyone who knows the place *and* likes it could take all of a month."

"Yes," agreed Estrada, "it's occurred to me that town politics isn't for everyone. Of course, honesty isn't really a prerequisite; in fact, it's probably a disadvantage. It took me a while to appreciate it, but half the time it isn't about what you can do, it's about what you make people *think* you can do. What the job needs is a sincere heart and the mind of a swindler."

"So you're looking for an honest crook to run your town?" I said. "Good luck with finding one of those."

Estrada smiled. "I've only ever met the one."

"Well," I told her, "you should probably ask them then. Of course, if they have half the sense you credit them with, they'll probably say no, and... Estrada, why are you looking at me like that?"

"Like what?" she asked.

"Like... like... Wait, you don't mean *me*?"

"Easie," she said, "you're selfish, rude, insensitive, and probably the most bloody-minded person I've ever come across in my life."

"Hey!"

"But from the moment I met you, I knew you could be far more than you were – and you haven't let me down. Look what you've helped accomplish in these last months: Moaradrid defeated, the giants rescued, a war averted. You do things your own way, and it's invariably the wrong way... but I'd say the results have been worth it."

Suddenly my heart was beating far too fast. Had the woman gone mad? I couldn't imagine anything worse than politics – and after my recent experiences, my imagination had plenty of scope. How did she think I could look after an entire town full of people, when I could hardly even look after myself?

Reading my reaction from the dread surely etched across my face, Estrada added gently, "Look at it this way, Damasco... can you honestly tell me you have anything better to do?"

I was ready to turn her down. The words were halfway to my tongue. Had Estrada said something else, *anything* else, I would have refused, and kept refusing until there was no breath left in my lungs.

Somewhere beneath the whirling panic that my thoughts had become, a small, detached voice observed that the woman had come to know me too damn well. Because, could I truthfully claim I had anything better to do than be mayor of Muena Palaiya?

I couldn't. I really couldn't.

There was no getting around it; I just wasn't the thief I'd been. And maybe, just maybe, that meant it was time to try something new. "When I accidentally burn the town down," I said, "or single-handedly start a war with Shoan, it will be on your head. You understand that, don't you?"

Estrada smiled. "It's a risk I'm prepared to take."

I offered her my hand. "Then in that case, I accept."

She shook. "I thought you would."

As she released my palm, I fought against the dizzying sensation that my world had finally, irrevocably tumbled off its axis. How had I come to this point? I'd accidentally crossed a lunatic warlord, inadvertently stolen something of inconceivable value. I'd fallen in with dangerous sorts like Estrada and Alvantes, the kind of people who believed in such perilous notions as heroism and self-sacrifice. I'd learned, to my great shock, that when I made mistakes, people other than me got hurt. And at the beginning of it all, I'd rescued a giant who wanted to fight even less than I did, never once imagining I might end up calling him my friend.

But Saltlick was gone – and the thought that he wasn't here to share in our victory, that he'd never even know he hadn't left us to our deaths, twisted like a cold blade in my guts. I finally, truly understood then the choice he'd had to make; save his people, or abandon everything he believed in to try to rescue his friends. It was a choice, and a sacrifice, that were bound to torment him for the rest of his days.

I couldn't have that. And I wasn't willing to let my friend go, either – not without a fight.

"A horse," I cried. "Estrada, I need a fast horse!" Then I remembered my past experiences of riding. "But perhaps not *too* fast," I added.

EPILOGUE

It was early afternoon by the time I caught up with the giants.

Had I thought the expedition through, I'd have taken along some water and a little food for my lunch. By the time I crested a rise and the giant column came into view in the far distance, I was parched and dusty, intent upon the grumbling of my stomach. Yet seeing them there, like pale pebbles cast upon the smudged grey of the road, knowing that the tiny figure at their head must be Saltlick, I realised that for once I was surprisingly unconcerned with my bodily discomforts.

Once I'd reached the tail end of the giant line, I rode along beside them, slowing so as not to agitate my horse. She was a good-tempered chestnut mare, and I was grateful to her for managing a commendable balance between speed and not scaring me half to death. Now, though, she was clearly unsure what to make of her enormous travelling companions, however much she tried to affect nonchalance.

As we passed the giants one by one they glanced down at us curiously, and I tried not to notice in turn what a bizarre sight they made, pacing with their heads bobbing at the level of the treetops. I was perhaps halfway to the front when Saltlick registered the clack of hooves over the tramp of giant feet and looked around. In a moment, his face was transformed: by astonishment at first and then, straight after, by joy. "Easie alive!" he roared.

"Of course I'm alive, you idiot," I shouted back. "Did you really think anyone could kill Easie Damasco?"

"No fight?" he asked, as I drew nearer – and it was odd to hear those oft-spoken words of his posed as a question.

"No fight," I agreed. "No war. No king breathing down our necks with his army. Not anymore. It's over, Saltlick."

I doubted anyone in Altapasaeda had looked as relieved by the news as Saltlick did just then. He held up a hand and spoke a word in giantish, and as the instruction was passed along, the column ground to a halt.

Once I caught up to him, I hurried to dismount. I was glad to note that Saltlick still wore the crown of Altapasaeda around his neck; it was better off in the world of giants than men, I was sure Malekrin could manage without it, and it was strangely comforting to know that at least one thing I'd stolen had managed to *stay* stolen.

"It's good to see you," I said.

Saltlick beamed down at me. Yet now that his initial delight had passed, it was impossible to miss the curiosity hovering in his eyes. I knew he'd never be so indiscreet as to ask what I'd come for, why I'd ignored his explicit request that I leave him and his people alone. Still, the questions were there, just waiting to be answered.

"Saltlick, I haven't forgotten what you told me," I said. "But I needed you to know Altapasaeda was safe. And there was something else I wanted to say too... I wanted to tell you that you were right. Your people will never have peace so long as they're around my people. We don't seem to be good for much except fighting, do we? Just because we avoided it this time, doesn't mean it won't happen again, sooner or later."

I tried to gather my thoughts. It had all seemed so obvious on the way there, so simple.

"The thing is, though, I'm not sure you can just go back to hiding from the world. You're not a myth anymore, not legendary beings that someone's great-grandfather saw once after too much wine. Everyone knows you're out here. Everyone knows you're real."

Here was the most crucial part. Yet now that Saltlick's features had settled into their usual, impenetrable pattern, I wasn't even certain he was following what I said.

"So going home, keeping away from people, getting back to how things were before Moaradrid came along... those are all fine ideas. But here's the thing: sooner or later there'll be another Moaradrid."

Saltlick nodded pensively. So he *was* following; and only then did it occur to me that I was telling him nothing he didn't already know. Of course he had tormented himself with the possibility of another warlord arriving at the giant gates; of course he understood that the sight of colossi tearing apart walls and wielding prodigious weapons was a memory that wouldn't soon fade. He was a good chief, and a good chief was bound to recognise such threats.

So did that mean I was about to waste my breath on a proposal he'd already discounted? For a moment, all of the pain and fear of the last days threatened to swamp my thoughts like floodwater; better to say a quick goodbye and leave, I knew, than to pour my heart out and still find myself friendless and alone.

Only, I wasn't there for myself – or not just. I wasn't there because I needed Saltlick, but because I'd finally come to realise he might just need me.

For what use was a good chief without good friends to advise him?

"Saltlick," I said, "what I'm trying to say is, if you cut off anyone who wants to help you, who'll be there to stop the ones who'd hurt you? You can turn your back on our world, but you can't make it turn its back on you. So what you giants need... I mean, what *I* think you need... is an ambassador."

"Ambassador?" asked Saltlick, chewing over the strange word as if it were a particularly stodgy morsel.

"It means, someone who understands the world outside of their own. Someone who knows people... people in the right sorts of places. Someone who could visit every once in a while, to Altapasaeda, maybe even as far as Muena Palaiya, every year, every six months even, and catch up with the news, perhaps share a meal with somebody who'd... well, you know..." I gulped. "What I mean is, a friend who would miss him if they were never to see him again."

Saltlick took a long moment to mull that over, his features working unconsciously with the effort. Then his cavernous mouth broke into the widest smile I'd yet seen there, a grin so cheerful and unrestrained that I could hardly believe it hadn't cleaved his head in two.

"Ambassador," he bellowed, loud enough that I thought my eardrums would explode.

Sat upon the roadside, I watched the end of the giant column disappear over the next hill. Idly, I imagined them arriving at their high, hidden mountain enclave with Saltlick at their head: a leader bringing his people home, just as he'd sworn he would.

We hadn't set a time for his visit, merely said a hurried farewell. Even I could see that Saltlick would have his hands full for a while. Still, I was confident that he would keep his word. I'd go to Muena Palaiya, see what I could make of this new life that had somehow fallen into my lap – and one day there would come a knock like thunder at the town gates and I'd know my friend had returned. It was a good enough thought that I could live with a little uncertainty.

Soon I'd have to go back to Altapasaeda. Soon, but not just yet. The sun was still shining. The breeze was still cooling. The grass was soft beneath my rump. For the first time in longer than I could remember, I felt no need to think; not about Moaradrid or the giant stone, not about Panchessa or Mounteban or my many, many brushes with death.

The past was the past, and somehow I'd survived it. The future was the future, and it would surely take care of itself.

I looked over to my horse, where she was cropping a late dinner from the verge nearby, paying me no attention whatsoever.

"You know," I told her, "all things considered, this could probably have worked out a lot worse."

ACKNOWLEDGMENTS

Thanks to Tom, for assistance beyond the call of duty, and to Jobeda, for her love, support and patience.

ABOUT THE AUTHOR

David Tallerman was born and raised in the northeast of England. A long and confused period of education ended with an MA dissertation on the literary history of seventeenth century witchcraft that somehow incorporated references to both Kate Bush and H P Lovecraft.

David currently roams the UK as an itinerant IT Technician-for-hire, applying theories of animism and sympathetic magic to computer repair and taking devoted care of his bonsai tree familiar.

Over the last few years, David has been steadily building a reputation for his genre short fiction and increasingly his writing has tended to push and merge genres, and to incorporate influences from his other great loves, comic books and cinema. David's first novel, *Giant Thief*, was published in January 2012. *Prince Thief* is the third book in the series.

davidtallerman.net
twitter.com/davidtallerman